The kiss started out damn near perfect, a sensual merging of lips that felt as natural as shifting to wolf had earlier.

It felt…*right.* More than that. Perfect. Braden had dreamed of this, ached for this, in truth ever since he'd first heard the sexy sound of her throaty voice.

Crazy. Foolish. And not at all like him.

Despite this, he craved more, much more. He wanted to do things with her that someone like him had no business wanting to do with a royal princess.

And that was enough reason to make him realize he needed to stop. Right this instant.

He broke off the kiss and moved away, feeling oddly bereft. "My apologies," he told her, stiffly formal. "I shouldn't have done that."

"I didn't mind." Rather than furious, she sounded strangely elated. "Why apologize for something we both clearly enjoyed?"

Enjoyed?

Books by Karen Whiddon

Harlequin Romantic Suspense

The CEO's Secret Baby #1662
The Cop's Missing Child #1719

Silhouette Romantic Suspense

**One Eye Open* #1301
**One Eye Closed* #1365
**Secrets of the Wolf* #1397
The Princess's Secret Scandal #1416
Bulletproof Marriage #1484
***Black Sheep P.I.* #1513
***The Perfect Soldier* #1557
***Profile for Seduction* #1629
Colton's Christmas Baby #1636

Harlequin Nocturne

**Wolf Whisperer* #128
**The Wolf Princess* #146

Silhouette Nocturne

**Cry of the Wolf* #7
**Touch of the Wolf* #12
**Dance of the Wolf* #45
**Wild Wolf* #67
**Lone Wolf* #103

*The Pack
**The Cordasic Legacy

KAREN WHIDDON

started weaving fanciful tales for her younger brothers at the age of eleven. Amidst the Catskill Mountains of New York, then the Rocky Mountains of Colorado, she fueled her imagination with the natural beauty that surrounded her. Karen now lives in north Texas, where she shares her life with her very own hero of a husband and three doting dogs. Also an entrepreneur, she divides her time between the business she started and writing. You can email Karen at KWhiddon1@aol.com or write to her at P.O. Box 820807, Fort Worth, TX 76182. Fans of her writing can also check out her website, www.karenwhiddon.com.

THE WOLF PRINCESS

KAREN WHIDDON

ISBN-13: 978-0-373-88556-5

THE WOLF PRINCESS & ONE EYE OPEN

This edition published by arrangement with Harlequin Books S.A.

For questions and comments about the quality of this book please contact us at CustomerService@Harlequin.com.

www.Harlequin.com

Printed in U.S.A.

CONTENTS

Dear Reader,

Nearly every little girl dreams of being a princess, which made me wonder if princesses dreamed of being...ordinary. Not boring ordinary, but a regular person who could go to college, hit the mall for sales and stroll the beach without notice. And a shape-shifter princess would have it far worse—the only time she could be like everyone else would be when she became a wolf.

The Wolf Princess is about such a woman. The youngest daughter in the royal family of the fictional country of Teslinko, she is sought after, stared at and talked about. And when a blind doctor travels from America to study her, that seems to be the last straw.

Instead, she learns her new life has just begun.

The sequel to this title, *The Wolf Prince*, will be out next year. Both brother and sister have their own journey and, though they might seem diametrically opposed, they are actually pretty similar—both headed toward love. After all, that's what life is really all about.

Sincerely,

Karen Whiddon

To all the readers who write to me, whether by email or paper and pen, thank you for your notes. They mean the world to this busy writer. Again, thank you.

THE WOLF PRINCESS

Chapter 1

Princess Alisa of Teslinko's first hint that the man waiting for her at her family's table was trouble was the fact that he wore dark glasses—even inside the palace dining room, where the candle-illuminated table made the light relatively dim.

Her second hint, his unabashedly scruffy appearance—from his rumpled black hair to his disheveled, too-casual clothes. Usually when suitors—even those from other countries—visited royalty, they made sure to look their best, even for her. The fact that he hadn't bothered told her he either honestly didn't care, or worse, didn't know any better.

Either way, as she made her way toward him, she grudgingly admired him for his boldness in daring to be different. She had to admit, it pricked her interest, especially since she was different herself. Someone like him was a welcome change from the usual ass-kissers who came seeking her hand. Though she knew she'd eventually have to choose one of them, so far she hadn't been able to get past the fact that every single one of them felt more infatuated with her money and status than her.

And now this man, apparently the latest in a long queue of minor Pack royalty.

Head up, dark glasses obscuring his face, he ignored her as she drew closer. This gave her pause. He didn't turn toward her and flash his teeth in a patently false smile or dip his perfectly cleft chin in acknowledgment or even give any outward sign that he noticed her approach. Except for the slight flaring of his nostrils, he might have been completely oblivious.

Barely stopping herself from rolling her eyes, she made her way to the table, affecting a pleasant smile that she hoped hid her frustration. Lately her parents had been focused obsessively on marrying her off, as though they had some sort of checklist of their children's names and hers was the next one on it. It didn't help that she was not as beautiful as her two older sisters or that she was known around Teslinko as a bit of a brainiac.

And here sat yet another one of her parents' finds.

There was a second or two of extreme awkwardness when she reached them. Her father gallantly stood, while her mother and the stranger remained seated. Alisa couldn't believe it. She'd never had a visitor—suitor or otherwise—act in such a deliberately boorish manner.

Finally, as though by second thought, he pushed back his chair and stood, tilting his head as her father performed the introductions. His title and name—Doctor

Something—barely registered as she studied him, wondering why he looked so familiar, when in fact she knew they'd never met.

"Princess Alisa, I'm honored to meet you."

About to make some pithy comment, Alisa froze. Stunned, she couldn't at first form a reply. The richness of his sensual voice rolled over her like molten caramel. Her reaction shocked her. Quite frankly, she hadn't been expecting this at all.

Despite herself, she shivered. Hellhounds.

Gathering her shredded composure, she inclined her head. She could do this. After all, she was a princess, well schooled in affecting grace in all sorts of unique situations. One rude stranger with a voice as rich as sin couldn't even put a dent in her composure.

Regally, she held out her hand, absently wondering if he'd kiss it or simply take it in a weak clasp before releasing it. When he did neither, her heart rate increased and her face heated. Swallowing hard as this next bit of discourtesy forced her to slowly lower her arm, she glanced at her father to see how he was taking all this. Such impossible behavior should not be tolerated. At the very least, this man should be given a severe dressing down. Or, even better, sent packing.

But instead of wearing a thunderous frown, King Leo simply pulled out her chair for Alisa, indicating with a dip of his chin that she should sit.

Really? Biting back a retort, she did. Once she'd gotten seated, Dr. Rude-with-sunglasses-still-on did the same.

Great. Her parents weren't going to let her off the hook so easily. She'd have no choice but to smile and somehow get through what promised to be the dreariest hour she'd spent in weeks. Months, even. Which just went to show exactly how far her parents were willing to go to procure a husband for their plain and brainy daughter. They refused to accept the fact that Alisa did not want to get married. Not yet, maybe not ever.

Barely curbing her impatience, she schooled her face into a bland sort of pleasantness. Though she realized how excruciatingly long this luncheon just might be, part of her job as princess was making sure her visitor had no idea that she wanted to be somewhere else. Anywhere else.

But still…glancing at the man wearing his dark sunglasses, she sighed. Discourteousness had a way of begetting impoliteness. Maybe she could help move things along if she simply cut to the chase.

Leaning across the table, she flashed him her most brilliant smile, even though she knew smiling only detracted slightly from her plainness. "Doctor, I'm afraid I missed your name. But since you're here, why don't you tell me why you think I should consider marrying you rather than someone else? We can save a lot of time that way."

To her astonishment, the doctor nearly choked on the wine he'd been about to drink. Carefully setting the glass down, he blotted his mouth with the napkin before he cocked his head toward her. "I think you misunderstand," he began. "Actually, I believe you're a bit confused as to the purpose of my visit."

Again she had that odd reaction to his voice, which both infuriated and inexplicably energized her. And for him to say she was confused? Now that was fresh. Most of her prior suitors had carefully avoided commenting on her intelligence, even though that was the one thing she truly liked about herself. Brains over beauty, this had been the hand she'd been dealt. She'd long ago stopped longing to be more like her glamorous older sisters.

"Misunderstand what?" Her tone came out a bit sharper than she'd intended, causing her father to reach over and cover her hand with his in a gentle warning.

Taking a deep breath, she continued in a much softer voice. "Are you or are you not here because you want to apply for my hand in marriage?"

King Leo cleared his throat and started to speak. To her shock, the doctor held up a hand to silence him. The king. He dared to silence the king. Hiding her glee, she waited for the eruption. Any moment now, all hell would break loose.

To her surprise, nothing happened. Her father's always-mercurial temper appeared to be on hiatus. Instead of acting infuriated as he should be, her father appeared to find this man hugely amusing. What she didn't understand was why. Had her parents truly given up all hope for her?

Apparently completely unaware, the doctor leaned forward. "About your assumption that I'm here as your...what, suitor? I'm not. Not at all."

"Really?" she repeated. "But—"

He continued on as if she hadn't spoken. "That's a bit arrogant of you, isn't it? Do you automatically believe that any man who visits has some sort of over-reaching desire for you?"

Arrogant? He really didn't know her at all, did he? She would have thought the man would have at least bothered to do some research on her before his arrival.

Opening her mouth, she eyed his blasted dark

glasses. Her father's glare and her mother's slow shake of the head made her close it without giving any sort of rebuttal.

"I can assure you," he said, his low, impossibly rich voice vibrating with certainty, "I have absolutely zero interest in marrying you, or anyone else for that matter."

Stunned, she sat back in her chair. To further the surreal aspect of it all, neither of her parents commented. At all. Even if he wasn't here to court her, even though it was the twenty-first century, who talked to a princess like that? Who talked to anyone like that? Honestly.

As she pondered how to respond, her mother leaned forward and took Alisa's hand, gently squeezing. "Honey, Dr. Streib is here because we asked him to come for medical reasons. You know we've been concerned about your health. And even in America, Dr. Streib learned of your situation. He's traveled all this way because of that."

Mortified and horrified, Alisa finally realized what Doctor what's-his-name was doing here. "They called you because they think I'm sick." Saying this, she felt queasy.

Expressionless, sunglasses still hiding his eyes, he nodded. "I am a doctor, yes. But—"

This time she interrupted him. "Honestly, I'm sorry they wasted your time. Which they have." Turning her attention to her most likely ally, her father, she tried to keep her voice level. "Dad. There is nothing wrong with me. Just because I haven't shifted into wolf lately…"

"Six months is not 'lately.'" Despite the steely look in his eyes, like her he kept his tone mild. "You know as well as I do that you need to change more often. Everyone does."

"I don't. I've told you—"

"Yes, you have. And your story has become well known in not only our country, but all around the world. So much so that Dr. Streib contacted us from the United States and expressed a wish to examine you. Your mother—and I," he added pointedly, "are both very concerned over your mental well-being."

"I'm fine." She'd grown weary of the old argument. Ever since she'd first shape-shifted, with no inclination or yearning to do so again on any regular basis, her parents had worried. Until she'd become a teenager, her mother had made shifting to wolf a family event, something that they did every weekend, as regularly as other families went to church or to the mall. This had been their way to ensure Alisa changed regularly. She'd actually come to enjoy these little outings, the royal pack of wolves running and hunting and playing together in the rugged mountains near the palace.

But once she and her siblings had grown older, her sisters had gotten married, and her mother had weddings to plan and grandchildren to dote over. The family get-togethers had stopped and Alisa had changed less and less frequently.

Unlike apparently everyone else in the Pack, she didn't feel a craving or compulsion to become wolf. In truth, she hadn't cared if she remained human forever. Actually, she hadn't even been aware six months had passed since the last time she shape-shifted. And she certainly hadn't realized her parents were still keeping track.

Now, they were so concerned about her mental health that they'd invited this man into their home. Was he a psychologist? Because according to conventional wisdom, her ability to remain in her human form for a longer period of time than most meant that she should be stark raving mad.

The fact that she wasn't continued to astound everyone.

"Then you are here to psychoanalyze me?" she asked, hurt despite herself. "You are going to make sure I'm not crazy, is that it?"

"No. I'm not that kind of doctor," he began.

"Doctor Streib is a top neurosurgeon," her mother said, still holding Alisa's hand. "He has also made a career out of studying the brain. He is here because he believes that your ability could have great benefits for our kind if it can be replicated."

Replicated? Eyeing her parents, who until now had seemed remarkably indulgent of her many imperfections, she began to wonder if they were only making up this nonsense to soothe her wounded pride over the fact that they believed she needed a psychiatrist.

"Do you think I've gone mad?" she asked bluntly, holding her father's gaze.

King Leo blinked before slowly shaking his head.

"Good." Now Alisa turned to face her mother. "How about you, Mom?"

"Of course not," Queen Ionna hastened to reassure her, while her father watched, amusement glinting in his bright blue eyes. All of the family had those same sapphire eyes, except Alisa. Hers were the color of sea foam.

"I don't think you're crazy, dear," the queen finished.

"No? Then why have you sent for this man?" she wondered out loud. "Have I shown a single sign of mental instability?"

"No, of course not," her father said, his mouth twitching in an obvious attempt to keep from smiling. Her mother shook her head in agreement, while the boorish doctor continued to stare, his sunglasses reflecting back her distorted image.

"Then why?" Shooting a wry look at both her parents, she waited for someone—anyone—to state the obvious—that this had been a colossal mistake.

When no one did, Alisa glared at the doctor and did it herself.

"I'm fine," she repeated. "Dr. Streib, I assure you I'm doing perfectly well. There is nothing wrong with my brain, I promise. So there's no reason for you to be here, no reason at all. You're wasting your time."

"I'm not concerned with your mental health." When he spoke for the third time, the timbre and resonance of his voice was like whiskey and silk. Smooth and dangerous at once. Damn his voice. She had to force herself to focus on his words instead of melting into the sound of him.

"You're not?" she managed, looking from her mother to her father and back again. "Then why are you…?"

"As your mother mentioned, I am—was—a neurosurgeon," the doctor said. "I don't believe there is anything wrong with your brain, not at all. But I do believe that there is something different in you, something that enables you to do this thing that no one else can."

Alisa picked up on a single word. The *was*. "You *were* a neurosurgeon, you said. But you're not now?"

"No." A man of few words, this doctor.

"Dr. Streib no longer performs surgery," her father said, before she could ask the doctor to elaborate. "Even though he no longer operates, he's the foremost Pack expert in research that may someday enable all shifters to do as you do—to go longer periods of time in human form without going mad."

"Research. Interesting." She frowned, even though her mother kept reminding her a smile made her look prettier. Straightening her shoulders, she took a deep breath, not sure she liked the direction this conversation appeared to be heading.

Though she suspected she knew the answer, she had to ask anyway. "That's nice, but what does that have to do with me? Don't tell me he wants to study my brain."

Though she said the last as a joke, no one laughed. Instead, both her parents continued to regard her intently.

"That is exactly what he wants to do," King Leo said. "And more."

"More?" she said faintly, looking at her mother for help. The queen's serious expression told her she couldn't expect assistance from that quarter.

"Dr. Streib has been given copies of your blood work. He also has requested both blood and tissue samples."

Eyes gleaming, King Leo practically rubbed his hands together. "We've had numerous conversations on the phone. Throughout Pack history, there have only been a few documented cases of shifters who could do as you do."

Great. Briefly she closed her eyes. Yet another well-intentioned reminder of how different she was.

"Dr. Streib seems to feel your brain might hold the key. You, my dear daughter, might have the answer that could help millions of our kind."

Horror growing, she stared at her sire. "But—"

Expression regal, he held up his hand to stave off her

interruption. "I haven't finished. This is an honor, both to our country and to our family name. If by studying you, he can determine how you do what you do, your name will go down in history."

"Studying me?" she asked faintly.

"Yes. Dr. Streib has requested permission to do some tests, none of which, he's assured me, are harmful to you in the slightest."

"Tests?" Appalled and ashamed, she jumped to her feet. "I don't believe this. Why would you even consider such a thing?"

"Because without tests, he can't determine if his theory is correct."

"These are non-invasive tests," Dr. Streib hastened to reassure her, his voice still rolling over her like whiskey and honey. "I will not be cutting into you."

"I should hope not." Both furious and hurt, she shook her head at him before turning to glare at her parents. "Am I hearing this right? You want me to be this man's guinea pig?"

"I wouldn't put it quite like that," Queen Ionna began.

"No? How would you put it, then? This is unbelievable. What's next? Are we filming a reality show about life with the royals?" Snatching up her glass of wine, she took a long, deep drink.

"Now, Alisa. There's no need to be ridiculous."

Alisa nearly choked on her wine. "You find me ridiculous? Me? That's rich. I refuse to let this man experiment on me. I want you to tell him to leave."

Before either of her parents could speak, Dr. Streib pushed back his chair and stood, facing her. He was a very tall man, lean and lanky, wearing his rumpled clothing as though at home in his own body.

"Princess Alisa, I think you should reconsider. You could help lots of other shifters—hundreds of thousands of them, if not more—if you help us to find the secret to what you do."

"Has it ever occurred to you that such a thing cannot be replicated?" she said. "You're a doctor. More than a doctor. A *neurosurgeon.* Surely in your years of practice, you've come across things that cannot be explained. I believe my ability is like that. It just *is*. No amount of testing or studying is going to change that."

"Stop being so selfish," he said, his sensual mouth curling. He delivered this in such a smooth, even tone that it took her a second to realize she'd been insulted.

Then, while she was still gaping at his most recent rudeness, her father stood also, his expression thunderous.

"Enough. Alisa, you will be helping Dr. Streib." King Leo sounded cool, since he knew full well if he ordered her to do something, it would be so.

"And, once he has formed a conclusion," her father continued, "if he is able to make some sort of drug to enable others to do what you do so effortlessly, Dr. Streib has generously agreed to allow the manufacturing plant to be based in Teslinko."

His stern gaze pinned her. "I know I don't need to tell you what a boon this will be for both our economy and our people."

And there he had her. If she refused—which, as the youngest female child and the second most spoiled after her younger brother Ruben, she still could, even though it'd mean a lengthy fight—she'd come out the bad guy.

And even then, there was a definite chance she'd probably still lose, as strange as they were acting. It didn't help that her parents knew she was just as passionate about their people and their country as they were.

Defeated, she swallowed, forcing herself to think rationally. An opportunity such as this was too good to pass up, no matter the personal cost.

Besides, running a few tests shouldn't take too awfully long. Dr. Streib would be merely a momentary annoyance, that's all. But still…

"Let me see if I have this right," she said slowly, eyeing her father. "You want me to be this man's experimental lab rat in exchange for a possible promised factory? Even though there's a distinct possibility that he may never find the secret and even be able to make the medicine he's aiming for?"

Both King Leo and Queen Ionna looked at the doctor.

Instead of responding, Dr. Streib continued to watch her, the blasted dark glasses still hiding his eyes.

"Fine." Alisa exhaled when it seemed no one else would comment. "How long is this going to take?"

"Not forever," her father hastened to reassure her. "I've put a time limitation on this."

"How long?"

"He has one month, no more. If after two fortnights he doesn't have his answer, he will have to go back to the United States empty-handed."

Now would have been the time to chime in, but still Dr. Streib remained silent, his sunglasses hiding his eyes. Her resentment toward those soulless dark glasses of his increased by the minute.

"If he fails and, as I've said all along, discovers that

I am perfectly normal in every way, what then?" she asked. "How will we be compensated for my time?"

Now Dr. Streib chose to interject. Now, when she'd been talking to her parents rather than him. "What will you get out of it? You'll have been given a chance to help your people. You'll know you gave it your best shot."

Again, one corner of his well-shaped mouth twisted in what could have been either the beginnings of a smile or of a sneer. "What more can a royal princess ask for?"

Biting back her immediate surge of anger at his sarcasm, she made her tone icy. "Actually, I wasn't asking you. I was speaking to my father."

If she'd expected him to feel intimidated, she was wrong. Instead, he tilted his head and eyed her the way he might have studied a small, poisonous insect before crushing it under the heel of his boot.

"Are you really going to continue these objections?" he asked. "While you are a princess, you aren't even the next in line for the throne. Your time isn't all *that* valuable."

Stifling a gasp, she eyed her mother and father, noted that they were watching with amusement plain on their aristocratic faces, and felt a flush of shame.

Shame? Really? Swallowing, she lifted her chin. She, who prided herself on her sharp intellect and emotionless demeanor, would not lose her cool. She hadn't since she'd been thirteen. Now twenty-four, she took a sort of grim pleasure in her reputation as the princess who got the brains rather than the beauty.

"For the last time, this is a private matter between my family and me," she said evenly. "Please, stay out of it. And," she added for good measure, "why don't you take those sunglasses off? There's no need to wear them inside the palace. The light is not even all that bright, especially in this room."

Staring hard at him, daring him, she ignored her mother's wordless sound of dismay and her father's muffled protest. Instead, she continued to watch the doctor, curious as to how he would react.

"Take the sunglasses off," she repeated, waiting, watching as his hand came up and he slowly, finally removed the dark glasses.

The instant he did, her world shifted on its axis as she realized she'd been more than insensitive.

First, the sunglasses weren't a fashion statement or an attempt to be cool or rude or any of the things she'd initially suspected.

Dr. Streib was blind. He'd been covering up his beautiful, sightless eyes.

Yet he was Pack. She could see his aura. How could he be blind? This wouldn't be possible if he was a full-blooded shifter. Full shifters healed rapidly from any injury except fire and iron.

Which meant he had to be Halfling, part human. They did not always heal from their injuries so easily.

Still, with all his resources, why hadn't he sought the help of a healer? She'd heard one existed in the United States, living in Texas. The woman, Samantha something-or-other, had been hailed as a miracle when her remarkable abilities to heal Halflings had been discovered.

But his blindness and his Halfling status weren't the only things she recognized now that she could get a good look at his face. Oh, no. The man standing before her with barely curbed impatience twisting the corner of his sensual mouth was someone she'd been waiting to meet most of her life.

Her mate. The One.

That is, she reined her thoughts in, if she actually believed in such things. Which she didn't. The concept of true mates was nothing but romantic nonsense.

Still, a part of her couldn't help but wonder.

When she'd been a teenager with raging hormones, devouring two or three romance novels a week, she'd often imagined her type. She'd firmly believed he was out there somewhere, waiting for her. Waiting to complete her.

This man, this Dr. Streib, with his dark, craggy features and ancient, sightless eyes, wasn't remotely what she'd pictured or even what she found herself attracted to. Yet, as improbable as it might be, she felt an instant, senseless certainty that he was The One. The only One.

Of course, she immediately discounted that, preferring to consider those few seconds as a bit of romantic foolishness left over from her teenage years. One last shred of the silly adolescent she'd been, rising from the depths one last time, only to be ruthlessly quashed, never to appear again.

Dr. Streib, she told herself, was nothing to her. Nor would he ever be. She'd suffer through his ridiculous tests, let him pretend he had the slightest chance of learning the answer, and then send him home with his metaphorical tail tucked between his legs.

As far as she was concerned, the day couldn't come fast enough.

The sooner she got rid of him the better.

Chapter 2

As soon as Her Royal Highness Princess Alisa of Teslinko opened her mouth, Dr. Braden Streib knew he was in Trouble with a capital *T.* Because his wolf reacted strongly to her voice.

Strongly being the understatement of the year. Throughout his thirty-eight years, he'd periodically fought with his lupine half. Everyone did. When the wolf wanted out, he wanted out. The place or time didn't matter to the beast. Most times, subduing the urge to change was a simple matter, using a light touch and a firm resolve.

Not so, this time. This time, his wolf fought like a caged, wild thing driven mad by a long captivity.

At first stunned, Braden successfully battled the beast back into submission, trying to understand what had just happened.

For some reason, whether from the sound of her voice or her intriguing, feminine scent, Princess Alisa affected his wolf, intensifying his urge to shape-shift.

This made absolutely no sense. Braden had no scientific rationale on which to base this supposition. Yet simply being in the same room with her resulted in an epic battle between his human and wolf natures.

Something about her mere presence in his proximity spoke to him on a subconscious level. Something primal, compelling. And completely without reason. The scientific part of him abhorred such illogic.

But the part of him that was wolf didn't care about reason, or logic, or even common sense. The wolf inside him reacted simply to external stimuli, which in this case was her. Princess Alisa was, for some unknown reason, the catalyst. His wolf reacted to her with a violent certainty.

Making him at war with himself.

Not good, especially since his first impression of her wasn't a good one. The woman was stubborn and arrogant. He could hear it in the impatient, irritated tone she used.

Of course, he supposed that was to be expected. She was royalty, after all, not used to mingling with common mortals like himself. Presented with an opportunity to do something that might help not only her own country but shifters around the world, she'd balked. No doubt she planned on sulking like a spoiled child and making things as difficult as possible when they worked together, hoping to shorten the amount of time he would require her.

Her ploy wouldn't work. He'd tough it out. He might not like her, but he had no choice. If he could have chosen another subject to use in his research, he definitely would have.

But her kind was rare. In fact, she was the only one he'd heard of who could go so long without changing and continue to exhibit no outward signs of madness. So he would have to use her, whether he or she liked it or not. Life wasn't always a bowl of cherries, something that had been proven to him over and over.

She'd imperiously demanded he remove his dark glasses. He'd complied. After he'd done so, he waited for whatever pithy comment she'd come up with.

He heard the sharp intake of breath that indicated she'd only just realized the extent of her rudeness. Waiting for the inevitable apology felt a bit anticlimactic, so he decided to head her off at the pass.

"Now, about the experiments… I was thinking four hours in the morning before lunch, then if you can spare the time, another two hours in the afternoon. Will that work for you?"

His rapid change of subject worked as a distraction. She sputtered, whatever half-hearted apology she'd been about to utter forgotten. "Six hours a day? That's impossible. I have way too much to do to be able to agree to that large a block of time. I was thinking more along the line of an hour a day." Her tone made it clear she thought she was being generous.

Braden bit back a retort. He couldn't help but wonder if the king and queen enjoyed watching them spar the way spectators did at a tennis match. Whatever they were doing, they were awfully quiet. He didn't like quiet people—silence made it difficult for him to visualize them.

"Dr. Streib?" The princess touched his hand, sending an odd frisson of electricity through him. "Are you listening to me? I cannot possibly work with you for more than an hour—or two at most—a day."

"Ah, so we're going to barter for time?" Facing in her direction, eyebrows raised, he gave her a look plainly meant to tell her what he thought of her. To strengthen the effect, he left his sunglasses lying on the table in front of him, right next to the bowl of what smelled like fresh salad that the servers had just placed in front of him.

When she didn't immediately respond, King Leo cleared his throat. "I think we've had enough discussion for now. Let's enjoy our lunch, shall we? And then surely you two can work something out afterward."

The reply Princess Alisa made to her father's barely veiled command was unintelligible. Braden hid a smile as he fumbled for his fork, glad he finally would get to eat something more substantial than the dry breakfast bar he'd taken from the meager supply of snacks he'd packed for the trip. Across from him and next to him, he heard the clink of silverware on china as everyone began to eat.

Funny, how he pictured this place and these people. Judging from his booming voice and jovial tone, King Leo would be a robust man, with a full head of wavy hair and maybe even a short beard. Queen Ionna would be blonde and tiny and petite, with the kind of regal beauty found only in the movies.

While Princess Alisa… He puzzled briefly over her. No doubt she resembled a Barbie doll, all curves and plastic perfection.

Still pondering the images, he turned his attention to the meal. The salad was fresh and crisp, the dressing delicious, melting on his tongue. He barely got to enjoy the amazing explosion of subtle flavors before he finished the last bit of watercress and the servers began whisking away the bowls. Hurriedly, he put his fork down and instantly, someone removed his empty bowl. A second later, someone else placed another plate in front of him.

The next course, some kind of baked fish and evidently the main luncheon, smelled so good his mouth watered. He didn't want to continue stuffing his face like a cretin, so he let himself savor the smell. "What kind of fish is this?" he asked politely.

"This is nase, one of our native fish and our chef's specialty," Queen Ionna said softly. "It's a particular favorite in our country. I hope you like it."

Her lightly accented English was pleasing to the ear. Thanking her, he nodded, well aware that even if the nase tasted like baked sawdust, he'd have to choke it down with a complimentary smile on his face.

Luckily for him, the first bite proved as wonderful as it smelled, which was no small feat. These days, since losing his vision, he was all about the scent, even as human. This had the added benefit of making him feel much closer to his lupine nature.

A companionable silence fell while they all dug in. Though ravenous, Braden couldn't help but be über-conscious of the princess, or as he preferred to think of her, his subject, seated directly across from him. Even though he couldn't actually see her, the odd pull he felt toward her was quite strong. He listened for some sort of signal that she'd finished her meal so he could once again bring up the subject of their schedule.

One of his flaws—and to be honest, he was aware he

had many—was his absolute devotion to routine, especially these days. After all, maintaining a sort of precise order was the only way he could keep control of his now dark and sightless world. If he was to have a prayer of completing his research in the time the king had allotted, he had to make certain Princess Alisa would consent to more than a mere hour or two a day. Perhaps if she understood that at that rate, the testing would take months rather than weeks, she'd be a little more generous with her precious time.

As if his was worthless.

A light touch on the back of his hand made him start. "Did you enjoy the fish?" the princess asked, her dulcet tone sweet enough to constitute a warning that she was up to something. He didn't know her well enough to know what, exactly.

Instantly alert, he murmured a polite response. Carefully keeping his posture relaxed, he waited for her to drop the bomb.

"If I am to spend copious amounts of time in your laboratory, then it's only fair that you return the favor," she told him. "I have need of an escort to attend several formal affairs with me."

Sensing her parents listening with interest, he pretended to give her words serious thought. "While I would be honored, of course, are you sure you've carefully thought this out? I am unable to see, after all. As such, my usefulness would be quite limited."

There. Sitting back and folding his arms, he waited for her response. No one, especially not a beautiful princess, wanted to walk around with a blind man on her arm. Now let her try to back out of that one gracefully.

"Don't worry. I'll help you," she said, barely missing a beat. "As long as you know how to dance, I can keep us pointed in the right direction. Other than that, your main duty will be holding my arm and trying to look interested while other people babble inanely to us."

Surprised, he barely suppressed a snort of laughter. "Sounds like one of a hundred faculty gatherings I have to attend at CU, the university where I occasionally teach."

"Then you agree to do this?"

Against his better judgment, he found himself nodding. "I'll be your escort. That is, if you can agree to spend at least four hours in the mornings at my lab."

Her affirmative reply, edged with amusement, made him duck his head so she wouldn't see his smile turn into a grin.

Interesting. Something about this princess intrigued him, something beyond the fact that she was an anomaly. Being around her made his wolf restless and made him…what? Curious to know more? Of course. That was why he'd come here, after all.

Yet, in his analytical way, he knew it was more. He liked that she could keep him off balance, something few had ever been able to do despite his recent loss of sight.

Oddly enough, for reasons he'd yet to fathom, the princess was dangerous to his equilibrium. He'd have to try to keep his mouth shut and work as fast as he could. Because of what she was, who she was, he couldn't risk offending her too badly. The quicker he could conduct his experiments and analyze the data, the better.

The reason why she wanted him to act as his escort escaped him. But he'd do it, if doing so meant she'd consent to spend more time in his research lab. But even there, he had to be careful. Too much time alone with her and he just might pop off and say the wrong thing. Or worse, grab her and plant a hard kiss on that smart-ass mouth of hers.

Shocked at the thought, he shook his head at his own foolishness. That wouldn't be good on so many levels it boggled his mind.

Still, something about her…

"Penny for them?" the princess asked, startling him out of his thoughts.

While he searched his brain for something safe to say, his wolf half began to stir, inexplicably restless.

"Dr. Streib?" Her voice again, slicing through his thoughts. "Are you all right?"

"Call me Braden." His response was automatic as he prepared to lie. "I'm just mentally reviewing some of the tests I need to run on you in the morning."

"I see. Have you finished with your fish?"

It dawned on him that one of the serving staff stood at his elbow, ready to remove his plate. "Yes," he answered. "It was very good."

Immediately, someone whisked his plate away.

"I'm particularly looking forward to today's dessert," King Leo pronounced.

"Dessert?" Startled, Braden rubbed the back of his neck. "I'm stuffed. I couldn't possibly eat another—"

A light touch on his hand shocked him into silence.

"It's his favorite." The soft warning in Princess Alisa's voice made his wolf even more restless. "You can at least have a taste, can't you?"

His mouth had gone dry, so he nodded, hoping he successfully masked his expression. Unfortunately, as though sensing weakness, his internal wolf chose that moment to go on the offensive, fighting to be allowed to surface, to break free.

Damn. Braden did a quick mental calculation. How long had it been exactly since he'd last changed?

After a quick internal struggle, he wrestled his beast back under control, all the while keeping his head down so the Teslinko royal family wouldn't know.

He usually was more careful. Changing often enough to keep his wolf satisfied. This level of discord had never happened to him before. His wolf felt nearly out of control. Why this furious need? Why now? Was it them? Or her? He suspected the latter, though it made no sense. Why would being around this woman affect his beast in such a visceral and urgent way?

As scientist, he desperately deduced that one reason had to be simply because being blind, he experienced everything more sharply in his lupine form. He didn't miss his vision nearly as much as he did while human. With wolves, scent was the dominant sense. Scent told him almost everything, as much as vision did for humans.

And Princess Alisa smelled perfect. Feminine and flowers and vanilla, all in one.

Hellhounds, this wasn't good. Counting back, he tried to calculate how long it had been since he'd changed. Ruefully, he acknowledged that too much time had passed. He'd been so occupied with his research and securing the permission of King Leo and Queen Ionna, and then traveling here and getting settled in, that he'd managed to completely ignore his own needs. His own wolf's needs.

He needed to change. As soon as humanly possible. Perhaps, since he wasn't going to work with the princess today, this afternoon would be a good time to find a secluded, wooded place to shape-shift and let his caged wolf run free.

Even thinking about this brought his wolf back, roaring to life. The beast inside him rushed the invisible barrier, testing the mental bounds Braden had imposed.

Finishing the fight, he raised his head, suddenly aware of the yawning silence. No doubt they were all staring at him, wondering if he'd completely lost his mind.

"Dr. Streib?" Queen Ionna asked gently. "Are you all right? You haven't even touched your dessert."

Forcing a shaky smile, he turned in the direction of her voice. "Yes, I am. My apologies. I was thinking of all that must be done. I am very eager to begin."

On his other side, Princess Alisa made an odd noise in the back of her throat. "Try your cake," she said, her tone perfectly level. "You do not wish to disrespect the king, now, do you?"

Put that way, what could he do? Fumbling for his fork, he finally located it and managed to scoop up some of the king's favorite dessert. Not sure what to expect, he was surprised to find it melted on his tongue. In addition to chocolate, he tasted peanut butter and a hint of something else. Cinnamon. And a lot of sugar. A whole lot of sugar. So much that he felt vaguely queasy.

"Excellent," he lied, taking a second bite and manfully choking it down.

"I told you." King Leo sounded pleased. "There is a reason this is my number one sweet."

Nodding, Braden continued to eat, shoveling the cake into his mouth as quickly as he could while still having some sort of table manners.

"Take it easy, dear," Queen Ionna admonished. "You'll choke if you continue to eat so fast."

Polishing off what felt like the last bite, he swallowed, before taking a large gulp of his now lukewarm coffee. "Very good. I'm sorry if I seem to be rushing, but I have much to do to get ready to begin testing the princess tomorrow. If you'll—"

"Our daughter is eager to begin as well," King Leo interrupted before Braden could get out the words *excuse me.* "Isn't that right, Alisa?"

"Of course," she said, sounding about as sincere as he felt when forcing down the sickeningly sweet cake. "Where is your laboratory? I will meet you there in the morning."

Braden took his time answering, figuring King Leo would interrupt and tell her the rest of it. Not only had the royal family allowed him the rare privilege of analyzing their youngest daughter, but they had set up a fully functional laboratory down the hall from his bedroom. This was on the same floor as hers, though in a completely different wing.

But neither the king nor the queen spoke. Apparently, they were leaving it to him to relay the news.

"Well?" she repeated, her rich voice curious and mildly exasperated, all at once. Once again, just the sound of her had the same effect on him, like a jolt of raw energy sending his wolf into a frenzy.

Again, damn it. Gritting his teeth, he battled back his other half. This had not happened since he'd been a teenager, full of raging hormones. It took him a moment to get his beast under control, luckily. Though this time, he lost more ground more quickly. If the beast kept fighting him, he'd have to do something quickly or there'd be a major embarrassing incident. He could only imagine that it'd be in extremely poor form to shape-shift in the palace while lunching with Pack royalty.

He had to get a grip on this thing, whatever it was. Taking a deep breath, he wondered how much longer he'd have to wait to manage to politely excuse himself.

"Your laboratory, Dr. Streib?" Princess Alisa repeated, speaking slowly as though she now thought him a simpleton. "I asked you where I might find it."

Lifting his chin, Braden explained the situation in a few short sentences. "My understanding is that I am actually working on the same floor where you also reside."

"At the opposite end," King Leo put in. "This is a very large palace, Dr. Streib. Your living quarters and your laboratory are in the west wing. Princess Alisa occupies most of the east."

Thankfully, the princess didn't comment. Braden wasn't sure he could take another assault of her voice on his wolf self. Now if he could just get out of there until he got his beast under control.

"I'm glad we got that settled," King Leo said, amusement warring with preoccupation in his voice. "We have also provided you with an assistant, Dr. Streib. Katya will be there to help you first thing in the morning."

"Thank you," Braden said, pleasantly surprised.

"You are most welcome." The king heaved a satisfied sigh. "Now, if you two will excuse us, the queen and I will leave you to finish your discussion. Come, my dear."

Braden pushed to his feet as well, standing politely as the King and Queen of Teslinko exited the room. When he finally took his seat again, he sensed the princess studying him. He wanted nothing more than to bolt, but knew he had to do something to satisfy his wolf.

He had no choice but to enlist her help. He needed to change badly and he had no idea where to go.

The servers offered more coffee. They both accepted, waiting while the beverage was poured.

She sighed. "You are different than I would have expected."

If she wanted to make polite small talk, he thought he could manage, as long as he kept a death grip on his wolf. "How so?"

"Well," she mused, "despite your generally ruffled and disheveled appearance, you are actually a very attractive man."

Heat suffused him, which both infuriated and intrigued him. "Though a bit backhanded, I'll accept the compliment."

She laughed, a low and musical sound that sent a heated shiver through him. He felt his grip on his wolf slipping and frowned, concentrating on regaining control. "Now it's your turn," she said, a smile making her voice light.

"My turn?"

"To compliment me."

Was she *flirting* with him? He could think of no reason why someone like her would do so other than to mock him. But why? They were alone. Did she mock him for her own amusement? Considering he knew absolutely nothing about her personally, such a thing was entirely possible.

Taking a deep breath, he considered his options. Even when he'd been able to see, flirting had not been his strong suit. Fleeing would not only be cowardly, but slow and ungainly since he was unfamiliar with the path he'd need to take. In reality, he knew he could withstand much from her, considering how badly he needed her for his research.

Rapidly searching for a vapid, non-offensive bit of frippery, he settled on the first thing that came to mind. "You have a sensuous voice and a beautiful laugh."

The instant the words left his mouth, he knew he'd made a huge mistake. Too personal and too true. Not at all the purpose of light, playful flirtation. He should know this—intellectually, he did. But because he sucked at flirting, abhorred it in fact, he'd given her truth when she wanted falsehood.

As if she knew this—of course she did—she inhaled sharply. Any moment now, he suspected she'd let fly with a bit of scathing commentary, merely to point out what kind of social pariah he was. And if she did, he knew he wouldn't be able to rein himself in. He'd respond in kind. While he wasn't good at flirting, he was excellent with cutting retorts.

Which would only make things worse between them. He needed to get along with her if he wanted her cooperation for his experiments.

His tenuous grip on his wolf slipped. Out of his depth, he took the only option that made sense. Leaving before he either said something truly awful or worse, before his wolf broke free and he shape-shifted right there in the dining room of the royal palace.

Pushing to his feet, he murmured a quick excuse and headed out. She made no move to help him, despite the fact that he'd forgotten his cane.

Halfway in his struggle toward the door, he turned

in her general direction. "Please come see me in the morning in my laboratory. I'm eager to begin my work."

Without waiting for her to answer, he left the room, cursing his social ineptitude and cursing the fact that he hadn't managed to ask her to assist him in finding a place to change.

Once again, it appeared he was on his own. He and his wolf, both blind, sharing the same, desperate need.

Chapter 3

Strange man. Watching as he struggled to get to his feet and leave as quickly as he could with his head up and his dignity intact, Alisa wondered why the doctor had so much difficulty engaging in what she considered normal small talk between a man and a woman.

He'd been affronted and offended, acting as if she'd insulted him when in fact she'd meant no harm. Honestly, she didn't know any other way to converse with a man who wasn't either family or in her employ. Truth be told, she'd always hated it. Growing up watching her older sisters, Alisa had known she wasn't beautiful or sensual or even very interesting. Still, she'd known what had been expected of her and so she behaved accordingly. Young or old, married or single, they flirted and she flirted back. It meant absolutely nothing. It was all a game and everyone did it.

Everyone, that is, except Dr. Braden Streib.

When he almost walked into the doorframe instead of through the door, she rose from her seat to go to him and offer her assistance, but he corrected himself at the last moment. Which was good, because she knew he probably wouldn't welcome her help in any way.

Strike the *probably*. He would *not* want her assistance at anything other than his research tests.

Noted. Not only was he arrogant, but stubborn and rude to boot. One of those intellectual types who looked down on people who weren't.

Which stung, because he apparently hadn't bothered to learn anything about her other than her ability to go a long time without shifting. She wasn't the stereotypical fairy tale type of princess, spending her days shopping and partying. Instead, she'd taken stock of her assets and realized early on that her intelligence would get her much farther than her looks. So she'd gone to university, earning both her bachelor's and her master's in short time. She was currently on track to work on her doctorate.

Few people knew that about her as it was something she took care to keep hidden from the world. The last thing she wanted was paparazzi following her around campus with cameras. She enjoyed blending in, loving a place where she wasn't judged in the shadows of her two sisters' amazing looks.

Once again, someone wanted to put her in the spotlight and highlight her differences.

Dr. Streib claimed to have researched her. Evidently, he'd only checked into her medical history, which seemed oddly shortsighted. For all he knew, her mental ability could have something to do with the way she needed to change less often than others. If anything, she would have expected a researcher of his caliber to be more thorough.

So he thought her a dim-witted party girl. Fine. Lots of people—those that didn't really know her—did. One more shouldn't have bothered her, but it did, oddly enough.

She'd long ago stopped wishing she was prettier. With a blind man, looks wouldn't matter. If he'd been different, more approachable, they could have conversed in a purely intellectual manner. She would have enjoyed that.

Obviously, that wasn't meant to be.

She'd have to figure out another way to deal with him. Too bad. This had been the first time in a long time that she'd actually been more than mildly interested in a man.

As for his research, she knew beyond a doubt that her blood, body or cells didn't contain some magical, mystical difference that would give him the secret to her ability to remain human for long periods of time. It was just who she was, a little bit of extra she'd gotten since she'd clearly been passed over in the beauty department.

With a small shrug, she rose and smoothed down her dress. They'd have to figure out a way to get along. After all, they'd be spending a lot of time together in his laboratory—more than she'd intended or imagined, if he had his way. Of course, she didn't plan on working with him for six hours a day, every single day. She had her volunteer work and her education, as well as her horses and her painting.

Out in the hallway, she took a leisurely stroll to the

staircase, wincing as she imagined him trying to navigate the labyrinth that was the palace. She should have helped him, regardless of his antagonism, as she would have assisted any guest. In the future, she resolved that she would. No matter what he said, she wouldn't let him get to her.

She would help him do his experiments and tests and hopefully, when he found nothing, he'd accept that with good grace and go back to America where he belonged.

There. Problem solved. She'd do her duty, her father would be happy, and Dr. Streib would go away knowing he'd tried. Now she could relax and try to go about completing her duties for the afternoon.

Though she bustled around the palace on various errands, Dr. Streib was conspicuously absent the rest of the day. He didn't attend the evening meal and when she inquired, she learned he'd chosen to eat alone in his room.

Since her parents were entertaining friends with an elaborate formal dinner and her brother had gone out on one of his numerous dates, Alisa also ate alone. This happened more frequently than not, as she preferred quiet evenings at home with a good book to going out on the town partying with a group of people she had to pretend were her friends.

As usual, that night she took her meal in a small table in the kitchen. The ginger chicken with black beans was tasty and she ate slowly while she read.

Oddly enough, though normally she relished the peace and quiet, this night she found she would have welcomed company. Not just any company, but Dr. Streib's. For some unfathomable reason, she realized she found their verbal sparring invigorating.

After she'd finished her meal, she grabbed a pot of fresh tea and headed up to her room to read. Aware she had to be at the laboratory early, she got ready for bed, crawling beneath the covers right as her clock chimed midnight. She had a touch of a headache, though she felt too tired to get back out of her bed and search for a pain reliever.

If she had any dreams, she didn't remember them.

The next morning she woke to bright sunshine and birdsong. Testing her head, she found the headache had retreated. Good. Stretching, she tried to decide what she'd do that afternoon. Normally on a day like this, she'd go for a horseback ride or a long walk with her dogs. Since she knew she'd be confined to the house helping Dr. Streib with his pointless research in the morning, maybe she'd do some of her favorite activities that afternoon.

Stretching, she reluctantly climbed from her super-soft bed and padded across the room to the shower. She elected not to call in any of her numerous assistants, preferring to perform her late morning preparations in privacy. She'd long ago learned that her day went better if she kept the fussing and pampering to a minimum. Of course, if there was a special event, she used all the help at her disposal. But for day-to-day, routine life, she preferred to do as much as possible on her own.

Ninety minutes later, hair scooped back in a jaunty ponytail and minimal makeup skillfully applied, she wandered out into the hallway dressed in jeans and boots and a soft cashmere sweater. Despite the bright sunshine, the weather forecasters had predicted a cold front coming in from the mountains later that day and she wanted to be ready.

A quick glance at her watch showed it was nearly noon. She'd overslept. Next time, she'd be sure and set an alarm. After having an egg-white omelet for a late breakfast, she took her second cup of coffee with her as she made her way to Dr. Streib's laboratory. She wasn't sure what exactly to expect, but she doubted any of it would be fun.

Focusing intently on listening to any sound from the hall outside the room he'd been given to use as a laboratory, Braden tamped down his rising irritation and impatience. Where was the princess? He'd asked her to be here at eight and he'd of course arrived early, grabbing some kind of pastry from the kitchen and asking for a pot of coffee to be sent to his room.

He tapped his wrist, grimacing as his audible watch stated the time. Princess Alisa was nearly four hours late. At this rate, it would be lunchtime and the entire castle would come to a grinding halt so everyone could eat some sort of huge meal.

Had she meant to stand him up? Was the no-show her way of quietly rebelling against her father's dictate that she submit to testing?

Cursing under his breath, he went over placement of his equipment for the six or seventh time. The first things he'd planned to do would all be routine medical tests. An EKG, some blood work and a urinalysis. The king had even, at no doubt great expense, brought in an MRI machine and a CT scanner and set them up in separate rooms.

He planned to do everything both to her and to himself, so he could use his results as baseline.

When he'd finished, all of the data would be analyzed and digitally encrypted in his computer. Voice recognition software would enable him to dictate and he had an audio program in place to keep him informed of the results.

He'd already run his own panel of tests. The only thing missing was his subject. Princess Alisa herself.

He cursed again. Virulently. If he'd been able to see, he would stride down the hall and locate her himself, bringing her back to the lab posthaste. As it was, without sight he couldn't actually stride, though he could do some damage with his cane if he felt so inclined.

His watch again announced the hour. Straight up and down noon. They should have gotten started hours ago. Hours. If his subject wasn't royalty, she'd be in for a tongue-lashing when she finally showed up. Assuming she did show up.

He began to pace the length of the small room, having predetermined there were no obstacles to trip over. Despite what pre-conceived notions he might have had of spoiled, selfish princesses, he truly hadn't expected this.

To her, this might be all fun and games. Something she had to do to keep her father happy so he wouldn't cut her off. But to Braden, this was more. This was his life's work, something that could make a difference as much as his work in surgery had. Discovering a cure for the madness that plagued those who didn't change often enough would be epic. Legendary.

The implication was unfathomable. He could only imagine how such knowledge would broaden the horizons for so many. Pack members would be able to serve in the navy, travel on submarines and ships. They could work on oil rigs and drilling platforms, and other places where it was impossible to change.

If he could discover the secret. He was so close. And if he actually believed in anything as esoteric as gut feelings, he'd say that he could feel it.

Princess Alisa held the key. He knew this with unshakable certainty. For this reason he had jumped through diplomatic hoops, secured the necessary permissions and gathered supplies.

Now he'd cleared all the hurdles and made the journey to Teslinko. The ordeal had taken far too long to come to fruition. Now, the time had finally come to begin.

Then this. His subject hadn't shown up. She knew the key lay with her and didn't much care. A pampered princess from some obscure European country. No doubt she'd like nothing better than to dismiss him and stroll away, laughing all the while.

Which she couldn't do. He wouldn't let her. He'd go back to King Leo if necessary. Princess Alisa was vital to his research, the sole living shifter who could go six months to a year without changing shape and—most importantly—without going mad. Such a thing was virtually unheard of, except in the dusty old legends of their kind.

Consumed by his thoughts and his pacing, he almost missed the sound. There. High heels tapping on marble. Princess Alisa had finally deigned to grace him with her presence.

Braden clenched his jaw, steeling himself for her arrival. When she entered the room, his wolf sat up and took notice. He could have sworn the atmospheric pressure changed, or something else completely unscientific. Either way, it made him uncomfortable and he didn't like it one bit.

He busied himself with pretending not to notice her arrival and rechecking his equipment.

"Hello? Earth to Doctor." A trace of amusement colored her husky voice.

He started, still playing her game, all the while suppressing the urge to lash out with some comment about the time. "Ah, Princess Alisa. I didn't hear you arrive."

"Obviously," she drawled. "Well, I'm here. I'd like to get this over with as quickly as possible. Shall we get started?"

He couldn't help it—he saw red. Over with as quickly as possible? They could have been halfway done with that morning's tests if she'd actually showed up when she'd agreed to. This—and more, in fact all the remonstrations he wanted to say—simmered right at the tip of his tongue.

Rather then spewing them, he swallowed hard, taking a deep breath, trying to compose himself. If he gave in to his temper, he'd make things even more difficult.

He wasn't used to exercising such restraint.

His watch chose that time to speak the hour. Twelve-fifteen. More time wasted. Perfect.

And then his stomach growled. Loudly.

"Have you had your lunch?" he managed, hoping there was the smallest semblance of civility in his voice.

"Lunch?" Again she laughed. "I'm not hungry. Since I overslept, I barely just finished my breakfast."

Which would explain why she was only now showing up. She must have slept in. Of course she'd slept in.

If she'd been a graduate student at CU, he would have given her a severe tongue-lashing. Instead, he fiddled with the EKG machine, aware she'd have no idea that he wasn't resetting it or something.

Restraint, he told himself. Restraint. Difficult to maintain when his agitation had stirred up his wolf even more, making the beast restless and angry.

"I ate breakfast hours ago," he said, wondering if she'd take the hint.

"Yes, you mentioned you were an early riser."

When her cheerful comment got no response, she moved closer, bringing with her that fresh fragrance of peaches and vanilla. "Are you all right, Dr. Streib? You sound sort of…strangled."

Perceptive, wasn't she? To a point, that is.

"I'm fine." He ground out the words. "Let's get you hooked up to this machine." Pointing to a curtained-off area in the corner, he worked hard at keeping his voice level and emotionless. "You can change there. Put on the robe, making sure it opens to the back. My assistant will hook you up to the electrodes."

"Your assistant?" She sounded skeptical. "We're alone in this room. I see no helper."

Jaw aching from clenching it, he counted to three for patience. "That's because I sent her to have lunch. She was hungry." After they'd waited nearly four hours for the princess to put in an appearance.

"I see." She was on the move, her voice drifting to him from around the room. "What did my mother say her name was?"

"Katya." He hoped she wasn't messing with any of his equipment. "Your parents were kind to offer her. I believe her normal duties are as personal assistant to the queen."

"Ah, okay." Now she spoke from his left. "I know

her. And how long do you think it will be until she returns?"

"Not long. She should be back any minute now." He hoped. "She'll need a urine sample and then will draw some blood."

She made a sound, no doubt meant to convey distaste, but since he couldn't see her expression, he couldn't be positive.

"What about you? What will you do while I have this test?"

"I'll be eating." Using his cane to guide him, he stomped toward the door, needing to escape her before his anger boiled over. "I'm hungry. As I said, some of us ate breakfast hours ago. In the morning, when most people do."

Unable to resist that parting shot, he shook his head. Hopefully he could get his temper under control so that when he returned, he could participate in the experiments himself without thoroughly pissing her off.

He could always hope. Maybe food would do much to calm him down.

He passed Katya the personal-assistant-turned-research-assistant as he rounded the first corner. "The princess is waiting for you," he told her. "I'll be back after I grab some lunch."

"Are you sure I should do this on my own?" Katya asked, a hint of desperation in her heavily accented voice. "I've never done this before and I'm afraid I'll do something wrong."

Good Lord, even she didn't want to be alone with Princess Prima Donna. "You'll be fine," he said.

"Before I go to the lab, I think you will need my help?" Katya persisted. "I can show you the way to the dining room. It is a very long walk, though it is on the same floor."

"I'll be all right." He shook his head. "Don't keep your princess waiting. Please do the EKG like I showed you. Also, see if she will give you a sample for the urinalysis, would you?"

Without waiting for her answer, he moved off in the right direction, at least judging by the scent of food. He'd gotten quite good at following his nose.

After he'd eaten, he got to his feet and made his way slowly back to the lab, dreading the next confrontation.

At least Katya should have finished the preliminary tests by now and hopefully she'd managed to coax the princess into cooperating. Since they needed to make up for the time lost that morning, if he had anything to say about it, the princess would be spending the entire afternoon in his lab. Luckily for him, his wolf appeared to be sleeping.

"Here he is," Katya said immediately when he entered the room.

"Did you enjoy the meal?" the princess asked, without inflection.

"Very much." He wondered if Alisa was smiling or frowning, then decided he didn't really care. Instead, he directed his next question at his assistant. "Katya, have you run all the tests?"

"Yes, Doctor. The computer has done all the analysis and the report is ready for you to hear."

"Hear?" Princess Alisa chimed in. She actually sounded interested, which surprised him.

"I have a computer program that reads to me, since I obviously can't read myself. It assimilates all the data, computes a result and then relays that result to me."

He inclined his head, dismissing his assistant. "Katya, thanks for your help. I won't need anything else from you today. You can leave now."

He got a sense of the other woman curtsying to him, which almost made him smile. His imagination apparently had become particularly vivid since arriving here in Teslinko. He'd actually started seeing things despite having no way of knowing if they were actually happening. This blindness thing was messing with his mind. Not good for a scientist. Not good at all.

"Thank you, Doctor," Katya said, moving past him so quickly he felt the disturbance in the air.

Leaving him alone with the high and mighty one. Who was no doubt glaring at him this very instant. A second later, he scoffed at himself. He usually went with facts, not suppositions.

"I'm glad she's gone," Alisa finally said, surprising him. "I don't like her."

"Why not?" he asked, curious despite himself.

"Good question." Silence while she appeared to be musing over her answer. "I don't know. I don't like her energy. She doesn't give me a good feeling."

Energy. Feeling. Next she'd be talking about vibes. Par for the course. He wouldn't be surprised if she mentioned she studied astrology or the healing powers of crystals. After all, how else could a bored and rich princess amuse herself?

Rather than comment, Braden concentrated on his equipment. Fumbling on the tabletop—he hated fumbling—until he located his headphones, he flashed an utterly fake smile in her general direction before he slipped them on and pressed the play button.

Listening while the mechanical voice relayed data,

he frowned. Nothing out of the ordinary. The complete blood panel and the urinalysis contained nothing different or abnormal, nothing that wasn't common to every other shifter on the planet. Not one single blasted thing. Except for blood type, his results and hers were exactly alike.

How could this be? Though he certainly hadn't expected this to be easy, there had to be at least one thing out of place, one anomaly. Something. Anything.

The machine finished spitting out data and went silent. Had he missed something? He punched the replay button, and the audio stream started again, repeating the same test results.

A moment later, her arm brushed his as she reached around him and clicked the machine off, cutting the mechanical voice off mid-syllable.

His wolf came instantly awake.

Slowly, he removed his headphones, pushing back a surge of justifiable anger. "Why did you do that?"

"Surely you don't expect me to sit here and twiddle my thumbs while you listen to music or whatever," she drawled. "A little conversation would help pass the time."

Calling on his rapidly dissipating patience, he shook his head. "Princess, we aren't here for social hour. This is work, plain and simple. Tests were run, and I need to listen to the results."

"But I'd like to hear them, too," she protested. "Play them out loud. You don't have to wear the headphones."

For the love of... He cleared his throat. "You wouldn't understand them if you heard them. Next time, why don't you bring a book or something to amuse yourself."

Her sharp intake of breath told him she hadn't taken

his comment favorably. "How do you know I won't understand? You might be surprised."

"I doubt it." Again the sharp hiss of breath. His wolf had begun pacing, telling him he faced another epic battle if he didn't wrap this up and find a place to change.

"I'm not going to argue with you," she began.

"Good. Now, if you don't mind, I need to review the data one more time." He reached for the audio button and listened again as the robotic voice replayed the numbers. This time, she did not interrupt.

Chapter 4

Finally, after listening for the third time, he clicked it off and removed his headphones. "No answers," he said with a sigh, wondering if she was still there. "Not a single, solitary clue."

"I'm sorry," she said. "But do not ever do that to me again."

Honestly surprised, he cocked his head. "Do what to you again?"

"Shut me out." A thin thread of anger made her melodic voice vibrate. "I'll let you have a pass this one time, but if you want me to be part of this, you've got to make me a full part. I need to listen in. I'm not just a lab rat."

With his wolf on full alert, he considered her words. For the first time he wondered if he might have a completely wrong picture of her. Maybe there was more to this princess than met the eye. Why else would she even care what he found out?

"My apologies." Executing a half bow, hoping that such an old-fashioned gesture would please her, he managed a smile, even as he struggled to keep his wolf subdued. "You're right, of course. It won't happen again, I promise."

"Thank you." Rather than gloat, she sounded relieved. "I've been tested before, you know. There's nothing abnormal about me. My parents have already consulted the foremost medical authorities in Teslinko and also in Rome."

"So I've been told." If she wanted to participate, then she needed to know the truth. "But those other doctors were looking for an illness, some hint of madness. I'm looking for something else entirely."

"Like what?"

How could he explain, when he could hardly articulate what he knew even inside his own head? "As unscientific as it sounds, I'm trying to find the unthinkable. Magic that actually can be explained by science."

"Very poetic," she commented, pleasure thrumming in her tone. "I like that."

His wolf stirred again, restless, eager to run. Slamming the lid back down on the place in his mind where his wolf-self resided, he took a moment to compose himself before answering. "Thank you, I guess."

"You're welcome."

He cleared his throat, uncertain how to respond. "Let me check my notes one last time," he said evenly, putting the discussion back where it belonged. Business. "Give me a moment, then we'll start the next round of tests."

To his surprise, she left him alone while he recalibrated his machines and readied his slides. This lasted all of five minutes.

"How did you lose your vision?" she asked, her voice an interesting combination of determined and hesitant. "I heard that you were involved in an accident. Is that true?"

Braden set down a slide and considered. Though normally he disliked talking about what had happened, he figured he owed her an explanation. After all, he'd already given one to the king.

"Yes, though I suspect it was no accident. I'd completed my surgery for the day and stopped by my lab at the university to retrieve some materials before giving a lecture."

He took a deep breath, seeing it all again inside his head. "A few minutes after I arrived, there was an explosion in my lab. A fire. I was injured, badly burned but not incinerated since the explosion knocked me out of the lab itself. They found me unconscious in the parking lot."

"You're lucky you weren't killed."

With a nod, he acknowledged the truth of her words. "So they said. I had burns, a concussion and a few broken bones as well. They healed, but my vision did not come back."

When she spoke again, her voice was low and serious. "Since you are Halfling, I know you don't heal as quickly as a full shifter, but why have you not visited the Healer? I looked on a map and Texas is not all that far from Colorado."

"I did visit her," he said reluctantly. "Her name is

Samantha. She's a very nice woman and really tried to help."

"And?"

"She put her hands on me, did whatever foolishness she apparently does. It didn't work."

She gasped. "I've never heard of a Healer failing."

"Neither had she." He shrugged. "She was shocked. She said there was no reason for me not to see."

She'd also told him his blindness was all in his head and that she thought he felt he needed to make retribution for something. More bullcrap. Of course Samantha hadn't been able to heal him, despite her much-touted successes with other Halflings.

But he was no ordinary Halfling. He was a doctor, a scientist. And, in the history of both mankind and Pack, snake charmers were never successful around those that really questioned.

He didn't say those thoughts out loud. In the past, whenever he'd dared to voice them, the reactions had ranged from anger to derision. At him, rather than the Healer.

A brief, uncomfortable silence fell, during which he refused to fidget or otherwise reveal how uneasy this line of conversation made him feel. Instead, he went back to reviewing his notes, listening as the mechanical voice replayed them for the fourth time. This time, he eschewed the headphones and played them out loud so that she could hear, too.

Listening with him, she waited only a few moments before interrupting. "Do you mind if I ask you a question?"

With a sigh, he pushed Pause, then clicked the machine off. Why not? He wasn't getting anywhere with these test results. "Another one?"

"Yes." She must have leaned closer, because he caught a whisper of her unique scent. She smelled feminine and delicious, making his head spin and sending his wolf into bouts of pacing again.

"How did you manage to talk my parents into agreeing with this nonsense?"

He lifted his chin, wishing he could see her expression. "Your parents are honestly worried about you," he told her. "After all, your ability to remain in the human form for so long *is* abnormal. Since this usually brings about madness, they didn't want you to go insane."

"Always? You said usually. Does it always bring about madness? Surely someone, somewhere has done this without going crazy?"

Aware that she—unless she'd been living under a rock—already knew the answer, he nodded. "Without exception, not changing often enough has always meant madness. Until now, until you. That's why you're such a puzzle."

"In that case, let me give you another aspect to look at." She sounded triumphant, as though he'd played right into her no doubt elegant and perfectly manicured hands. "How do you know I'm not already mad?"

After a second of startled silence, during which he imagined the horrified faces of her worried parents, he couldn't help it, he threw back his head and laughed. Long and robustly and full of genuine amusement. Part of him was amazed. He hadn't laughed like that since the explosion.

"I'm glad you find me humorous," she finally said,

her voice an interesting combination of frosty and hurt. "It was a serious question."

"No, it wasn't." Crossing his arms, he tilted his head in her direction. She intrigued him, with all her apparent contradictions.

"What do you mean?"

"You know you're not crazy. Therefore, your question was completely rhetorical. Though I do promise if you have real questions, ones that actually pertain to my work, I'll do my best to answer them."

She muttered something that sounded like a curse, and then he heard the scraping sound of her pushing back her chair. Murmuring her apologies in a falsely sincere voice, she hurried off without another word to him, her high heels clicking on the floors.

Rubbing his chin, he listened to her go. Damn. Despite his best efforts—and what he considered success in keeping himself reined in—he'd still managed to anger Princess Alisa, cutting short his already inadequate time to work with her.

For maybe the fifteenth time, he wished he'd been able to locate another subject. He'd certainly searched hard enough. But every single time he'd thought he actually might have found someone, when he'd checked them out he'd found their story to be false.

In that regard, he'd spoken the truth to the princess. Not changing often enough meant madness for shifters, whether full or Halfling. Every single time.

Until now. He had verification from her parents, her teachers, her friends and her doctors. Princess Alisa was the lone exception known in the entire world. And for that reason alone, she was vital to his research.

But working with her wasn't going to be easy. Not

with the way his wolf reacted to her. If not for the possible magnitude of the reward to his kind once he was proven right, he knew damn good and well that he'd already have decided this was too much trouble and hightailed it out of this tiny European country and back home to Boulder, Colorado, to work on something else. Hounds knew he had plenty of interesting projects on the back burner.

Yet none of them were vital. Not like this. Why, if he were to discover a way for any shifter to maintain their human form longer than a few weeks, then a Pack astronaut could actually go to the space station. Or on a ship out to sea without having to be confined to a tiny cabin to shift in misery and unhappiness. A wolf that couldn't hunt and roam wasn't pleasant to deal with. To say the least.

Rolling his shoulders, he smiled ruefully. No matter how unpleasant the chore might be, he must figure out a way to work with Princess Alisa and to make it as painless as possible. For both of them.

The doctor was a bore. Eyeing him, shaggy black head bent over his machine, she couldn't figure out what it was about him that was different. But he was. He infuriated her, enraged her, and made her wolf restless and uneasy.

He also made her feel alive.

Which made no sense. Alisa had always had an analytical mind. Though she'd had her share of crushes when she was younger and affairs through college, without exception she'd been able to dispassionately examine every single one. She'd known why she'd been attracted to Damian (sex appeal), or Theo (rakish charm), or Ian (blond good looks combined with a brilliant, acerbic mind). In the past, she'd chosen male companions for their ability to make her laugh, or because they had an interesting hobby (like Christoff with his hang gliding). She'd had no delusions at all why they wanted to be with her—she was the proverbial brass ring, bringing with her a title and riches, despite her dismaying lack of beauty.

Dr. Streib cared little for either the money or the title.

So despite being aware of her attraction to Dr. Braden Streib, she was fully cognizant of the exact reasons why she *shouldn't* be even remotely interested in the man.

One, he was not the usual type of man she attracted. He was rough-hewn rather than polished, disheveled rather than neat, his craggy features were compelling enough to warrant a second look, but no more than that.

Second, his personality left much to be desired. He was rude, not charming or deliberately sexy, and apparently the man had absolutely no sense of humor.

He was brilliant, true. But intelligence by itself made a cold bedfellow.

The only good thing she could say—if one were to consider this good—was that her wolf had the hots for his wolf. It was true. Her beast wanted to do the nasty with his.

This alone was reason enough for her to sit up and take notice. In all her relationships, her wolf side had affected bored disinterest at best.

Now, though, for the first time since childhood, her wolf refused to be contained, pacing and whining and snarling. Wanting out.

It grew worse every time she was around him. This afternoon in his laboratory, while verbally taunting him, keeping her wolf contained had required so much effort that she'd finally had to leave the room. Which she'd hated, since doing so felt so much like retreating and Alisa never retreated.

Perhaps she should give in, let her wolf win just once, and suggest that the good doctor and she find a place and shape-shift together. Later, in the normal rush of arousal that always accompanied the change back to human, they could make love with abandon. No strings, no messy emotions, no ties.

Even as the thought flashed into her mind, her long-suffering beast went wild with joy. Definitely something to consider. Taking a deep breath, she did an abrupt about-face and headed back to the lab. Because, after all, Alisa never retreated from a challenge.

Even with the sound of her high heels announcing her return, Braden sensed her presence the instant she stepped into the room, though he didn't acknowledge her.

"I'm back," she finally said loudly, as though he'd lost his hearing as well as his sight. Of course, to be fair, he *was* wearing headphones.

Still, he didn't immediately answer, grateful for the distraction of his computer program that relayed information from the sensitive sensors on his fingertips to the auditory program playing in his headset.

Though she had no way of knowing, he hadn't yet turned the audio portion on yet. In fact, he'd been debating the wisdom of even bothering to do so. After all, how many times could he listen to the same information?

"Hello?" Again the heels clicking on the hard floor.

Tap, tap, tap as she crossed the room to stand near him. Though he couldn't see her, even with his limited human olfactory senses he could smell her. Absently he made a mental note to find out what brand of perfume she wore and have it analyzed—the stuff smelled absolutely wonderful. From this day forward, he'd be unable to smell vanilla and peaches without thinking of her.

"Good afternoon," he said, removing the headphones and forcing a smile all at the same time. "I'm glad you decided to come back. How are you feeling now?"

"Better," she answered, then took a deep breath. "I'm sorry I left earlier. Nature called."

Accepting her obvious lie without comment, he gestured toward the area where she could take a seat. "Please, sit. We'll get started in a moment."

She didn't move. Naturally. If he wanted her to sit, he should have insisted she stand.

"Get started on what?" she asked.

"Tests. Nothing you need to concern yourself with. I won't bore you with the details."

Again he heard her sharp intake of breath, telling him that once more, albeit unintentionally, he'd offended her.

"I'll pretend you didn't say that," she said.

"Okay." And he waited, knowing there would be more.

He wasn't wrong. "How about this?" she asked. "Why don't you tell me what you're working on today and what you need from me? I'd like to know the schedule in advance, before we get started."

"The schedule?" He caught himself wishing he could read her expression, because her voice gave nothing away. If she was taunting him, he couldn't tell.

"Yes," she drawled, making him imagine her studying her no doubt perfectly manicured nails. "Surely you've planned out the rest of the afternoon's tests, have you not?"

"Yes." Sort of. "It's actually not a strict kind of plan. We're simply going to run as many tests as we can fit in."

"How long will each one take?"

"I don't know. I don't work that way."

Still, she persisted. "What kind of tests?"

Focusing on her amazing voice instead of his irritation, he debated how much to tell her. As a socialite whose main concern was no doubt the latest fashion or which party to attend, he didn't expect her to know much about science. *Much?* Ha. Change that to *anything.*

So how many details should he reveal? His research, though complicated, could be simplified, put into layman's terms that would be easy enough for an average high school student to understand.

But would she even care? Judging from the bored impatience with which she greeted his every statement, he doubted she would. Which meant she only asked in order to annoy him. Fair enough. He refused to give her that much satisfaction.

Instead, he'd give her information.

"We'll start with your voice. I want to run some sound tests, to check out your pattern of speech. Then I'll do more blood work and take tissue samples, especially of your hair, skin and even your nails, if you can spare one."

"My nails?" She sounded surprised rather than offended, interested instead of bored. "I don't know about that. If I cut one, I have to trim all the others so they're all the same length. Why do you need them?"

"I'm going to run several tests on your DNA and I want to run the same test on different bodily sources. I'd like to try to isolate the areas where you are different."

"Different?" She sounded both haughty and…hurt? "There is only one way I'm different. I'm descended from centuries of royalty. My Pack lineage can be traced back to those who made up the first Pack. Beyond that—I'm the same as everyone else."

Though his research had already turned this information up, hearing the words said out loud made him realize what an incredible opportunity this was. There were very few shifters anymore who could trace their heritage back to the first Pack.

Of course he couldn't help but wonder if this rare pure blood contributed to her amazing abilities.

And then there was the single anomaly. Both her parents had blond hair and blue eyes, as did her two sisters and one brother. From what he'd read, Alisa was a brunette, with green eyes. Though not common, this was not impossible. Still he had to wonder how her genetic makeup differed from the rest of her family.

"None of your siblings can do what you can do." He spoke his thoughts out loud.

"No. But still—"

"Then your lineage is irrelevant."

Her audible gasp made him smile.

"Insulting me isn't going to help," she said.

"I wasn't insulting you. I said irrelevant, not unremarkable. Don't confuse the two terms."

After a second, she laughed. "Thank you for clearing that up. By the way, you should do that more often."

Confused, he cocked his head. "Do what more often? Clear things up for you?"

"No." She laughed again, the husky sound sending a second shiver through him. "Smile. It becomes you."

"Oh." Unsure how to take her words, he returned his attention to fiddling with the microphone, even though his wolf had gone completely and utterly still at the compliment.

Compliment. Hmmph. Pushing away the rush of warmth, he willed himself to concentrate. Nothing but the science and his work mattered. Nothing. Least of all his insane and inappropriate attraction to a spoiled princess.

"Excuse me, Dr. Streib?" Her voice brought him right back to where he didn't want to be—the present. "You keep zoning out on me while I'm talking. Are you all right?"

"Zoning?" He raised a brow. Sometimes he thought she sounded more like she was from Boulder than he did. "That's a very American term."

"True. But then, I went to school with a bunch of American kids."

"School? You went to an international high school?"

This time her laugh sounded a bit forced. "Not high school. College."

"You went to college?" He didn't know why he was so surprised. "Where?"

"California," she shot back. "And you don't have to sound so surprised. Many royal families send their children abroad to universities."

"True, but I thought most of them went to Cambridge or Princeton or Yale."

"Harvard, MIT, Stanford and John Hopkins were all

good schools, but University of California at Berkeley was fifth ranked."

"In what?"

"Initially, I went for molecular biology."

"What?" He dropped the microphone. Facing her, he realized his mouth hung open and closed it. "You're kidding me, right?"

"No." The smile in her voice spoke volumes. "I'm not kidding. And yes, I graduated. I received both my bachelor's and my master's degrees. I have to decide whether to go back in the fall to finish working on my doctorate."

"In molecular biology?"

She sighed. Loudly. "Yes. Now you see why I wanted explanations about the tests."

Dumbfounded, he tried to process this information. Obviously, the brief bit of research he'd been given was inadequate. Seriously lacking. He made a mental note to fire that particular research assistant when he got back in the States.

"No offense, Dr. Streib," she continued, "but time is wasting. We need to move things along here. I do have other duties besides working with you."

"Call me Braden," he said without thinking, still feeling a bit foolish.

"Then you can call me Alisa," she graciously granted. "Now, let's get started."

"All right." He forced himself to focus as she took a seat in his chair. Readying the needle to prick her finger, he considered. Doing such things was difficult while blind, but not completely impossible, as long as he wore gloves and took care not to contaminate the sample. Still, this was too important to take the risk.

"One moment," he told Alisa, then pressed the button on his console that would summon his assistant.

A moment later, Katya arrived. "Yes, Doctor?"

Explaining what he wanted, he waited while she took the blood samples. When she'd finished, he directed her to place the slides under the multi-faceted microscope for his machine to view and analyze. Though Katya didn't know, along with Alisa's were the samples he'd taken of his own blood earlier, for comparison purposes.

Katya did as he directed and pushed the button for the machine to begin to analyze. This process would take several minutes.

"Will there be anything else?" Katya asked.

"That will be it for now," he told her.

Murmuring something about calling her if he needed her again, Katya left the room, leaving him alone again with Alisa.

As he turned to face her, he braced himself for more questions. He wasn't wrong.

"Tell me about your work. I'm very curious how you are a neurosurgeon when you cannot see," she mused. "Or, was that something you only did before the explosion?"

No tiptoeing around for her. This time, her bluntness didn't surprise him. In fact, after months of colleagues avoiding the issue, he actually welcomed talking about it. And of course, he'd lost the capacity to be wounded shortly after he woke up in a Denver burn unit with his head wrapped in bandages, unable to see.

"I *was* a surgeon," he said, careful to keep all traces of bitterness from his voice. "Past tense. Before the explosion, I was an excellent neurosurgeon, working in Denver. One of the top ones, at least among the Pack.

Three days a week, I'd operate on someone's brain, or spine, or peripheral nerves. I also taught medical students and gave some lectures to residents. In my spare time, I did research for the Pack."

"Spare time? That sounds like you didn't have much."

He shrugged. "I did what I could when I could. I was happy. I made good money, so my wife was happy as well."

"Wife?" A certain watchful stillness came over her voice. "I didn't know you were married."

Chapter 5

He forced a smile, trying to swallow. Again he had that awful taste in his mouth, like copper. This happened more and more frequently whenever he tried to relive the past. "Again, past tense. I was married. I'm not now. She left me immediately after the accident, and filed for divorce before the week was over."

If she had comments on what kind of woman would do such a thing, she didn't voice them. He supposed he shouldn't be disappointed.

"I'm sorry," she said instead, the warmth in her voice making his wolf nudge him playfully.

A simple, heartfelt response. He welcomed it, glad she didn't ask him a thousand follow-up questions that he had no desire to answer.

Yet. He waited, and still she said nothing else.

Despite that, or maybe because of it, he found himself continuing. "I met Camille—my ex-wife—when I was in residency. She was a nurse, a newly minted RN. Looking back, I think she loved the idea of being married to a doctor. I'm not sure she ever entirely loved me for who I am rather than what I was."

And when he'd been unable to be her status symbol, when his hope of resuming his career as a top neurosurgeon had disappeared, so had Camille. In reflection, he hadn't even really been surprised.

When Alisa squeezed his shoulder, he realized how tense he'd gotten and tried to force himself to relax.

"Was your ex Pack, too? Or human?"

"Oh, she was Pack. She was a full-blooded shifter, not a Halfling like me." And later, when the divorce was under way and he'd dared disagree with something she'd wanted, she'd thrown that up against him, as if his bloodline was something to be ashamed of.

For all he knew, most full-blooded shifters secretly looked down on Halflings. He had no way of knowing.

Raising his head, he debated asking. But Alisa was not only a full-blood, but a princess. Definitely not the right person to answer. And really, what did it matter now? He was what he was. That part of himself he couldn't change. He had much more pressing issues to worry about.

While lost in his thoughts, to his shock, Alisa got out of her chair and hugged him, letting him know without words that her spirit was nothing like Camille's. Either that, he thought wryly, or he really was a sap.

He allowed himself a few seconds to fully appreciate her efforts, before firmly taking her shoulders and moving her back. "Thanks," he managed, wondering when his machine would be finished analyzing so he could return his attention to the business at hand.

The chair creaked as Alisa resumed her seat. "A brain surgeon," Alisa mused. "Odd, but you look nothing like how I would picture a neurosurgeon to look."

This amused him. He could imagine what she thought. Pocket protectors, glasses and bad haircuts. One out of three wasn't bad. "You actually pictured a neurosurgeon?"

He wondered if she blushed. "You know what I mean," she said.

Strangely enough, he did. "Better or worse?" He hated himself for asking, and then realized with no small measure of amazement that he actually was flirting with her. Something he'd never quite gotten the nuances of.

Flirting. As she'd tried to do the day before.

"Oh, definitely better." Not appearing to notice, she cleared her throat, as if embarrassed.

Though it shouldn't have, her comment pleased him.

His machine chose that moment to beep, signaling that the analysis was complete.

"All right. We should get back to work," he said with no small measure of relief, aware of his wolf, watching with silent amusement.

"Are there more tests?"

"Yes," he told her. "Though first, I want to listen to these results."

"After that, what would you like to do to me first?"

Her innocent question brought about such vivid carnal images that he had to grip the counter to keep from staggering. What the hell was *wrong* with him?

Again he began to try to analyze. Possibly the fact

that he hadn't been with a woman since months before his ex-wife walked out on him. Yeah. Between that and the length of time he'd gone without shifting into wolf, he was an explosion waiting to happen. That had to be the reason for his bizarre behavior.

He breathed deeply, willing his heartbeat to slow. Now that he knew why, he could deal with the issue. Logic always triumphed in the end.

"Let's listen to the results first, then we'll decide what other tests to run," he said, managing to sound normal.

As the robotic voice droned on, Braden grimaced. Nothing. Of course, he hadn't truly expected this to be easy.

Since he couldn't glance at his watch—a former bad habit of his that had taken his blindness to break—he touched the little audible timepiece he wore on his wrist and grimaced as it announced the time.

Three o'clock. Cursing himself, he wondered how he'd managed to completely overlook the time. He'd have to make apologies to her and scratch the rest of this day off as a lost opportunity.

If he made it that far. The familiar fatigue had begun creeping up, and he knew from past experience that soon he'd have no control over what happened.

"Since it's rather late in the day," he said, infusing his voice with a sort of resigned cheerfulness. "Let's plan to try again tomorrow. In the morning this time? As in eight o'clock."

"I have the rest of today free," she insisted. "Why waste time?"

"Not today," he said shortly. "We'll meet back here at 8:00 a.m. sharp."

"I'm really not a morning person," she told him. "Why can't we start in the afternoon? Let's keep going."

She had him there. Of course she had no way to know about the weariness that overtook him in the afternoon, the debilitating exhaustion that forced him to take a nap for an hour or two every single day. That is, if he wanted to be able to function at dinnertime.

Since he was rapidly fading, she was about to find out.

"It's my nap time. You know, siesta?" he said helpfully, battling back both the tiredness and his ever-vigilant wolf.

The way she sighed told him she was no doubt rolling her eyes. "Wrong country, Dr. Streib. You could at least learn our native language since obviously you plan to be here awhile."

As he fumbled for a response, exhaustion charged through his body like a storm surge in a hurricane. Dizzy, he fumbled to find the stool near his makeshift work space and dropped onto it.

"Are you all right?" Now she sounded concerned.

Wearily, he nodded. "Yes. No. I will be, once I get some rest."

"Did you not sleep last night?"

"Yes, I did. It's not that. Ever since the explosion, this happens every afternoon around the same time."

"This?"

"Yes, this." His gesture encompassed both him and the entire room. "It's like I simply shut down. I have no control over my own body."

"Why? What's wrong with you?"

He swallowed, wondering how much to tell her. Since they were going to work together for the foreseeable future, he decided to go with the truth. After all, she clearly already believed him weird. What could one more bizarre bit of information hurt?

"There's nothing wrong with me, according to the numerous medical specialists that I consulted, including the non-medical Healer."

"What did she say?"

"Like my blindness, she said it was all in my head." Hearing the bitterness in his voice, he tried to gather his scattered thoughts. But he lacked the focus or the energy to do so. He took a halting step forward, swaying.

Alisa grabbed his arm, steadying him. "Are you all right?"

Swallowing hard as another wave of dizziness swamped him, he fought a wave of nausea. "No. I'm not."

"You look terrible. Is there anything I can do to help you?"

Though he hated to ask, his rapid disappearing energy left him no choice. "Will you help me to my room?"

"Of course. Do you have your cane?" Then, without waiting for an answer, she leaned across him, her full breasts brushing his chest. Despite his human exhaustion, his wolf blazed to life, eager and ferocious and willing to fight for freedom.

Braden wasn't sure he had the strength left to keep the beast contained. But he had to. He had to. What a horrible, unforgivable breach of etiquette changing inside the palace would be. A wolf running amok inside a giant, lavishly appointed cage could do a lot of damage.

From deep inside his inner core, he pulled forth

strength and wrestled the wolf back into furious submission.

But doing so used up his last reserve of energy.

He swallowed, stifling a groan as his wolf readied himself for another attack. If he spent too much time with her in his weakened state, he didn't know how much longer he could hold the beast at bay.

"Stop that." Her sharp voice felt like a whip as she moved away. "If you're so tired, why are you exhibiting signs of getting ready to change?"

"My wolf wants out," he told her simply, knowing she might not understand. The instant he finished speaking, a wave of severe dizziness swamped him, so strong he stumbled, nearly falling to his knees.

Instantly, she was beside him, sliding under his arm. "Here's your cane," she said in her dulcet voice, so close her breath tickled his cheek. She helped him move forward. This time he was ready for his wolf's instant reaction, and he kept himself under better control, even though his legs felt as though they might give up on him.

"Lean on me," she said. "Let me help you get to your room. We're nearly there."

Nearly being the operative word. Not good enough, as he knew he was losing the battle. He could no longer walk. Even breathing became too much of an effort.

"I'd better call the royal physician." She gasped as he stumbled, nearly taking her down with him.

"No." Summoning strength from some inner reserve, he straightened so he no longer leaned on her, using his cane instead. "This happens every day. I'll make it."

But after he'd taken three steps, he realized even that was doubtful.

Inside, his wolf waited, watching for any opportunity. The animal part of him didn't understand or care about complicated things like human frailties. The second he let his guard down, the beast would attack.

A disaster waiting to happen. "How. Much. Farther?"

"Not far," she said, this time taking his elbow, more to direct him with than anything else.

He tried to nod, which turned out to be a colossal mistake. As he dipped his chin down, the entire floor shifted, as if a giant earthquake had rendered the castle foundation unstable.

His legs gave way and he crumpled. With his last bit of strength, he tried to direct himself away from her, not wanting to harm her or pin her beneath him as he fell.

He never knew if he succeeded or not.

When Dr. Streib—Braden—collapsed beside her, Alisa didn't stand a chance of holding him up. The best she could do was to direct his fall so he didn't hurt himself, or her.

She only partially succeeded. He'd tried to twist himself away from her as he went down, but since he appeared to have lost the use of his limbs, he didn't quite make it. Instead, he knocked her sideways.

She hit the carpet hard, rolling so that her side took the brunt of his body. The fall knocked the breath from her.

While she sucked in air, trying to breathe, she took stock of the situation. Completely unconscious, Braden lay on top of her, his torso on top of her hips, completely pinning her to the marble floor. She had no idea how much he weighed, but by twisting and pushing at the same time, she was able to move him maybe three centimeters. Not good. Her legs were already feeling a bit numb.

Worse, she'd left her cell phone in her purse on her dresser. She hadn't thought she'd need it while working with Braden. Now, she wished she had the blasted thing. At least she could call a few of her family's brawny bodyguards for assistance.

As things stood, it looked like she was on her own.

Bit by bit, she wiggled herself free. Finally, after what seemed like forever but was probably only a few minutes, she managed to scoot out from under him. Legs numb and aching, she climbed to her feet. Braden still lay unmoving on the floor, his disheveled black hair in violent disarray, his limbs at odd angles.

Staring down at him, she felt the oddest sensation deep inside her chest. Her wolf, suddenly alert and restless. Even as she tried to understand, her beast made a swift attempt to force her to change, rushing her, taking her completely unaware.

What the…? Stunned, Alisa easily controlled the animal. Where on earth had this come from? Such a move was shocking. Her wolf had been content to remain dormant ever since Alisa had changed for the first time at thirteen. Back then, she'd simply shown the beast who was in control and that had been that. Since then, there had been no challenges, no rushed attempts for escape, nothing. She and her wolf had existed in complete harmony.

Until now. Why? Deep inside her she knew this had something to do with the man lying unconscious in the hall.

Speaking of whom—Alisa rushed into one of the empty rooms and picked up the nightstand phone to call the family's personal protection unit. Moments later she hung up. Help was on the way. She'd deal with her miscreant wolf later.

Wakefulness came as suddenly as the loss of consciousness had earlier. One moment he was out, the next, fully aware.

Despite his lack of sight, Braden opened his eyes and turned his head, reaching out to see what his fingers encountered. Soft sheets, the luxurious feel of Egyptian cotton. Relief flooded him. He was in his room, on his bed. Apparently he'd made it back here after all.

"No, you didn't." Princess Alisa spoke from a chair near his suite's fireplace. "You weren't fortunate enough to get back here before you passed out."

He frowned, wishing he could see her expression. "Did I say that out loud or did you read my mind?"

"Neither. Your thoughts were easy to read on your face."

Letting that go proved beyond his capabilities. "Sorry, since I lack the ability to read your face, I wouldn't know."

She continued as if he hadn't spoken. "You dropped in the hallway, as quickly as if you'd been shot."

Suddenly he remembered and winced. "My apologies."

"Accepted," she said, sounding slightly prim. "Do you want to hear the rest of what happened?"

"There's more?" Horrified, he wondered if his wolf had somehow managed to wrest control before he'd blacked out. But even if the beast had, when one lost consciousness, so did the other. He knew there'd not been enough time for him to shift.

"Oh yes, there's more." The smile in her voice had him feeling slightly better. "When you fell, you pinned me to the floor. It took me a good twenty or thirty minutes before I could extricate myself."

"Hellhounds." He closed his eyes, a habit from the days when doing so would have blocked out an unwelcome or embarrassing sight. "I apologize again."

"No need." Now she sounded positively cheerful. Was she really taking delight in his misfortune?

Clearing his throat, he hoped not. "How did I get back to my room?"

"I called a couple of my father's off-duty bodyguards. They came and carried you here."

Picturing this, he shook his head. "I'm actually glad that I wasn't awake for that. That's way beyond mortifying."

She crossed the room to him, bringing with her that amazingly tantalizing scent. "Don't look at it that way. You were sick, they helped you. Nothing more, nothing less."

Since he had no choice in the matter, he nodded. Pushing himself up on his elbows, he winced at the stabbing pain in his head. "Migraine," he said. "Sometimes this happens after I pass out."

"Ah, I can help with that." Talking as she moved away, she turned on the tap and filled a glass, returning to his side. "Hold out your hand. I have just the thing for your head. This works wonders for me."

Instantly suspicious, he squinted up at her as though he could really see her. And—strangely enough—just for a moment he was able to pretend that he could. Just her silhouette, a lighter shade of gray against all the black. But when he tried to fixate on this, it vanished.

Proof that once again, his mind was playing tricks on him. This in itself was enough to make him scowl.

"It's nothing dangerous," she said, nudging his hand with the glass. "One pill. Just a simple, over-the-counter migraine medication, derived from an ancient Teslinkian remedy. It works miracles, I promise."

Because his head really was pounding, he accepted the glass, then held out his hand for the pill.

Once he'd washed it down, he let her take the glass from him and allowed himself to sink back against the pillow.

"Rest a second," she told him. "Give the medicine time to work."

"I hurt too badly to do otherwise." Trying to relax, he closed his eyes. To his surprise, a few minutes later, the tight band of the headache began to ease.

"Are you okay?" she finally asked, leaning in close and bringing a whiff of scent that made him want to reach up and touch her.

Clearing his throat, he focused on her question. "Surprisingly, I feel better."

The second he spoke, his wolf decided to rush him. Though weak, he was able to bat the animal back into submission.

Still, the problem had to be dealt with immediately.

"I need your assistance," he told her. Past experiences had taught him in urgent situations directness worked best. "You know how I told you my wolf wanted out? It's more than that—I can barely keep him contained. It's been far too long since I've changed."

"How long?" she asked, genuine curiosity in her voice. Again he stifled the urge to reach up and cup her chin with one hand while exploring her face with his other. The fact that he'd be fumbling to find her gave him pause, as well as knowing she'd find this a shocking invasion of her privacy.

"I don't actually remember," he admitted. Then, before she could make some comment about how she'd thought she was the only one who had trouble keeping track of changes, he continued. "I'd appreciate it if you could help me find a place where my wolf can run."

At first, she didn't respond. Then, she moved closer still, so close that her breath tickled his face. Keeping perfectly still, he refused to react, though his heart had begun to pound in his chest.

Finally, she did the unthinkable. With her soft fingers, she brushed the hair from his forehead. He shuddered, unable to hide it.

"Of course I will," she said. "When do you want to do this?"

Though her touch had his pulse leaping, he managed to sound relatively normal. "As soon as possible. Now."

"Do you feel up to it?"

Curse her, though she wasn't touching him, she didn't move away. If he'd been more certain of her motives, he would have captured her wrists and pulled her to him.

Even the brief thought made his body stir. His wolf, waiting for the smallest sign of weakness, waited alertly.

"Yes. I have to. Now."

"I'll have someone drive you to the forest," she said.

His stomach sank. Inside, his wolf growled, furious and disappointed.

"That won't work." He blurted out the first thing that came to mind. "I'd like you to go, too."

"Why?" Her sharp voice told him she wasn't fond of the idea. Some people—and evidently she was one—

found the act of shape-shifting too intimate to share with total strangers. Most shifters, when they changed back to human, were completely aroused physically. Lovers often took advantage of this state, while others simply ignored it politely until it went away.

He had no interest in copulating with Princess Alisa. He wondered if telling her so would be too bold and offend her.

"Because I'd like you to change as well. That way, my wolf can observe you while you're in that form."

"Observe me?" she repeated. "Are you telling me that when you're a wolf, you can see?"

He frowned. "You know as well as I do when we're wolves our nose is our primary sense. So no, I can't see with my eyes. But I can smell."

His wolf made yet another full-scale attack, snarling and biting in a furious attempt to make him change.

After he'd managed—barely—to subdue the beast, he took a deep breath. "Did you see that?" he asked quietly.

"Yes. And my wolf has been reacting to yours."

This surprised him, though he didn't have time to ponder any possible ramifications.

"Reacting how?" he asked, though he already suspected.

She was silent for so long he'd begun to doubt she would answer.

When she did finally speak, her tone had gone scornful. "My wolf seems to think we could be…mates."

Stunned, he found himself at a loss for words.

"That's…"

"Ridiculous?" she finished for him. "Believe me, I

know. I don't believe in woo-woo nonsense like true love or soul mates, so don't worry."

"I wasn't." He cleared his throat, changing the subject. "I really need to change. Can we go now?"

"Are you able to get up?" Leaning in, she took his hand, her touch soft and warm, her scent and her amazing, sensual voice electrifying.

He couldn't help it, he jerked away. Not out of repulsion, but from fear he'd do something crazy, something they'd both regret, like yank her down onto the bed on top of him.

"Sorry." Her sharp tone told him she'd taken his abrupt movement as a rebuff of her friendly attempt to help.

Since there was no way in hell he could tell her the truth about what her touch did to him, he simply pushed back the thin sheet that covered him and swung his legs over the side of the bed. "I'm ready now."

"Come on," she answered, her tone more distant. "Let me send for my car and I'll take you to our hunting grounds in the Sjmelka Forest. That's where my family goes when we wish to change. We used to always go there and run together as a Pack." She sounded wistful. "That was the one time I felt like every other shifter."

This, he could understand. In the world of the wolf, there was no such thing as royalty.

Keeping his thoughts to himself for now, he followed the precise *click-click* of her heels as she strode down the hallway. The length of her quick stride made him believe she must be a tall woman. Athletic possibly, since she didn't seem to have any quickened breathing or other signs of strenuous physical exertion.

Unlike himself, he thought wryly. He'd spent so

much time hunched over computers, books and microscopes that he'd quit working out, except for the occasional bike ride around Boulder. Of course he'd even had to stop that once he'd lost his sight.

"Watch your step," she said. Immediately, he slowed, not sure if he'd be stepping up or down or what. He'd been so antsy about getting to the woods to change that he'd completely forgotten his cane.

"Where?" he asked. The last thing he needed was to fall or injure himself. He had enough problems with the perpetual blindness and daily exhaustion as it was.

"Here." To his surprise, she took his arm. Her hands were soft, too, the smooth, pampered skin of a rich, royal woman. "We're about to go outside. There are six steps down, and then we'll be waiting while someone brings my car around."

Once again, she'd managed to surprise him. "You drive yourself?"

Her laugh was low, husky and sensuous. "Of course. I have the most lovely automobile."

He couldn't help but smile at that, picturing a powder-pink Volkswagen Beetle or candy-apple-red tiny convertible or something silly like that.

She led him outside, allowing him a moment to pause and inhale deeply of the clear, dry air.

"Now the steps," she said, helpfully steering him in the right direction. He couldn't help but wonder why she was suddenly being so nice to him, especially since she'd made it plain she didn't want him around.

Just then he heard the throaty rumble of a sports car.

"Here's my car," she said. "It can go from zero to sixty in a few seconds."

Chapter 6

A moment later, the vehicle pulled to a stop in front of them. Someone got out and opened the passenger-side door, helping Princess Alisa herd Braden inside.

"Buckle up," she said, a smile in her voice. "I tend to drive very, very fast."

Doing as she asked, he wondered if he should be glad that he couldn't see. Back before the accident, he'd loved nothing more than speed. Now, with everything else completely out of his control, he wasn't so keen on the idea.

They took off, burning rubber, and then shooting forward so quickly he was thrown back in his seat. Beside him, he could hear her change gears, letting the engine play out to maximum RPMs before shifting.

Grudgingly, he realized she was a good driver, methodical despite her apparent love of driving fast. But then of course, he could only go on what he heard. If he'd been able to actually see, he wondered if he'd feel differently.

Inside, his restless wolf made his displeasure known. Braden soothed the beast, letting the animal know he would soon be able to run free. Grumbling with displeasure, the wolf finally settled in to wait impatiently.

Alisa cursed, then downshifted rapidly, slowing their speed considerably. "Traffic," she said. "It's rush hour and everyone is trying to make it home from work."

Dread curled in his stomach as his wolf snarled. "How far is it to this forest?"

"It's actually a short distance," she told him, sounding slightly grim. "Normally, that is. Traffic like this will add another half hour to our drive."

The vehicle felt as though it was barely moving.

Again, he struggled with his wolf, trying to make his beast understand the delay. Enduring this, he could well understand how one would go mad—refusing to let the animal side have its time had already taken a toll on him, and it hadn't been more than a month or so. He hadn't meant to let it go so long, but with the trip here and all the arrangements he'd had to make to ensure his lab at home was able to run, time had slipped by too fast.

"Tell me about this forest," he asked, wanting to distract his now-pacing wolf.

"Hold on," she said, downshifting rapidly. "Traffic is breaking up in the fast lane. I'll need to do some maneuvering to get there." She then tromped on the accelerator, running through the gears in rapid succession.

The sports car responded, shooting forward as they weaved left, then right, then left again. Braden found himself envying the powerful machine and actually respecting the skill with which Alisa controlled it.

"We did it," she crowed. "We've broken free of that knot of cars and there's nothing but clear highway ahead. Sjmelka Forest, here we come!"

Braden nodded, sheepishly releasing his grip from the door handle. As he did, they took a curve to the right, moving so quickly and so sharply that he was thrown up against the door.

He barely stifled a curse.

"Sorry," she said, sounding completely unapologetic. "Now to answer your earlier question, our forests are well known among the European Pack. It is thought that our founding wolf-mates met here during a hunt."

"Founding? As in the beginning of your family?"

"No. Broader than that. As in the beginning of our country. The Teslinko Pack."

Mildly curious, he settled back in his seat, enjoying the melodic sound of her voice. "How long ago?"

She laughed. "I take it your research didn't bother to track our ancestry either?"

"No." Once again, he made a mental note to fire the research assistant, who'd obviously been lazy compiling what he considered necessary information.

"The Teslinko Pack was one of the earliest Packs studied. It is believed that our mated pair traveled here separately about the time Atlantis fell."

Startled, he swallowed back a snort of derision. "Atlantis? Atlantis is a myth."

"Is it? Like werewolves and vampires are myths?"

This time, he did snort. "Just because one set of fables is real doesn't automatically render them all factual."

"Everyone is entitled to their own opinion. Anyway," she continued, apparently not wanting to debate him, which was a pity. There were few things he enjoyed more than a rousing debate.

"These two shifters, each alone, traveled the forest in their wolf form. Legend has it that they were both hunting the same deer. The male brought it down and the female moved in on his kill."

"Which can be asking for death," he said, interested despite himself. When he'd been a small boy, he remembered his mother telling him stories about their own ancestors.

"Yes." He could hear the smile in her voice. "Only in this situation, the male was so smitten that he not only didn't challenge her, but he let her have the heart and liver of the kill."

This made him smile. "Classic behavior of a mate."

"Exactly," she said. "Hold on, we're about to leave the pavement. The road is dirt from here on."

He barely had time to grip the door handle before they careened sideways, hitting what felt like a crater. The rest of the bone-jarring, teeth-rattling ride felt like it went on forever, especially to his still bruised and sore body.

"How much longer?" he forced out, trying like hell to sound as if he didn't care and only half succeeding.

"Almost there," she answered. Then he could have sworn she deliberately swerved so they'd hit a pothole straight on. Though why would she? She'd been nothing short of friendly since his accident and collapse in the hallway. She'd seen the bruises and scrapes. She had to know he was hurt.

When the car finally stopped, he had to unclench his

jaw and take a deep breath. There was little he liked less than being out of control. Being blind had taught him an instant lesson in acceptance, as there was nothing less in control than being blind and forced to depend on others for everything, including transport.

Honestly, it sucked. But he'd learned to cope. After all, he had no choice.

"We're here," she said, sounding so cheerful that he once again wondered if she had something up her sleeve. Then he chided himself and his suspicious nature.

Fumbling with the seat belt, he finally got it open and located the door handle. His wolf, already wide awake and more than ready, increased his pacing, aware release was only a matter of minutes away. The beast was chomping at the bit to be set free.

Pushing open the door, he climbed out, stretching. The princess touched his shoulder, sending another of those strange, electric-type shocks through him.

"Let me know if you need me to help you walk this path. There are a lot of stone and tree routes, as well as branches."

Once again, cause to hate his blindness. Once again, he'd learn to cope. "I think I'll be fine. Just stay close, if you don't mind."

She bumped her shoulder to his, the casual gesture of a friend. "No problem. I won't leave your side."

He couldn't help but wonder if she might be playing some elaborate game.

She took his arm, startling him back out of his thoughts. "Careful," she murmured, a huskiness lingering in her voice that sent yet another shiver straight down his spine. "There's a lot of underbrush. I wouldn't want you to fall."

His wolf snarled. The irony of her remark didn't escape him. Right now he had to fight the urge to drop to all fours and let the change rip through him, clothing and decorum be damned.

But she was a princess and he was a guest in her country. His research depended on her goodwill. Clenching his teeth, he struggled to maintain self-control. He would wait, his wolf would wait, even though the beast inside him cared nothing for human conventions and hovered near the edge.

"I know the perfect place. It's this way," she said, tightening her grip on his arm. Even this, the slightest of touches, felt painful, as though his skin was raw. Another side effect from waiting so long to change? He made a mental note to investigate this, even as his wolf snarled inside him, ready to run.

"Do you feel the ancient magic of this forest?" she asked, evidently not having had near the problem with her wolf that he was having with his. Of course not. This was the woman who couldn't care less if she changed.

"I—" About to tell her how urgent his need had become, he bit down on his cheek and forced himself to be silent.

"There's so much here," she continued. "The scent of the pines, the damp earth, the leaves. I love the way it fills the senses. Oh, and the wildlife. The hunting is good here." Her soft murmur invited him to quit focusing on his internal thoughts and instead, experience her forest's wild beauty.

If not for his wolf, he would do exactly that. Struggling, he contained the beast for a few more moments, lifted his head and inhaled.

Scent assaulted him. Musk and moist soil and leaves.

Heaven. He could almost swear he smelled sunlight, even though he knew such a thing was only wishful thinking. Underfoot, leaves whispered beneath his uneven tread and, though he technically hated the fact that he had to be led around like a blindfolded child, he was grateful for her steadying grip.

Finally, she squeezed his biceps. "Here we are." Letting go of his arm, she took his hand, guiding him to touch something made of boards. "There's a large wooden box where you can store your clothes. I'll change on the other side of the box and you can shift here. Is that all right with you?"

If she'd said he had to change while climbing a tree, he would have done so. This, this was perfect, even if he continually felt as if she was moving in slow motion.

Nodding, he briefly wondered if she felt awkward, especially since a blind man would become a blind wolf—a distinct liability any way she looked at it.

She probably wondered if she'd have to hunt for him, too, but he planned to disabuse her of that notion. Even without sight, his olfactory senses were sharp enough that he could easily take down a rabbit or other small game.

Even the thought made his mouth water. Shuddering with the effort of trying to control the change, he silently counted to three. Then, rapidly, he began shedding his clothes. This time, when the wolf surged forward, he didn't try to hold him back.

He barely had time to drop to all fours, the leaves rough under his hands, before his wolf burst free, forcing a change so fast it slammed into him, excruciatingly painful. A cross between a snarl and a groan escaped him as the change continued to rip through him, his bones rapidly elongating, his teeth, claws and fur appearing as though by magic. Too quickly, but he was powerless to stop it now. It had been too long coming.

The last human thought he had was wondering if the normal swirling lights that always accompanied shape-shifting were also fast-forwarded, more of a blur than a shimmering light show.

Finally he stood as wolf, all four paws planted firmly in the damp earth. There was another wolf here, someone both familiar and not. The princess.

He swung his snout in her direction, using his nose to locate her whereabouts. Her scent as wolf was even more delicious than he could have imagined. His wolf was eager to explore it further.

With a low growl he took a step forward, luxuriating in the feel of the soil beneath his paws. Fully wolf, he wanted to run, to celebrate his lupine existence. He started to leap forward, ignoring the ever-present blackness, then stopped, the dimly human part of him remembering she'd told him that they were in a heavily wooded forest.

As wolf, he snarled, furious, irritated. He couldn't run. Not like he needed to, full out and wild and completely free. He wanted to throw his head back and howl with frustration, well aware that he'd been too excited about the upcoming change and way too stimulated by being around her to really think things through. He should have explained that he needed a meadow.

Spinning, he tried to find her. He scented her a half second before Alisa as wolf bumped him with her flank. Turning his head, he blinked as she touched her nose to his.

Then she nudged him, as if to say, "run with me."

Joy leaped in his chest as he realized that if they stayed side by side, she could direct him and steer him clear of obstacles.

He could run! For a second, human Braden hesitated to believe. Wolf Braden wanted to go all-out.

As though she wanted to prove it, she nudged him again, then took off. He didn't wait, leaping forward and moving with her, only a split second behind, as the path widened and became something larger. A clearing? No, a meadow.

Side by side, they ran, their tails streaming in the wind. Braden's wolf was savagely happy, tongue lolling from his mouth, as they finally slowed to a lope. Ah, this was living! Life the way a wolf lived it—in the moment. Now. He bared his teeth in a wolfish grin, as happy as he could ever remember being, at least since the accident. How could he have waited so long to let his wolf free? How could anyone? He'd needed this, and he owed Princess Alisa a debt of gratitude that he fully intended to repay somehow.

The breeze tickled his fur as their lope slowed to a trot. He caught the scent of rabbit, apparently at the same time as she, because she nipped him lightly. Often considered a form of foreplay, the gentle bite, he knew in this instance, was meant to let him know they were going hunting.

Immediately, they slowed to a walk before they quickly hunkered down. Bellies low to the ground, together they crawled forward, following the hare's pungent scent trail. Their prey had passed by here not too long before they'd appeared. Hopefully, the smaller animal was still somewhere in the vicinity. Suddenly ravenous, Braden found his mouth watering. He hadn't eaten freshly caught game in a long time.

A rustle of leaves from nearby had them up, instantly alert. The rabbit, no doubt catching their scent, took off, crashing through the underbrush, fleeing.

Heart pounding, he started forward, just as Alisa nudged him again, letting him know he couldn't follow. He understood. In this, if she wanted a prayer of catching their snack, she had to go it alone. She leapt forward, taking off in full-out pursuit, while he was forced to remain behind.

Unhappy, he panted and waited. He did not like this, not at all. But even as wolf, he knew he had no choice. In the hunt, at least here in this forest, his lack of sight was too much of a liability. If she'd tried to guide him and keep him with her, he would only hinder the success of her hunt.

Her hunt. This went against all the laws of nature, of his kind. While male and females often hunted in pairs, he knew of no male who sat on his haunches and waited for his female to bring him food.

But because, hampered by his blindness, he could do nothing else, he waited, exploring only the immediate area until she returned.

Luck was on his side that day. Leaves crashing told him the pursuit had turned back in his direction. As luck would have it, the terrified rabbit reversed course and blundered right into his clearing. Right into him, as though the space between his paws represented a safe haven.

Hah! Not so. One jump and a snap of his powerful jaws and he had it. The rabbit squealed as it died. A moment later his mouth filled with its blood, warm and fresh and delicious.

A second later, still in hot pursuit, Alisa ran up, panting. Startled, he dropped the dead rabbit at her feet, letting her have first choice of meat even though he'd made the kill. Common courtesy, for all she'd done for him.

Also, the behavior of a mate.

The instant the thought occurred to him, he reconsidered, but it was too late. Apparently as ravenous as he, she snatched up the prize, tearing into it. The sounds of her obvious enjoyment made his mouth water and he had to restrain himself from snatching what was left of the meat away from her.

Finally, after what seemed like an eternity, she touched her nose to his, letting him taste the coppery blood. The rest of the meat was his for the taking.

He barely hesitated before he ripped into the remains of the carcass. Seconds later, it was gone, bones and all. Too quickly. A small, thin rabbit. Barely a snack.

When she nudged him again, he understood. She wanted to forage again, side by side. More of an appetizer than a meal, the slight taste of fresh meat hadn't been enough for either of them. They both were hungry for more.

Flank to flank they moved forward. When she turned, he did the same, intuition and a kind of mind-melding giving him a gracefulness that had been long absent and sorely missed. In this moment, he felt closer to his old self than he had since losing his sight.

A few minutes later they caught the scent of another small animal, a squirrel this time. One touch of her nose indicated she meant to take chase and leave him standing alone, though he didn't feel quite as utterly useless as he had before.

In the instant before she moved, a sound—the crack of a twig—alerted them that something else, something larger than prey, was near. They both froze, she trying to locate the threat with her eyes, he doing the same with his nose.

Braden heard the report of the rifle a split second before the bullet hit the tree. A second later, Alisa slammed into him, knocking him down and sending him rolling. He didn't need words to know what she meant. They needed to run. Fast and far, keeping low to the ground. Right. Now.

Go. She nudged him again, flipping her tail against his face. He understood, opening his mouth and clamping down on the edges of her furry tail with his teeth. He barely had time to think before she sprang forward, leaving him no choice but to do the same.

They ran like the wind before a storm, the way he had before blindness had overtaken him. The sensation was unlike any he'd felt since the explosion.

Before losing his sight, he'd always loved the jolt of his paws slamming into the earth, the wind blowing his fur. But never before had he moved so much in unison with another wolf, snout level with her right flank, the tail an indicator in case he accidentally turned the wrong way.

They ran together in perfect harmony, full out, low to the ground. Out of deference to his blindness, she kept to as straight a path as possible, rarely veering between trees. He supposed she did so only when she had to, in order to keep him safely with her.

Finally, after several minutes of running, she slowed,

panting. Finally, he let go of his mouthful of her tail, nudging her once to give wordless thanks and an apology in case he'd somehow hurt her. She nudged him back, once. He supposed this meant that she was okay.

In the silent forest, they listened. Flank to flank they stood, sides heaving. No sounds of pursuit, no human blundering through the underbrush after them. No more shots.

She nudged him once more, and then he felt the air around him ripple with energy as she changed. Though he felt a sharp pang of regret—he had not remained wolf long enough for his beast—he knew it was necessary.

A moment later, no longer in her wolf form, she spoke. "Your turn, Braden. Time to shift to human. My father keeps a hunting cabin near here. We'll go there until we figure out what to do and how we'll get back to the palace. If we don't return soon, my parents will worry."

Dropping low to the ground, he closed his eyes and did as she asked. A moment later, as man once more, he climbed to his feet, his arousal jutting out proudly before him. Though he of course could not see her, he was well aware that she could see him. Even so, he refused to feel shame. Especially since such a sexually aroused state was normal for both men and women of their kind once they changed from wolf to human.

Commonly, unless both parties were attracted to each other, the polite response was to ignore it.

Which she did.

He couldn't help but feel a bit disappointed. The thought of her being aroused made it difficult for him to breathe.

"Are you all right?" she asked, mistaking his silence for something else.

"I'm fine. You'll have to lead me again, I'm sorry." he said.

"Of course." A moment later, she slid her small hand into his. After a startled second, he closed his fingers around her, refusing to acknowledge that even this slightest of touches increased his impossible and irrational desire for her.

"Come with me." The trace of huskiness in her voice told him she wasn't completely unaffected. Of course, neither of them could or would act on their inappropriate desire, but his shredded ego rejoiced in the small boost her possible arousal gave it.

To distract himself, he focused on what he could discern of their surroundings.

"The sun must be going down," he commented. "The breeze is beginning to carry a distinct chill."

"Actually, we're much higher up in the mountains now, very close to the no-tree line. That's another reason it feels colder."

This made no sense to him. "Why go up? With less trees, it'll be much easier to spot us."

"Because whoever is trying to shoot us, hunters or not, is between us and my car, so we ran the opposite way. The cabin isn't far."

"I suppose we're nowhere near our clothes?" he asked, well aware that they were probably moving in the opposite direction.

"You supposed correctly. Don't worry, these are private, royal lands. We shouldn't encounter anyone else."

"Good to know," he said.

With a sigh, she tugged on him and kept on marching forward. "I doubt our stalker will want to follow us up the mountain."

"Maybe so, but we'll have to come down sometime," he pointed out, overly conscious of his firm grip on her delicate and smooth-skinned hand.

They were both buck-naked. He tried not to picture her body without clothes and failed. If anything, his arousal grew stronger. Foolish and humiliating. For all he knew, she could be the opposite of everything he found attractive in a woman.

"True, we will have to go down eventually. But I'm thinking whoever shot at us won't wait around too long, unless they're simply hunters, right? Right now they're probably searching for us close to my Jag." Her grim tone told him that this, at least, she took seriously. "I can only hope they don't destroy my car."

The worry in her voice sounded real, unfeigned. Odd. "Someone as rich as you are can surely buy another."

"My family may have a lot of money," she said, her tone dripping ice, "but that doesn't mean I spend it unwisely. And while I definitely can buy another vehicle, that's beside the point. I love that car."

He didn't have a response for that, so he said nothing. Princess Alisa often felt like a walking contradiction, making him wish he could take the time to find out what made her tick. But that wasn't why he'd made the journey to Teslinko, and he couldn't afford to allow himself to be sidetracked.

Though he really needed to know why someone was trying to kill her. Or them. He didn't think for one second the shooter had been a misguided hunter.

Chapter 7

They continued walking, still hand in hand.

"What's it like, being blind?" she asked, surprising him with her bluntness. But her voice was kind, so he gave her question serious consideration.

"The truth? It stinks. I keep telling myself I'll get used to it, but the darkness is so limiting that I doubt I ever will."

"You've truly tried everything? Even Halflings like you eventually heal."

"And those that don't, visit the Healer." He shrugged. "It's kind of like me trying to find out how you can do what you do. No one seems to be able to figure out what's wrong with me."

"What happened?" she asked softly. "After the explosion? Do you remember?"

"Yes." He refused to dwell on the images that flashed before his eyes. "I woke up in the hospital, heavily sedated. I was severely burned, with broken bones and a head injury. All the hair had been singed off my body and they kept me doped up so I wouldn't be in too much pain."

"I'm so sorry." She squeezed his hand, apparently totally comfortable with her nakedness. "How long were you in the hospital?"

His shrug was deliberately casual, as words could not be, at least when discussing this pivotal moment in his life. "A very long time. Too long."

They kept walking and for a while she didn't reply. Normally, he would have welcomed the silence—he'd grown to despise talking about the accident. But with her, he couldn't help but wonder what she thought. At least his arousal had begun to subside. He was thankful for that.

When she spoke again, she asked another question. "Did they ever find out what caused the explosion?"

He made a sound, something between a laugh and a growl. "Not what, but who. My lab was sabotaged."

Her gasp told him he'd shocked her. "Why?"

"I don't know." And he didn't. "The police didn't seem too worried about finding the answer. I'm not sure they believed me."

"Then what did they think happened?"

"Who knows. An experiment gone awry, maybe. It's been known to happen."

The thoughtful silence that followed told him she was considering exactly that possibility. He couldn't blame her. He would have done the same.

"Do you have proof that the explosion was sabotage?" she finally asked.

"No. If I did, the police might have taken me more

seriously. I was badly injured and on the edge of death, from what they told me. They eventually put me into a medically induced coma until my burns healed, to keep me from excruciating pain."

He took a deep breath, trying to keep his voice detached and unemotional. "By the time I was coherent enough to even talk to the police, any proof I might have been able to gather had vanished. They, of course, found nothing."

Next she asked the only question that made sense. "How do you know, then? How can you be one hundred percent certain that it was sabotage and not an accident?"

He gave her the simple truth. "I can't. But I know, believe me. There wasn't a single thing in that lab capable of causing that explosion. Not one single thing. Whoever caused it meant to kill me."

"Why? Why would anyone want you dead?"

"I can think of a thousand reasons," he replied, aware his brutal honesty would no doubt shock her. "In my profession, I'm at the top. There are always others who would like to see me knocked down a peg or two."

"Maybe so." She acknowledged the frailties of their humanness in a wry voice. "It's like that being royalty, too. But I would think it would be different for you. You're a doctor. You help humanity. I can't help but find it difficult to believe that someone would actually kill to do so."

"You have no idea." Shaking his head, he decided that rather than attempt to enlighten her, he would list other reasons why someone would attack him. "And even if that wasn't the reason, there's always my research."

"Research? You mean *this* research."

"Among others."

She sighed. "I'm sorry, but I think you're really overreaching now. As if any shifter would want to stop you in your attempt to figure out a way to enable them to remain human longer."

"You just don't comprehend the atmosphere in the scientific community. It's dog-eat-dog. Whoever makes a major breakthrough in something like this will have made their name among the Pack."

"I understand," she said, but he knew that she didn't.

Again a companionable silence fell. Though often she seemed to be brimming with questions, small talk and flirting, now she was quiet. He wondered how he was able to feel so comfortable being led through a forest and up a mountain, stark naked in broad daylight.

Finally, he realized they were heading downhill rather than up. He commented on this, asking her if they were nearly at the cabin.

"No." She squeezed his hand, as though for her own reassurance. "We're not going there. I changed my mind. We've begun to double back. We'll criss-cross a path toward where we left our clothes. Once we retrieve them, we're going to try to make it back to my car, assuming it's still drivable."

Nodding with approval, he squeezed her hand back. "I like your boldness."

"Thank you." She sounded pleased. "But it's not really all that bold. If the persons who shot at us are still around, they are somewhere else hunting us. The last thing they would expect is for us to head back here."

He had to agree. "I take it that you haven't seen any

sign of the shooter? No tracks, nothing to give us any idea who it might be?"

"No." She sounded grim. "Believe me, you'll know if I see anything. I left my cell phone in the car. As soon as I can get to it, I'm calling royal security so they can get out here and take a look."

A few moments later, he smelled the faint coppery scent of blood. It had to be from their earlier kill. "We're almost there, aren't we?"

"Not almost. We are here." She shoved his clothing into his arms. "Get dressed. And hurry. I'd like to get out of here quickly, just in case our enemy comes back."

Resisting the urge to mock-salute her, instead he did as she asked. When he'd finished, running his fingers down the middle of his shirt to make sure it was buttoned correctly, he waited for her signal or touch. He was ninety percent sure he knew which way to go, but couldn't be positive. If the wind hadn't shifted direction since they'd arrived, he could make his way to her vehicle as surely as if he had sight.

"Are you ready?" This time instead of taking his hand, she locked her fingers around his wrist. Without waiting for an answer, she tugged him forward. "Come on, then. This way."

He'd been right. He would have been able to walk there unassisted.

"My car looks undisturbed," she said, clearly pleased.

"Did you lock it?" He prayed she had, even though the chances were slim. After all, they were in the middle of nowhere.

"Probably. Force of habit, you know." She moved forward and he could tell she was checking the doors. "Yes. Thank goodness for routines."

A beep sounded as she unlocked the vehicle. He moved forward without waiting for her to lead him and connected with the car, fumbling for the door handle. Sliding inside, he buckled in while she did the same, locking the doors immediately.

Putting her cell phone on speaker, she dialed. While it was ringing, she started the car, put it in Drive and took off.

Someone finally answered, speaking in the Teslinkian language. Braden understood none of the rapid-fire exchange that followed, with Princess Alisa sounding increasingly calm and the other man growing more and more agitated.

Finally, Alisa concluded the call. "Can you believe that?" she asked, sounding furious.

"Since I didn't understand any of the conversation, I have to take the fifth," he said drily.

"The what?"

"Sorry." He realized he might have well been speaking his own private language with that phrase. "It's an American reference to our Constitutional Bill of Rights. It basically means that I refuse to comment."

She tsked. "Why didn't you just say that? Much cleaner and more simple. My bodyguard was angry that we came out here unaccompanied."

"I can well imagine," he said drily.

"There will be hell to pay when we get back."

A sudden burst of fury shook him. Delayed shock, most likely. "There should be. I don't know about your country, but in the rest of the world an assassination attempt is a big deal."

"Believe me, I am taking this seriously."

"Are you?" Heedless, he let his anger show in his

voice. "You don't sound like it. You should be worried or, at the very least, afraid. Most women would be terrified."

"How do you know I'm not?" she shot back.

If she hadn't been driving, he would have kissed her. As it was, he could only seethe and battle the adrenaline coursing through him like liquid fire.

"You could have been killed," he said. "Both of us could have."

"I'm well aware of that." Her voice had gone stiff, formal. "I'm a princess. I'm not allowed to overreact."

Instead of replying, he listened as she changed gears. Their speed increased and for a while the perfect hum of the car's finely tuned engine as she negotiated the winding curves was the only sound.

He thought of the explosion and how there'd been rumors of espionage. If he was successful, his work would have far-reaching implications to change for the better—the existence of his kind. In the wrong hands, he supposed such knowledge could be used as an instrument of power.

And then there were those who viewed such a thing as unethical, contrary to the nature of their beasts. Would they be willing to kill him to stop its development?

Finally, she broke the silence. "I still don't understand why someone wanted to make an attempt on my life."

"If that is what happened, it had to be because you're a princess."

"True, but I'm nothing in the scheme of things here. I'm way down the list of succession, I'm not married to anyone influential, and I have no power. How would anyone benefit from my death?"

He took a deep breath, aware how his next words might sound. "Maybe they weren't trying to kill you at all. It's entirely possible that whoever blew up my lab traveled here to finish off their attempt. The shooter might have been gunning for me—assuming they weren't simple hunters."

"Aiming for you?" Alisa tried to hide her shock. In her experience, most doctors had a healthy-size ego, but this took the cake. "How is it possible that you honestly believe that everything is ultimately about you?"

"Because I—" he started to say.

But she wasn't finished, not by a long shot. "You are in Teslinko now. No one here knows you. On the other hand, I'm royalty, a princess, for hound's sake. My family is constantly worrying about death threats and kidnapping attempts. That's why we have bodyguards."

Frowning, he didn't appear convinced. "But still..."

She swatted at his shoulder, frustrated. "You know little of my country or my family and nothing about me beyond my ability to remain human for longer than most consider normal."

"I know more than you realize," he interjected, sounding nearly as annoyed as she. "I did study your family quite extensively before leaving America."

"Not extensively enough. You didn't even know that I went to America to go to college."

"I had a crappy research assistant," he said. "Sue me."

He still didn't get it. Fine. She'd lay it on the line for him. "For an intelligent man, you understand nothing.

Please think about this for a moment, Braden, er, Dr. Streib. Because if you truly believe someone is after you, I will have to inform my family. I can assure you that my father will end my participation in your experiments if he must worry about my safety."

She glanced at him. He faced straight ahead, scowling. His lack of response told her that the thought hadn't even occurred to him.

When he finally did speak, the husky tone in his low voice sent an involuntary shiver through her. "Perhaps I was wrong."

She grinned, glad he couldn't see her. "Perhaps you were."

"Then you do want to help me with my research?" he asked, turning toward her.

Surprised that she didn't even have to think about it, she nodded, more for herself than him. "Yes, I do. If by my existence, I can aid other shifters, then I definitely am willing to assist you."

Though she waited, he didn't respond, not even to say thank you. But when she glanced at him, the pleased expression on his craggy features made her smile widen.

A strange man, this Dr. Braden Streib. But the more time she spent with him, the more she found she liked him.

"Describe this place to me," he said abruptly. "I would like to know how everything looks, from the inside of the palace to the lands without."

Glad of the distraction, she smiled, even though he couldn't see it. "Many people find our palace beautiful. It's primarily constructed of white marble and is designed to mimic the Palace of Versailles in France, except we have no hall of mirrors."

"Something in your tone tells me you don't agree."

Startled by his astute observation, she shrugged, before remembering to give a verbal response. "I find the palace to be rather cold. It's like an icicle glittering in the sun. Lovely to look at, but if you hold it too long in your hand, it will begin to melt."

He lowered his brows at her remark but didn't comment.

"The real beauty here is in the wilderness," she continued, letting a note of pleasure infuse her voice. "Our mountains make a jagged slash in the bright blue sky, the snowcapped peaks a gorgeous backdrop for our deep, deep forests and flower-strewn meadows."

"And does the air come alive with the sound of music?" he asked, grinning.

She swatted at him. "The movie? Did I sound like a poorly written travel brochure?"

"No," he replied, becoming serious. "You sound like someone who really loves their country."

"I do," she said, thinking that she could love something—or more specifically, someone—more, if given the chance.

The thought should have shocked her, but she'd been living with this awareness simmering inside her for a while now. In fact, she'd felt a twinge of it the first time she'd ever seen him. Currents of electricity, sizzling in the air between them. She wondered if he'd felt it as well.

She could easily come to love this man.

The instant they arrived at the palace, her father's bodyguards swarmed them, surrounding the car. Despite her protests, Braden was hustled off separately from her. The muscular, stern-faced men refused to listen to her protests, urging her along.

"The king is waiting," one said sharply, arms crossed.

Of course. Her father would be furious. Not with her, but because of the fact that someone—anyone—had *dared* to make an attempt on her life.

When they reached her father's private chambers, the men surrounding her did not follow. As she entered, both her parents crossed the space to her, enveloping her in a huge hug. Her mother's perfume and her father's scent of pipe tobacco made her instantly feel better.

Finally, they broke apart.

"Thank the hounds you are okay!" Queen Ionna cupped Alisa's face in her hands and leaned in close as though to examine her for signs of injury. Her blue eyes were suspiciously bright.

As her father seconded that sentiment, he pointed to a chair. "Sit. Sven has questions for you."

"Sven?" She glanced around. Finally, she saw Sven standing unobtrusively in the back of the room. One of her father's most trusted aides, he'd been head of security for the last eight years.

As she made her way to the elaborately carved hardback chair, she forced herself to forget Braden's suspicions about the shooter, preferring instead to focus on what she did know.

Still, he should be here for the questioning.

"Where is Dr. Streib?" she asked. "Don't you want to talk to him as well?"

"He is being questioned separately, Your Highness." Sven's tone might be courteous, but his harsh expression told her he would brook no argument. "Now, tell me what happened today."

Fine. She straightened her shoulders. In as crisp and clear a tone as possible, she relayed that day's events, sticking only to the facts. They'd driven to the forest, changed, and someone had shot at them. "And that is all I know," she finished.

Expression unchanged, he studied her. "How did you escape?"

"We ran." Her shrug implied their escape had been no big deal. They all knew otherwise. "Since the doctor is blind, he took my tail in his mouth and followed me. Once we judged the assailant had left, we returned to the area where we'd left our clothing and changed back. Then we got in my car and returned home."

"Alisa Marie!" Speaking for the first time, her mother appeared on the verge of fainting. "How can you take such risks?"

Before Alisa could answer, her father spoke. "She exhibited quick thinking, my dear. She would not have risked returning to her clothing and vehicle unless she knew for certain there was no danger."

Sniffing audibly, the queen lifted her chin and glared at her husband. "I want to know why she was shape-shifting with Dr. Streib in the first place."

"Good question," Sven said. "Please explain."

"He is doing research on me." Keeping her eyes on her father, she waited for him to confirm her statement and save her from further explanation. When he did not, she reluctantly continued.

"He needed to change and he wanted to see what I was like once I changed, for research purposes." She looked down, reluctant to share details of what had been an intimate and fun afternoon, at least until the gunshot.

"And?" Sven prompted.

Refusing to let him intimidate her, she met his gaze. "And that's all. I changed, he changed, too, and someone shot at us. You know the rest."

With a nod, Sven looked past her, at the king. "I believe I have enough. If I may be excused, Your Highness?"

King Leo nodded. "Close the door behind you. We wish to have a word with our daughter in private."

Great. Squaring her shoulders, she forced a smile, aware that she probably wasn't fooling them.

Sven bowed and left. The instant the door closed behind him, Queen Ionna crossed to an ornate, embroidered settee and took a seat. "Sit," she ordered, patting the cushion next to her.

Alisa sat. "Mother? What's this about?"

"You, of course," the king responded, standing in front of them and eyeing Alisa. "Both your mother and I are very concerned."

"Please, don't worry. I'm sure your security detail will find the person that shot at me."

"Oh, I'm certain they will." Her father raised a brow. "But that part of your safety is only one of my concerns."

Now her mother interjected. "You are acting completely out of character, Alisa. What on earth possessed you to shape-shift with a perfect stranger?"

"A perfect stranger?" Agitated, Alisa jumped to her feet. "I fail to see how shifting with him is any more intimate than submitting to endless medical exams and tests."

Her father turned away and her mother made a sound of impatience. "You know why. You are a young, beautiful woman. A princess. He is a virile man. I know you are aware of what happens once you change back from wolf to human."

Flushing red, Alisa shook her head in disbelief. "Mother, for the love of… He cannot see!"

"He can still touch," the queen responded grimly. "As well as do other things."

Completely and totally embarrassed, Alisa glanced sideways at her father's back. He stood stiffly, staring silently out the window, a flush creeping up his neck.

"First off, you both know I am not beautiful." She held up her hand when her mother started to protest. "Secondly, I can assure you that any interest the doctor has in me is strictly for his research."

"You are very beautiful to me," her mother put in softly. "And that is why I am concerned."

"You have absolutely nothing to worry about," Alisa said to both her parents as she headed toward the door, face flaming. "I can promise you that."

Then, aware she didn't have permission to do so, she left anyway, fleeing down the long hall toward her bedroom.

After being completely and thoroughly grilled by two harsh-voiced men from the king's security detail, Braden was finally permitted to go to his room. He'd been unable to provide many details, since he hadn't seen anything.

Once he'd made his escape, he hurried down the hallway, concentrating on putting one foot in front of the other while using his cane to tap out a path before him. His wolf had finally quieted, as physically exhausted as his human self was mentally.

When he reached the sanctuary of his room, he had

barely enough energy to make it to the bed. Yanking back the sheets, he climbed up, fully clothed, and pulled them over him. The instant his head hit the pillow, he closed his eyes and willingly let the blissful oblivion of sleep overtake him.

He woke on his own. Still groggy from the brief but intense nap, he pushed himself up on his elbows and checked his watch. Nearly dinnertime. His stomach growled, making him realize food would be his next major concern. But he didn't want to trudge back down to the kitchen. If he were staying in a hotel rather than the palace, he'd simply pick up the phone and call room service.

Did the palace offer a similar convenience?

A soft tap at his door interrupted his musings. Braden hoped that it would be someone from the kitchen with a late afternoon snack.

Smoothing down his no doubt rumpled clothing, he put on his dark glasses and pulled open the door. "Yes?"

"A message for Dr. Streib," a deep voice intoned formally.

"All right." Braden waited. "What is it?"

"Here." The man bumped him with a silver tray. "Please take it."

Braden did. The paper felt heavy and fine, with ornate engraving at the top. "Nice paper." He handed it back.

"Sir?" The poor man sounded bewildered. "You haven't looked at it."

Obviously, this servant wasn't familiar with him. Slowly removing his sunglasses, Braden gave the man time to take note of his sightless eyes. "Since I obviously can't read it, would you be kind enough to tell me what the note says?"

"Your presence is requested to escort the princess at a formal dinner tonight," the servant intoned. "The event will be held in the main ballroom at eight o'clock this evening."

An elaborate dinner. On the same day that an attempt had been made on their daughter's life. What were they thinking? Of course, planning an event like this took time. No doubt this dinner had been planned for weeks, even months. The king and queen must have weighed the risks with their security detail and decided to go ahead and have it. After all, canceling at the very last minute would cause their invited guests major inconvenience. Braden would just bet the security would be extraordinarily tight.

Three hours away. His stomach growled again, reminding him that he needed to eat now. If he could just find something, preferably some sort of protein, like a thick, juicy steak, cooked rare, to tide him over. Then he'd gladly go to the formal thing. Hounds knew he could easily eat twice.

Thanking the man, Braden closed the door and grimaced. Formal. That meant a tux. Not only did he not own one, but he'd honestly never worn a tuxedo in his life. Even when the faculty had dinners or parties, a simple sports jacket and slacks had been deemed dressy enough. But that was academia and the extremely casual town of Boulder, Colorado. Not the royal court in Teslinko.

Ignoring his hunger pangs, he sat down on the edge of his bed. Right now, he had two options. He could pretend he'd never received the invitation and take a meal in his room or he could put on his best and only suit and pretend not to understand what the word *formal* meant.

In the end, he guessed he'd better go. If he skipped out, the royal family might take insult and toss him out on his ear. If he at least made the attempt, at the worst they'd simply assume he was an ignorant American and laugh at him behind his back. He didn't care much about that. All his life he'd been considered different and odd and had trained himself to either ignore unkind words or to rise above them.

Fumbling in his closet, he found the jacket and slacks and a button-down shirt. Since he couldn't decipher colors, he had developed a system. He'd had Xs sewn on the label of each shirt. One X meant white, two blue, three yellow, and so on.

He'd shower and then get dressed. Maybe if he was lucky, he could put in a token appearance at this dinner, scarf down some food and make a quiet and unnoticed escape.

In addition to avoiding Alisa and his disquieting feelings for her, he needed to do some quiet investigating to determine who had been the target earlier. If it was him, he could deal with that.

But if it was the princess, he had to figure out a way to keep her safe until the perpetrator could be caught.

Chapter 8

Alisa despised formal dinners. Her sisters were fortunate in that since they'd married, they no longer lived at the palace and weren't required to be present. She and her younger brother weren't so fortunate. Since her parents considered marrying Alisa off to be their next project, these events had become a sort of sophisticated torture. The king and queen always made sure to invite numerous eligible bachelors and had given Alisa strict instructions to be pleasant so she could be eyed the way a farmer eyes a new mare.

And she had to pretend as though she was actually participating, as though she possibly could consider one of these men as her potential mate.

Which meant consenting to dances, allowing them to bring her drinks and tidbits of food, and smiling through excruciatingly dull conversations. Worse, she wasn't allowed to leave for at least three hours. And after the last dinner, when she'd indulged in one too many glasses of wine in order to make the boredom more palatable, she'd been told she could not have more than three glasses of wine. The entire night long. They were so strict with this rule that they hired one person solely to keep an eye on her.

Since he'd agreed to be her escort, she knew Braden would attend as well. This lightened her heart. At least she'd have an ally, someone she could talk to instead of being constantly badgered by uninteresting men attempting futilely to gain her favor.

And, if she admitted the truth to herself, she could fully explore her inner wolf's belief that Braden was her mate.

Though she still wasn't certain there even *was* such a thing, she couldn't deny her attraction to him.

Because it was expected of her, she rang for her maids and allowed them to dress her in one of her new, sparkly designer gowns. Daydreaming while they applied her makeup and piled her hair on her head in an elaborate updo, she thought about how much she'd enjoyed her time as wolf earlier in the day, before the idiot had taken potshots at them.

For the first time in a long while, she'd actually found joy in her lupine half. She could only believe that Braden changing to wolf with her had been the reason. The more time she spent with the man, the more she wanted. If he was her mate, she assumed making love with him would be phenomenal. Just thinking about it made her quiver inside.

Turning the corner, she saw that his door was open and her heart skipped a beat. He must be about to leave for the dinner. Maybe they could walk down to the main dining hall together.

Moving quietly, well aware of his excellent hearing, she crossed to the doorway and stopped without entering the room.

He stood there facing the doorway, as though he'd been waiting for her. He wore a suit. And he wore it really well, considering. For a moment she lost her ability to breathe, watching him as he turned and moved confidently throughout the maze of equipment, his lack of vision not appearing to hinder him in the slightest.

In her long, custom-made designer gown, she watched him, her mouth dry, her heart in her throat. She wondered why he didn't wear a tux, then decided it really didn't matter. He looked wonderful and dangerous and insanely attractive as it was.

And therein lay the crux of her problem.

She didn't know why, but this man made her insides melt and her heart ache. In an odd way, she found him beautiful, with the unique kind of confident presence of the truly original. His assurance, despite his disability, along with his intelligence and—she refused to lie to herself—his boyishly rumpled good looks and tall, lean body drew her to him even more.

Which was not a good thing at all. Though she knew she had to keep this foolish attraction under control, she couldn't seem to make herself stop feeling it, no matter how she rationalized.

"Alisa?" The sharpness of his tone told her how much he hated not being able to see. Then, a heartbeat later, he nodded. "Is that you, Alisa?"

Could he actually discern her scent from clear across the room?

"Yes, it's me. I'm here." Schooling herself for the absurd tightening of her body that was her reaction to him, she kept her tone as cool and detached as possible. As though the mere sight of him didn't make her tremble in some deep, visceral place. Which managed to both infuriate and intrigue her.

He went absolutely still. After a moment, he turned to face her, dark glasses still in place. Though he'd somehow been able to coordinate his suit, shirt and tie, he'd also managed to button his shirt unevenly, completely missing the second button, so the rest of them did not align.

She debated for a heartbeat before crossing the room and reaching for his buttons.

As soon as she touched him, her stomach lurched with excitement. He tried to move away. She stopped him with a firm grasp of his arm.

"Hold still," she ordered. "I need to fix your shirt."

His jaw tightened, but he nodded. "Thank you. I usually check it myself, but I'm a bit tense over this dinner. As I'm sure you know, I've been summoned to be your escort tonight."

"Of course you are." Deliberately keeping her tone light, she couldn't keep herself from smoothing down his tie. "You promised, after all. I have to say, you look very handsome, all dressed up."

"Don't do that," he said as she finished fixing his buttons.

Suddenly she remembered. "The flirting thing?"

"Yes. I hate it."

Circling him slowly, pretending to search for a flaw in his appearance, she made it back to the front of him and sighed. "Didn't you ever flirt? You must have, back when you were younger and carefree."

"Never. It's a colossal waste of time, as far as I'm concerned."

She sighed. "You won't hear any argument from me there. I have to attend these dinners at least once a month, sometimes more. And flirting is expected of me. So, I've learned to be quite good at it."

He nodded, apparently at a loss for words.

"It'll be fine," she said, feeling like a breathless girl about to go on her first date. "You might even have fun."

"I don't know about that." Looking at her, she saw determination in the rigid set of his jaw. "But I'm ready."

Despite his closed-off expression, she could sense his vulnerability. "Then let's go."

He didn't move. "Since I'm your escort, will you stay by my side?"

Her heart lurched. "Of course."

"Thank you. I've got my cane, so I can find my way back here if you end up making other plans. It's just that there are going to be a lot of people, from the sound of it, and I don't want to risk breaking anyone's kneecaps or ankles with my cane flailing." His tense expression relaxed into a hesitant, but utterly beautiful masculine smile.

She laughed, her chest aching. "You made a joke! I'm delighted."

And then, just like that, his smile disappeared. "Never mind," he told her, backing away. "I've changed my mind. I don't need an escort. As a matter of fact, I'm reconsidering even attending at all."

Refusing to let his harsh tone deter her, she advanced

on him. "Why? Just because I gave you a compliment and took pleasure in your humor?"

"I've already told you, I don't play those kind of games."

"I'm not playing anything," she protested. "I really meant what I said."

"Then you need to be careful." Rather than retreating, he stood his ground as she advanced on him.

Something made her want to be wild and reckless. "Why?" she asked. "Why do I need to be careful?"

"Because if you keep up this skillful flirting of yours, I'm likely to do this." And he caught her by the shoulders and crushed her to him, slanting his mouth hard over hers.

The kiss started out damn near perfect, a sensual merging of lips that felt as natural as shifting to wolf had earlier. It felt...*right*. More than that. Perfect. Braden had dreamt of this, ached for this, in truth ever since he'd first heard the sexy sound of her throaty voice.

Crazy. Foolish. And not at all like him.

Despite this, he craved more, much more. He wanted to do things with her that someone like him had no business wanting to do with a royal princess.

And that was enough reason to make him realize he needed to stop. Right this instant.

He broke off the kiss and moved away, feeling oddly bereft. "My apologies," he told her, stiffly formal. "I shouldn't have done that."

"I didn't mind." Rather than furious, she sounded strangely elated. "Why apologize for something we both clearly enjoyed?"

Enjoyed?

He scratched the back of his neck, momentarily dumbfounded. "Because you're a princess, and I'm just a man." Brutal honesty seemed the best way to go.

"That matters nothing to me." The happiness still echoed in her voice, inviting him to smile with her.

Instead, he forced himself to continue as though she hadn't spoken. "And I'm blind and you can see."

"Don't." She placed her hand alongside his cheek, the warmth of her soft touch both startling and arousing him. "You cannot help that. Don't ever apologize for what happened to you."

"Why shouldn't I? You can see when my shirt isn't properly buttoned, or if I have on the wrong color shoes. You know my hair color, my features and how I'm built. While I don't even have the slightest idea what you even look like."

She paused before speaking. "Does that honestly matter?"

"Yes, it matters." He cursed, aching and furious and afraid, all at once. "I could pick your scent out of a crowd of a thousand others, your voice is as familiar to me as my own, but I have no idea as to the color of your hair, or your eyes, or whether you are fair-skinned or dark. It's strange to know someone as well as I feel I know you and have no idea how to picture them."

"I can remedy that," she said, still standing far too close for his piece of mind. "My hair is brown with red highlights, my eyes are green and my features are unremarkable."

Unremarkable. Only someone totally comfortable in their own skin would say such a thing. He wondered if she spoke the truth or merely the truth as she saw it.

"I'm not lying," she said calmly, as if she'd read his

mind. "But if you doubt me, if you really want to know, you can touch me and see for yourself." And without waiting for his response, she took his hands and placed them on her face.

At the first feel of her silky skin under his fingertips, he froze, his blood roaring in his ears.

"Go ahead." She held herself perfectly still.

He could swear he still heard a trace of desire in her throaty voice. He swallowed tightly, his body instantly responding with a fierceness that astounded him.

"Touch me," she urged, trembling under his hand, which only unnerved him more. "Please."

Heart thumping erratically, he took a deep breath. Then, as though unable to help himself, he let his fingers glide over her skin, slowly, gently, aroused and curious and feeling awed, as if he stood in the presence of something holy.

Alisa. This was Alisa.

Exploring her face, he tried to form a picture. She held her breath, he held his, and when they exhaled at the same time, breaths mingling with each other, his arousal swelled to unbelievable proportions.

Despite the intensity of his desire, he kept himself in check. This was too important to give in to base, carnal needs, no matter how powerful. The scientist in him—no, the *man* in him—needed to know her face. Needed to know more than merely a voice and a tantalizing scent. Needed to know *her*.

Memorizing each hollow, each swell of cheekbone and chin, he trailed his fingers over her smooth, silky skin. She stood motionless, and trembled again when he stroked her lush lips, parting them for him. Sweeping slowly up the curve of her cheek, he placed his fingertips on her temples, where the slightest pulse beat riotously. He lingered there, then gently and reverently swept over her eyes. Her lashes were long and thick, framing eyes that seemed to have a faintly almond-shaped curve.

Dropping his hands, body throbbing, he stepped back, trying to form a mental image. With shock he realized his princess was beautiful, heart-stoppingly gorgeous. Of course she was. Weren't princesses usually?

For some reason, this knowledge disconcerted him. Uncomfortable, suddenly ill at ease, he kept his hands at his sides and took another step back. Once, beautiful women had flocked to him, but that had been before his accident. Now, they avoided him like the plague. No one wanted damaged goods.

Except Alisa. Even as he had the thought, he questioned it. She could have anyone—rich and handsome and royal and famous. Why would someone like her want him?

Yet she'd kissed him. She'd been the one to invite his touch. Now knowing of her beauty, he could find no logical reason.

From somewhere, he found his voice, dredging up the necessary words. "Thank you. I now have a better idea of your appearance." Even to himself, he sounded like he'd swallowed a bucket of rusty nails.

"And you're disappointed." The hurt in her voice told him she'd taken his reaction differently than he'd intended. She breathed in quick, shallow gasps, as though holding back a very raw, very powerful emotion. "I should have warned you. I'm not very pretty."

"Not pretty?" Stunned, he hesitated, blinking in bafflement. "I can only tell you what I saw with my fingers. And you are a very beautiful woman."

A soft gasp escaped her. For a moment, he thought she might be about to argue, but instead, she rushed over and gave him a quick, nervous hug.

"Thank you."

"You're welcome. I mean it," he told her.

"I know you do." The disbelieving tone of her voice told him she thought he was lying to her, if out of kindness or as a means to an end, he didn't know.

"Stop." Unable to help himself, he reached out and traced the line of her cheek once more. "You know I don't flirt. I'm telling you the truth."

Her breath hitched, making him wonder if the experience might have been as shattering for her as it had been for him.

Despite everything, despite knowing she was out of his league in more ways than he could number, his desire had not quieted. Instead, his need had grown stronger. He burned for her, ached for her, his body throbbed for her.

Heart hammering in his chest, he took a deep breath, and then decided the hell with it. Reaching for her, he pulled her closer and slanted his mouth over hers a second time.

Instead of pulling away, as he had half feared she might, she moaned and opened her mouth to his. Heat flared, blazed as their tongues mated. His skin tingled where their bodies touched, the jolt of her nearness making his insides jangle.

Still, he tried to maintain some semblance of control, even as it rapidly shredded around him. His body, already more aroused than it'd ever been, swelled even more, straining the front of his trousers. He craved her, ached to bury himself deep inside her, to experience the thrill of her wrapped tight around him.

Evidently, she felt the same way. As she curled her body into him, he realized the rest of her was as perfectly proportioned as her features.

Inside, his wolf watched silently, radiating approval rather than actively fighting him. His beast wanted this as much as he did.

She moaned and pressed her lips against his, her wordless cries asking for more. As he covered her mouth with his, the hunger inside him grew. Craving more, he deepened the kiss. She tasted like she smelled, yet better, more sensual and womanly and…his.

Damn it. He froze. She wasn't his. She never would be. Only an idiot would even entertain such a thought.

What the hell was he doing?

Pushing himself off her, he took a staggering step back. Breathing harshly and completely disoriented, he took little consolation in the knowledge that she sounded equally off balance.

Still, that didn't make him any less of a fool.

"That shouldn't have happened." He ground out the words, knowing if anyone had to apologize, it should be him. "I'm sorry."

"Don't be." Her flippant tone was laced with what, oddly, sounded like pain. "I enjoyed it as much as you did, just like the first kiss."

For an aching moment, he wished he could gaze down into her face and see the look in her beautiful eyes, drown in the desire he knew must have darkened her gaze.

Removing his dark glasses, he dragged his hand

across his eyes, fervently wishing it could be so. As he did, there…on the very edge of the darkness… Was that a shape, different from the nothingness that was all his eyes were able to perceive?

For a second he felt dizzy. Wishful thinking? Or reality? He blinked, trying again to make sense of what was happening, and then inhaled sharply.

He wasn't sure he entirely believed what he was seeing. Yes, *seeing.* Instead of complete and utter blackness, there was a distinct lightening at the edge of the darkness. A sort of shadowy gray that gave a hint of the possibilities beyond.

Could it be that his sight, believed to be lost forever, might be returning to him in tiny increments? How was this possible and… The thought was so staggering he felt it like a punch to his stomach.

Was this miracle due to Alisa somehow?

He must have cried out, made some sort of sound.

"What's wrong?" she murmured, touching him again. "Braden, talk to me. Are you all right?"

All right? He was better than that, a thousand times better. If he dared let himself believe…

Yet hope and optimism and magic were not part of the repertoire of a physician who all too often saw the worst life could throw at people. Inoperable brain tumors never miraculously healed, Alzheimer's never magically vanished. So why would he believe he could be any different? Why would his sight suddenly reappear?

Had it really? Or had he imagined that brief, wonderful moment when black became gray? He needed proof, something tangible that he could measure and probe.

Failing that, he needed…her. Wrapping his arms around her slender back, he pulled her close.

"Alisa," he began, hesitant and uncertain yet wanting her to understand. "For just a nanosecond, I thought I could actually, almost, *see*."

She gasped, mouth pressed into the hollow of his throat, making him realize just how tall she was.

"Are you certain?" She sounded hopeful and breathless.

Though they hadn't known each other all that long, he felt like their connection was more intimate than he'd ever experienced with a woman. With her, he could only share the truth. "No. Not at all. It might have only been wishful thinking. But I swear there was a lightening at the edge of my vision, a dark gray rather than the black nothingness."

"Really?" Drawing back, she gripped him by the upper arms. "Is it still there?"

He stared ahead, squinting slightly, considering. Longing, wishing. "No. It's gone."

"But still… That's a reason to hope, wouldn't you say?"

Hope. He swallowed hard. As foreign to his line of work as Darwin's theory was to a Southern Baptist preacher. He shoved his dark glasses back on his face.

"I don't believe in hope," he finally said, aware of the sharpness of his reply. "I don't believe in miracles."

Then, as she sagged against him, he realized she did. Of course she did. "Listen, Alisa. If you're waiting for a magical cure, a lightning bolt to shoot out of the sky to suddenly make me normal, you need to face reality. I'm blind. I can't see. That's how it is."

He could feel the tears on her cheek as she shook her

head against his chest. "But surely it's not permanent. If you'll just let yourself believe."

He hardened his heart at the optimism in her voice, aching. In that instant, he realized that if he could, he'd give her anything she wanted. Anything within his power to give. Which, at this point in his life, was absolutely nothing. No matter what he'd once been, he couldn't give her this.

"Alisa," he said gently. "I've seen numerous doctors. The best of the best. My blindness is permanent. I told you. Even our Pack Healer—she who can cure anything and anyone—failed."

"Because you didn't want to be healed," she cried. The pain in her voice nearly broke him. That she could feel so deeply, so strongly, when they'd only just met. This should have terrified him. Oddly enough, it didn't.

But because he could do nothing else, he straightened his shoulders and squared his jaw. "That's not why. It's not even logical."

"You know what? Sometimes things happen in life that can't be explained away by reasoning."

Now she sounded angry, which was good. Much better than sorrow, at least. Anger he could respond to in kind. He refused to let himself mourn. Not his lack of sight nor…her.

"Why do you care so much?" he asked her, genuinely curious and frustrated, all at once.

Silence. Then, pushing herself out of his arms, she moved away. "Do you really have to ask? I know you're leaving here eventually, but still…"

Like a sucker punch to the gut, her words registered. She was right. In the midst of this crazed obsession with her, he'd managed to forget that once he'd concluded his experiments and went home, he'd most likely never see her again.

Though intellectually he'd been aware of this fact ever since the instant he heard her wonderful voice and breathed her tantalizingly feminine scent—how could he not?—emotionally, the very concept of spending the rest of his days without hearing her or feeling her touch was enough to make him want to give in to grief for the first time and howl.

So not like him. What the hell had happened to him?

Throat aching, he tried to force his thoughts elsewhere. His eyes stung. Glad of his dark glasses, he cleared his throat and turned away. Damn emotion. The one part of life that continually defied logic and the one thing above all others that he sought to avoid.

Her soft touch on his arm stopped him. "Don't you want to have your vision back?"

"What I want has nothing to do with anything." He spoke harshly, well aware she wouldn't understand the double innuendo. "Life isn't like that. The sooner you realize the truth, the better off you'll be."

The soft hitch of her breath as she released him was the only hint that he'd hurt her.

Yet when she spoke, her voice was strong and even and as courageous as ever. "Do you know how many people have said that to me over the course of my life?"

Frustrated, he shook his head. "Then why haven't you listened? You're going to be badly hurt if you don't."

"I don't understand you," she retorted. "At all."

"Good." Each word felt like it was ripped from his throat. "It's better that way."

"Better that you refuse to see endless possibilities? How is closing yourself off better than daring to dream?"

"How easily you say that," he mocked, "when all I want from you is the secret to your ability to remain human. That's all I want from you."

The instant the words left his mouth, he realized how hurtful—and false—they were. A lie, when he wanted more, so much more. He'd spoken without thinking, another pitfall when he let emotion win over logic. "I'm sorry," he said. "I didn't mean—"

"Apology accepted." The crisp tone to her voice told him she had taken his statement exactly the way he hadn't meant it. "There is a formal dinner to attend. If we don't want to be late, we need to leave now."

Dinner? He'd managed to completely forget about that.

He shook his head, the tightness in his throat almost impossible to force words past. "I've changed my mind. I'm not going. You'll have to attend without me."

She went silent for a moment, no doubt trying to judge whether or not he was serious.

"All right, then," she finally said, sounding like someone else. "Have a nice evening." Then, judging from the sound of her footsteps, she turned and marched away without him, leaving his door as wide open as his heart had been.

Chapter 9

Alisa barely made it around the corner before the tears started, running silently down her cheeks like rain. Why she was crying, she didn't know. But she felt like a hole had been ripped in her chest.

All she could think about was to wonder what had just happened back there, in Braden's room? She barely knew this man. But they'd kissed and it had been…unexpected. Wonderful and earth-shattering and… Sweet hounds of hell, she was a complete and utter fool. Why had she allowed him to kiss her? Allowed? She'd practically begged him for it.

The intimacy of his fingers whispering across her face had brought to roaring life the desire that always seemed to simmer inside her when she was around him. She'd wanted him then and—if she was perfectly honest with herself—she wanted him still.

She thought of her sisters and how they'd be absolutely appalled if they were to find out she'd kissed the American doctor. She pictured her parents' shock and her younger brother's amused laughter. For once, he wouldn't be the one who'd messed up. It would be she.

And Braden had even admitted to her that all he wanted from her was the answer to her ability. She was an experiment to him, a lab specimen. Nothing more.

The low, insistent throb of another of her headaches threatened. Covering her face with her hands, she shook her head, then winced at the pain. No one could know. She knew what they all would say because she'd heard it before, though never in relation to her love life.

No common sense. They'd been saying that to her for years. Too much education coupled with too little actual experience, walking around with her head in the clouds, while wearing permanent rose-colored glasses—she'd heard them all and pretended the words didn't wound her.

But they had. Deeply. Her intelligence canceled out her glaring lack of beauty. Even so, her detractors had tried to strip that from her by claiming she had no common sense. For the most part, she'd ignored them.

Until now, the only area no one had ever been able to find fault with her had been her love life, because she didn't have one. She hadn't wanted to. She'd gone on dates, flirted, and pretended she cared. But she hadn't. Not until now.

Oh. My. She was attracted to not only an American, but a man who'd made it abundantly clear his only interest in her was scientific. No doubt he had some research or experimental motivation for the kiss.

Worse, she wanted to kiss him again. She wanted to

feel his hands on her body and to run her own fingers over his. She wanted him.

And all she could do apparently was rub her throbbing temples and ache and cry like a blubbering fool. Which she most certainly was not, despite what anyone else might think.

She'd get over this. She had to. And as long as Braden—and everyone else—didn't know, she'd be fine.

Straightening her spine, she wiped at her eyes with the back of her hand. Wait a minute. Why on earth was she crying, anyway? She was Princess Alisa of Teslinko. So she and Braden—Dr. Streib, she reminded herself—had shared a kiss. So what? She found him fascinating, likely because he was different. It wasn't as though she'd never kissed anyone before. In her halfhearted efforts to find a relationship, she'd kissed plenty of men. Just because none of them had started that simmering spark low in her belly, it didn't mean she would go and do something foolish, right?

Exactly. So what. If she admitted the truth, she'd been wanting to kiss him for a long time, ever since she'd first seen his craggy features and heard the rasp of his masculine voice. So she'd finally given in to temptation. Nothing more. She didn't need to make a big deal out of this. Being overly dramatic had always been another of her faults, at least according to her siblings.

She could deal with this. She would. She had to.

Still, no other man's kiss had ever made her feel so…delicious. She shivered, touching her lips with her fingertips.

His kiss had been magical. And if she felt cheated just because she wanted to kiss him again, well, she'd get over that. Because it could not happen again.

Decision made, she squared her shoulders and blotted at her face with a tissue from her clutch purse. Hopefully she hadn't managed to ruin her makeup. She had a formal dinner to attend.

Stopping short, she cocked her head. Damned if she was letting him weasel out of this event because of a single stolen kiss. She needed an ally and he'd promised to be hers. Now she'd hold him to his word.

Stomach turning somersaults, she pivoted and marched herself right back up to his room.

With the door still open, she was able to steamroll herself inside. He remained where she'd left him, motionless, apparently lost in thought.

She had a fleeting thought—had the kiss affected him as much as it had her?—then banished it. The kiss didn't matter, couldn't matter. They both needed to forget that it had ever happened.

As far as she was concerned, it hadn't.

"Excuse me," she said politely from a few feet away, aware he'd been so lost in his own mind that he hadn't heard her return. He spun around, the expression on his rugged face so intense that she instinctively took a step back.

"What do you want?" he practically snarled. Then, appearing to collect himself, he dragged his hand across his mouth. When he spoke again, he sounded completely different. Cultured and polite, as one should be when speaking to a princess.

He also sounded distant. She realized that she didn't like it one bit.

"What are you doing here?" he asked quietly. "You're going to be late for your formal dinner."

"I came back to get you." Bravado and determination

moved her closer. "You promised to assist me tonight. I'm not letting you weasel out of this dinner so easily."

"Weasel?" He cocked his head. "Did you pick that up in college also?"

She refused to be sidetracked. "Of course I did. Even if English is not our native tongue, we know slang, just like anyone else. Now please, Braden. Come with me."

Still he didn't respond, just continued to face her with his dark glasses obscuring his sightless eyes.

"Please," she tried again. More flies with honey and all that.

When he didn't reply, she realized she had to go with the truth. "Honestly, I'd really like you to go."

"Why?" His expression might have been made of stone. "So you can parade me around in front of your friends like some kind of freakish curiosity?"

"No." Taking a step closer, she dared to reach out and place her hand lightly on his biceps, thrilling at the way his body quivered under her touch. "The truth is, I hate these things. My parents trot me out like I'm their prize, up for sale to the highest bidder. I spend the entire night listening to suitor after suitor expound on his charms. They ask me to dance, I get my feet stepped on so much that I can barely walk, and then I return to my chair for more conversation about them. When one leaves, another takes his place. I need you to help me discourage them."

"How?" He crossed his arms. "I'm not royalty, nor am I one of your suitors. Most of them will probably deem me as below them." And he sounded as though if one did, he'd love to punch him in the face.

She smiled at the thought. Though she hated to even think such a thing, and the consequences would be disastrous, a fist fight or any kind of altercation would certainly liven things up.

Still, she owed him an answer. "Act like you're my escort. If you don't ever leave my side, it will be more difficult for them to approach me."

First he started to shake his head. Then he laughed, a deep, masculine sound full of such mirth that she would have laughed along, if the source of his amusement had been someone else. "Don't you have any friends who could do this for you?"

"Friends? Once again, you prove that you know nothing about the life of a princess. Look, I know I sound pitiful," she said defensively. "But you have no idea how awful these things can be."

When he clapped his hand on top of hers, still resting lightly on his arm, she froze. For one heart-stopping, thrilling moment, she thought he might kiss her again.

Instead, he squeezed her hand and released her, taking a step back. "Fine, I'll go. On one condition."

Relieved, she smiled up at him before realizing yet again that he couldn't see her expression. "What's that?"

"We leave when I want to leave. No discussion, no arguments. Agreed?"

First she nodded, and then belatedly found her voice. "Agreed."

In response, he gave her a savage grin of such dangerous beauty that it made her chest ache. "Then let's go," he said, reaching for his cane. Then, appearing to change his mind, he left it where it was, moving forward without hesitation.

She reached for him to help him, then thought better of it. After a moment's hesitation, she decided to simply ask. "Is it all right if I take your arm?"

"Because you want to help me get there?" he asked. "And then you'll drop it once we reach the general area of the banquet hall?"

"Why would I do that?" she countered.

"Because while you want me to help you fend off other men, you don't want to send out a public statement that we're together."

"But you have difficulty around large crowds of people," she countered. "I think that outweighs something silly like worrying about what other people think, don't you?"

Though he shook his head, he didn't reply with some kind of sarcastic comment, which she considered a minor victory. "Fine. Take my arm."

Feeling ridiculously self-conscious, she slid her hand into the crook of his elbow.

Arm in arm they walked around the corner and approached the throng of people milling about near the double doors leading to the banquet hall. Her father had stationed uniformed guards there and each person was required to produce an invitation. The name on the invite was then checked against a list.

Smiling and waving at a few people she recognized, Alisa breezed to the front of the line, tugging Braden along with her. In the crowd, she noticed several people staring and whispering to their companions, but she kept her head up and gave them her back.

Of course the guards let her and her companion through immediately.

Once inside, she scanned the room for her parents. As usual, they were holding court at a table up on a raised dais. Throngs of admirers waited to pay tribute. Good. They were far too busy to notice her and her escort.

At least until the time came to be seated. Then, Alisa would be expected to take her seat up on the dais with the rest of her family. Since Dr. Streib was a guest in the palace, he would be expected to sit there also.

Breathing a sigh of relief, she tugged at Braden's arms so he would bend down closer. "You'll be meeting my brother here tonight. No matter what he says, don't let him provoke you."

Dark glasses firmly in place, he nodded. "He's that big of a pain?"

"If you could only imagine," she began. At exactly that moment, she spied her brother heading directly toward them, the devilishly intent look on his aristocratic face spelling nothing but trouble.

The swell of noise notwithstanding, the mixture of scents and bodies disconcerted Braden. Glad of Alisa's grip on his arm, he followed her lead and tried to shut out all the distractions. But her brother?

"He's heading this way," she murmured, sounding distressed. "Don't let him get to you."

He nodded. Now that she mentioned her brother, he remembered he'd read about him while researching her family. The youngest child and only male, Prince Ruben was not only the heir to the throne, but a hellion and dedicated playboy to boot. Braden could easily understand why some people might find him annoying. Aside from that, everything he'd read made the prince seem harmless.

Judging from the way Alisa stiffened and the panic in her voice, he was about to find out.

"Well, well. Who's this?" a masculine voice drawled. "Lisa, aren't you going to introduce me to your friend?"

Lisa? Somehow the completely Americanized version of her name seemed to fit her. If she hadn't been a princess, that is.

Alisa sighed. "Ruben, since you've somehow managed to avoid meeting him the entire time he's been here, this is Dr. Braden Streib. Braden, meet my brother Ruben."

"Prince Ruben," her brother corrected. "Pleased to meet you, Doctor."

Braden raised his head, putting on a bland smile and affecting bored disinterest as he stuck out his hand for the prince to shake. As they did, he noted with cautious approval that the prince had a firm, confident grip.

"Lisa, I'd like to talk to your doctor," Ruben said as soon as he released Braden's hand. "Alone."

Then, without waiting for anyone's consent, he took Braden's arm and steered him away.

Mildly amused, Braden allowed this. He could well imagine exactly what Alisa's brother wanted to say to him. Some variation of "Hurt my sister, and I'll break your legs," no doubt.

"Stop frowning," Prince Ruben said over his shoulder, presumably to Alisa. "I'll bring him back in just a moment."

Instead of going to a quiet corner, the prince shepherded Braden to an entirely separate room, closing the door behind them as he released Braden's arm.

In this moment, more than anything, Braden hated the all-encompassing blackness. He would have given much to read this man's expression or body language.

For all he knew, Alisa's brother might punch him in the stomach.

"I wanted to talk to you in private," Prince Ruben said, all traces of amusement gone from his voice. "I understand you were shot at while running as wolves."

Braden raised a brow. "That's correct. Has your security detail had any luck in finding out who or why?"

"No. At least, nothing concrete. But we have our suspicions." Ruben's grim certainty put Braden on full alert.

"'We'?" Braden crossed his arms. "Are you working with the security detail personally?"

"I am." Ruben sounded grim. "I have been head of security for the last five years. I'll have to ask you to please keep this to yourself. Neither my mother nor my sister know about this. Sven works for me now."

Braden thought back to the information he'd read on the royal family and shook his head. "Actually, no one knows about this, do they?"

"Correct. And my father and I would like to keep it that way."

Nodding to show his compliance, Braden waited.

"About your attack. We were concerned that such a thing might happen. My father debated briefing you on the situation, but decided against it."

That was not good. "'The situation'?"

Prince Ruben cleared his throat. "There's more going on here than appears on the surface."

Could he be any less informative? "Please, enlighten me."

"Would you like to take a seat?" Ruben asked, pulling out a chair close by. "Let me direct you to it and—"

"No need." Braden waved him away. He thought of

Alisa, waiting out in the crowd. "Is this going to take that long?"

"No." Ruben's tone grew clipped. "I'll keep it as brief as I can. There is a certain group of European Pack members who don't want the secret of Alisa's abilities to be found."

This so boggled the mind that Braden couldn't find words to express his shock.

When he didn't immediately reply, the prince continued. "There have been numerous attempts on my sister's life ever since word got out about what she can do. We've been trying to infiltrate the group and capture the ringleader, but so far we've had limited success."

All Braden could think about was Alisa, blithely living her life, completely unaware that she was in any danger. "Why have you kept this from her? I would think she needs to know."

"I tend to agree with you," Ruben said drily. "But our father wanted her to have as normal a life as possible. Until the day you and she went alone to the mountains to change, we always had someone unobtrusively shadowing her and watching over her."

Braden nodded. "And when she and I traveled alone the day someone shot at us? What happened to her escort then?"

The prince sighed. "You were in the car with her. You see how she drives. She simply outran the men who were following her. They lost her and they were disciplined accordingly."

Was that a trace of reluctant admiration in Ruben's voice? He was right about one thing, though. Thinking back, Braden remembered Alisa driving like a bat out of hell. “That car of hers is awfully fast. Anyone would have had trouble keeping up.”

“Yes, I know.” Ruben sounded both amused and weary. “Keeping Alisa safe from herself is another full-time job, never mind worrying about a group of extremists. I’ve been trying to talk my father into making her drive something a bit more sedate.”

“She’ll never go for it.” Listening to himself talk as though he’d known her for years.

“You’re correct. Also, my father refuses to deny her anything. But I find your insight most interesting.” The prince moved closer, bringing with him the scent of mint and masculine aftershave. “You seem to know my sister quite well.”

“We spend a lot of time together,” Braden said lightly, trying to defuse the sudden tension. “No worries there, I promise.” He cleared his throat. “Back to these extremists or whatever they are. Please explain. Why would any shifter not want to have the ability to remain human longer? All the jobs that Pack members can’t take, including the military, would be within our reach. Our horizons would be significantly broadened. Opposing such a good thing makes absolutely no sense to me.”

“I agree. Yet for all that they’re a militant group and highly organized, they appear to be an intelligent crowd as well. From what I gather, they feel more connected to their wolf selves. They believe remaining human for longer than a week or two is an abomination to their true natures. They even use terms like ‘wolf abuse’ and consider those of us who live normal human lives as sellouts to our own kind.”

“Sellouts?” Once again Braden was stymied. “I’ve

not heard one word of this, ever. Not in the U.S. or in Europe. Is this new or has it been going on long?"

"Long enough." Prince Ruben swallowed hard. "We think they might have been behind the explosion in your lab last year. Though I believe they meant to kill you rather than blind you."

Damn. "You definitely have my attention. And this was because of my work researching Alisa's abilities?"

"Right. You are known worldwide as the foremost researcher seeking to bring our kind the ability to remain human longer. They believe if they could eliminate you, your death would essentially stop the research cold."

"They were right." Stunned, Braden tried to process what he had heard. "Why wasn't I informed of this?"

"I tried." The prince sounded as frustrated as Braden felt. "I didn't want you to come here. I argued with my father, but he refused to hear me. Having you and Lisa in the same place makes an enticing target. One strike would take out both risks at once. These extremists are not stupid. They have already tried to take advantage of the situation once. I have no doubt they will do so again."

"So King Leo wouldn't listen to you?" Braden scratched his head. "Again, I fail to see the logic. Why did he want me here? Your argument makes better sense."

"Because he doesn't want my sister to spend her life looking over her shoulder. He is using you to draw the militants out so he can bring them down."

"In other words," Braden drawled, "I'm bait."

"You're a target. That's why I'm letting you know. I don't want you to become a casualty of this rebellion."

"Rebellion?" Braden picked up on the word. "What are they rebelling against?"

"Progress," Ruben said, bitterness coloring his voice. "Their creed is similar to that of the Ferals. They abhor living among humans and prefer to live as wild savages in the wilderness."

"That's their choice. But you're telling me they can't see that others would choose differently?"

The prince began pacing, reminding Braden of the way Alisa acted when she was agitated. "They see nothing beyond their own desires."

Heart sinking, Braden knew that there was only one thing to do.

"Thank you for telling me. I will pack my things and arrange to leave immediately." Though he hated to abandon his unfinished research, he saw no other choice.

"You can't." Sounding angry, the prince again came to a halt close to Braden. "You don't strike me as the kind of man who would give up so easily. If you go, you'll be admitting defeat."

Braden shrugged. "I can't see an alternative choice. I would do nothing to endanger your sister."

"That's just it. Your leaving will not help. The danger will not end once you've returned to America. Her life is still at risk. She makes a game out of avoiding her security detail. At least if you stay by her side, you can help protect her."

The concept was so mind-boggling that Braden couldn't help but wonder if Prince Ruben mocked him. "Protect her?" he asked bitterly. "I can't even see to identify the threat. If anything, I'm a liability to her."

"Ah, but there you're wrong. You can slow her down.

If we can make her believe you are in danger, she will take steps to protect you, thus protecting herself."

What a tangled web of lies. Braden hated deceit and playing games worse than anything. "Why not just tell her the truth?"

"We have." Exasperation plain in his voice, the prince began pacing again. "She refuses to hear it."

"Like father, like daughter." Braden shook his head. Like it or not, he couldn't abandon Alisa now. "What do you want me to do?"

Relief and satisfaction mingled in the prince's voice. "Stay with her. Continue your research. How close are you to finding the answer?"

For some reason, Ruben's offhand question sent up red flags. Maybe because no one in the royal family—including Alisa—had asked about results. Braden didn't know if they were trying to be polite or what, but he'd certainly expected to be questioned before now.

And now, this instant, the prince had asked at the worst possible time, when everything seemed doubtful.

Still, Braden would answer. Unfortunately, he could only tell the truth. "Not close at all. I don't understand it. I've run every analysis I can think of and Alisa tests normal every single time."

"Well, keep at it." Slapping Braden on the back, Ruben sighed. "Now, are you ready to go out there and circulate among the sharks?"

Braden nodded. It seemed Alisa wasn't the only one who despised the formal dinners.

When they emerged from the room, Ruben touched Braden's shoulder. "Fair warning. My sister is waiting for you across the room and she doesn't look happy. She has two men on either side of her, each trying to get her attention. She's glaring at us. If looks could kill..."

"I can't blame her. I promised to be her escort and help her fend them off."

"That's certainly above and beyond the call of duty," the prince drawled.

"Maybe." Braden shrugged. Truthfully, he didn't mind helping Alisa out. In actuality, he sort of relished the idea that someone like her was willing to let everyone think they were together, even if only for one night.

"Well, it's your funeral. I'll walk over there with you and you can get busy fending. Those men can be rather intent when the prize is a princess."

The carefree laughter was back in the prince's voice, full force. Braden wondered if Ruben presented a lighthearted facade deliberately to throw people off.

Chapter 10

Staying close to the other man, Braden followed. A moment later, they reached Alisa.

"Here he is, sister of mine," Ruben boomed heartily, still using that falsely jovial voice as he kissed Alisa loudly on both cheeks. "And I'd say none too soon if he wanted to make sure none of your gentlemen friends would steal you away from him."

The two men who were with Alisa murmured excuses and walked away.

"Thank you, Ruben." Alisa's voice dripped with so much icy, aristocratic culture that she almost sounded like a stranger. "It's about time you two returned. I don't like my escorts to keep me waiting."

"Sorry." Ruben sounded anything but.

Shaking his head, Braden held out his arm. An instant later, Alisa took it, gripping him tightly.

"Shall we go?" he asked, pitching his own tone to sound as formal as hers.

"Definitely." She squeezed his arm hard. "Since you disappeared for so long, we don't have time to mingle. We must be seated when father rings the bell for dinner to begin. We cannot be late."

"She's right. I'll see you two up there in a minute," Ruben added. He didn't appear to be in as big a hurry as his sister, but he probably got a lot more leeway since he was the only male child and the heir to the throne. If he was late, the king probably waited for him.

Braden sighed. Sorting through all this royal protocol gave him a headache. With Alisa leading him, they moved off, her arm firmly in his.

Getting through the crowd of people was a bit nerve-racking. Though he guessed they tended to move apart for Alisa, sort of like the Red Sea parting, the noise level in the packed room made him tense.

Plus he couldn't help but worry that the attacker might have managed to infiltrate this dinner in order to make another attempt on either his or Alisa's life.

A crash from his left made him jump, and he half turned by reflex in case he had to fight.

"It's all right," Alisa murmured. "One of the wait staff dropped something."

He nodded. Feeling slightly paranoid after Ruben's talk, and progressively more uncomfortable as always in the ever-moving crush of people, he mumbled apologies as he tried to avoid stepping on feet.

"I'm like a bull in a china shop," he said. "I wish now that I'd brought my cane."

"Sorry." She squeezed his arm again, pressing in close to his side. "We're almost there," she told him, as if she sensed his growing unease. "There are three steps leading to the dais. I'll tell you when to step up."

At her words, he stopped, pulling her to a halt with him. "Dais? Surely you don't expect me to sit up on a platform so everyone can stare at me."

"My family sits there and that's where I have to take my meal. Of course my escort will be seated next to me."

Of course. Except her normal escorts were a bunch of rich, spoiled aristocrats vying for her attention. Enough was enough. "Maybe you should choose one of the others," he said. "I'm not up for this. Not now."

She stopped, still gripping his arm, and turned to face him. "What on earth did my brother say to you back there?"

"Nothing to do with this, I promise you."

"Then why are you acting so strange? You promised to be my escort. Believe me, I appreciate your help."

Resigned, he nodded. She was right. He'd given his word.

"Never mind," he told her, coming to an instant decision. "I'm sorry. Of course I'll sit on your dais with you." He even managed a pained smile. "Lead the way."

For once, he was glad he couldn't see the people who were no doubt staring at him, talking behind their hands about the blind man who didn't own a tuxedo.

Since he didn't speak the Teslinkian language, which was the predominant language in the room, he had no idea what anyone was saying. Nor, he told himself, did he care. None of that was important. What worried him was how he could protect Alisa if he couldn't even see the threat coming.

A bell rang and the noise in the room grew to a crescendo.

"That's the signal for everyone to take their seats," Alisa told him. "In a few minutes, there will be another bell and the staff will begin serving our meal."

Exactly as she'd said, another, louder bell rang barely two minutes later. Plates clanked, silverware and crystal tinkling as the service commenced. Though he couldn't view it with his own eyes, Braden could picture a small army of servers, balancing trays with covered plates, going around the packed room.

Finally, the meal was served. An expectant hush fell over the room.

"Next my father will stand and make his speech and give the traditional blessing."

Listening as the king spoke, the musical cadence of his native tongue lyrical and exotic, Braden inhaled the odd aroma of the food. It smelled like mashed potatoes and gravy, with a side of roast beef. Though he had no idea what they were serving, his mouth watered.

Finally relaxing, he thoroughly enjoyed the room's relative quiet while the king gave his speech.

As King Leo finished, another bell pealed.

Immediately, as though someone had flicked a switch, the noise swelled up from the floor.

"Now we may eat," Alisa murmured in his ear, sending a shiver of heat through him.

Groping for his fork and knife, Braden cut into his food and raised a piece to his mouth. Even after a taste, he still had no idea what it was, though he guessed it was some kind of beef dish. He continued to eat, chewing the food methodically, trying to force it down despite his lack of hunger and the strange, unfamiliar taste.

"You don't like your dinner?" The laughter in Alisa's husky voice warmed him to his toes. His body stirred.

"It's, er, interesting," he murmured back, pushing it around on his plate with his fork. "What exactly is it?"

"In English, you call it liver."

Unable to suppress a shudder, he gripped his fork and nodded. No wonder he couldn't stomach it. He smiled and forced himself to take another bite, trying not to gag.

The next three courses were better, and he began to relax. Finally dessert arrived, some kind of pudding that he actually enjoyed, though he really didn't want to know what it was. He ate this with gusto, keeping a pleasant expression for the onlookers.

Finally, the plates were cleared away. "Let's go," he said.

"Already?" Was she feigning her disappointment, or was she serious? "The entertainment has not yet started. My father likes to play the piano and my mother enjoys singing."

He resisted the urge to grimace. "Then we're leaving just in time. Come on."

Because she, too, had promised, she got to her feet and took his arm. They descended the dais arm in arm, sweeping through the now milling crowd. This time, since most everyone remained seated, they made it to the door without incident.

Only when they were outside the banquet room and well down the hall did he slow his pace and take a huge breath of relief.

"Thank you for doing that for me. You were a wonderful escort." She leaned in close, bringing him the heady scent of her perfume. "I still want to know what Ruben said to you."

Now that the dinner was over, he saw no reason to lie. "He told me about the danger facing you and how you won't listen."

She pulled her arm free. "There is no danger. My brother exaggerates."

"Really? Did he exaggerate the shot, too?"

"That was not related," she sniffed. "You said so yourself. The shooter was after you, you said so yourself."

"I said that before I knew about these extremists who want to kill you."

"There is no proof that these people even exist. I think they are a figment of Ruben's imagination."

He snorted. "Listen to yourself. Funny, but you don't seem the type to avoid reality."

From her sharp intake of breath, he saw his barb had hit home. "I'm not avoiding anything. What my brother tells me doesn't make sense. Why would anyone not want to have the ability to remain human longer?"

"So, because your idea of reality doesn't mesh with theirs, you're saying theirs does not exist?"

"If it does, you must understand one thing. Ruben counts himself among those who would rather be wolf than human. If I believe what he tells me, then I have to consider my own brother a threat!"

As soon as she said the words, tears welled up in Alisa's eyes. She couldn't believe she'd just spoken out loud her most private fear. Accusing her baby brother of something so sordid felt akin to being heretical. She knew he loved her and would never hurt her. She wished she'd kept her mouth closed.

"You can't be serious." Braden's stunned response only made her feel worse. "Your brother wouldn't do anything to hurt you, would he?"

"Of course not," she hastened to reassure him as well as herself. "That isn't what I meant. Ruben would never be a threat to me. I know he would protect me with his life. And honestly, my brother is extremely loyal to our family and our Pack. I just meant that not all shifters who'd rather be wolf are crazy."

Frowning, Braden didn't appear convinced. "I've never met anyone who'd even admit to such a thing. Your brother appears to be a nice guy. How certain are you that he feels that way?"

She huffed. "I'm positive. Believe me, if he were offered a choice, Ruben would prefer to remain wolf, only changing into human when necessary."

And in anyone else…

Braden's frown told her he'd arrived at the same conclusion. "I wonder why he didn't mention that tidbit to me when we were talking earlier."

"He probably didn't feel his personal views were relevant," she told him. "As members of the royal family, we're taught at an early age to keep quiet about how we feel on most major issues."

"That stinks." While this might be true, he wasn't sure he bought into it.

"Maybe, but I don't mind. We are allowed to have differing views, but must not express them publicly."

"Why not?"

"My father believes we must all show support for

his policies for the sake of peace. This is probably why Ruben didn't say anything to you."

"Possibly." Still, his frown darkened. "But talking to me is not the same thing as making a public declaration."

"Maybe not to you. But you are American, after all. And well-known in the scientific community. If you were to mention that Prince Ruben of Teslinko preferred his wolf state to his human, the international repercussions among the Pack would be enormous."

"I would never—"

"But Ruben doesn't know that," she interrupted.

Slowly, Braden shook his shaggy head. "One minute you're practically accusing him of siding with the enemy and the next you're defending him."

Alisa opened her mouth to respond, and then closed it. He was right. "I love my brother," she finally said. "And just because he identifies more with his wolf side doesn't mean he's a bad person."

"I agree." Braden smiled, surprising her. "I didn't say he was."

The way his smile transformed his craggy face into something else fascinated her. He looked beautiful, in a purely masculine way. Watching him, she found herself aching to reach up and remove his dark glasses so she could see his striking, albeit sightless, eyes.

If she reached her hand toward his face, she'd be lost and she knew it. Plus the man had said he was only interested in her for research. She felt a sudden perverse urge to see if she could change his mind.

"Come on," she urged instead, tugging on his arm. "Let's keep moving, especially if we're going to talk about something so sensitive."

After a moment's hesitation, he did as she asked, though he walked so slowly she felt as if she was dragging him down the hall. This made her wonder—should she try to do this? Was it wise? And then she smiled, aware she'd never been one to take the easiest course of action.

When they reached the elevator, she pressed the button to take them to his floor. "Do you want to go to your lab or to your room?" she asked.

"What time is it?" he countered, sounding weary.

"Nearly ten." Again she studied him, letting her gaze roam lovingly over his rugged features, then down his broad shoulders to his flat stomach and narrow hips. She flushed as she wondered what he'd do if she actually touched him, trailing her fingers down his chest to the place where his shirt met his slacks.

His breathing changed, becoming rough and labored, as though he knew. Not possible, she told herself. After all, he'd been very plain in his denial there was anything between them. Of course it was possible he'd lied. She supposed she'd find out the truth in a moment.

"Your room or the lab?" she repeated.

"My room, please." His voice sounded strained.

When the elevator doors opened again, she took his arm. Side by side, her hip bumping his, they walked down the long hall toward his room.

Once she'd guided his hand to the door knob, she hesitated. Normally she wouldn't go inside unless he invited her, and if he did…well, that'd be asking for trouble. She hadn't been able to stop thinking about the feel of his mouth on her, his lean and hard body pressed up against her.

Foolish, but she couldn't change the way she felt. She

wouldn't be responsible for her actions if Braden asked her inside. His kiss had only left her wanting more. Much more. And Alisa had never been shy about taking what she wanted.

As he opened the door, he turned to face her. She held her breath, waiting, hoping against hope, though she wasn't sure whether she truly wanted to go inside with him or play it safe and head back to her own room.

"Despite the dais and the strange food, I mostly enjoyed this evening," he said gruffly.

She couldn't help but smile. "I did, too." She leaned in and squeezed his arm. "Thank you again for accompanying me."

An expression akin to pain crossed his face. Dipping his chin in a curt nod, he stepped inside. "Good night, Alisa," he said, then quietly closed the door in her face.

Well. Stunned, relieved and, oddly enough, amused, Alisa shook her head. That settled that. Though the night was still young and dancing would be starting at the dinner party downstairs, she trudged along to her own room. A hot bath and a good book might help her forget what her body wanted. And if not, she could always send for a bottle of wine.

After he'd shut Alisa out of his room for the night, Braden headed directly to the bathroom, shedding clothes as he went. A cold shower would do much to dampen the constant state of arousal he found himself in whenever he spent time with the princess.

He wanted her. More than that—he craved her with a fierceness that shocked him with its intensity. And this was one hunger he would have to ignore. After all, it wouldn't do much for diplomatic relations if he were to make love with the king's youngest daughter, even if she was an adult. He had the doctor-patient relationship taboo to consider as well, though technically he wasn't her doctor.

After his shower, he thought about listening to an audio book, but he could barely stay awake. Finally, he just gave up, turned out the light and went to sleep.

Something startled him awake from a wildly erotic dream about Alisa. Listening for half a second, he realized someone was in his room. Since to him, darkness was constant whether day or night, his clue wasn't actually another sound, because the intruder had taken pains to be silent, but the barely discernable odor of cigarette smoke that clung to the stranger's skin. The scent tickled the edge of his nose, sending him from sleep to wakefulness instantly.

Though he couldn't judge the time, he guessed it was somewhere around two or three in the morning. He took a split second to decide not to speak and alert the intruder that he'd come awake. Hopefully, the other clue—the change in his breathing—would be overlooked.

Instead, he pushed himself up and hurled his body in the general direction of the smoke smell. He lucked out—he connected. The intruder went down with a muffled *oomph.*

Braden was able to process a few quick details. Male, slender, wiry build. Easy to subdue, since he was taken by surprise. Braden twisted his arms up behind his back.

"Why are you here? What do you want?"

The man/boy muttered something in the Teslinkian

tongue. Though Braden wasn't one hundred percent certain, it sounded like a curse.

Pushing down harder, Braden increased the pressure on the guy's arm. "Answer me."

Though Braden's grip was nowhere near his neck, the man started making choking sounds, low in his throat as though gasping for air. Braden eased up a little, and bam—the guy broke free.

Shoving Braden back against the wall, he took off, slamming the door open, running away down the long hall.

Stunned, Braden climbed to his feet. The ruse had been an effective one. Fumbling along the edge of the bed, he located the bedside table and the phone. Snatching up the receiver, he pressed the zero, hoping the palace had some kind of night operator or something.

"Yes?" The feminine voice sounded exceedingly cheerful and awake, especially given that it was the middle of the night. Tersely, Braden relayed his need for security to come to his room, right away. She promised to send immediate help.

Heart still pumping from adrenaline, he hung up and waited. He couldn't help but wish he could pace the room like everyone else did when they got nervous, but since he'd end up stumbling along in the darkness, he knew better than to try.

Instead, he got up and closed the door, locking it just in case the intruder decided to come back and finish off the job.

After what felt entirely too long but had to be only a few minutes later, someone knocked: three sharp raps. Security? Or… Since they didn't announce themselves, he had to find out. "Who is it?" he asked, wishing like hell he could look through the peephole like a normal person.

"Security. There are two of us."

Aware he had no way of verifying their identity, he took a chance.

Opening the door, he waved them into his room. One of the men fumbled on the wall and apparently switched on the lights, then cursed under his breath. They both smelled like stale cigarette smoke.

"I'm Thomas. What happened here?" One man wanted to know. "The room is trashed. It looks like you had a fight."

Quickly, he filled them in on what he knew, which was precious little. "Do either of you have a cigarette?" he asked casually, waiting to see which man was the smoker. It was a long shot—lots of people smoked, but still…

"Sorry," Thomas answered. "I'm all out. What about you, Igor?"

Igor grunted. "Not now. Maybe later. Are you hurt?"

Braden answered in the negative.

"Was anything stolen?"

With a shrug, Braden gestured around the room. "You can probably answer that question better than I can. Does it look like anything is missing?"

They made a halfway decent show of stomping around him, presumably checking.

"Not at first glance," the second man finally offered. He hadn't spoken before, and his heavily accented voice sounded deeper and more authoritative that the other's.

"And you are?" Braden asked.

"My name is Igor."

For now, Braden had no choice but to take their word

for it. Most of his equipment and notes were all in the lab anyway, and he kept that door locked.

But then, this door had been locked also.

"We need to check the lab," he said.

"We will, in good time. First, you need to tell us what you think the intruder was after."

Clenching his jaw, Braden shook his head. "I have no idea. Anything I have of value is in the lab. We need to go there now."

"Fine." Igor sounded impatient. "Let's go."

Grabbing his cane, Braden followed them as they strode down the deserted hallway. He couldn't help but wonder if this seemingly random act of violence was related to both the shooting in the forest and the explosion in his lab in Boulder. If Prince Ruben was to be believed, then the assailant would have simply shot him, killing him while he slept in his bed.

Unless...for some reason, perhaps this militant faction believed him to be close to discovering the secret. In that case, they'd want his research rather than him. Whoever controlled the knowledge would have all the power.

There was only one problem with this theory. Braden was nowhere close to discovering Alisa's secret.

In which case, perhaps Alisa herself was in danger.

"We need to check on the princess," he announced, barely managing to keep the panic from his voice.

Immediately, the two guards grabbed him, one on each side. "Why?" Thomas asked, suspicion in his voice.

"I'm afraid the man who broke into my room might be after her. Take my word for it."

"We'll check," Igor said harshly. "Wait."

Shaking his arm free, Braden listened as Thomas spoke quietly on what must have been a headset or cell phone.

"She's safe," Thomas announced a moment later.

"How do you know? Did someone check on her?"

"We have a guard stationed down the hall from her room. No one has come and gone on her floor. Now come on." Thomas took Braden's arm again. "Let's go check out your lab."

Braden broke away. "No. Not until you take me to Princess Alisa's room so I can be sure."

Thomas gave an exaggerated sigh and began conversing with Igor in Teslinkian. Finally, he agreed. "But we will not be waking her. We will go to her room, speak to the guard, and that will be enough."

"I would like the guard to open her door and check on her."

"We cannot wake the princess in the middle of the night!" Thomas sounded appalled and horrified.

"We don't need to wake her. If her guard will do a quick check to make sure nothing has been disturbed, that will be enough."

Again the men spoke to each other in their own tongue.

"Fine," Igor finally spat his agreement. "We will do as you ask. Far be it from you to put our positions in jeopardy because you don't believe her security detail can do their jobs."

This time when Thomas grabbed Braden's arm, he allowed it. From his door they turned right. He counted forty-seven paces before they made another right turn. At any moment, Braden expected them to encounter Alisa's guard, but no one stopped them.

One more right turn put them on the opposite side of the building. Here, they met up with another man and Braden's two escorts spoke in hushed tones with him. More smoke-smell. Did all of the guards use tobacco?

"He will go check the princess's room," Igor said quietly.

"We'll follow him." Braden's tone left no room for argument.

This time, they simply humored him. He counted ten more steps to Alisa's room before they stopped.

"Rok will go inside now," Igor announced in a low voice.

Braden listened intently as Rok opened Alisa's door, closing it softly behind him. After a moment, the door opened again and he emerged.

"She is fine, sleeping soundly. Her room has not been disturbed."

"Thank you, Rok," Igor said, satisfaction thickening his accent. "We will leave you to your post."

Braden counted steps again as they went back in the direction of his room. He didn't know what, but something was off.

"Now, we will check out your lab," Thomas announced.

Still not entirely certain, Braden allowed the man to propel him forward. As they turned a left corner, he knew they were growing closer to his lab.

His escort's footsteps slowed. "Wait here," Igor ordered tersely. "The door is open."

Chapter 11

Damn. Braden's heart sank. He'd left the lab securely locked up. This could only mean someone working with the assailant—or the assailant himself—had also searched the lab. They were looking for something. Obviously, for whatever reason, they thought he was further along in his research than he actually was.

But why?

He itched to know what they'd done to his lab. But since he couldn't tell without touching things and thus contaminating the evidence, he stayed in the hall, waiting.

A moment later Thomas returned. "They have wrecked the place," he said brusquely. "Do you have any idea what they were after?"

"No idea," Braden said, telling the truth. "How bad is it?"

"Very bad." The other man sounded grimly certain. "The king will have to be notified of this."

"Good." Though doing so wouldn't change things. One thing would—catching the crooks. "Do you have security cameras in the hall?" Braden asked, hoping against hope that they did, just as he hoped they were who they claimed to be. As his sense of wrongness increased, he was beginning to wonder.

"We do." Voice slightly surprised, Thomas called to his coworker in the native tongue before turning back to Braden. "Igor knows where we can view the footage. We'll review the tapes and get back to you."

"I want to know." He was frustrated that he couldn't see anything, not the damage that had been done to his lab or the face of the intruders on the surveillance tape.

Clenching his hand into a fist, he silently counted to three. Punching the wall would do more harm than good and would accomplish absolutely nothing.

Again, he thought about Alisa. Was she truly safe? Though he had nothing concrete, something had been off. Braden needed to make sure she was all right and, once he knew that, he wanted to discuss this with her, get her thoughts, see if she had any idea who could have done this and why. This had all the makings of an inside job. Someone or multiple people in the palace were members of the group that didn't want Braden's research to be successful. Ruben was right. Both he and Alisa were in danger.

"What time is it?" he asked abruptly, picturing the other man checking his watch.

"A little after three."

He made a sudden decision. "I'd like to go back to my room. I've got a busy day scheduled tomorrow and

I need to get some sleep. I'll deal with all this in the morning."

No doubt eager to be rid of him, they dutifully escorted him back to his room.

After they left, he waited a good ten minutes to be certain they were truly gone. Then he grabbed his cane and slipped out his door.

He'd check on Alisa himself.

As soon as he got out in the hallway, Braden turned right and retraced his steps, counting all the way. When he encountered Rok the security guard stationed outside Alisa's door, he planned to tell the man that the princess herself had called him and summoned him to her room.

Even if Rok didn't believe the story, he'd still have to check with Alisa. Either way, it seemed a foolproof plan.

Except Braden didn't encounter Rok. Either the man had left his post to take a bathroom break or had gone to bed for the night.

Which made absolutely no sense. He was supposed to be guarding the princess.

Heartbeat accelerating, Braden took a deep breath outside of Alisa's room.

Then, putting his hand out blindly, he tried the knob. It turned easily in his hand. Slipping inside, he closed the door behind him. Moving carefully, he went forward, hoping he didn't crash into anything.

A garbled sound made him freeze mid-step. Alisa? On the verge of calling her name, something made him hesitate. Then he smelled it—the same human smoker smell that had caused him to come awake in his own room.

The intruder. The same intruder was here.

Lifting his head, he inhaled again, pinpointing the intruder's location.

Then, trusting in blind luck a second time, he launched himself forward, miraculously connecting with a body. A masculine one, the same man he'd subdued before.

He swung wildly, hitting hard, the stench of cigarette smoke and unwashed body growing stronger. Yep, same guy.

The other man landed a good punch to Braden's chest, sending him staggering back. Braden swung again and missed. Fighting blind gave him a distinct disadvantage, but his larger size helped.

As he pulled back to try once more, the intruder sucker-punched him. First, hard in the stomach and then, while Braden was doubled over, gasping for air, he got in a quick uppercut to the jaw.

Braden went down like a shot. Kicking him as he ran past, the intruder took off, slamming the door closed behind him.

Struggling to pull in air, Braden managed to get to his feet, all the while mentally cursing his ineptitude. Another muffled sound—a groan or a cry—from behind him had him turning, heart pounding. His princess.

"Alisa," he said again, moving slowly forward, hands outstretched, praying to a higher power when he'd never prayed before. She had to be all right, she had to be. Anything else was simply unimaginable, unacceptable, unforgivable.

There. He found her. Alisa. Still alive. But how badly was she hurt? She squirmed against him, making muffled sounds, as though trying to speak past a gag. Keeping his touch gentle, he let his fingers roam over her, exploring. No blood, and he noted that she was still clothed, although the skimpy shorts and tank top must have been what she wore to sleep in.

Softly, hating that he had to fumble, he located and removed the gag, which seemed to be some sort of cloth placed in her mouth and tied behind her head.

The instant he got it out, she took a deep, shuddering breath. "Thank goodness," she said, her voice shaky. "I felt like I was going to suffocate trying to breathe through my nose."

"Are you hurt?"

"No." She sounded furious. "Now please, untie me."

She helped him as he removed the restraints around her ankles and wrists. As they struggled to free her, her unrestrained breasts brushed against his arm and then his chest, igniting a different kind of trouble inside him.

Though he tried to hide the hitch in his breath, she went from struggling to absolutely still.

"Braden?"

Mouth dry, he answered. "I'm right here."

"I need you to hold me," she said, the slightest quaver in her silky voice. "I really, really need you to hold me tight."

The urgency in her tone swept aside his misgivings. Though he dimly realized she probably wanted only reassurance, desire flared again, dangerously close to raging out of control. He couldn't think, couldn't breathe. All he could do was blindly try to offer her comfort without frightening her with the force of his arousal.

He could do this, he thought, gritting his teeth. He could. And would.

Tilting his body at an angle, he reached out to pull

her gently into his arms. Instead, she stunned him by meeting him halfway, yanking him down on top of her so that part of him straddled her, the very part he'd been trying to keep her from feeling.

Now, she felt it all right. She most definitely felt it. And pressed up against her lush, feminine curves, he swelled, feeling her as well.

Stimulated by touch, fueled by adrenaline, desire roared to life, his feeding off hers and vice versa. Hell-hounds, he wanted her, needed her, craved her. And, judging by the fervor with which she kissed him, she wanted him just as badly.

"Touch me," she gasped, arching her back. So he did.

Now, more than ever, his fingers were his eyes. He let them have free reign, exploring her, experiencing her and arousing her. Somehow, he helped her shed her clothes, and as she tugged his shirt from his trousers, then loosened the button and unzipped him to free his huge arousal, he realized if he didn't put a stop to this, they were going to make hot, passionate love.

And she was a royal princess of Teslinko, his host's daughter. Plus, they had no way of knowing whether the attackers would return.

Gathering up the shreds of his self-control, he pushed himself back from her. Breathing in great, gasping gulps of air, he tried to think. Somehow, he must make an attempt to get back to normalcy.

"Your adrenaline rush is making you do this," he managed. "It's a common enough occurrence. You were attacked and now you want to reaffirm life. First, we need to contact—" he began, but she pulled him back down to her and silenced him with a deep, sensual kiss.

His body pulsed again as helplessly he pushed himself mindlessly against her.

Still, he could still stop, should stop, and with that in mind, he tried again to regain control. As long as she didn't touch him…

Then, as though she'd heard his unvoiced thought, she reached inside his pants and wrapped her small hand around him. That did it. He completely lost the capacity for rational thought. Hell, he could barely breathe. She moved her hand and he surged into her touch.

Just like that, he surrendered.

All he knew was her. All he craved was her.

Damn. Buried deep inside her. That's where he wanted to be. The thought that they might be interrupted only poured fuel on the fire.

"Stop," he gritted, staying the movement of her hand by gripping her wrist. "It's been too long and I don't know if I can hold back."

"I don't want you to hold back." The smoky desire in her voice made him shudder. A second later, she grabbed his arms and straddled him, her moist sheath slipping over him as though they were made for each other.

Then, just when he thought he'd actually proven the existence of heaven, she began to move. Moist heat, searing him. Delicious, enticing, and his. All his.

His wolf surged to life inside him, and he growled, grinning savagely as she returned the sound in kind. Even their wolves joined in this, this mating.

Mating? What the…? He raised his head, trying to think. Then she kissed him again, clenching herself around him. Waves of ecstasy shook him with each pulse of her body. Raising to meet her, thrusting from below as pleasure shattered his thoughts and he forgot to be concerned.

She rode him with a fierce intensity, dancing on the edge of control. If she kept this up, he'd explode inside her now, too soon. And this, he couldn't allow. With a swift movement, he lifted them both, flipping her onto her back.

Claiming her with his gaze, he savored the raw act of possession as he pushed into her deeply, filling her, and held himself there while she quivered around him, before he slowly withdrew. She moaned, begging him to go faster with incoherent sounds and her hot, demanding body, but he knew he had to slow things down or this would be over before either of them wished it to be.

Slowly he pushed back inside her and withdrew again, letting the exquisite sensuality of the movement make an entirely different rhythm as passion arced between them.

"Shhh," he whispered against her lips, thrilling to the heat radiating from her body. "Let's enjoy each other first. There'll be time enough for the crazy mad rush to fulfillment later."

"Even now you sound like a scientist," she grumbled. "But I want you hard and fast and furious."

She began to move to match her words, still under him, clenching him with her body and releasing him, pushing him to drive into her harder and faster, making him completely lose control.

A second later, she shuddered around him, a rush of honey bathing him as she cried out. Her release pushed him over the edge, sending him hurtling down a dark precipice until he shattered into a thousand pieces, exploding inside her.

In all of his thirty-eight years, he'd never made love like this. Ever.

A knot filled his throat. He held her while his hammering heartbeat slowed, smoothed the hair back from her face gently and reverently, unable to believe what had just happened. She curled into him with a sigh, her breath fanning his cheek. "That was…"

He silenced her with a soft kiss. "I hope you don't regret this in the morning."

"Do you?" She sounded fragile, vulnerable. Exactly how he'd feared she might be. "Why would I?"

"Because you were attacked and tied up. Adrenaline fuels desire. It's only normal that you would want to make love to show yourself that you were alive."

"You said that before. And you really believe this is why I…we…?"

He shrugged, ignoring the ache in his throat. "It's a scientific fact."

"I see. Do you?" she asked, sounding a little stronger now. "Regret this, that is?"

He could only be honest. "I know I should, but no. I don't regret anything." Though that would certainly change, if her brother or her father found out.

"Excellent." Burrowing her face in the hollow of his throat, she kissed him.

"Alisa?" He pushed himself up on his elbows. "We need to talk about what just happened."

She sighed. "I suppose you're right."

"And we need to let your father know."

"I know." She didn't sound happy. "He's going to freak."

"As well he should. Someone attacked you inside the royal palace. That's not good."

"He'll probably place me under heavy guard."

Braden knew he would, if he had the right. "I can't say I blame him."

"But—"

"No buts." He kissed her once, hard and fast.

"Come on now." Pushing himself to his feet, Braden held out his hand to help her up. "I'm guessing it's close to four in the morning. We'd better get dressed and go find your brother." He made his tone brisk.

"Ruben? Why?"

Hounds, he'd forgotten she didn't know. The hell with it. Maybe it was time she did. "Ruben heads palace security. Someone broke into my room and the lab as well as yours. The security detail appears to have vanished. This entire incident will have to be reported."

"I don't think I can talk to Ruben right now." She sounded alarmed, as if she'd rather stay in bed or walk barefoot over hot coals than get dressed and face her brother.

He couldn't really blame her. "There's no way he's going to know about us. Now come on," he said lightly, reaching until he connected with her hand so he could pull her up. "You have to. You were attacked and tied up. It's either Ruben or your father. Your choice."

"Ruben, then." She pushed herself up and disappeared into her lavatory.

After they'd gotten dressed, Alisa led him to the security offices on the main floor. "I'm not sure if Ruben will be here or not," she warned him. "If, as you say, he's in charge of security, I doubt he'll be here this early. He's probably asleep in his room. Sven usually heads up security, you know."

"I'm sure they'll summon him." Of course they would.

After they made their report to security, he'd have Ruben tell her what he'd told him. She needed to understand that the extremists were real and the amount of danger she was in. The danger they were both in, actually.

When they entered the security offices, Alisa tugged on his arm. "Wow. My brother actually is here. He must have come right after the party. I wonder when he sleeps."

"Hello," Ruben greeted them. He sounded tired, but relaxed, which meant that he had no idea what had just happened.

Speaking quietly, Braden told him as concisely as possible. Of course, as Braden had known he would, Ruben locked in on the fact that an intruder had been inside his sister's room.

"He tied you up?" Anger simmered in the prince's voice. "Lisa, were you hurt in any other way?"

"No, Ruben. Nothing like that." She kept her tone soothing. "This was the same man who broke into Braden's room and also trashed his lab."

"I've already reported this to your men," Braden said. "I can't believe they didn't inform you."

"My men?" Ruben sounded bewildered. "We have a skeleton staff on from midnight until six. Most of them have been patrolling the grounds. Who took your report?"

"There were three of them. Igor, Thomas and Rok."

Ruben said nothing, but Braden knew. "They don't work for you, do they?"

"Their names are not familiar." Ruben sounded grim. "Let me pull up the surveillance video."

"Does it have audio?" Braden wanted to know. "That way I can at least listen in."

"Yes." The prince moved away. "Let me cue it up. I'll put it on the big monitor over here."

Braden started to move forward, then stopped, realizing that not only had he forgotten his cane, but he had no idea what obstacles might be in his path.

Alisa slipped her hand into his. "Come on. I'll show you the way."

Since all Braden could do was listen while the others watched, he held himself perfectly still, focusing on the voices. Since the cameras were only trained on the hallways, the sound went silent when the men entered a room as there was nothing to see or hear.

Ruben uttered a word in the Teslinkian tongue that sounded like a curse. "None of them work for the palace security detail," he said. "And worse, the man you called Rok was the same one who broke into both your and Alisa's room."

Braden swore. "I knew something was off. That means the entire time I was with what I thought was security, I was actually with men who are part of the extremist group?"

"It would appear so."

"Extremist group?" Alisa chimed in. "Are you really serious about this?"

Braden stayed silent, giving the other man the opportunity to tell his sister the truth. If he didn't, then Braden would.

Perhaps the prince sensed Braden's resolve. Talking quickly, Ruben told Alisa what the two men had discussed earlier.

"You've mentioned this before, but never with this amount of detail. How long have you known about this?" she asked, once Ruben had finished.

"A good while." At least the prince had the grace to sound ashamed. Braden realized he actually respected the other man for this.

Alisa, on the other hand, sounded furious. "Why did you hide this from me?"

"I tried to tell you, in a roundabout way."

"That wasn't enough. I don't understand why you didn't think I needed to know this information."

"Because our father ordered me not to tell you." Tone steely, Ruben now sounded every inch the heir to the throne. "Even now, I am disobeying him by talking about this."

"Honestly?" Now bewilderment rather than anger colored her tone. "What is his reasoning? If I'm aware of the threat, I can better protect myself."

Braden's thoughts exactly, though he knew enough to stay silent. He saw no need to insert himself into this family mix.

"I'm sorry, Lisa." Ruben turned away. "At least you know now. I've got to make a full report to Father pretty quickly, even if I have to wake him up. We've got to find out how those men were able to get into the palace to begin with."

"What about the front desk girl?" Braden asked. "She might know something. She's the one I called when I awoke and found someone in my room."

"Front desk girl?" Both Ruben and Alisa spoke at once.

"I punched zero on my bedside phone." Frowning,

Braden crossed his arms. "Some woman answered and said she'd send security."

"The switchboard," Ruben said. "There were two girls working earlier when you called down there. We need to talk to them. Let me make a call."

Braden and Alisa waited while he did. A moment later, he hung up the phone and cursed. "Unfortunately, both of the women who were working the switchboard have gone missing."

"Both of them?" Alisa sounded shocked.

Privately, Braden figured they'd been murdered. And for what? These extremists were trying to steal a secret that didn't even exist.

Chapter 12

Alisa felt brittle, as though made of glass, the kind that might shatter if anyone touched her.

As she'd predicted, her father had placed her under heavy guard. Two armed men stood outside her bedroom door and accompanied her wherever she wanted to go.

The dark mood inside the castle felt oppressive, matching her mood.

If not for the pleasant ache of her body, she thought she might have dreamed the powerful lovemaking she and Braden had shared.

The events of the prior evening had changed her, shattering her safe existence and making her realize nothing was exactly as it seemed.

Early in the day, the two missing women were found. They'd been tied up, in a supply closet. They were shaken, but otherwise unharmed. Unfortunately, they claimed to have no idea who had done this to them.

Now she was on her way to be questioned by his top security officials, at her father's urging. Her mother accompanied her to the sitting room, her silence telling Alisa how worried she was.

When she entered the large drawing room, her mother walked to the other side and began talking on her cell phone, too quietly for Alisa to hear. Frowning with worry, King Leo pulled out a chair and waited until Alisa was seated before giving her a quick hug.

"Are you all right?" he asked.

She nodded. "I think so."

His skeptical expression told her he didn't believe her. "Your mother is beside herself. Though I've asked her not to, right now she's calling both of your sisters."

Alisa groaned. "If you don't do something, they'll all come home and surround me like a gaggle of clucking hens."

He grinned at her description. "You've been listening to me and your brother, haven't you?"

"Maybe," she allowed. "But I don't want them coming here. The risk is too great."

"Exactly what I told your mother. I've forbidden any of your sisters to come home until the perpetrator or perpetrators are caught."

"Good." She exhaled in relief.

"Your mother wants to send you to visit one of them instead."

"What?" Alisa sat up straight, opening her eyes wide in alarm. "Please don't do that to me. With all the guards, I should be safe enough."

"I know," he replied, the twinkle in his eyes telling

her he'd twisted words to get her to accept a twenty-four-hour guard. "Now my security people want you to watch some surveillance video."

"All right." She waited while they brought her a laptop, watching as they keyed up a video. While she watched, Ruben's top man peppered her with questions.

Though she answered him and viewed the surveillance video at least four times, she knew she wasn't of much help. Until Braden had come crashing into her room, she hadn't even gotten a good look at her intruder.

"I was asleep," she repeated. "It was dark and then he tied me up and gagged me. I never saw his face."

"Perhaps you should speak with the court psychiatrist," her father said.

"I'm not traumatized," she emphatically told him. "I was only a captive for a few minutes. Braden rushed in and rescued me and that was that."

When the grizzled security officer expressed doubts about how much help a blind man could actually be, Alisa bristled.

"He was plenty of help. He charged the intruder and knocked him down."

The older man crossed his arms, apparently not convinced. "But he did not detain him?"

"No." Appealing to her father, who watched silently, she swallowed. "But he freed me."

As she spoke, she couldn't help but blush as she remembered how wonderfully the night had ended. She and Braden had made slow, sensual, passionate love. They'd connected in more ways than merely physical. That trumped everything else, even her attack.

Her father squinted at her, reminding her that he had no idea what had transpired after Braden had rescued her. She prayed no one noticed the discrepancy between the time the intruder had gone running from Alisa's room and the time she and Braden had emerged to call security.

Apparently, no one did. Comforting her with a bear hug, King Leo peered down into her face. "Are you certain you are all right?"

"I'm fine," she said.

Concluding her phone call, Queen Ionna came over, phone still in hand. "I would feel so much better if you would talk to a counselor."

With difficulty, Alisa summoned up a smile. "Thank you for your concern, Mom," she said. "But I really am fine. I promise."

Exchanging a look with her mother, who had already begun dialing another number, King Leo told Alisa she could go. Relieved, she didn't wait to be told twice.

On her way back to her room, she couldn't stop thinking about what had happened.

She'd been attacked inside her own home. She didn't care how many guards she had; she wasn't sure she could ever feel safe again.

What she didn't understand was *why?* Why would anyone want to hurt her? Was this, as Braden seemed to think, tied in to her ability to go without shape-shifting for longer than what was considered normal?

If so, was she now consigned to spending the rest of her life watching out for the next attack?

To distract herself, she forced herself not to dwell on it. Instead, she thought of Braden, of making love with him.

They'd fit together perfectly, like their bodies had been made just for each other. The physical part of their joining had been amazing, transcendent, unreal. Even her wolf had been involved in the act.

Odd how something so wonderful could come out of something so horrible.

Even if he had told her he only cared about the research. His body said otherwise.

Though she had to wonder, how one-sided was this situation?

After all, if she were to be totally honest with herself, she'd wanted Braden ever since the first moment she'd laid eyes on him. Since shifters couldn't get STDs, and she faithfully took her birth control pills, she hadn't worried about protection. Instead, she'd let passion and desire take over. She couldn't say she regretted that. Even if she did want more.

If making love with him only involved her body, she'd be in his room every single night, giving herself over to the sensual pleasure of sharing herself with him.

But this involved her soul. It was way more than just recreational sex. The depth of the emotion she felt toward him frightened her. She couldn't stop thinking about him or longing to be with him. Not just sexually, but in every way that mattered. She wanted to wake up next to him, to laugh and talk over coffee and breakfast, to welcome him at the end of the day with a full-body hug and a smiling, silent promise of more to come.

But he didn't want that. He'd been completely honest about that.

Could she live with a relationship based on sex?

Ah, but such sex.

Vital, hot and furious. She wanted more of that, too. Much more. But she knew if they continually joined their bodies together, expressing physically the close connection they felt for each other, the emotions she felt would just deepen and solidify.

She would be hurt. More than that. Destroyed.

And this, she could not allow. Romantic involvement with Dr. Braden Streib would be a disaster of epic proportions on so many levels, just thinking about it made her head ache more than during one of her normal migraines.

Reaching her room, she went inside and closed the door, still pondering. She fought the urge to pick up the phone and call him on some pretext of checking to make sure he was all right. He'd see through that in a heartbeat.

Foolish. Then again, part of her wanted him to know, regardless of how he regarded her. Braden was bruised and damaged, broken and battered. He lived in his own insular world, behind walls he'd built himself, inviolate and untouchable. One day, he'd realize he was painfully lonely there in his lofty ivory tower. Alisa knew she could touch his life, even if only briefly. He needed to know she cared.

Ah, but was she brave enough to tell him? Trusting him enough to share more than her body with him would be a huge leap of faith on her part. Such a thing could be sheer stupidity, a leap into an abyss of such foolishness that she'd regret it the rest of her life.

But, she suspected, not nearly as much as she'd regret never having loved him.

Since the intrusion, she now had two guards stationed outside her bedroom door. There were two more guarding the lab and yet another duo outside Braden's room. With all the intensity focused on the hallway, sneaking into his room at night would be downright impossible.

During the day, they met in the lab for him to run his infernal tests, so at least she'd get to see him there. Speaking of which…

Checking the clock, she realized her sentimental musings had made her late again. She'd promised Braden she'd be at the lab right after breakfast to help him get everything back in order. Of course, she'd slept late and assumed he would have as well, considering how they'd both been awake for several hours the night before.

Ah, well. Scooping her hair back into a ponytail, she ran a tube of lip gloss over her mouth and headed out the door.

When she arrived at the lab, she found Braden already hard at work. To her surprise, Ruben was assisting him and had evidently been there for a while, since the place looked almost exactly the way it had before the break-in.

She stood in the doorway for a few minutes and watched them work. Neither man noticed her. Finally she moved and that caught Ruben's eye.

"Well, hello," he said, smiling. "It's about time you showed up. Did you get something to eat?"

Though she nodded and briefly glanced at her brother, she couldn't tear her gaze from Braden. He'd gone perfectly still, his head cocked in that intent way he had when he was listening. She had the craziest urge to go to him and wrap her arms around him and just hold on. But of course she couldn't. Not in front of Ruben.

Instead, she forced a polite smile and moved into the

room. "Sorry I'm late. I didn't sleep well last night." She directed this last comment to Braden, taking small satisfaction in the way he flushed. "What can I do to help?"

With a shrug, Ruben glanced from her to Braden. "I think we've got it all fixed up as good as new. What do you think, Braden?"

Suddenly busy rearranging what looked like different-sized test tubes, he barely raised his head. "You can take the day off, Alisa. I'm not going to be running any tests, so I won't be needing you today."

Oddly enough, that stung. She knew what she should do, what the old Alisa would have done. She'd make some sort of mocking joke before sauntering off to do something else.

If he didn't need her, she had other places to go. Except she didn't want to. She wanted to be with him.

And he obviously didn't want to be with her.

Studying her hands while she tried to figure out a course of action, she looked up to find her brother staring at her. "Lisa, are you all right? You look a bit shell-shocked. I mean, with all that happened last night, maybe you should talk to someone, you know?"

"Not you, too." She sighed. "I just left our parents and I'll tell you the same thing I told them. I'm not traumatized. I want to catch those men as badly as you do."

He studied her face. "Are you sure?"

"Yes." Though she felt herself flush, she didn't dare look in Braden's direction. "I promise you, I'm fine."

Relaxing, Ruben nodded. "Dad's furious. But then I'm sure you know that if you just spent time with him."

"I do." Did she ever. Though King Leo had become a master at shielding his emotions, she and her siblings and their mother could always tell. "I just spent an hour with him, watching him pace the room while I answered the security man's questions. Meanwhile, Mother made phone call after phone call."

"Really?" Braden's golden brows rose. "Who was she calling?"

She grimaced. "The entire family. It's almost like she's assembling the troops. She called our sisters and their families. I'm guessing that they, as well as all the aunts, uncles and cousins, will be here this next weekend."

Ruben looked properly shocked. "Why? I don't understand how Mother would think that could help."

"Maybe she feels there's safety in numbers." With a shrug, she cut her eyes at Braden and then jerked her chin toward the door in a silent plea for Ruben to leave.

Eyes widening, Ruben glanced from her to Braden and back again. She made a shooing motion with her hands.

"Maybe I should go," Ruben finally said, frowning at her.

She nodded vigorously, glad Braden couldn't see her.

"You can stay if you want to," Braden put in, telling her without using the actual words that he didn't want to be alone with her.

Tough. He wasn't getting off that easily. They had things to discuss.

"It's all right. Go," she told Ruben, playfully pushing him toward the door. "I'll be up for the evening meal, so I'll see you then."

Shaking his head, Ruben went, his thunderous expression letting her know she'd have some explaining to do later.

She followed behind him, keeping far enough back

that he couldn't ask her any questions. Back stiff, Ruben continued on, still frowning.

As soon as her brother had turned the corner in the hall, Alisa closed the door to the lab and locked it. Suddenly, unaccountably nervous, she decided she'd lead up to the topic she really wanted to discuss.

"About the break-ins," she began, trying not to smile at the nearly palpable relief in his expression. "What do they want? Obviously, they don't intend to kill me or they would have done so when they broke into my room."

"You don't know that for certain," Braden said. "I might have interrupted them before they could complete their task."

"No, I saw the video. It shows the guy—Rok or whatever his name was—entering my room and you coming to my door a good five minutes later. If his mission was to kill me, he had ample time to do it."

He blanched, considering her words. "All right. Let's say I believe that they don't want to kill you. But it's perfectly obvious they want me dead, based on the explosion in my laboratory back in Boulder."

"Come on. You don't even know if that explosion was related to this," she protested. "And even if it was, I doubt the same people in your country were involved here in Teslinko."

"Ruben thinks they were."

This stopped her cold. "He does?"

"Yes. These extremists will apparently do anything to keep us from finding out how you remain human so long."

"That makes no sense," she protested, feeling vaguely ill. "Even if you discovered a potion or a pill people could take, it would still be strictly voluntary. Why deny others the right to choose to do what they want?"

"Because it's always that way. A few people think they own the right to determine how others live." He started to turn away, then, almost as an afterthought, turned back toward her. "Now, Alisa, if you don't need anything else, you can go. I've got a lot of work to do."

"We need to talk," she blurted, crossing her arms, wishing her heart wasn't pounding.

He winced. "No. We don't. I do need to apologize—"

"Don't you dare!" Furious now, she had to take several deep breaths to keep from blurting out something she'd regret later.

"Alisa, last night was a one-time thing, a huge mistake," he continued, apparently oblivious to her anger. "Don't make it into more than it has to be."

She refused to let him know how his words stung. Or would have, if she truly believed he meant them. "That's odd," she said, her voice silky smooth. "I could have sworn we both enjoyed ourselves."

Dragging a hand through his already mussed hair, he sighed. "Of course we did. That's not the point."

"Then what is?"

"You're a royal princess. When all my testing is done, whether or not I have definitive results, I'll be going home. Back to the U.S., back to Colorado."

She waited for him to get to the point. "And?"

"And you can't go with me." The grittiness in his voice, as well as the tightness in his jaw, told her how difficult he found making that statement.

"Go with you?" she repeated, feeling a rush of tenderness as well as surprise. "Are you asking me to—"

"No." The single word sounded so harsh that she recoiled. "I'm not asking anything of you, Alisa. Except to leave me alone."

She refused to acknowledge the sharp stab of hurt. "That would be pretty difficult to do since you still have to do your little experiments."

Strolling around the large lab table, she walked right up to him and poked him, hard, in the chest. "Or have you possibly given up on your research?"

His mouth twisted. "I haven't finished testing you. We must have contact professionally out of necessity. But that is all it can be. We cannot have a personal relationship."

She couldn't help herself, she laughed. "I think it's a bit too late for that, don't you?"

"I've already tried to apologize," he said. "But you won't listen to me. You hear the words, but refuse to acknowledge their truth. I know you're royalty and as such, used to getting exactly what you want, when you want it, but this time is going to be different."

"Prejudice of a different sort," she said. "Tell me, Mr. Logical Scientist, on what facts have you based this finding?"

She had him there. She could tell by the dull red that spread up his neck to his aristocratic cheekbones.

Finally, he inclined his head. "Again, it appears I must apologize."

This time, she said nothing. Instead, she strolled closer to him, standing as near as she dared without actually touching him.

He swallowed hard, his only reaction to her.

But it was enough.

For a moment she watched the rise and fall of his chest as he breathed. While he might try to pretend to be completely unaffected by her, she could tell her closeness disturbed him.

Satisfied, she gave him a little space. "Isn't that what's important here?" she asked softly, circling around him again. If she kept moving, she might not touch him. "At least to you?"

He swiveled his head, following the sound of her with an uncanny motion that made her wonder if he could suddenly see. "Of course. It should be to you as well."

A pulse beat strong and hard in the hollow of his throat. He wanted her, she knew. As much as she wanted him. At the thought, desire swept through her in a wave of heat so strong it blindsided her.

Swaying, she put out a hand to steady herself, connecting with the cool metal of the stainless-steel countertop. She felt pulled to him as strongly as if by powerful invisible magnets, and actually leaned toward him. Because all she wanted was to feel his hard, masculine body against her, touch his heated skin, feel his mouth slant across hers.

He must have felt the same compelling impulse, because suddenly somehow they were wrapped around each other, melded together like molten metal.

Exactly where they should be.

When the floor moved beneath them, at first Alisa thought this was in her head, a reaction to the heat of his kiss.

But the second time, when she heard a loud boom and the motion was so violent that test tubes and beakers went crashing to the floor around them, she realized something else had happened. Something awful.

"Is this an earthquake?" she gasped, holding tight

to Braden so she wouldn't fall, bracing herself for another tremor.

"It might be," he said grimly. "Though judging from the sound of things, I think a couple of bombs just exploded."

Chapter 13

As the seconds ticked away, seemingly in slow motion, a flurry of other sounds echoed through the walls and reached them. Sirens, another series of smaller booms. Screams. Then…nothing.

Amidst the shocked hush, a hiss as the overhead sprinkler system came on, soaking them.

"Damn." With a sinking heart, Braden realized he'd been right. "I think at least two bombs went off in the palace, close enough to shake the floor and rattle the walls. And now there's a fire somewhere. This isn't good."

"Bombs?" She sounded frightened. Then, not waiting for an answer, she moved closer to him. Instinctively, he put out his arm and pulled her in tight, trying in vain to shelter her from the cold water cascading from the ceiling.

"Surely not a bomb. It could have been a hundred other things, couldn't it?"

"What else could it be?" he asked, wishing he had an umbrella. Already drenched, she felt smaller and much less royal, more human. More Alisa.

Shivering, she sneezed. "So you're telling me that you think they're attacking the palace?"

The icy water raining down on them didn't help him think clearly. Still.

"An outright attack?" she repeated, sounding incredulous. "I can't believe they dared."

"We don't know for sure it's them," he tried to point out, reasonably he thought, trying in vain to shield them both from the sprinklers with the jacket he'd draped over the back of his chair.

"We don't?" Rather than sounding afraid, anger vibrated in her voice. "Who else would have wanted to attack the royal palace of Teslinko?"

She sounded as though at any moment she wanted to go hunt them down, like a warrior woman of old. Damn. The king and the crown prince would never forgive him if he let her place herself in harm's way. And he'd never forgive himself if anything happened to her.

"Alisa, listen to me. We don't know for certain that it's an attack." He kept his voice soothing. "For all I know, it might be a military exercise gone bad."

Though he didn't really believe that. Just in case she didn't either, he wrapped his wet coat tighter around them, effectively keeping her in place.

"We've got to do something," she pointed out, holding herself tensely, but not pulling away or ducking out from under the coat. Yet.

The instant the thought occurred to him she struggled to push away.

"What are you doing?" he asked, managing to sound only marginally concerned. "You can't go out there."

"Can't I? I'm a princess, true, but more importantly, this is my home. My family is out there somewhere. I need to make sure they're safe."

"But what can you do?" he pointed out.

"I don't know, but there's no way I'm simply going to hide away in here and let some extremist group overrun the palace. My palace."

She had a point. But still… How the hell was he supposed to keep her safe if she insisted on throwing herself out into the fray?

He thought fast. "Why don't you call Ruben and see if he can tell you what's going on?"

She took a deep breath. "That's a good idea." At least she sounded calmer. "That is, if I can keep my phone from getting drenched."

Muttering a curse word in her native tongue, she finally crawled under the lab table. "At least this helps somewhat. Are these sprinklers ever going to shut off?"

"I was hoping you could tell me that."

Instead of answering, she snorted. "All I can think of is that they're keeping the building from burning down."

He nodded, listening as she messed with her cell phone. After a moment, she sighed.

"It goes straight to voice mail," she told him. "What if Ruben was hurt?" A thread of panic crept into her voice as she stood back up. "Come on. We've got to go make sure he's all right."

He grabbed her arm as she tried to duck away and brush past him. Her skin was wet and clammy. And soft. "We'll do no such thing. If the extremists are here in the palace, they want one thing. You. Ruben—and your father—would want me to protect you at any cost."

Though she grumbled under her breath, he could tell she realized the truth of his words.

"You have a point," she finally said, shivering. "But listen to me. By staying here getting soaked, we've become targets—wet, ineffective targets. Is that really what you think is the best course of action? What if a team of enemy commandos comes crashing through the door at any second?"

About to tell her not to be foolish, he closed his mouth. Now that he thought of it, she might not be too far off in her supposition.

"Fine then. Come on," he told her. "We won't stay here. First thing we're going to do is find a safe place to go. Hopefully, a dry place. Please keep trying your brother."

Her shivering had gotten worse. Now she'd begun shuddering. "I will. And my parents, too. If anything has happened to them..."

He wanted to pull her close again and try to warm her up. Instead, she took his hand. "I'll lead the way."

Again forced to acknowledge the limitations of his blindness, he let her lead him from the room, trying to push away a dash of resentful self-loathing as he went. She was a princess in need of a knight, but he was only half a man. How the hell could he protect her from what he couldn't even see?

Together they moved through the door. Squinting, trying hard to focus, he searched the blackness of his vision, hoping to find the lightening at the edge, the faint gray he'd noticed once before.

Instead, he saw only darkness. Disgusted with himself for hoping, he gave up the effort. Best to use his other senses to the fullest extent rather than try to make one manifest that was never going to be there.

Once out in the hallway, the acrid smell of smoke was stronger, though the sprinklers continued to douse them with icy water.

Braden barely even noticed them anymore.

"Our guards have vanished," she said, still gripping his hand. "They must have run off to help the others."

"And abandoned their posts. That's not good."

"No, it's not." Her grim tone told him she took this seriously. "I will make sure my father and Ruben know about this. They will be reprimanded."

If they aren't dead. Neither one spoke the words out loud. Instead, they continued moving forward. The odor of smoke grew stronger, polluting the air, making it difficult to breathe. Despite that, the sprinklers continued to pummel them with increasingly foul-smelling water, making him wonder what exactly the sprinkler system used as a reserve.

Still, Alisa pulled him along, moving without hesitation, as though she sensed no danger in the dank and wet halls.

Feet sliding in what had to be an inch or more of what felt like a swamp, yet again he found himself cursing his lack of sight. Would he ever get used to being blind? Apparently not, especially not now.

"How bad is it?" he asked. "Can you see in front of you, or is it really hazy from the smoke? Do you think there's a fire on this floor?"

She never even slowed. "If there is, I'm guessing the sprinkler system would have taken care of it."

Now that they had taken action, she sounded fearless. He couldn't help but admire that. Many women—especially those raised as sheltered as he imagined a princess must have been—would be cowering and afraid of their own shadow right about now. Not Alisa.

Still, she hadn't exactly answered his question about the potential fire.

"How far ahead of you can you see?" he asked again.

"Far enough." Still she kept her hold on his hand, leading him forward the way a woman leads a small child. "Come on, we've got to hurry."

Suddenly, he'd had enough. Jerking his hand away, he stopped, concentrating. He thought hard, clenched his teeth and willed himself to see.

Of course, nothing changed.

Feeling slightly foolish—he was a scientist, after all, and thus should know better—he tried again.

"What are you doing?" Impatience coloring her tone, she reached once more for his hand.

Scowling, he eluded her grasp. "Give me a minute," he growled. "Please."

"Fine."

Again he concentrated, hoping against all rational thought, all logic, that he could somehow harness the power of his mind and lift the permanent blinders over his eyes.

See, he roared to himself, inside his own head. *See, damn it. See.*

For the space of one heartbeat, he thought he saw a flash of lightning. Blinking, he tried to find it again and failed. Of course. What had he been thinking? He of all people knew better. In the real world, miracles never happened.

Shoulders sagging, he reached out to find her hand. "I give up," he said. "Lead the way."

She didn't immediately help him out. "What were you doing? And don't say 'nothing.'"

"I was being foolish." Disgusted with himself, he lurched forward, hand outstretched like some ridiculous music-video zombie. When he connected with her fingers, he closed his fist around them and held on tight. "Please, let's continue on. Let's go."

With a loud sigh, she started forward again, tugging him with her. They sloshed through the flooded hall, with bitter, smoke-tinged water raining down on them, and neither spoke.

Finally, after the trudging seemed both endless and pointless, he used his free hand to slough water from his face. "Where are we going?" he asked. "What's your plan?"

"We're going through a part of the house that's less traveled. I want to make sure my family is all right. Since it's obviously not safe to take the elevators, I've decided that we should go for the stairs."

"Good thinking." At least one of them was showing common sense. "Is there a back way out of the palace?" He coughed. His worthless, useless eyes were watering from the soot-filled water. Of course they were.

"Yes." She coughed, too. "But first, I'm going to see that my family is okay." The sharpness in her voice told him she meant it.

He set his jaw, preparing in advance for her protest. "Alisa, it's not safe."

"You know what?" Her fierce tone had his wolf sitting up and taking notice. "I don't care. This is my family. I refuse to abandon them."

He couldn't exactly blame her. Even his wolf approved. But still, it fell to him to try and keep her from harm. "Try to call your brother again."

"I will, after we get out of this water and away from this smoke. Let's go."

As she spoke, the sprinklers suddenly shut off. It seemed oddly silent without the loud hiss and shower of water.

"Thank the hounds," she said. "I'm guessing this means the fire is out."

"Maybe." He sniffed, inhaling sharply. "Or maybe not. The smoke is getting worse."

And it was. Though he couldn't see, he'd smelled this kind of smoke before. Black, roiling smoke, uncurling like a snake, rolling ahead of the storm with a threat of heat.

Which meant that somehow, somewhere, despite the sprinkler system's deluge of water, it hadn't been successful in putting out every fire. One, at least, still burned somewhere.

But how? If everything was sodden… Then he realized. An accelerant had been used. The only kind of fire that water wouldn't extinguish was a grease fire, but that made absolutely no sense. Not in this instance. He'd heard the bombs. If it had been up to him to guess, he'd say gasoline or kerosene had been the accelerant. But if either one had, water should have put it out.

The heat and smoke grew more intense, nearly beating them back. "The fire must be on the other side of a wall," he rasped.

"It's bad," she choked. "I can't breathe."

"We need to get low to the ground." He pulled her

down with him into the warm, dirty water. "There's more oxygen down here."

Gasping for breath, they huddled together for a moment. Already soaked and chilled, they found the additional dampness made absolutely no difference. Moving as one, they crawled forward until his arms and back and sodden kneecaps ached. And if he hurt, he knew she had to as well. Yet she never protested or complained. His admiration for her grew in leaps and bounds. Had he ever truly thought her a pampered, spoiled princess? Now, when it truly mattered, she did better than him.

She stopped suddenly and he bumped into her. Raising into a half crouch, he lifted his head and sniffed the air. The smoke seemed to be dissipating. Good. The filthy, acrid water, however, was not.

"I feel like I'll never be dry again." Her wry tone made him smile.

"I hear you. Are we almost there?" he asked.

Her cough seemed deeper this time. "I'm not sure. It's hard to see in all this smoke, but it shouldn't be too much farther. It's really making my head hurt. I get migraines and I feel one coming on."

Concerned, he squeezed her hand. She sounded weak, on the edge of collapse. Dizzy himself, he knew if they didn't get away from the smoke, they weren't going to make it.

"Can you run?" he asked her suddenly. "It may be our only chance."

"I think so," she wheezed. "Hold on to the back of my blouse and we'll try."

Heart pounding, he jumped up and leapt forward when she did, willing his air-starved body to press on.

He had to—they had to. If they failed, the consequences were too horrible to contemplate.

"Here," she grunted, gasping as she slammed up against a door. Pushing it open, she pulled him through. He kicked the door closed behind them.

Fresh air. Arms linked, they stumbled forward and both dropped to their knees, dragging in great, gasping breaths. Next they needed to check on her family and then he—or they—had to get Alisa to a safe place. Starting now.

The instant he tried to stand up, dizziness overwhelmed him. Interesting that he could still get dizzy when he couldn't see. Holding the wall, he struggled to find his equilibrium. But as soon as he did, he doubled over, coughing and wheezing, trying to clear his lungs. Dimly he was aware of her next to him, doing exactly the same.

Finally, he was able to inhale without coughing.

"Are you ready?" she sputtered.

"Yes. We need to get moving. It won't be too long before smoke makes its way into the stairwell."

Taking his hand in hers, she directed his other hand to the rail. "Let's go."

"How many flights?"

"We were on the sixth floor."

Great.

Down they went, the metal stairs clanging underfoot. Around and around at each level, the closer they drew to the main floor, the louder the clanging sirens became.

"I don't know what floors are on fire," she said. "Surely they weren't able to hit everything at once."

"Unless they had people inside again."

She went silent, remembering the three men who had posed as security guards.

Finally, they ran out of stairs and came up against the final door.

"This comes out by the kitchen," she told him. "I don't think they'll be looking for us there."

"Lead the way."

As soon as she pushed the door open, noise erupted from another part of the building. Screaming and shouting and the panicked sounds of people trying to make sense out of what was happening. Once again, water sloshed underfoot and the air still stank of smoke, though only faintly.

"My father's offices are on this floor. I'd like to check there first."

"Let's go."

As they darted through the kitchen area, her leading him, he thought again about trying to will his eyes to see, but saw no reason to subject himself to the foolish and completely unscientific hope.

The smoky air had slightly dissipated, which meant the fire had to be out on this floor.

The kitchen appeared to be deserted. Apart from some debris that they had to dodge, they had a clear path to the door.

"We're almost at the exit," she exclaimed. "I can see the big red exit sign glowing over the door."

Saying nothing, he simply continued moving.

"We're here." She placed his hand against metal that was still a bit warm. "It seems to be stuck."

He nodded, thinking of all the action movies he'd seen back in his sight-filled days. "We're going to have to ram the door. On the count of three."

"Do you think it will work?" She sounded dubious.

"It has to. One, two, three." He slammed up against the door in unison with her. Miraculously the metal gave and wedged open, bringing a rush of cooler air though still tainted by smoke.

"We'll have to try once more." This time, she counted out and they hit it again. Stepping through, Braden braced himself for what might be on the other side.

To his surprise, they were greeted by the sound of… nothing. The noise they'd heard earlier, the shouts and crashes, had ceased as abruptly as if they'd been only a recording.

"What the…?" Alisa started to ask.

Before she could finish, a woman screamed.

"Wait here," Braden ordered, and then charged forward, rounding the corner without her.

"Wait here?" Stunned, Alisa repeated his words. Really? Was he crazy? First off, she'd never been very good at standing around doing nothing. Princess or no princess, she couldn't hide like a cowering child and let some big, brave, *blind* man do all the dangerous stuff.

So, after losing maybe three seconds to her understandable confusion, she went after him. Dodging water still spraying from broken sprinklers, past sooty marble that had once been blindingly white, down the long, long hallway that no longer resembled a palace, but instead a war zone in some other country. Or a medieval artist's version of hell.

Worse, the hallway stretched out in front of her, long and water-filled and clear. Where was he? How had he managed to vanish so quickly? Cursing under her breath, she picked up the pace.

Walking along the hallway as it turned, she still saw no sign of him. Or of anyone else, which was really odd.

Why had she let him go off without her? The man couldn't even *see,* for hounds' sake.

Or could he?

Remembering his brief flash, when he'd claimed the blackness had lightened, she wondered. Had his sight been miraculously restored to him, and if it had, why wouldn't he have told her?

A sound up ahead—men fighting?—made her try to run, sloshing through the deepening standing water, frantic to get to wherever Braden had gone.

When the man jumped out in front of her, she slammed right into his outstretched arms. Instinctively, she lashed out, fighting with determination born from panic. She landed one good right hook before he grabbed her hands.

"Lisa, Lisa, hold on." Her brother Ruben's face swam into focus. Then, before she could get a single relieved word out, he crushed her to him in a giant bear hug.

"Thank God you're all right."

Blinking, she hugged him back, then pushed out of his arms. "Ditto. But, Ruben, we've got to find Braden." Quickly, she told him what had happened.

"There's no way he could have disappeared like that." Ruben eyed her like he thought she might have hit her head. "Come on, sis. He's blind. It's difficult enough to move fast in all this water when you can see, but—"

"I know. And he only got a few seconds' head start on me. That's why I think someone got him." Clamping her teeth together to keep from getting hysterical, she went to move around him. "Either that, or he's hurt somewhere. We've got to find him."

Ruben didn't budge. "First, let me tell Father and Mother that I found you and that you're all right."

Before she could protest, he dug out his phone and typed in a quick text message. "I'm not calling because you know Father would order me to bring you in immediately and then where would we be?"

As he pocketed his cell, the ringer went off to notify him that he had an incoming call. Glancing at the caller ID, he hit the decline button so the call would go to voice mail. "See? What'd I tell you? That was him."

Jittery with impatience, Alisa nodded. "Come on. The more time we waste standing here, the less chance we have to help Braden."

"Fine." He grabbed her hand. "You really care about him, don't you?"

Glaring at him, she swallowed hard. "Does it matter? He's a famous scientist and I consider him…a friend. We can't just let him die in our home."

"You didn't answer my question."

"Ruben!" She punched him. "Let's go. Now."

"All right. But I'm not letting you out of my sight. You check the rooms on the left, I'll get the ones on the right. Okay?"

Giving him a terse nod, she started forward, hating that she practically had to drag him along with her. If not for the obvious danger, she'd yank herself free and search for Braden alone.

Chapter 14

Braden felt like a fool. Only an idiot would have gone charging after what had sounded like a woman in distress. Really, what had he imagined he would do once he reached her? Fight her assailants effectively despite being blind?

Luckily for him, the sound he'd heard hadn't been a woman at all. Instead, he'd literally stumbled across a large and very wet dog, trapped and highly distressed. He'd mistaken its whimper for a woman's cry.

When Braden followed his ears into one of the small drawing rooms, he splashed right into the animal. With a stuck paw, the beast was up to its belly in water in what seemed to be a small closet.

Braden knelt down in the chilly water and reached out. Again, the dog tried to bump him sideways, this time nearly knocking him down with the sheer force of his stocky body. Luckily, the animal was friendly. Despite the pain it must be in, it seemed to recognize that he was there to help.

What had trapped its paw? Feeling along under the water, he found some kind of opening, like a loose board. An opening in the wall that had partially closed on the dog's foot. He pulled and tugged and finally used his own foot to wedge the board wide enough for the animal to free its paw.

Once he'd done so, the shivering and sodden beast had gone wild with joy, leaping on him hard enough to send Braden back on his butt in the smelly water. Now he just had to find Alisa.

Murmuring soothing nonwords to the animal while it licked his face, Braden heard a masculine voice talking out in the hall. At once, he fell silent, though he continued to hold the dog close by the collar. The last thing he needed was for the dog to begin barking and potentially notify his enemies of his location.

Standing tall and alert, the dog began to wag his tail—his entire body actually, trying to pull away. Listening closely, Braden realized what he'd heard were not enemies at all. The voices belonged to Alisa and Ruben.

Relieved, he rose from his crouch and, keeping one hand on the collar buried in the dog's scruff to keep him in place, called out.

"Braden?" Alisa cried. "Where are you?"

"Right here." He leaned partially out of the closet entrance. "I found a dog."

"York?" Ruben sounded joyful. "You found my York? Come, boy."

With a joyful yelp, the dog broke away and bounded forward, splashing through the water. Braden had no choice but to let him go. He started to follow, but Alisa beat him to it, running up to him and slamming into him with a full-body hug.

After she released him, she took his hand and held on tight. Outside, in the room itself, they could both hear the sounds of Ruben and his pet's happy reunion.

"York's been missing for a couple of days now," Alisa said, a smile in her voice. "We thought he'd gotten outside and run off, though no one claimed to have seen him do so. We didn't have any idea what happened to him. Ruben feared the worst."

"I guess he got lost in the palace. It's certainly big enough to do so."

"Maybe." She sounded doubtful. "But we searched every room on every floor. Teams combed the entire palace. Ruben really loves that animal. I'm just glad you found him."

"What kind of dog is it?"

"A German shepherd," she told him. "He's a very large eleven-month-old puppy."

"What about you?" he asked, curious. "Do you have a dog, too?"

"No. Me, I keep cats. They're more of a challenge."

Braden couldn't help but laugh. Most cats, unless raised around shifters since they were kittens, could sense the wolf inside and took an intense dislike to anyone who was Pack.

Straightening up, he winced as a sharp pain stabbed him across the forehead and eyes.

"Are you all right?" Alisa asked, slipping her arm around his waist and again hugging him close. "You gave me quite a scare."

"I'm sorry. Bit of a headache, but I'm sure I'll be fine."

"Ah, headaches. I certainly can relate to them. Braden, you shouldn't have run off like that." Though chiding him, she continued to hold him close.

"I know. But the dog's whimper sounded like a woman in trouble and I didn't think, I just reacted."

"You two look…cozy," Ruben said flatly, startling Braden. "Mind telling me what's going on?"

Alisa moved away as though guilty of something. Braden went to shake his head, then winced at the pain. The last thing he needed was Ruben learning that his sister and Braden were lovers. Even imagining this made him clench his jaw. Before he could frame a suitable response, Alisa gasped.

"Ruben, look. Down there, in the left corner. There's a door in the closet. It's partly open," she explained, no doubt for Braden's benefit.

"That's what trapped your dog's paw," Braden said. "What is it, anyway, a secret passageway?" He tried to make a joke to defuse the tension.

"Actually, it probably is." Rather than angry, Ruben sounded stunned. "Ever since Lisa and I were kids, we've heard stories about an interconnected series of tunnels that run throughout the palace. Though we looked, we never had any luck in finding them."

"Believe me, we looked," Alisa put in, her relief and awe almost palpable.

"That would explain how York was able to literally vanish right from underneath our noses."

"And," Braden said slowly, "this would also explain how the extremists are able to come and go undetected."

Ruben cursed.

"What exactly has happened out there?" Braden asked. "Were there explosions?"

"Yes. One device was a bomb on a timer. The other appeared to be some sort of Molotov cocktail, though it was tossed by someone inside the palace."

"Like a mole." Braden nodded to show he understood.

"A traitor," Ruben said flatly. "Two people on our domestic staff were killed."

"But Mother and Father are all right?" Alisa asked.

"Yes, of course. Though Father is spitting mad. On top of trying to secure the palace, we've now got to investigate for someone working from the inside."

"Well, the tunnels can explain a lot of that."

"Yes," Ruben agreed, grim-voiced. "They certainly can."

"Let's go check this out." Alisa pushed on Braden's back, trying to propel him toward the back of the closet and the door.

"Alisa, wait."

"If you're worried about our safety, don't be. Ruben's armed, so we should be safe enough."

"Not necessarily." Braden refused to move. "We have no idea how many of them might be in there or how heavily armed they are. Ruben's one weapon would be worthless against five or ten armed men."

"He's right." Still sounding grim, Ruben agreed. "Let me call security. We need a small, armed force to accompany us. Perhaps I'll simply have them investigate these tunnels."

"Ruben!" Alisa protested. "How can you say that? We've got to check the tunnels out ourselves."

"Lisa, you will not be going in there under any circumstances, do you understand?" Ruben ordered.

Since his tone brooked no argument, Braden figured that would be the end of that. And it might have been, if York hadn't started growling furiously.

A second later, the dog blew by Braden, brushing against his legs as he dashed past, into the closet.

"Grab him," Ruben shouted, too late.

Alternately barking and snarling, York disappeared through the doorway, into the tunnels.

Cursing, Ruben went after him. Barely hesitating, Alisa grabbed Braden and pulled him along, too.

Up ahead, sounding as if it came from a great distance, they could hear the dog barking. Ruben shouted, without success, ordering York to come. He ran off ahead of them, calling over his shoulder for Braden to keep an eye on his sister.

Still leading the way, Alisa's footsteps became less certain. "It's really dark in here," she muttered. "Difficult to see. I wish I had a flashlight."

Now dark he could do.

"Welcome to my world. It's all the same to me," Braden answered, actually feeling as if this one time his blindness gave him an advantage. Though neither one could see, he was actually used to stumbling around in the darkness and she was not.

Raising his voice, he called to Ruben to wait for them. Ruben didn't answer. He didn't come back, either. And the sound of York's barking and Ruben's shouting faded into the distance.

How deep were these tunnels, anyway? Damn. Braden yanked Alisa to a standstill. "Listen," he whispered. "This is really not good. We can't even hear the dog. Even Ruben has gone silent."

"Then we need to keep going." She sounded unimpressed by his cautious words. "Come on."

"Alisa—"

"We're not abandoning my brother. Come on." Again she tried to pull him along.

"No." He refused to budge. "Not like this. Let me go first. I'm much more expendable than you."

Expendable. Hearing himself, he grimaced. The foremost neurosurgeon and Pack researcher in the world and he was the expendable one. Interesting how life could turn so quickly in an unforeseen direction.

"Either we do it my way or not at all," he told her. "Your choice."

After a second's hesitation, she released him and let him slide by her and take the lead. As he did, he couldn't help but relish the luxury of her soft curves momentarily flush against him.

Nice. Even in a situation like this, he couldn't control his desire for her.

And she apparently was oblivious. "Since you don't have your cane, I'll have to direct you as best I can," she said.

He snorted. "I thought you couldn't see in here."

"Up ahead, it looks like the light is getting a bit better. It must be artificial, but still…"

Since he had no choice but to take her at her word, he nodded. "Just keep me from running into the wall or anything else, okay?"

"Of course."

They continued forward, moving slowly and cautiously. The water and smoke had luckily not made much inroad into these passages. After the first fifty feet, the floor seemed barely damp, at least judging by the lack of water sloshing against his ankles. This was a good thing.

"Stop," Alisa ordered, digging her nails into his shoulder. "There's a wall about ten feet in front of us. We can either go left or right. I have no idea which way Ruben went."

Under his breath, he counted to three. There had to be some scientific, logic-based way to choose, but he couldn't think of any right this instant. Instead, he did something he never did—he went with instinct, gut reaction. "Let's go right."

About fifty feet into the new tunnel, the wall he'd been using to feel his way abruptly ended.

"Wait," she said.

He stopped.

"Wow!" Alisa exclaimed. "It's not dark at all in here. This is where the light was coming from. There are lamps—either electrical or battery-operated."

"Yes, but where are we? Why has the tunnel ended?"

"It hasn't ended at all." Grabbing hold of his shoulders, she turned him to the right. "We're in a room. It looks like some kind of living quarters. It's about the size of one of the receiving rooms on the main floor. There are bunk beds, stacked three high, enough to sleep twelve people. There's even a refrigerator and a camp-stove-type thing that looks like it runs on charcoal. I don't see a shower or any kind of loo."

A clanking sound behind them had Braden spinning to face it, instinctively moving to block Alisa from view.

"There you are." It was Ruben's voice, a softly growling York behind him. "I went the other way at the split and found only more tunnels. Then York decided he wanted to backtrack our steps, so we did and found you."

At the growl, Braden's wolf woke up and took notice of the alert dog, then dismissed him as beneath him.

"Ruben, you shouldn't have disappeared like that." Alisa's strong tone matched Ruben's from earlier. "You spout off all this nonsense about protecting me, and then you run off and leave me alone with—"

"A blind man?" Braden interrupted, disappointment and anger and hurt coloring his voice.

Both Alisa and Ruben went silent. He imagined them staring at him, then glancing at each other.

"I was going to say 'an unarmed man,'" Alisa put in quietly. "You must stop being so hard on yourself."

"Why should I?" he exploded, driven by frustration and resentment. "I'm a liability here. You two have to guide me everywhere and if the bad guys were to show up right now, you'd have to protect me. I sure as hell can't defend myself when I can't even see."

Silence again.

Finally, Alisa spoke. "Are you quite finished? I'll allow this one instance of self-pity. When you think you might have finished wallowing in it, it will be time to pick yourself up and go on. Let me give you a few moments."

Silence, except for the faint sound of her counting under her breath. When she reached ten, she exhaled.

"There. Finished. Are you quite done now?"

Her tone, so proper and regal and completely unlike the Alisa he knew, had Braden fighting not to smile. Then, deciding the hell with it, he shook his head and laughed out loud. "Yes," he said. "I'm quite done. Sorry about that. Now, what do you two want to do next?"

"I called for a security detail," Ruben answered. "I gave them instructions on where to find the door to the tunnels, but they won't know which way to go. Perhaps we should retrace our steps so we can meet with them."

Once they'd done so, they exited out the same closet as before, to find the security team Ruben had called for milling around in the hall, apparently very confused.

All the fires had been put out, though none of the perpetrators had been caught. Braden could sense that the mood was very grim.

King Leo had put the entire palace on lockdown. No one was to come or go until the bombers were located. The discovery of the tunnels had sent the entire security team into an uproar, especially since one of the team leaders was among the more severely injured.

King Leo summoned Alisa and Braden to his chambers. Ruben accompanied them.

When they entered the room, Braden and Ruben stood silently while Alisa and her parents had an emotional reunion. Alisa returned to Braden's side once all that was finished, taking his arm.

"The palace is not safe," the king said, his voice weary and stressed. "Ruben has informed me that these extremists want Alisa and Dr. Streib."

Queen Ionna made a sound of distress and her husband took a moment to comfort her before continuing.

"Because I cannot protect either of you here, I am sending the two of you away. Ruben has concurred with my decision."

"Where?" Alisa demanded, speaking for the first time.

"You do not need to know," King Leo declared.

"We've worked out details privately. Your mother and I, as well as Ruben, are the only ones who will have this information."

"And your chaperone, of course," Queen Ionna put in.

"Chaperone?" Alisa sounded incredulous. "Why on earth do we need a chaperone?"

Ruben laughed, though from the royal parents' silence, Braden judged they didn't find her comment at all amusing.

"Come on, Lisa," Ruben teased. "You know as well as I do that a royal princess can't disappear with a man, even if he is a doctor. Imagine the gossip and the damage to your reputation."

Wisely, Braden remained silent. No way was he getting into the middle of this debate. After all, Alisa's brother was correct. She did need a chaperone, if not only to protect her from him, but from herself.

"What about you, Father?" Alisa finally asked, worry coloring her tone. "Are you and Mother going somewhere, too?"

"We are not," Queen Ionna spoke sharply. "We cannot leave the kingdom. Fleeing would seem not only like an act of cowardice, but we would be abandoning our people."

"But you must stay safe," Alisa argued. "Father, at the very least, send Mother with us. She can be my chaperone."

The king sighed. "I've already asked your mother if she wished to go with you. She declined, saying she prefers to remain by my side, as a queen should be."

While Alisa digested this, the king continued, his voice hardening. "You will have thirty minutes to pack what you wish to take. Ruben will drive you. We've also arranged for decoys to leave at the same time. If the extremists have a mole inside the castle—and it appears that they do—I want them following the wrong couple."

"Thirty minutes to get ready?" Alisa sounded intrigued rather than upset. "That's not very much time."

"No, it is not." The smile in King Leo's voice told them how even now, his beloved youngest daughter managed to amuse him. "So you'd better get busy. Ruben will accompany you both along with a small, armed detail, so each of you had better work quickly. We don't know when these terrorists will attack again."

"We will." Letting go of Braden's arm, Alisa crossed the room at a jog, from the sound of her footsteps. Braden imagined she hugged her parents before she returned to him and tugged him away.

"Come on," she said. "We need to go."

"Just a moment." Raising his head, he directed his question to the king. "Your Highness, what about my lab? If I am to be sent into hiding with your daughter, I would prefer to continue to run my experiments."

"I guessed as much. I've taken the liberty of having two of my most trusted guards pack your lab, or as much as they could," King Leo said. "The smaller machines have already been loaded. Some of them were, out of necessity, sent with the decoys. I hope you understand."

Braden inclined his head in what he hoped was a respectful bow. "Thank you." Most of the equipment belonged to the king anyway. Braden had brought very little machinery with him. Prior to his arrival, he'd sent a detailed list of what he'd need, and the king had provided everything.

He retraced his steps back to where Alisa impatiently waited and held out his arm. "Let's go," he said.

On the way up to their rooms, completely surrounded by armed guards from the sound of all the footsteps, Alisa went uncharacteristically silent, though she didn't relinquish her grip on Braden's arm. For this, he was grateful, especially since they were moving along at a fast pace.

"Here we are," she finally said. "Give me a minute to throw some things into a bag."

Ruben waited with Braden at the door while she packed. "Look, I don't know what is going on between the two of you," he said in a low voice. "But you should know you have no chance of a future with my sister."

Jaw clenched, Braden nodded, amazed at how much hearing the truth actually hurt. "Nor do I expect one."

At his response, Ruben leaned in close and gripped Braden's shoulder, hard. "You'd better not hurt her, do you understand me? Because if you do, I will come looking for you. And, blind man or not, you will wish you were dead by the time I get through with you."

The threat touched Braden rather than intimidated or angered him. "Understood," he finally said, turning away so Alisa's brother wouldn't see his self-deprecating smile. "If I had a sister, I'd be the same way."

"You're an only child?" Ruben asked, sounding more relaxed now that he'd delivered his message, though Braden really wished he could see the other man's face.

"Yes." Short answer, no elaboration needed. Braden knew perfectly well that all Ruben had to do was check out the file the royal family had no doubt made on him before ever allowing them access to their precious daughter. All his personal information would be in there.

"I think that's—"

"I'm finished," Alisa said, sounding slightly breathless as she interrupted whatever else Ruben had been about to say. "Let's go to your room, Braden."

He let her pack for him since he couldn't tell what he touched without feeling his little custom labels and they didn't have time for him to do this.

So he waited with Ruben, refusing to let the silence feel uncomfortable.

Luckily, he didn't have to wait long. As she'd done with her own belongings, Alisa finished in record time.

"We're ready," she said brightly. From the anticipatory tone of her husky voice, she appeared to regard this entire thing as an adventure rather than a hardship. This was good. Once, when Braden had to staff his neurosurgery office, he'd made sure to hire people with a positive outlook, believing they would balance out his own tendency toward darkness.

"Just a moment," Ruben said, no doubt after exchanging meaningful glances or some such nonsense with his sister. "I need to make a call and arrange to have your doubles meet us in the parlor. We'll have them come disguised, so the moles don't see them."

When he'd finished his call, they headed back downstairs. At least things had quieted somewhat.

"How is this going to work?" Alisa asked.

"We've got two body doubles. You will switch clothing with them—they are currently dressed as household staff. They will be sent off with a lot of fanfare, while you two—and your chaperone—will sneak off with me."

"Sounds like a good plan," Braden said.

"Yes, it does," Alisa agreed. After a moment of silence, she asked her next question in a too-casual voice. "Speaking of my chaperone, who is it?"

"I can't remember her name," Ruben said. "But you both are familiar with her. She's one of the household maids, I think. Father chose her. I'm guessing she won't speak English, just Teslinkian. That way, at least you two can have private conversations."

Neither Braden nor Alisa commented. When they reached the parlor, Ruben handed them each a household staff uniform.

"You'll be dressing like a butler," he said, clapping Braden on the back. "There's a small closet in the back of this room. You can change there."

"Would you mind pointing me in the right direction?"

Before Ruben could, Alisa grabbed Braden's arm. "I'll show you," she said as she walked with him to the closet.

He changed quickly, emerging to find Alisa still waiting outside the door.

"My turn," she said. "They've even given me a blond wig. Once we've finished, our decoys can get dressed in our clothes."

As plans went, it seemed like a good one. A few minutes later, Alisa rejoined him, taking his clothing from him, presumably to give to the man who'd be pretending to be him. Again they waited, this time while the others changed.

"Are we ready?" Ruben finally said, a forced sort of cheerfulness in his voice. He repeated the question in his native tongue, and two unfamiliar voices answered in the affirmative.

"Good," he said. "Alisa, you and Braden will go to the service entrance, unaccompanied. An unmarked van will be waiting there for you. Your chaperone is already inside."

"What about them?" Alisa asked, apparently meaning the decoys.

"I will accompany them. We have a limo waiting, as well as an armed escort on motorcycles. They will drive away with much fanfare. Hopefully, that will be enough to throw the extremists off."

"Make sure my decoy remembers to act blind," Braden cautioned. "If he forgets and someone sees him, they'll know he's not really me."

"We have that aspect covered," Ruben said. "I honestly believe we've taken care of every single detail, right down to the smallest."

Braden didn't comment. Even brilliant men made mistakes and working out the details of a complicated plan under stress was iffy. He, like the rest of them, could only hope for the best.

"But what if something happens to them?" Alisa persisted. "Are you certain you have taken adequate precautions? I refuse to endanger them simply because they wish to be of service to me."

"They wish to be of service to their country," King Leo boomed, his tone letting them all know that he'd finished discussing the issue. "We will make sure they are safe, as we will for you. Now, if everyone is ready, let's put this plan into motion."

Briefly, Braden wondered if the king watched a lot of American crime dramas on television.

"Come on." Alisa took his arm. "Are you ready to pretend you can see?"

"Easy for you to say," he grumbled, low enough that the king couldn't hear. "Why doesn't anyone think it will look odd if a maid is seen leading around a sightless butler?"

Chapter 15

They made their way down the deserted hallway, heads close together as though sharing confidences. Braden couldn't help but relish her nearness, breathing in her sweet scent and aching as she pressed her soft curves into his side. His pulse quickened.

"Good point," she whispered, her breath warm on his neck. "But if we pretend to be lovers on our way to a tryst, no one will think anything of us having our hands all over each other."

His blood heated at the thought. "Whose idea is this?" he managed. "Surely not Ruben's."

"Oh, no," she chuckled, a suggestive little sound. "If he knew about this, he'd be livid." Then, as though to prove a point, she leaned in and breathed a kiss on his jaw.

Damn. He shuddered, fighting back the urge to turn

his head and kiss her hard, right here in the hall. But this was so not the time or the place, so he kept putting one foot in front of the other as though her gesture had caused little response in him.

"You've got to put more into your acting," she chided. "We're supposed to be all over each other, not hanging back."

Gritting his teeth, he nodded. Apparently she didn't have the same worries as he did about losing control.

"Then kiss me," she ordered. "Or touch me or something. Hurry. One of the other maids is coming this way."

She turned into him as she spoke and giggled, exactly like a young girl flirting with her boyfriend. He responded in kind, nuzzling her neck while cupping her behind with one hand. As she pressed her full breasts into him, he had trouble remembering this playacting wasn't real. Hiding her face in his chest, she nipped him lightly with her teeth, sending his pulse skyrocketing.

As soon as the maid's footsteps disappeared, Alisa moved away, leaving him feeling like he'd been set adrift, desire making him dizzy.

"We're safe," she whispered. "She's gone."

Praying she wouldn't comment on the obvious sign of his arousal, he nodded. Since he couldn't find his voice to save his life, he continued trudging along beside her. He couldn't help but hope someone else would come along so he'd have an excuse to touch her again.

"Here we are." Releasing his arm, she moved away. The heavy clanking sound told him she was opening another door. Again, he wished fiercely that he could see, which pissed him off. How long would he keep longing for something he couldn't have?

"This leads into the parking garage for employees," she said, for his benefit. "Come on."

Stepping through with her, he waited while she closed the heavy metal door.

"There's the white van, exactly where it's supposed to be," she exclaimed as the van pulled up in front of them.

Once the vehicle coasted to a stop in front of them, though oddly reluctant to let go of Alisa's arm, he helped her up inside the van. He felt eternally grateful when she returned the favor by keeping her hand in his and guiding him up and to his seat.

"Hello, Dr. Streib," a softly accented voice said. "Princess Alisa."

"Katya?" They'd sent along his assistant?

"I am to be your chaperone," she said shyly. "I hope you don't mind, Your Highness."

"Of course not." Alisa's brisk tone would seem to indicate otherwise. "Braden—that is, Dr. Streib, certainly looks pleased."

"I am." Even though grinning wouldn't seem to be the best option, he couldn't help himself. "This is awesome. She's trained to help me with my research. Your parents have been more than considerate sending her."

"Yes," she said sourly. "They certainly have."

From the driver's seat, Ruben laughed.

Alisa settled back, seatbelt tightly fastened and a fixed smile on her face. This was for both her brother and Katya's benefit. The assistant certainly appeared pleased to be accompanying them to this secret location.

At first, Alisa had thought this must be because the

foolish girl believed that Ruben was staying with them as well.

But then she saw the way Katya watched Braden. *Her* Braden. Katya watched him like she'd like to eat him up.

Hounds over the moon. She, Princess Alisa of Teslinko, was jealous.

If that didn't beat all.

Driving slowly for him, Ruben switched lanes and gradually decelerated. "We're going to exit here," he announced. "I want to make sure we're not being followed."

As they coasted down the road, Alisa turned and looked behind them, even though Ruben continually checked the rearview mirror. They turned down a side street, drove into a wooded neighborhood of flats and the occasional house, then came back out on the same side street, heading back in the direction they'd come.

Though traffic was light, Alisa felt certain she didn't see the same car more than once.

"I think we're safe," she said.

"I agree." Ruben flashed a warm smile. "Now we can get back on the highway."

"Where are we going?" Alisa asked. "Since we're on the way, I see no reason why you can't tell us."

"It's one of our many houses—the summer cottage on the coast."

"I know the one! When we were children, we used to go there all the time, though you were really small and probably don't remember."

He shrugged. "Maybe not. Either way, Father says it's isolated and very easy to guard. You should be safe there."

Alisa nodded. "You know, I really hate running away. I'd much rather stay and fight."

"I know you would." He gave her a fond look. "But we must keep you safe. We can't protect ourselves if we're worried about you."

"That's right, put it back on me," she grumbled. She jumped when Braden put his arm around her shoulders.

"He's right, you know." His low—and if she was honest, sexy—voice rumbled in her ear. "Plus, we may have better success figuring out your ability if we're away from all distractions."

Ah, but who would protect them from the biggest distraction of all—their attraction toward each other?

Eyeing Katya watching them, Alisa didn't voice this concern. Something about the other woman set her off, though she couldn't put her finger on exactly what. Maybe it was the way the assistant, now that she was to be away from the palace, wore a low-cut blouse that prominently displayed her ample assets. Which made no sense, as Braden couldn't see. If she was trying to impress Ruben, she'd exerted absolutely no effort. She hadn't even looked at the prince once since they'd gotten into the van.

Alisa frowned, glaring at the other woman. She'd hoped whoever her parents chose as chaperone wouldn't even speak English. Instead, they'd sent someone who was not only fluent in the language, but who'd acted as Braden's research assistant as well.

At least Katya had the common sense to avert her gaze instead of glaring back.

"How long a drive are we in for?" Braden asked.

"About an hour," Ruben answered pleasantly. "At least you all are going to the most beautiful part of our country—the coast. While the beaches are a bit rocky, the sheer beauty of the cliffs more than make up for that."

"Do you go there often?" Braden asked.

"No. Like Lisa, I haven't been in a while. You know what, though? As soon as all this is over, I think I'll come stay for a few weeks. I remember coming here as a child. It's really the most amazing place."

"How do you remember?" Alisa asked. "You're two years younger than me."

He shrugged. "Maybe from all the pictures Mom took. Or maybe…" He grinned. "Because Dad and I come here fishing occasionally."

Though Braden only nodded and didn't reply, his pained expression told Alisa how much it bothered him that he couldn't view the gorgeous countryside.

She ached to comfort him with a touch, but both her brother and Katya's eagle eyes prevented that. Instead, she sought to distract him with words.

"As children, our parents would bring us to the coast every summer. I don't know about Ruben or my sisters, but those were among the happiest times of my life."

She told him about ordinary childhood pleasures—the building of sand castles and riding an inflatable raft over the smallish waves.

"I thought the beaches were rocky," Braden commented.

Exchanging a glance with her brother, she smiled. "They are. But our father had the area in front of our house dredged out and truckloads of sand were brought in. He created the perfect beach area in which to let his children play safely."

Finally, they arrived at the gated, winding drive that

led to the royal vacation cottage. The lane meandered through sheer rocky cliffs, upon which King Leo had placed a guard shack. Another guard post waited at the point where the road exited the cliffs, as well as another tall, wrought-iron gate.

Keeping up a running commentary, Alisa relayed descriptions of it all for Braden's benefit.

"Thank you," he murmured into her ear. "It's almost as good as actually seeing it."

And though his smile appeared tinged by sadness, his words lightened her heart.

Again, she ached to touch him, to pull his head close to hers and kiss him. She actually swayed, so powerful was the urge. Only Katya's deliberate cough stopped her.

"We're here!" Ruben said, sounding relieved. When he pulled up in front of the low-slung, stone house and parked, he lifted his hands from the steering wheel and flexed them. Watching this, Alisa realized he'd been much more tense than he'd let on.

"The house is made of native cedar and stone." As she walked Braden from the car to the front door, she kept up the running monologue.

"Wait." Ruben stepped in front of them. He spoke a few words into his phone, then dropped it back into his pocket. "I've asked the security detail to run a complete check of the interior. We're not going anywhere until I get an all-clear."

"How do you know you can trust them?" Braden wanted to know. "You had a mole back at the palace. Who's to say you don't have one here?"

"All of the people stationed here have worked at this location for ten years or longer." Ruben smiled as he spoke. "They are among our most trusted staff. That is one of the reasons my father chose this house out of all the others."

Braden nodded. Alisa squeezed his arm, standing a tiny bit closer than was actually necessary, but not so close that anyone would notice.

In fact, she had difficulty tearing her gaze from the house. The cozy, cottage-looking facade brought back so many childhood memories, all from a time before she'd fully understood what being a princess actually meant.

Odd how so many people viewed royalty as exalted and envied what they believed to be special, privileged lives. In her experience, being a princess meant one thing. She had to live her life apart and alone, never fully able to participate in the sometimes messy spontaneity of normal life like others did.

Instead of private school, she and her siblings had tutors. Instead of classroom and recess and friends, they'd only had each other. Their play dates had been arranged with carefully selected children, almost all of them the offspring of other nobles.

Her entire life she'd been scrutinized and criticized, carefully watched, often imitated, and occasionally mocked. Only here, at this house by the sea, had she felt able to let go of her public persona and simply *be* Alisa. Or Lisa, as Ruben called her.

Her brother was right. She hadn't been to this spot in years. Too long. She didn't even remember why they'd stopped coming here. Now, she got to experience the simple beauty and near-magical enchantment of the place once more. This time, she had Braden by her side.

If the situation wasn't so volatile, she would have said it couldn't get much better than that.

Finally, Ruben got the all-clear. "We can go inside," he said, giving Alisa a warning look that had to be because of how close she and Braden were standing. From the other side, Katya managed to mirror his expression exactly.

Ignoring them both, she pulled Braden up the sidewalk. Though he wouldn't be able to actually see the interior, she'd do her best to describe it for him.

"It's as different from the formality of the palace as night and day," she said excitedly. "In fact, this is the only house that my mother completely decorated herself instead of using an interior designer. She did it all in a beach motif."

"While not terribly original," Ruben drawled from behind them, "done right, it can be soothing. I'm guessing she did a good job, because I've always gotten a sense of peace when I stay here."

The front door swung open and the staff, many of them elderly, all of them smiling, had lined up to greet them.

Alisa went down the line, squeezing hands, kissing cheeks and murmuring hellos. At her side, Braden only responded when directly spoken to, though Alisa took care to introduce him.

"Excellent." Ruben waited for them at the end of the huge foyer. "I've taken the liberty of choosing Braden's room myself. It's at the other end of the hall from yours," he told Alisa with a smug smile.

"That won't work," she responded immediately. "Since he can't see, he needs me closer than that so I can help him get around."

"I brought his cane." Smile fading, Ruben's final remark won his counterargument. "Plus I don't want to make it so easy to take the two of you out at once. You'll be at opposite ends of the hall, with guards stationed outside both your doors. Katya will sleep in a room close to you, Alisa."

"But..." Alisa swallowed, unable to find fault with his logic.

"I am your chaperone, after all," Katya put in smoothly.

"As well as my research assistant," Braden said. "Now, if you don't mind, I'm extremely tired. If you could show me to my room, I'd like to get some rest."

Ah yes, she'd managed to completely forget about the fatigue that plagued Braden in the afternoon.

"And I've got a long drive back ahead of me," Ruben said. "Enough of the discussion." He looked at Melton, the head manservant. "Please show Dr. Streib to the room I've chosen for him. Anita will show you ladies to yours."

As Alisa turned to follow the manservant, Ruben surprised her by gathering her close and giving her a fierce hug.

"Take care of yourself, my sister."

She hugged him back. "You, too, baby brother. Always remember that you are heir to the throne." Though she hated to have to warn him, she knew well how devastated their parents would be if something were to happen to him. As she would be as well.

"I will," he responded, letting her go. Then, with a jaunty wave, he and his guard turned and exited the way they'd come.

Which left Alisa no choice but to join the impatiently

waiting Katya and the matronly Anita, and go with them to her room.

As she glanced back over her shoulder to see Braden, following three paces behind Melton, she knew she'd have to figure out a way they could be together. If not in their well-guarded bedrooms, they'd at least have lab time together. Assuming the research wasn't permanently suspended. She'd have to deal with Katya, lab assistant and chaperone, but it could be done. Then maybe she could convince him that she was more than a research subject. She was his mate.

Never in his career—hell, never in his *life*—had Dr. Braden Streib abandoned anything. He'd never performed any task half-assed, and actually considered himself thorough and reliable to the point of obsession. His ex-wife had mocked these very traits, calling him anal-retentive.

In a way, she'd been correct. What she hadn't realized was that he in no way considered the term an insult.

It was because of this dedication and drive that he had succeeded at every single thing he'd ever attempted. Every single thing.

Until now. He'd traveled to Teslinko, confident that despite his blindness, he would succeed where countless others had failed. He'd be the one to discover the secret behind Princess Alisa's amazing and extraordinary abilities. He'd even been optimistic enough to believe he'd do so in under a few weeks.

Thus far, he hadn't been successful. Less than successful, in fact.

And now the extremists had managed to interrupt his work. In the end, their bombing and attempts to hurt him and Alisa had worked in his favor. Banished to a remote location, alone with his equipment, Alisa and his research assistant—how much better could things get?

If he didn't find the truth here, he never would.

Such negative thoughts were completely unlike him.

This again got him fuming.

Three weeks and three days. Twenty-four days of work and experiments and tests, in between dodging extremist assassins and bombs and snipers.

His lab had been trashed, both he and Alisa had been individually attacked, and still he kept testing. Trying. Believing.

And the results never changed. Personal feelings aside, there was absolutely nothing unusual about Princess Alisa of Teslinko. Every single indicator matched his. Every result claimed she was perfectly normal. For a shape-shifter, that is. Not one single marker pointed to any abnormality that could explain her unique abilities. Not one.

Damn. None of this made any sense. When he'd heard about the woman who could go for close to a year without changing or going mad, he'd certainly expected to find anomalies.

He'd slept surprisingly well last night, considering he was in a new place and had an armed guard stationed at his door. Though he'd missed Alisa, the entire situation meant she was completely off limits, so he'd gone to bed alone and immediately dropped into a deep, dreamless sleep.

This morning, he'd awakened bright and early, feeling rested and ready to tackle the day. While showering, he'd had another of those incidents when the all-encompassing darkness that surrounded him had inexplicably lightened, teasing him with a tantalizing vision of what he still could not yet see.

The manservant named Melton had appeared at his door moments after he'd gotten dressed, almost as if the guard had reported Braden's status to him. After breaking his fast with a meal of oatmeal and fruit, they'd walked to the lab, where Braden was eager to get started once again, even without Alisa.

Until doubt had set in. He missed her, he truly missed her.

He tried to focus on the questions, reminding himself that an answer continued to elude him. But for nothing. All he could think about was the princess. *His* princess.

At the thought, his wolf stirred. His inner beast kept trying to tell him she was his mate. Though normally he trusted his wolf instinct above human, this time he wasn't sure what to think.

He wanted her. He needed her. But did he truly love her?

He suspected he did. If so, he had grown foolish and careless since coming here. Loving someone like her could only bring pain.

Chapter 16

Luckily, Alisa and Katya arrived a moment later, saving him from developing a true black mood.

"Good morning," Alisa said, sounding so impossibly bright and cheerful that he wanted to kiss her.

"Yes, good morning," his assistant-turned-Alisa's-chaperone seconded, reminding him of all the reasons he couldn't.

He responded as pleasantly as possible, considering the circumstances.

"What are we going to do today?" Alisa asked, her breath catching as though she shared similar thoughts.

"More of the same." He refused to let the grimness of the former results get him down. "I'm going to retest everything. There has to be something wrong with the results."

"Why do you say that?" Katya sounded curious, though oddly strained.

"Yes, why do you say that?" Alisa seconded.

"Because I've run a DNA profile, done every blood panel possible. I've viewed the results of the complete body scan that was done on you, plus done a CT scan of my own, and damned if I can find anything even remotely unusual."

Alisa snickered. "So I'm normal. I could have told you that. I'm just like anyone else."

"But that's it. You're not. No one else can do what you can do."

She sighed. "Sometimes I wish I couldn't, you know. I had no idea that people went crazy when they didn't change."

He felt a twinge of sympathy for her, which he immediately squashed.

"Pampered, privileged, perfect little royal princesses certainly aren't in touch with the real world," Katya drawled maliciously.

Her comment surprised him. She could be fired for such insolence. Until now, his assistant had hovered in the background, responding only when spoken to. After all, she was a personal assistant to Alisa's parents.

Still, Katya was right. Her comment served to remind him of the differences between Alisa and him. He needed to remember what she was, who she was, especially when he woke in the middle of the night alone in his bed with her name on his lips as he'd done last night.

Would he ever get over this craving for her? Logically, since they'd made love, that act alone should have slaked his thirst, not made him burn for more.

But nothing about Alisa inspired any kind of logic. Nothing.

His body stirred, even as he replayed in his mind

the carnal passion they'd shared. He'd never experienced anything like it, not even with the woman he'd once believed to be his mate, until she'd betrayed him. He couldn't help but wonder if he'd ever experience anything like it again. Once he left Teslinko and went back to America, he saw a barren emptiness yawning in front of him for the rest of his days. Life without Alisa.

Katya cleared her throat, reminding him of her presence.

Stop, he ordered himself. He'd never been prone to poetry or romantic thoughts of any kind. Why should he be different now? He needed to focus, get back on track. He'd always thought of himself as a scientist first and foremost, a man second, and didn't plan to change that now. Not for her, nor for anyone.

"Of course people go mad," he said. "Katya, what is the longest you've gone without shifting?"

"Me?" Obviously, his question surprised her. "I've gone three weeks tops. But I've always been afraid to go too long."

"Why?" Alisa asked, sounding curious.

"In my village, we had two aberrations. One was a man who tried to stay human too long, and he went mad. The other was a Feral who didn't want to leave her wolf shape. She too went mad. The Protectors from Italy came and got her. I never knew if she was exterminated or…" she stumbled over the unfamiliar word in English, her heavy accent making it almost unrecognizable "…rehabilitated."

"Protectors?" Alisa said the title as though the concept was foreign to her. "What do you mean?"

"Did you never hear of the Protectors?" he asked carefully.

"No."

Somehow, he was not surprised. "They hunted Feral shifters and tried to rehabilitate them. Many of those Ferals went mad from trying to remain in one form too long."

"One form? You mean human, right?"

"Or wolf," Katya put in. "Like the Feral from my town."

Braden cocked his head, considering. "I have to say I'd rather be human. Though I'm sure a lot of shifters would say wolf."

"I don't know." Alisa went on the defensive. "The thought has never occurred to me to stay wolf longer than I had to."

"And now?" He couldn't resist the question.

"I still don't find the idea at all appealing."

This conversation kept getting more and more interesting. He had a sense that they could be on the verge of the breakthrough he'd been looking for. But for some reason, he found Katya's presence unsettling.

"Katya, have you broken your fast?" he asked.

"Yes, of course. Food was brought to the princess's room and she and I ate together."

"Well, I haven't," he lied. "Would you mind getting me something to eat?"

"I cannot." Her response was swift and emphatic. "I have been charged with the duty of acting as the princess's chaperone. As such, I cannot leave you two alone together."

"That's ridiculous," Alisa interjected. "We're in the lab. We've worked together like this for weeks. What do you think is going to happen? And since when did a personal assistant have such power?"

Rather than answering, the other woman sniffed. Though Braden had no idea what she looked like, he imagined she watched them with narrowed, suspicious eyes and a pursed mouth.

"Enough." Alisa's sharp voice sounded regal. "Katya, I order you to bring the doctor something with which he can break his fast. The task should not take you longer than ten minutes. I doubt anyone can do anything untoward in ten minutes. So go. Now."

The other woman shuffled off, her sullen gait showing what she thought of the order.

As soon as the sound of her footsteps faded, Alisa wrapped her arms around him and held on tight.

"I've missed you," she murmured.

Gently, but forcibly, he disengaged himself and stepped away from her. "I've missed you, too, but we need to work."

"Work?" She sounded both hurt and incredulous. "I arrange for us to have a few minutes alone, and you want to work?"

"We're running out of time," he told her, keeping his voice gentle. "I've got to discover the answer before those rebels wreak havoc on the rest of your country. You don't want anyone else to get hurt, do you?"

"Well, no. But why can't we just take advantage of Katya's brief absence and enjoy each other? With all the guards, it's not like we'll get to spend the night in each other's bed."

If she only knew how badly he wanted to do just that.

Instead, he had to focus on his work ethic. He had to believe there was an end in sight, a solution to the question he'd been asking for weeks.

"I'm sorry," he told her, meaning it. "But I don't have

much time left to find out what it is about you that enables you to—"

"Remain human," she interrupted. "You know what? I like being human. I enjoy it. And if I decide to banish the wolf part of me forever, I will do so. Understand? That's all there is to it, nothing more, nothing less. I decide."

She took a deep breath. "I am tired of being probed and studied and tested like there's something wrong with me. I enjoy being human more than I do being wolf. Deal with it."

Something about her tone, her words… Some tiny hint, the meaning of which hovered just out of reach. If only he could decipher it.

"Why do you not enjoy being wolf?" he asked carefully. "Surely, you like it a little bit at least? We all do, after all."

"Enjoy?" She began to pace, her heels clicking. From this, he deduced that she was giving his question some serious thought. "It's okay, I guess. Fun when I'm in the moment. But I don't really crave it."

Interesting. Keeping his face expressionless, he pretended to concentrate on separating out two sets of glass slides. "But your wolf, what about her? Doesn't she fight you? Doesn't she long to run free?"

She stopped her pacing. "Why do you speak as though my wolf half is separate from my human side? We are one and the same, not two. We are each merely different aspects of the whole. My wolf is me and wants what I want. I control her and she accepts this."

She sounded as though she was smiling. "Back to the experiments. What happens now?"

Was it his imagination, or did she sound sort of

breathless? Deciding it didn't matter, he focused on her question, not wanting to push too much with his. Though he would need answers, he didn't want to badger her with a barrage of questions all at once. A defensive Alisa wasn't a helpful Alisa.

"We need to step back and reevaluate. Beyond that, I honestly don't know."

Her scent turned his head as she circled him, the way a stalking wolf circles prey. Though he couldn't actually see her, his sense of her was so strong that the strange awareness he shared with her *showed* him exactly where she was.

"Are you declaring your experiment a failure?" The taunting note in her voice was designed to get a reaction.

He refused to give her one. "My *research* has not concluded."

"Then what next?"

"Good question. For today, we will rerun the tests."

She came to a stop in front of him, her body a foot from his, awareness shimmering in the air in front of him. "You don't have an answer, do you?"

"Not yet," he said. "And until I do, I'll keep on. I'll ask more questions and record your answers. Run the tests once more. Whatever trait or gene you have that makes you special will occur to me with enough time."

He swallowed hard, trying to ignore the almost physical pull he felt toward her. "I will discover your secret."

"And what if I don't have one, Doctor? What then?"

"You do." He spoke with certainty. "I simply haven't found it yet." Now that he knew about how she had somehow merged her wolf into her humanness, he had a lot more to work on. Instincts told him that exploring this would lead the way to the answer he so desperately sought.

"You can't be certain of that." Now she definitely sounded husky. And closer. Much closer. His wolf stirred, growing agitated. Where the hell was that Katya? If he didn't know better, he'd guess she'd stayed away longer than she needed to on purpose, so she could catch them doing something they shouldn't.

Speaking of temptation…

Alisa sighed, her breath fanning his cheek. If he put out his hand he could touch her. He'd actually started to raise his arm before realizing what he was doing. Damn. Instead, he took a step back, refusing to let his beast rule him or let human desire govern his actions.

But that didn't make him need her less. Damn, he wanted her. Again. Making love with her one time hadn't lessened the craving. If anything, he desired her more.

Taking a deep breath, he forced himself to concentrate on what was really important here. His research. "I know that something unique to you gives you your ability. I've not yet exhausted the scope of available tests. In time, I will find out what that is."

"Will you?" She made a sound, something in between a snort and a laugh. "You keep running tests. My DNA, my blood, even my urine. All on my body. Has it ever occurred to you that what I do might be all in my mind?"

Her mind? Puzzled, he cocked his head. "What do you mean?"

"That I can control my mental stability myself because I only change when I want to."

"That's like saying you could fly without wings just because you wanted to. Obviously that's not possible."

"Obviously, it is." She mocked him. "I'm proof of that."

"What about your wolf? When you go a long time without letting her out, does she not begin to fight you for the right to be set free?"

Her silence told him she was carefully considering his question. "Since it appears you cannot understand what I tried to tell you earlier, let me rephrase. My wolf is well-trained," she finally said. "She is subservient to me and obeys me."

"Trained?" He jumped on the statement, which quite frankly boggled his mind. "Explain, please."

Now she moved away from him, making it easier for him to breathe. Judging from the sound of her footsteps, she'd begun to pace the length of the room and back.

"As much as I hate to use the analogy, from the time I was a child and my wolf a cub, I began to train her, the same way one might train a new puppy."

With difficulty, he kept his face expressionless. Most shifters would regard this statement akin to blasphemy. Comparing wolves to canines was considered the worst kind of insult. And the concept of training one? Wolves were wild beasts and as such, considered not trainable. Among the Pack, most shifters relished their wild lupine side.

Braden chose to ignore all preconceived notions and insults, focusing on the concept rather than the words. "Now you speak like you regard your wolf as separate from you, like she's an entirely different entity. Before you claimed there was no separation. Explain."

She stopped her pacing. "It's complicated."

"I think you can unravel it, if you try. Explain it to me."

"I believe I can." After a moment's pause, she spoke without hesitation. "But in the past, when I've spoken about this, others have acted as though I was strange and unusual. But surely everyone has to have some sort of control over their beast, otherwise we'd be shifting to wolf at the most inopportune times."

"True," he mused. "But your control goes deeper than most."

"There you are. I am not so different than you." She sounded relieved. "My beast is just better-trained. And while my wolf is part of me, her needs and wants and desires are completely separate from mine. I had to chose which would be more important."

"A conscious choice?" Fascinated, he stood still, wanting to hear more. "You're saying that at some point you realized that only one could be the leader, your wolf or you." A novel concept, though Alisa appeared to think it was nothing out of the ordinary, which explained why she hadn't mentioned it.

"Yes. She is very tough, my wolf. She fought me. She wanted to change when *she* wanted, not when I did. Training was necessary. To put this as simply as possible, I've trained my wolf that my human desires take precedence over her lupine needs."

Amazing. While all shifters did this to some degree, none had taken it this far. Their dual nature meant that at some point, both sides must have their share. Or go mad.

He still didn't understand how Alisa kept that from happening. "You must be very strong-willed."

"Of course I am. I always have been, even as a child."

Such a concept truly intrigued him, though he had to discount it immediately. If such a thing were actually possible, the repercussions were limitless, if people believed and could be taught. That would be no easy task, as he wasn't even sure *he* believed her. He would, he decided, need proof.

When he told her this, she laughed. "I am living proof. What more do you need?"

Still laughing, she swept past him, trailing her hand across his chest as she went. He caught her, grabbing hold of her wrist and yanking her to him.

Just like that, the air around them changed, becoming charged. Slowly, he reeled her in, pulling her to him. She didn't resist—instead, he felt her do a graceful sort of dance as she swayed into him.

And they kissed. This time, the third time, eagerness amplified by memory, her lips felt tantalizingly familiar.

Their mouths melded together and their breathing, in unison, became jagged. Raising his head, he held her, nose to nose, chest to chest, reveling in this perfect instant in time. Inside, his wolf, long past alert, began to rage.

Braden had to say something, do something, or this would rapidly escalate beyond his ability to control.

"I need to change soon," he said, his voice like gravel. "My wolf is fighting me. It'll only get worse."

She touched his arm, sending his senses into overdrive. "We can't here, not..."

"I realize we can't anywhere on the beach," he finished for her. "Isn't there somewhere close to here? I don't need a lot of room."

"Is this urgent?" Spoken with the true lack of understanding of someone who'd never had a fierce need to change. "How long can you wait?"

Still standing close to him, she drove him crazy with her scent. Meanwhile his wolf continued to fight for control inside him. "Not long," he rasped. "Not long at all."

Instead of moving away, she moved in closer, slipping an arm around his waist and pressing her side into his. He caught a whiff of her again, and more. This time, the tantalizing scent of desire drifted to him, igniting an answering fire inside him.

His body swelled and his wolf finally quieted. Waiting. Watching. Dangerous, that.

When she turned into him, he met her halfway. Hungrily, greedily, his mouth found hers. Like waves crashing against a sandy shore, desire rammed into him.

"Stop." The heavily accented voice had him jumping back guiltily. Katya. How had they managed to forget her? And who had given her so much authority?

"You will move apart this instant," Katya ordered, as if she had the right.

He was about to argue, but Alisa's touch on his arm carried a warning.

"Now!" Katya sounded both outraged and—as he'd known she would be—smug. "Get away from each other. Move. Right now."

Smiling faintly, Braden did as she requested. When Alisa clutched at his arm and refused to go, he wondered why.

Other footsteps entering the room alerted him that something was going on. He smelled the acrid odor of cigarettes and felt a flash of alarm.

"Braden," Alisa said, terror thrumming along the

perfect pitch of her voice, "we need to do as she says. Katya has brought armed men who are not with our protection detail with her. They have rifles, all aimed at us."

Chapter 17

The instant she saw the five men who entered with Katya, Alisa knew she was looking at the traitor. "You," she said, glaring at the other woman. "You've betrayed us."

"No," Katya snarled. "You're the one who's betrayed your own kind. You are an abomination." Her accent made the last word unintelligible, but Alisa got the drift.

Still. Katya as the enemy? Alisa could hardly come to terms with the idea. Katya's parents both worked in the palace and she herself had worked there since she'd been a teen. If anyone should have been loyal to the royal family, it was Katya.

Queen Ionna had even made her Braden's assistant, which perhaps was not so different from personal assistant to the queen.

"What is this?" Alisa demanded, as Katya and her

contingent of men pointed their wicked-looking silver pistols and long, black rifles at them. "Why have you turned against us? We've always been good to you."

Briefly, Katya lowered her gaze, showing she felt some measure of shame. But a moment later when she raised her chin again to face them, Alisa saw nothing but defiance in her hazel eyes.

"None of that matters now," Katya said softly, her tone unapologetic and strident. "This began when I was still a small child. When my people learned about you and what you can do, we began to see what you wanted to turn us into. You wish to erase the Pack from the face of this earth."

"That's not true! I—"

"Silence," one of Katya's men roared. "We are not here to debate with you the right and wrong of what we have done. You are our prisoners. You will do as we say."

"I am your princess," Alisa began.

"Shut up," the man ordered. When she opened her mouth again, he actually dared to raise his hand as though he would slap her.

Next to her, Braden made a sound of protest. Alisa squeezed his arm hard, begging him to be silent. After all, they might find him expendable while she, clearly, was not.

"Six of you," Alisa said scornfully, wanting to give Braden an idea of what they faced. "Katya, you brought five armed men to subdue a woman and a blind man?"

Busy squinting at her down the barrel of her shiny gun, Katya didn't answer, though one of her men must have understood English since he flashed Alisa a savage grin.

"We did not want to take any chances," he said.

As a matter of fact… Alisa did a double take. He looked familiar. Very familiar. An instant later, she realized where she'd seen him before. He'd been one of the men in the grainy video back at the palace, one of the three who'd posed as royal guards.

Braden's head snapped up. Apparently he'd recognized the voice as well. "Rok."

The other man's grin widened. "You've got a good ear."

Expression hard, Braden nodded. "I assume Igor and Thomas are here also?"

"That's right. They both have weapons pointed directly at you and the princess."

"Good." Jaw clenched, Braden looked furious. "As I remember, they do speak English, correct?"

"Only a little," Rok said. "Katya and I and George over there are the best English-speakers."

George was the one who'd acted like he wanted to hit her. Alisa filed this name away for good measure. If she ever escaped from this mess, she'd be sure that one was punished.

Evidently, Braden had a similar idea.

"Since they speak limited English, Rok, I want you to pass them this message for me. I want to make sure they understand it. Tell them when this is over, I intend to make them pay for what they've done."

Staring, Rok appeared unsure whether or not to take him seriously. Evidently, he decided he would not, because he laughed. "I'll do that," he said. "Another time."

Braden jerked his head in a nod.

"Now," Rok's amused tone changed, becoming icy and brisk. "We're going to have to split you two lovebirds up. You, Dr. Streib, will be coming with me and my men. Princess Alisa, Katya and two guards will escort you to your chambers."

Bad idea.

"I'd prefer to stay together." Alisa lifted her chin.

Again Rok laughed. "Your preferences mean nothing to me."

"He needs me," she elaborated. "I act as his eyes in unfamiliar places."

"Sorry. He'll just have to manage without you."

Trying to appear unconcerned, Alisa shrugged. "All right. I tried." She hadn't really thought they would let her, but at least she'd made the attempt.

"Let's go," Katya barked.

"Just a moment." Keeping her expression pleasantly blank, Alisa snagged her tote bag from the back of the chair. Her cell phone was inside and as soon as she could, she'd place a swift SOS call to Ruben.

"Let me have that." Without waiting for a response, Katya snatched the bag out of Alisa's hands. "I just need to take your phone."

Fishing the cell out, she turned it off before dropping it on the floor and smashing it to pieces with the heel of her boot.

"Next," she said, holding out her hand for Braden's.

Since he couldn't see, Alisa opened her mouth to tell him what Katya wanted. But before she could, Rok elbowed Braden in the side, hard enough to knock the breath from him in a startled *oomph.*

"Give her your phone," Rok barked.

"Consider yourself lucky you outnumber me," Braden snarled, his jaw clenched. Nevertheless, he dug his phone from his pocket and handed it over. It met a similar fate under Katya's heel.

So much for hope of escape. Struggling to control her racing heart, Alisa told herself they'd think of something. Of course they would. They had to.

Then Rok and his men surrounded Braden. Alisa stood watching helplessly as they slapped some sort of metal cuffs on him, hands behind his back, before he was taken away.

Marching along with his little contingent of guards, Braden knew he had to come up with a plan and quickly. Both his and Alisa's lives were in danger. What he didn't understand is why they'd been taken prisoner rather than simply killed on the spot, which would have been more logical.

Since the extremists didn't want them dead, obviously they wanted something else. But what?

As he was taken down the hall into another room, he cursed his lack of vision. Though he didn't want to be separated from Alisa, he went where directed, biting his tongue and wishing furiously that he could have one of those brief little episodes of sight. If only he could look upon the face of this man who sought to take everything from him. If only he could see his surroundings so he could judge the probability of escape.

No such luck. The ever-present darkness remained undisturbed.

"Your princess is going to die, unless you save her," Rok said. The heavily accented voice filled with hatred gloated, repulsing him. His wolf paced, fierce and furious and wild, ready to fight to be free.

Should he? Braden flexed his fists. Despite the fact

that they were chained behind his back, he had to suppress a desire to throttle the other man.

"In here." Rok shoved him in the back, sending him stumbling. He crashed into something made of metal. Window bars? Of course. To prevent his escape. Never mind that he had no idea what floor they were on, or what was actually outside the window. These people had planned for a situation, even the patently impossible.

Inside, his wolf roared, pushing impatiently to be set free. Braden's impotent anger fueled the beast.

Briefly, Braden considered his wolf's desire to change. Cuffed and chained as he was, the action would be foolish, especially since Rok was a shifter as well.

"Yes," Rok continued, as though Braden had responded to his earlier statement about Alisa. "Only you can keep her from dying a slow and horrifically painful death."

Again, Braden bit back a retort. If his captor wanted to torment him with words, Braden refused to give him the satisfaction of a reaction.

"Do you hear me, Dr. Streib?"

Slowly, Braden nodded, refusing to wince at the sharp pain the movement caused. "Have you hurt her?" he asked, demanding an answer. "What have you done to her?"

"She is being detained, like you."

"Is she hurt?" Braden took a step forward. "So help me, if you hurt her…"

The other man chuckled. "Threats? As if there was anything you can do, blind and bound and chained inside your little room. But I will tell you this—the princess is unhurt. As of right now."

Unconvinced, Braden lifted his hands. "Is she shackled like me? I don't think she'll be able to handle this. You mustn't put chains on her."

"You really care for her, don't you?" Rok seemed to find this hilarious. "Don't worry, she's fine. Her lily-white skin is unblemished. And her astounding ability to remain human still remains a secret, despite your attempts to discover how she does this."

"So you've been monitoring me. Since obviously you know I was not successful, why have you brought me here?"

"Unsuccessful?" Rok laughed again, the unpleasant sound skittering along Braden's nerves. "That's just it. About your research—your completely worthless research," he continued.

Braden refused to bristle. "What about it?"

"Don't you find it odd? You are, according to everything we read, the top Pack neurosurgeon in the world and one of our kind's foremost researchers. Yet with Princess Alisa, you failed miserably. Did you not wonder why you never found anything?"

Still refusing to be baited, Braden said nothing. His silence didn't seem to bother Rok at all.

"There's a reason for that," Rok continued. "Or, should I say, *we* are the reason for that."

Braden blinked. "Of course. How did I not see this before?"

Again Rok gave a chortle of mirth. "We've always had people working on the inside. Several people, actually. Katya served as your research assistant. Each time your results were loaded into that machine, she switched them for results we'd prepared in advance."

"You sabotaged me?" Though he still kept his face expressionless, Braden's heart raced. All this time, analyzing and re-analyzing test after test and finding nothing. No anomalies. Now he understood how such a thing could be possible. Someone had rigged his research to make sure he didn't find a single damn thing.

Which meant the answer—the key to Alisa's amazing abilities—was still out there waiting to be found. Unless it was all in her mind. Her amazingly strong willpower. He'd make sure they didn't learn about this.

Damn them all to hell.

"These tests," he said carefully. "My results. Did you have someone review them? Someone qualified?"

"We did." Rok sounded entirely too smug and self-satisfied. "We know what they say, but we did not have the opportunity to make your machine analyze them."

True. "That night you broke into my lab?"

"We'd planned to steal your machine. Only you showed up and stopped us. But this does not matter. After all, we knew you would wind up here as our prisoner eventually. You have your equipment, including that machine, and we have the actual test results. You will review them and when you have the results, you will share them with us."

And then you will die. The unspoken promise hung in the air like a poisonous mist.

As long as he had no illusions. Braden could see the logic in this and he was amazed that Rok believed he could actually live with it. Once he had the answer, he would be worthless to these people. Once he gave them what they wanted, he was as good as dead.

As was Alisa, he supposed. After all, what would they need her for once they knew all her secrets?

Of course, the machines would reveal nothing. He had to save her...

"Where is the princess?" he asked carefully. "And why do you wish to harm her?"

"Oh, *we* won't hurt her," Rok answered, sounding positively gleeful. "Not yet."

Again, Braden understood. As long as they needed her alive, Alisa was safe.

"Either way, Doctor, we've recalibrated your machines." Rok's voice now sounded cold. "I'll let your own machine give you your results in a language you'll understand. Remember, you have twenty-four hours to figure out what it is and to decipher the princess's secret."

Crossing his arms, Braden shook his head. Time to dig in his heels. "Why should I? You're going to kill me anyway. I think it's a safe bet that you won't be sharing my findings with anyone else. What's the point? What's my incentive to do the research now?"

"Ah, you think are a smart man." The smirk in Rok's voice set Braden's teeth on edge. "But you have missed one very important aspect to this thing. If you discover what gives the princess her special abilities, she will not suffer and we will let her live."

The raw hope slamming into him made his chest hurt. A second later, he cursed himself for a fool. "Once again, as you so succinctly put it, I am not stupid. If I discover the secret, you have no reason to let Alisa live."

"But we do. Because if her ability is genetic, it can be passed on. We will breed her and test the offspring."

This made no sense. He'd believed they wanted to *stop* the research. Not this.

Alisa as a brood mare? Every fiber of his being rebelled against the thought. This would be a life of pure hell, for both her and her children. He knew she would rather be dead. "I won't be a part of that."

"You have no choice. Either you do it, or we'll find another doctor. We don't need you as much as she does."

"Kill me now," Braden spat, hopefully somewhere near the other man. "Then you can go find some other doctor and pray he can interpret the test results."

Swearing a blue streak in Teslinkian, Rok grabbed Braden by the collar, and slapped him, hard enough to send him back into the hard stone wall behind him.

Cursing the darkness, cursing his bonds, Braden lurched forward, seeking some kind of retribution. Instead, Rok hit him again, twice as hard this time. Braden could feel the warmth of blood running down his split-open cheek.

"You will do what we tell you to do," Rok ordered. "Or your princess will die a painfully slow death in front of you. Too bad you won't be able to see it happen. Ah, well, hearing the sound of her screams will have to do."

Chomping down hard on the inside of his cheek, Braden nodded. Time. He needed time to try and figure things out. "I'll give you what you want. But I'll need my machines and all the results—the original ones that you took from me."

"They will be provided." Satisfaction rang in Rok's voice. "In a few minutes, guards will come to escort you to another room. The room is windowless and can only be entered by a six-inch-thick metal door. We have equipped it similar to a gas chamber."

Masking his rising horror, Braden winced. "You're going to kill me by gassing me?"

"If you don't achieve results, yes." The other man snickered. "All in all, it's not a bad way to die."

Easy for him to say. He couldn't possibly know about Braden's irrational claustrophobia. And, because if Rok did know, he'd use it to his advantage, Braden kept his mouth shut.

"Are you certain twenty-four hours is enough time?" Braden finally asked. "I'm certain there is a large amount of raw data to go through." Since he knew the data was worthless, he was merely buying time.

"Dr. Streib, we know as well as you do that your machine won't take long to give you results. I imagine it will be less than half an hour after you plug in the data and your computer reaches a conclusion."

"If you've reviewed the results..."

"We know what is wrong with the princess. You are absolutely correct. What we don't know is if this is what gives her the ability to remain human for so long. That is what we need you to tell us."

"Wrong with the princess?" Braden froze. "What do you mean, exactly?"

"You'll find out soon enough."

Braden scratched his head. "I don't understand. Why don't you just tell me? Why make me listen to all the results first, especially since you've given me such a short window of time?"

Rok went momentarily silent, though not for long. "Fine," he said, a grim satisfaction ringing in the harshness of his tone. "You want to know what's wrong with your princess? She has something on her brain."

"Something on her brain?" Braden had difficulty following Rok's line of thought. "Could you be a little more specific? What do you mean?"

"Remember when you took a CT scan early on in your visit?"

"And an MRI. Both of which showed absolutely nothing," Braden began, then realized that those results had most likely also been switched out. Again he cursed under his breath. So much time wasted.

"Oh, they definitely showed something," Rok practically chortled. "Now, I'm no doctor, but even I can tell when there's something in an X-ray that shouldn't be there. I'm thinking your princess has a tumor or something. Maybe cancer. Very advanced, I'd say, judging by the size of the blotch on her brain."

Blotch on her brain? In his career, he'd seen a thousand such films. None of them had boded well for the patient.

That didn't mean anything, he told himself firmly. Rok was not a trained medical professional. And who knows what he'd actually seen? For all he knew, the Teslinko machine was damaged, or faulty in some way. Still…

Braden opened his mouth, then closed it. "I doubt there is anything seriously wrong with her," he said coldly. "Princess Alisa has exhibited no other symptoms. No headaches, loss of balance, speech or thought problems. A subject with a dark spot on the film of the brain would exhibit some symptoms, especially in an advanced stage."

"All I know is that she has a dark spot—our doctors called it a mass—inside her brain. Some kind of tumor. I'm not a doctor. You are. You figure it out."

A mass? Alisa? Braden's heart stopped for a moment. Then, pushing himself into professional mode, he swallowed. "Did a Pack medical professional view the image, or is this just some local family practioner saying this?"

Coughing, Rok made a great fanfare out of chugging down some sort of drink and then clearing his throat. "We had a local doctor look at it. He's not Pack, but he is a doctor."

"You know our brains look different than those of humans."

"True, but not that different. If you could see the image, you'd know what I mean. Anyway, the doctor said it looked like a brain tumor to him. He advised us to get her to the hospital as soon as possible."

The MRI had been done weeks ago. Still, no reason to panic. He knew this better than most.

"There are over one hundred and twenty different types of brain tumors," Braden said coldly. "Many of those are not fatal and can be surgically removed. If this 'mass,' as you call it, even is a brain tumor, the location is of paramount importance. Regardless, it's highly unlikely a brain tumor would give Alisa—Princess Alisa—the ability to remain human longer than most. If anything, a large brain tumor would take away abilities rather than give them."

"Whatever." Rok sounded supremely unconcerned. "Our doctor seemed to think the prognosis was very bad. He specifically said that without surgery, she would die."

Damn. Suppressing the flash of panic, Braden straightened his shoulders. "Is he a neurosurgeon, then?"

"Like you?" Rok mocked. "No, he is not."

"Then there is no way for him to make such a determination." Braden suppressed his relief. "Many more tests would be necessary."

"Hmmm." Rock delivered his final comment. "Odd, then. Why don't you see if your machine agrees with him."

"I will." Braden trusted his machine. He'd designed the program himself. Still, even if she did have a brain tumor, this was not as worrisome as it would have been if she were human or Halfling. Since Alisa was a full-blooded shifter, she'd be all right. While tumors and cancer did occur among shifters, due to a full-blood's accelerated healing powers, such ailments were never fatal to them.

Halflings, on the other hand…

"Either way, fatal or not," Rok continued, almost as if he'd read Braden's mind, "the tumor itself is not that important to us. All we want to know is if that tumor has messed with her brain to the point where she can stay human longer. If it has, our scientists will try to figure out if the effect can be replicated artificially."

"Replicated? And endanger people's lives? Why? I thought you people were against the whole thing."

"We are against this, in the hands of others. But knowledge is power. Whoever controls that knowledge will have all the power." Rok laughed. "And we want that control."

About to speak, Braden inhaled sharply as the blackness lightened and a blurry image of a man—Rok—danced into focus before fading away. Gray to black. A fuzzy sort of light tantalized the edges of his vision before darkening to the complete and utter absence of the same.

He stood still for a moment, almost unable to believe it. Finally! These spells had been happening with much more frequency now, giving him tantalizing glimpses of restored vision. Which meant that regaining his sight was actually possible, though Rok didn't need to know that. He—as well as Alisa—were safer if Braden remained a blind man.

Hopefully, very soon, he would be able to see. Very, very soon. Before these crazy people had a chance to kill him and the woman he…

The woman he—what? Braden winced. No need to go there, not right now when the last thing he needed was any kind of distraction.

"Lead me to my machines," he said. "And if you want me to continue to research this, I'll need the princess as well. I'll need to rerun some of the tests, so I can check the accuracy of the results."

"I will think about that," Rok replied. "For now, you work alone."

"I won't get results as quickly."

"Twenty-four hours," Rok reminded him. "That's all you get."

And there it was.

Though he nodded, Braden knew that even if he did find something, he wouldn't reveal it to this man. And he'd continue to insist that he needed Alisa, just to keep her close in case a way opened up for them to escape.

He followed slowly as Rok took him to his machines.

"They have been loaded with the correct test results," the other man said, handing him his earphones.

"What if I need more time?" Braden asked.

"Work through the night."

As if he wouldn't already. Still, he had to do something to buy more time. "Seriously, I need—"

"Tick, tock." Rok laughed. And with that, he left,

closing the door behind him. A second later, Braden heard the latch turn and click, locking him in.

With a great sense of dread, he took a seat in front of his custom-designed diagnostic machine. Since Rok claimed they'd already entered in the actual data, he grabbed the remote and pressed the large play button.

A moment later, the robotic voice began to speak, confirming what Rok had told him.

Alisa had a primary brain tumor, very large in size, most likely a glioblastoma. These were very aggressive tumors that grew rapidly and tended to spread. Despite her full-shifter blood, she'd probably need to have surgery to have this tumor removed. Since she was full-blooded, it wouldn't kill her. But it could and would cause her major issues until her body overcame it. He couldn't help but wonder if this, rather than her strong will, was responsible for her extraordinary ability to remain human longer. Either way, the tumor had to go.

There was no one among the Pack better qualified to remove a glioblastoma of this size than him. Except for one huge problem. Unless he regained his sight, his blindness would prevent him from being able to operate.

His only other option would be to escape and bring her to Texas to see the Healer.

Chapter 18

A gloating Katya locked her in a small, windowless room that Alisa suspected might have once been a storage closet, and left. Feeling as though her breath had been cut off, Alisa began to pace. Not only did she hate being confined to small spaces, but being separated from Braden felt oddly akin to the sensation of missing a limb.

This was new and wasn't good. Despite making love, Braden still had not mentioned feeling connected to her in the way mates were. If he didn't…she'd have no choice but to learn to live without him. And if this awful, yearning ache was any indication, she'd be finding life after Braden unbearable, to say the least.

Assuming, that is, she lived that long. She didn't understand why the extremists had separated them to begin with. Actually, since they plainly viewed her as some sort of deviant, she wondered why they hadn't simply killed her on the spot.

Perhaps they realized the repercussions from her father and his allies would be too fierce. But they had to know also when her family realized she and Braden had been abducted, no stone would be left unturned as they searched for her. Maybe they intended to ransom her.

Pacing, she took a second look at her cell. Whatever the space's original purpose, no one had bothered to paint the gray cement walls or floor. Cold, damp and musty. This place looked like either a basement or a storm cellar. Either way, she saw no way to escape.

At least her prison cell had a small lavatory, complete with a sink and a commode. Every comfort of home, she told herself, furious at the knowledge that she was helpless, completely at their mercy.

While Braden… As she dropped onto the thin cot that comprised her bed, fear and anger knotted inside her. Were they torturing him at this very moment, seeking to pry information from him that didn't yet exist? Though she hated to think so, she had to be realistic. Otherwise, why would they have taken him?

Swallowing, she couldn't help but feel that this was all her fault. If only she could have been normal, at least on the surface. Such a thing would have been very easy to do. Just shape-shift at regular intervals and keep her mouth shut. No one would have been any wiser. Instead, she'd become a sort of minor celebrity among the Pack. The girl who wouldn't change.

She couldn't remake the past, but she sure as heck could try to influence the future. She'd have to watch, be vigilant, get ready to take a chance. As a royal, she had never lifted a hand to anyone or anything. These people wouldn't expect her to fight back. When the opportunity came, and she had to believe it would, she'd take it. For Braden, if not anything else. She couldn't let him pay for her imagined sins.

Though he didn't know it yet, every part of her belonged to Braden. Her heart, her body and her mind. As well as her wolf. Despite the apparent fact that he didn't feel the same, she believed he was her mate. Wolves mate once. When their mate dies, they remain alone for the rest of their lives.

And now, more than anything, more than she'd ever been in her entire life, Alisa was wolf.

Finally, from sheer exhaustion and lack of anything else to do, Alisa curled up on the cot and willed herself to go to sleep. Maybe then she could quiet the ever-present dull ache in the back of her head.

Trying to accustom himself to the knowledge that he would need to magically recover his sight so he could perform brain surgery on Alisa, Braden felt surprisingly numb. After all, he knew for a fact that miracles didn't happen. Though she wouldn't die, the tumor would begin to exact its toll on her in other ways. In time, she'd be little more than a vegetable, trapped inside a useless body.

He'd do better trying to figure out a way to get her out of here and take her to see the Pack Healer.

But to keep Rok from killing them both, he listened to all the data for the second time, and thought logically about the possibility that the tumor's location had some effect on Alisa's ability to remain human.

This was entirely possible. Tumors sometimes gave as well as took away.

He had to convince Rok to let him see Alisa. He'd never been a good liar, but he'd have to become one now. Unfortunately, he hadn't been given any way to communicate with the other man.

Lurching to his feet, he headed toward the wall, knowing if he felt along it far enough, he'd reach the door. Once he had, he began banging on it with his fists, hoping the noise would bring Rok running.

After a moment, his strategy worked. Rok banged back. Braden backed away. He heard the key turning the lock and then his captor entered the room.

"Do you have my answer already?"

Taking a deep breath, Braden shook his head. "No. There's an…anomaly in the test results. I need you to bring Alisa and let me rerun the tests on her."

"Absolutely not." Rok didn't even hesitate. "You've done every test possible. You should have more than enough to form an opinion."

"That's just it. You say you switched the results, but now you've replaced them. I performed two sets of tests—one on Alisa and one on me. I wanted to use my results as a measure against hers, especially the CT scan."

"So?" Rok sounded patently disinterested. "What do I care about your test results? It's the princess's we are interested in."

Dragging his hand through his hair, Braden forced himself to unclench his teeth and speak calmly. "The thing is, both Alisa's and my results are exactly the same."

"That's not possible," Rok responded immediately.

"I know it's not," Braden replied. "Something got

screwed up and now these CT scans are both invalid. I can't consider either of these to be remotely accurate."

"We don't have a CT scanner here." Rok sounded irritated. "You can do the blood work, but not that."

"No go. I need to redo those tests in particular."

Rok didn't respond. Braden waited him out. As lies went, this was a doozy.

"That couldn't be safe," Rok finally said, as if he cared. "Too much radiation."

"It is safe. It's been a few weeks." He took a deep breath. "Without this, I won't be able to reach any sort of valid conclusion. We see a brain tumor, yes. The CT scan is the preferred modality for cancer, pneumonia and brain tumors. I need this. On both of us."

"I'll get back to you," Rok said. A moment later the lock clicked behind him.

Braden could only hope his strategy would work. If he could get them both out of their prison, they might stand a chance of escaping.

An hour later, he heard the key in the lock, and the door opened.

The instant Alisa entered the room, Braden knew. His skin tingled and his entire body felt as though he had come alive after a long, numb sleep. Though it cost him, he forced himself to continue checking and rechecking the calibration on his machine without acknowledging her presence.

"We're going to the local hospital north of here," Rok said. "This is the closest place with a CT scanner. The hospital staff has been told that both of you are dangerous prisoners who must be kept shackled at all times."

"Fine," Braden said. "But take care how you treat the princess."

"Ah, yes, the princess." Now Katya spoke. "Rok, I'm worried that someone might recognize her. Therefore, we will be cutting her hair before we go."

Alisa made a small sound of protest. Not much. Braden figured she knew she didn't have a choice.

"Wouldn't it be easier just to make her wear a wig?" he asked, trying to spare her at least this indignity. "When we came here, she wore a wig as part of her disguise. Just let her use that."

"That won't work," Katya answered, her voice dripping malice. "The brain scan will reveal it. So it's a cut for her."

"Who cares?" Alisa put in. "So what if I'm wearing a wig? Lots of women do."

But Katya refused to be dissuaded, most likely because it would give her great pleasure to make the princess look as awful as possible.

Braden listened while they cut her hair, the few snips of the scissors no doubt radically altering her appearance, at least to those with eyes to see her.

Pretending not to care, he pushed his dark glasses up on his face. They'd allowed him to keep these with him, knowing a blind man was much too noticeable.

"Now no one will recognize you." Katya sounded triumphant and gleeful. "Amazing what a bad haircut can do to a woman."

"Yes," Rok agreed. "She looks awful, not at all like a princess. Good job, Katya."

Alisa's audible sniff told him how much this forced transformation pained her, though she didn't articulate her feelings out loud.

"You still look the same to me," he told her quietly when she came to stand near him.

To his gratification, she squeezed his shoulder. "Thank you."

On the ride to the hospital, they sat hip to hip. He had to continually remind himself not to lean into her.

"What's going on?" she asked quietly.

Aware they had an audience, he spoke in a low voice. "We need to rerun the CT scan," he told her. "On both of us."

"I don't understand. Why would—?"

"Silence," Rok ordered. "Don't make me separate you."

They fell silent. Braden kept his shoulder right up next to hers, hoping she drew some comfort from it.

Once they reached the medical facility, Rok made quick work of shuffling them in, surrounded by guards. "Dangerous prisoners," he repeated over and over.

Of course they were immediately rushed through and put in a separate waiting room. The staff, egged on by Rok, hurried them through the CT scans. Once that was over, Rok began to argue with the technicians who, according to Alisa, wanted to follow protocol and have the results read by their own staff doctor.

Best as Braden could make out, since he didn't understand the rapid-fire dialogue in Teslinkian, the staff adamantly refused to do as Rok wished.

Persistently, Rok continued to try and convince them to let him take the results back with him. They steadfastly refused, exactly as Braden had hoped they would. He knew the instant that they saw the huge and lethal brain tumor on Alisa's brain, they'd want her admitted to the hospital stat.

A full-blooded shifter could still function normally with a tumor of this size. A human should already be dead. As far as these medical professionals knew, Alisa was human. They had a duty to try and make her final hours or minutes pain-free.

And if he was correct, he had a pretty good idea how Rok and his goons would react to that.

Now would be their best chance to either escape or summon help. He just had to find a way.

While he waited, hands cuffed behind his back, side by side with a shackled Alisa, Braden leaned over and, in a whisper, asked her if there were any phones in the room. Getting to a wall phone would be tricky, but it was better than nothing.

"No," she whispered back. "Though someone left a cell phone on the counter in the small washroom. The door's open and I can see inside. Since there are huge signs stating all phones must be turned off, I'm betting that one is."

Rok and the CT technician were still arguing. Rok grew louder and more impatient. At any moment, Braden thought he might blow.

"We've got to get you in there," Braden told her. "If you can grab the phone, do so. If you have the opportunity, call for help. If not, pocket it."

"Very good, but how am I to get in there?"

"Faint or something. Say your head hurts and act like you need to vomit." Which would be more appropriate than she knew.

Without hesitation, she immediately cried out and doubled over. "My head hurts," she moaned. A second later, she began making very realistic retching sounds.

One of the technicians rushed up and hustled her to the bathroom. Rok paused in his tirade long enough to order Katya to accompany them. Braden could only hope Alisa managed to scoop up the phone before Katya got inside with her.

As the door closed behind Alisa, another door opened. Someone else entered the waiting room and clapped his hands for silence. Miraculously, it worked. The newcomer, in a loud and authoritative voice, introduced himself as Dr. Moray.

"This woman needs to be admitted to our hospital right away," he announced. "Her life is in serious danger."

Braden dropped his head so no one would see his expression. So far, everything was going exactly as he'd hoped.

"We'll take her ourselves," Rok said, suddenly sounding very calm.

A sharp pain began behind Braden's left eye, the beginning of a headache. Not now. Not now.

The bathroom door opened and Katya and Alisa must have come out, because one of the technicians jabbered something that must have been akin to "There she is."

"Ma'am," Dr. Moray began. "We need to escort you to Admitting. You have a massive brain tumor and—"

"Nobody move," Rok shouted. He and his cohorts must have pulled guns, because the room went completely silent.

Except for Alisa, who continued to moan. "My head, my head."

And then, in what Braden hoped was only the best acting he'd ever witnessed, she must have pretended to fall.

Now. While they were all distracted, he began frantically to work free of the handcuffs. Though it hurt like hell, and no doubt bled profusely as well, he finally was able to get his right hand out. Success!

"She's down!" Dr. Moray said. "Please, whoever you are. Put away your weapons and let me help this poor woman."

"She's not just any woman," Braden said loudly. "She's the princess. These people are terrorists and are holding us prisoner."

All hell broke loose. Katya began shouting—whether explanations or threats, Braden couldn't tell. He imagined all the extremists still had their guns drawn and, as he squinted in the general direction of where he'd last heard Alisa's voice, he realized the black had once again begun to fade to gray. Faint outlines—people, machines, guns—swam into focus.

His heartbeat stuttered. Now. Come on. *Now.* If the Healer had been right, if it was all in his mind, then he needed to overcome this immediately. If he could only believe. In himself. In the love he felt for Alisa. In his destiny.

He wanted his sight back. And, despite his complete lack of belief in miracles, with every bit of his dual nature, he willed it to be so.

Staring blindly out before him, glad he still had his sunglasses, he inhaled, his face tingling, his body vibrating with newfound confidence. The shapes began to solidify, take on color, a dazzling brightness.

He clenched his jaw to keep from revealing even the faintest hints of joy and wonder. And as his vision returned to him full force, he realized no one was paying even the slightest bit of attention to him. In fact, Rok stood with his back to him, a deadly-looking silver pistol trained on a tall, stoop-shouldered man who had to be Dr. Moray.

Turning his head, Braden quickly took in the entire situation. A slender woman who had to be Alisa lay slumped over, as if folded in on herself, moaning in what he prayed was false pain. Another woman, one with a hard face and cruel mouth, stood at her side, occasionally glancing down at her, but keeping her silver handgun trained on two plainly terrified women who wore scrubs that identified them as X-ray technicians. A third woman in scrubs crouched on the floor, trying to soothe Alisa.

A cold knot in his stomach, Braden knew he'd never have a better chance. He rushed forward, slamming into Rok from behind. Taken completely by surprise, the other man stumbled and lost his grip on his pistol. The weapon fell, clattering to the floor. Both Braden and Rok dove for it.

Pushing himself left as he fell, Braden knocked Rok out of the way and came up with the gun. Rolling, he leapt to his feet and jumped forward instead of back, toward the other man rather than out of Rok's reach. Grabbing Rok in a choke hold, Braden put the pistol at Rok's temple.

"If you move at all, I'll squeeze this trigger."

Rok froze. Good. Braden addressed Rok's crew next. "The rest of you drop your weapons or your leader dies."

No one moved. They all stared at him, as though debating the merit of disobeying his order. Finally, Rok barked out a command. "Do as he says."

To his immense relief, they finally laid down their weapons.

The police arrived moments later. They, along with

the legitimate members of the royal guard, rounded up the bad guys. Once they'd been placed inside holding cells pending transfer to the royal army, Braden waited anxiously while the human doctors tried to make Alisa comfortable. They wouldn't even let him in to be with her.

Pacing, Braden marveled in his renewed and restored vision, though he kept his dark glasses on out of habit. More than anything, he wanted to see Alisa, to make sure she was all right.

The tumor would have to be dealt with. He would, of course, offer his services as a surgeon or, if she preferred, he'd be glad to accompany her to visit the Healer in Texas. Unless her willpower was strong enough for her to destroy it on her own.

But more important, he wanted to, at least one time, gaze upon the face of the woman he now knew was his mate. The revelation stunned him every time he thought of it. Because he loved her, he knew it would be better not to tell her how he felt. Instead, he'd fade into the background and let her get on with her life as a royal princess. As for his research into her amazing gift, he suspected once the tumor was gone, so would her ability to remain human for extended periods of time. He doubted it had been done by her willpower alone, despite what she'd said.

Dr. Moray had kindly explained that the king and queen, as well as Prince Ruben, were on their way via royal helicopter. The good doctor expressed great concern about the fate of their daughter, believing—since he thought she was human—she had only a very short time to live.

Eyes burning from lack of sleep, Braden tried to persuade Dr. Moray to let him see Alisa alone. He finally convinced the other man to research him on the internet.

Immediately upon learning that Braden was a prominent neurosurgeon, and leaping to the understandable conclusion that Alisa was his patient, Dr. Moray agreed to bring Braden to see her.

"She might not recognize you," the other physician said, one colleague speaking to another. "We've got her on a morphine drip. Now I'll leave you to your patient."

Braden nodded, aware that morphine affected shifters the same way it did humans.

Finally, heart pounding triple-time, he stood in the doorway of Alisa's room. She lay on her back, the bed slightly elevated, hooked up to an IV, with machines beeping all around her as they monitored her vitals.

Her eyes were closed, lashes sweeping down on her high cheekbones as he approached. Chest aching, he let his gaze roam over her, hungrily taking her in. Her delicately carved features and creamy skin, the sensuality of her generous mouth, took his breath away. The awful, spiky haircut Katya had given her enhanced rather than detracted from her femininity.

His breath caught in his throat. He didn't understand why she thought she wasn't pretty. In his eyes, she was the most beautiful woman he'd ever seen. No one other than her would ever have his heart.

But she had her own life to live, her own destiny to fulfill as a royal princess. He had no doubt she'd accomplish great things, if she wasn't led astray from her fated path by a man who wasn't nearly good enough for her. He could imagine the huge rift in her family, knew if she chose him, she'd lose everything she'd ever loved.

And because she deserved better than that, he turned

and left her room without speaking. He'd wait for the king, offer his services as surgeon and, unless they took him up on it, catch the first flight for home. Alone.

Lulled by the drugs coursing through her system, Alisa barely woke for the transport back to the palace. Ruben rode with her in the helicopter and held her hand, telling her in a low voice that the extremists had surrendered and were even now naming their accomplices.

Though she nodded groggily and tried to comprehend his words, she could barely keep her eyes open. Despite the morphine, she ached for Braden and realized he should have been here somewhere, but couldn't form a coherent enough thought to vocalize her concern.

When she woke again, she was in a bed in a private hospital near the palace. Pushing herself up on her elbows, she looked around the room, taking in the numerous, extravagant floral arrangements. Both King Leo and Queen Ionna were seated in high-backed chairs at the side of her bed.

Her mouth was dry. Licking her lips, she spied a water glass on the bed table and reached for it. The water was cold, hurting her throat.

Taking her hand, her mother explained why she was there.

"A brain tumor?" Alisa couldn't help looking past her parents. "Where's Braden, er, Dr. Streib?"

"He went back to America," her father said gently. "Now that his sight has returned, he has offered to perform the operation to remove the tumor if you'd like. Unless, of course, you feel you can take care of this on your own."

Dazed, she tried to understand. Dimly she remembered Braden jumping Rok. At the time, she'd wondered how he'd been able to leap so accurately, but her pretend headache had become startlingly real. The other words—tumor, surgery—had less of an impact than the thought of Braden being able to operate. "He can see?"

"Yes."

Again she looked around the sterile room, at the riotous color of the exotic flowers, and at her parents' worried faces. "Why am I here? You know this brain tumor cannot kill me. In fact, I can probably shrink it."

"True, but it can incapacitate you. After all, you weren't even aware of it." The king sighed. "Plus, due to what happened at the seaside hospital, the news of your tumor is all over the press. We had to move you to this Pack hospital so no one would talk."

"Of course." Numb inside, she gave them a polite smile. She'd deal with the tumor later. More important was the fact that Braden could see. "I'd like to leave now. I've got a plane to catch. I'm going to find Dr. Streib. May I use the private jet?"

"Of course." The tiny frown that marred her mother's perfect forehead cleared. "You're going to let him operate?"

Swinging her legs over the side of the bed, Alisa asked for her clothes. "I don't know yet. I've got to speak with him first." She had to know the truth. Did he feel the same as she—that they were mates? Or was she just another research subject?

Working late had become the norm in the ten days since arriving home from Teslinko. Braden's staff had been ecstatic to learn he'd regained his sight. The specialists at first had been skeptical, until he passed every test with flying colors. He got his surgical status reinstated with the state medical board, and threw himself right back into work.

"Your three o'clock appointment is here, Doctor," his secretary Mary announced, sounding oddly excited. "She's requested a private consultation. We've put her in exam room seven."

Distracted, he looked up from his computer and nodded. As per protocol, he'd begun to document the results of his testing on Alisa, including his suspicion that the large tumor was responsible for her abilities. He'd present this document to the next meeting of the Pack Medical Board.

This should have been gratifying, but he felt only hollow. The excitement he'd once found in his vocation, the joy he'd once gotten from his work, all that seemed to have vanished. For the first time in his life, he'd begun to consider taking some sort of sabbatical.

Hitting Save, he pushed his chair back. Now that he could see again, he'd gone back to the gym and resumed riding his bike around the hills of Boulder. It was still slow going—he knew he had to build up to where he'd been before. But he was getting there.

He'd begun healing the rest of his body, but he wondered if he'd ever repair the hole in his heart. He'd never be the man he'd once been, thanks to Alisa. Somehow he couldn't help but think he was better off now. And he hoped she was as well.

Shrugging off the sudden melancholy that thoughts of her brought, he straightened his shoulders and strode down the hall to exam room seven. He opened the door and his practiced greeting froze on his lips.

Alisa. Perched on the exam table, legs swinging, the ghost of a smile curving her sensual lips.

Alisa. His breath caught. He felt like he'd been punched in the gut.

"Hello, Braden," she said, gazing at him steadily.

As though her essence pulled him, he stepped closer. Her eyes—he hadn't seen her eyes before—were the color of sea foam and glowed as though lit from within by golden fire.

"What are you doing here?" he asked, belatedly realizing she must have come to talk about the surgery. Jamming his hands into his lab coat pockets so she wouldn't see how they shook, he wondered if he'd be physically capable of operating on her.

She cocked her head to one side. The awful short haircut had been professionally styled, and perfectly framed her gamine face, giving her an ethereal beauty.

"I never figured you for a coward, Braden. You ran off without a word to me. So I traveled all the way to America to get an explanation."

During the flight home, he'd composed a hundred viable explanations, thinking perhaps he'd write her a letter or send her an email. All of those vanished as he inhaled her vanilla-peach scent and ached to touch her once again.

Nodding, he realized he could only give her the truth. He owed her that much.

"I'm no good for you," he said. "There are a thousand reasons why your parents wouldn't let us be together, and they're right. You're young, you're beautiful, and you deserve so much better than anything I could offer you."

Lowering her thick lashes, she nodded. His gut

clenched. While he knew he was right, he hadn't thought she'd agree with him so readily.

When she raised her gaze to meet his, the emotion he saw blazing there made his breath catch.

"You didn't feel I deserved to make my own choice?"

"I didn't even think there was any such option."

"Just like you didn't believe you could see again?" she shot back. "And as soon as you became whole, you didn't need me anymore."

He made a choked, desperate sound. "It wasn't like that. It was never like that."

Looking away, she bit her lip. "I have an appointment to see the Healer. The day after tomorrow. Though I can probably deal with this tumor myself, I don't want to take the chance. Will you come with me?"

Relief flooded him, both that he wouldn't have to operate, and that she had taken steps to make herself well. "Of course I will," he told her. "I've got to let her know I can see again."

She made a choked sound. To his consternation, her beautiful eyes filled with tears. "That is the true miracle. Do you have any idea what happened?"

You happened, he wanted to say. *My mate.* But he didn't dare. Instead, he simply shrugged.

"About that," she finally said. "I'm happy for you. But I never minded your blindness, you know."

Caught off guard, he wasn't sure what she meant.

"I love you, Braden Streib." Pushing herself up from the table, she flung herself at him. "With or without the ability to see. And I know you love me. I dare you to tell me you don't."

He wrapped his arms around her convulsively, unable to help himself. And when she lifted her face to his, he couldn't hold himself back from kissing her.

The instant he did, all his doubts vanished. "I do love you," he said, nose against hers, his heartbeat slow and steady and sure. "But I can't let you ruin your life."

Eyes flashing, she pulled away, holding him at arms length. "Ruin my life? You would condemn me to a fate of royal dinners and putting up with all those idiots who wish only to marry me for my title and my money?"

"And your beauty," he couldn't resist pointing out.

With a snort of derision, she shook her head. "I'm average, nothing more."

"Why do you believe you're not beautiful?" he asked, touching her silky short hair, still awed by the love he saw in her doe-like green eyes. He could see his own reflection there. Love bouncing right back at him. A second miracle, and one he'd tried foolishly to turn his back on.

She ducked her head to hide a pleased smile. "You can only say that because you've never seen my sisters."

Tentative joy blooming in him, he kissed her again.

"I'm never going to let you go," she told him fiercely, when they came up for air. "Mates are like that."

Tightening his arms around her, he nodded. "They are. Alisa, I wasn't brave enough to hope for a future with you. My own fears nearly cost me my heart. I won't make that mistake again."

"I should hope not." With a happy sigh, she snuggled against him. "And before you ask, yes. I'll marry you. My father approves and my mother is already planning the wedding."

"They don't have a problem with you marrying a commoner?" he asked, surprised.

She grinned, looking fierce and vulnerable, all at once. "After what happened with the brain tumor, I was able to persuade them it was a good idea to have a neurosurgeon in the family."

He gave a short bark of laughter, before claiming her mouth again. He had a feeling he was in for a lifetime of surprises, spent with this princess by his side.

"Mate," she reminded him, as though she could read his thoughts.

He nodded, reaching deep inside for his wolf and finding the beast approved. "Once you're better, do you want to celebrate with a run in the woods? Wolf to wolf, true mates together."

Her eyes lit up and she nodded. "Definitely. And just think, we can hunt together for the rest of our lives. Mates do that, you know."

Leaning in, he kissed her. "I didn't, not really, but I'm a quick study. And I'm sure you'll show me, especially since we have the rest of our lives to do it."

Kissing him back, she promised. "I will."

"For the rest of our lives."

* * * * *

ONE EYE OPEN

To my best friend and critique partner, Anna Adams, for all your valuable insight and immeasurable support—thanks from the bottom of my heart. And to Lucienne Diver, my agent. Your unflagging belief and enthusiasm have meant more than I can ever express. I appreciate you dearly.

Chapter 1

"I never pay for sex."

It took a minute for the tall man's words to register. When they did, Brenna suppressed a smile. "That's good, because I'm not selling it." She couldn't blame him for thinking she worked the seedy bar. Apart from two waitresses, she *was* the only female in the place. And the snug fit of her worn jeans with the black leather vest didn't help, either. Maybe that explained why she felt as if she was being watched.

"I want to talk to you."

The corners of his mouth twisted. "Sure you do."

She took a deep breath. "I heard you're looking for The Wolf."

Icy contempt flashed dark in his eyes. "Maybe."

"I have information," she lied. "I know him well."

From his skeptical expression, she could tell he didn't believe her.

"We need to talk." Though insistent, she kept her voice low, showing none of her rising impatience.

"Outside. That is—" his gaze slid over her, dismissing her too-suggestive apparel with a frown "—if you can stand the cold."

She'd worn the biker clothing to fit in. Gritting her teeth, she nodded once. Her heavy parka lay on the bar stool next to her. She picked it up and slid her arms into the sleeves without answering.

Outside, the full moon shone bright and silver through the threadbare tangle of trees that fringed the small parking lot. If she'd been a Hollywood-style werewolf, this man would be dead, his throat ripped out in seconds.

"Look, before we start—"

"I seldom pay for information, either," the man drawled. "And then only from known sources."

His words barely registered. There was something else… She sensed a threat in the frozen night breeze. Carefully she let her gaze drift past him to the dark and shadowy underbrush that surrounded them. Though she couldn't put her finger on it, there was wrongness to the night.

Someone was watching them.

Every nerve on edge, she forced her attention back to the stranger. "I don't want money. I want an even exchange. My info for yours."

His dark brows lifted. "What makes The Wolf your business?"

She would tell him her name, in case he knew of her. "I'm Brenna."

"So?" He made a dismissive motion with one gloved hand.

So he didn't know. Time, then, to play her trump card. "The Wolf is my brother."

Nothing on his rugged face indicated she'd shocked him. Instead, his insolent gaze again raked over her, making her shiver despite the warmth of her parka and relative anonymity of her hood.

"Sure he is."

Hounds help me, she thought, and clenched her jaw. "I'm telling the truth."

"Alex doesn't have a sister." His voice sounded flatly certain.

The use of her brother's first name jarred her. But only for a second. "You talk like you know him."

"I do—or did."

She cocked her head, considering. "He never mentioned you. Are you a friend?"

Instead of answering, he took a step closer. "Alex always said he had no family."

That stung. But only for a moment. Most likely Alex had tried to protect her.

Since she couldn't speak her thoughts out loud until she determined this man's intent, Brenna contented herself with a small smile and a shrug.

"Maybe you didn't know him as well as you thought."

He conceded her point with a dip of his head. "So you're a biker babe, huh? You don't look it now."

She dismissed the inconsequential remark with a shrug. "How I look doesn't matter. Your purpose for hunting my brother does. Why do you want him?"

His jaw tightened. "Personal reasons."

"Not an answer. Friend or foe?"

He laughed then, his breath a plume of white frost in front of his face. "Look, lady, it's ten below. I don't have the time or the inclination to stand here all night. Do you have information or not?"

Her sense of *wrongness* increased. The back of her neck tingled. Every sense urged her to change, which meant the danger was great indeed. She needed to stall this man until she could assess the risk, take care of it and then somehow get the information she needed.

But how? Ever since this stranger had appeared in the same places she'd haunted, asking questions about her brother, the same questions she herself had asked, she'd planned this confrontation. While normally her kind avoided conflict, retreating into the shadows, she'd known if she wanted to find Alex she had no choice but to deal with the threat, face-to-face.

"My information for yours." Lifting her chin, she tried to scent the night air unobtrusively. "You go first."

Harsh lines in his face belied his anger. "I could run a check on you. One phone call and I'll know everything about you."

She stared. "Are you threatening me?" Humans usually had sharper instincts.

"If you have reason to feel threatened."

If he looked for arrest information on her, he would find nothing. She'd never broken a law in her life. Since blending in with humans was one of her people's first and most important rules, she, like most others of her kind, lived an exemplary life. She worked as the sole librarian in the tiny upstate New York town where she lived. A librarian on leave.

Having no fears of a police record, Brenna studied the human. His dark eyes carried many shadows; his rugged features bore an unmistakable stamp of pain.

She needed to find out what this man knew about her brother. Without causing him harm, if possible.

Though patience had never been her strongest virtue, she took a deep breath. "Please. I need to know. Why do you want to find Alex?"

He took a step closer, his long shadow menacing, though he kept his hands jammed in his coat pockets. "Do you know what your brother is?"

His words slipped like icicles down the back of her parka. "I do," she retorted, though she knew they were speaking of different things. "The question is, do you?"

A metallic click from the trees behind them made her spin. She'd once had the misfortune of being in the forest during deer hunting season, and she recognized the sound.

"Down!" she yelled, dropping to the pavement at the same time. To his credit the big man didn't hesitate, going to the ground immediately. A millisecond later the sharp crack of a gunshot confirmed her guess. With her preternatural hearing, she heard the bullet whiz past harmlessly.

Immediately another shot rang out, again barely missing them. She stayed down. Though she had many powers, immortality was not one of them. A bullet would do the same damage to her that it would to any human.

Her companion swore. "Stay here." Without waiting to see if she would obey his terse order, he was up and running for the trees, crouched low. Bemused, she watched him go, though her senses told her the shooter had fled.

Who had shot at them? Though this man's questions bothered her people, she doubted any of them would take such a drastic step. Especially since she was the only one who truly believed Alex's life was in danger. She alone was hunting for him; her goal was to find her brother and make certain he was safe. The sudden appearance of this stranger with his numerous questions worried her, confirmed her fears. Alex was in grave danger.

Again she inhaled. The icy sigh of the winter wind in the trees told her that the danger was past. Standing, she wiped the snow off the front of her wet jeans and waited for the stranger to return.

A moment later he did, jogging awkwardly in the soft snow. He slowed as he approached her. Narrow-eyed, he shot her a look more icy than the glaciers of her ancestral homeland.

"Who was it?" Moving with a speed that startled her, he grabbed her arm. "Are you with them?"

Anger flared, clogging her throat. Jerking away, she stepped backward. "With whom?"

"Right." He cocked his head. "I'm taking you into custody."

Custody. "So you are a cop?"

"Of sorts."

"Odd choice of words." Hands on hips, she stared at him, unafraid. "So you think you're arresting me? For what?"

"Your own protection, maybe?" His deep voice dripped with sarcasm.

"I had nothing to do with that gunshot."

"Maybe you did and maybe you didn't. Still, they've been trying to kill me for a long time. I wouldn't put it past them to send a woman. Either way, you're coming with me. As insurance."

About to protest again, Brenna reconsidered. Going with this man might not be a bad thing, especially since she had no other leads to Alex's whereabouts. If she spent more time with this stranger, she might be able to get him to tell her what he knew. And if his intentions were evil, her physical presence might help keep her brother safe.

But she would make him suspicious if she seemed too eager.

"I don't even know your name," she said. "Or who you are or what exactly you do."

"Well, Brenna." The menacing way he spoke made her wonder. "You've had the bad luck of trying to prey on a DEA Agent. Special Agent Carson Turner. Pleased to meet ya."

Stunned more by his word choice—how he had known that she'd considered him prey—Brenna simply stared. After a moment she realized he was waiting for her to respond.

"D…E…A." She enunciated each letter deliberately. "Interesting."

"Come on." Indicating a snow-covered SUV, he reached again for her arm. "Let's go."

With a simple step she evaded him. "I want proof."

"Proof?" All but snarling the word, he reached into his pocket and, fumbling with his gloved fingers, withdrew a plastic-covered ID, holding it up for her inspection.

"'Drug Enforcement Agency,'" she read out loud. "'Carson Turner, Justice Department.'"

"Yeah." Pocketing the ID, he flashed her a humorless smile. "That's me. Now get in the car."

She examined the black Tahoe parked to the side. It

was one of only two four-wheel-drive vehicles amid the seven or eight motorcycles in the parking lot. He pressed his remote control, and the vehicle lights flashed as the doors unlocked.

"I need to get my bag from the car." She started forward.

"I'll get it," he said. "Toss me your keys."

Without another word she did as he asked. So he worked for a government agency—was that good or bad? Since Alex wouldn't do anything illegal, what would the DEA want with him? No one in the Pack used drugs of any kind. Doing so could seriously impair the ability to change, causing far greater damage than any brief moment of pleasure would be worth.

Climbing in after her, Carson tossed her duffel bag in the backseat and started the engine, turning on his wipers to clear the powdery snow from the windshield. She waited until he'd backed from the parking lot and pulled out onto the road before trying again.

"Tell me what you want with my brother."

He gave a rude snort, shooting her a look of fury that felt like a slap. "I thought you said you knew what your brother was."

Holding on to the shreds of her patience, she gave a slow shake of her head. "Alex disappeared over a year ago. No one in the Pack—" she stopped, heart in throat, then shook her head "—I mean, no one in my family has heard from him. I'm worried."

Only the quiet rumble of the motor broke the silence.

"You know, if I didn't need to keep my hands on the wheel, I'd clap," he said. "You sound really sincere. Family. Right. Academy Award material, that."

She gave him a blank look. "I don't understand."

"I'm not going to argue the point now, but I'll tell you what—" disdain underscored his savage tone "—when you level with me, I'll level with you."

Having learned long ago that there was no way to deal with irrationality, she stared out the window at the dark landscape as it flashed past. Being called a liar was a new experience and one she couldn't say she particularly liked.

But none of that mattered. None of it mattered at all, if she could only find her brother and make certain he was safe.

"What, no elaborate explanations?" Carson taunted. "Surely Alex gave you a better cover story than that."

"Enough." Turning to look at him, she was careful not to show her teeth. "If you really believed I was a criminal, you would have searched me for weapons before allowing me in your truck. You'd need a hell of a lot more proof of some kind of crime before you could legally arrest me."

He swore under his breath. She continued as if she hadn't heard him.

"So, in the spirit of honesty—and legality—" she allowed a trace of her own anger to show in her voice "—why don't you tell me why you're looking for my brother? Or I'll start to believe—" she met his stare directly, ignoring the cynicism she saw there "—that you yourself are engaged in some sort of illegal activity. I won't allow you to threaten my family."

"Won't allow?"

Though she'd spoken one of the most important creeds of the Pack, he didn't seem to recognize it, which was good.

"No."

He smiled. "Short and sweet. I like that."

Crossing her arms, she waited. Finally he shrugged. The look he gave her was laced with mistrust.

"Ever heard of Hades' Claws?"

Puzzled, she mentally reviewed every magazine article she'd read, every television show she'd watched, in preparation for this trip. "No."

His mouth thinned. "Right. The Wolf is your brother, but you don't even recognize the name of his biker gang?"

Biker gang? No way. Not Alex. Like her, he'd gone to college, gotten a good job. He worked in marketing, with a large Long Island firm.

"You must be mistaken," she said, her certainty showing in the flatness of her normally melodic voice. "Alex doesn't even own a motorcycle."

"Then why did you call him The Wolf? And why were you looking for him in a biker bar?"

She frowned. "The Wolf has been his nickname ever since third grade. And I heard he'd been to that bar, that's all."

With a quick motion, he peeled off his right glove, keeping his left hand on the wheel. Reaching into his coat pocket, he pulled out a much-folded sheet of paper and handed it to her.

Though grainy, the black-and-white photo in the center of the page was unmistakable. Alex.

Quickly she scanned the text. An FBI datasheet, the paper went on to describe how a biker gang, Hades' Claws, had committed numerous crimes, including several drug-related murders up and down the East Coast. Her brother was believed to be one of its high-ranking members and was wanted for questioning.

Feeling numb, she handed the paper back to Carson.

Accepting it, he kept his bleak stare on the darkened road ahead.

"Time to share again," he said. "Since you know why I'm looking for The Wolf, now you can tell me who shot at us."

She raised a brow. "Why do you think I would have that information?"

"You obviously were forewarned. You knew when to hit the ground."

"I heard the gun cock."

"Right," he said. "Who was the shooter?"

"I really don't know." She shrugged, careful to keep her expression neutral, while her head spun and her heart ached. Was the datasheet right? Was her brother hiding because he'd turned to crime? Or, as her premonitions suggested, was he in real danger?

"Damn." Carson went still, focusing on the rearview mirror.

Glancing over her shoulder, she saw headlights approaching fast on the otherwise deserted road.

"Are they—"

"Hold on." His low-voiced order was terse. He accelerated. The Tahoe leaped forward. The speedometer crept past eighty, then eighty-five. Ninety. The cab began to vibrate. She hoped that the road would remain straight and flat; at this speed, the slightest curve might send them into a skidding rollover.

Checking to make sure her seat belt was securely fastened, Brenna glanced over her shoulder. If they were going over ninety, the other vehicle had to be traveling in excess of one hundred, for it still seemed to be steadily gaining on them.

"I can't kill the headlights." Carson swore again.

A green highway sign loomed ahead. Wicket Hollow—One Mile.

"I'm gonna take it," he said. Still, he kept his foot on the accelerator, his hands locked in place on the steering wheel.

"Not at this speed. If we crash—"

"We won't."

Oddly enough, his calm certainty appeased her. She bit the inside of her cheek, forcing herself to relax her death grip on the door handle.

She told herself not to be afraid. Yet one thing kept running through her mind. If they crashed and she was mortally injured, she would be unable to keep from changing. She would have to drag herself away from the crash scene and die in her natural state far from human eyes. This was the law of her people. To do otherwise would risk bringing discovery and possible ruin upon them all.

Closing her eyes, Brenna began to plan. Just in case.

"There's the exit."

At his words, she opened her eyes. "Too fast," she snapped, as they blasted past the sign and left the highway.

"Seventy-five." Satisfaction sounded in Carson's voice. "One curve, then, straight shot."

She sat up. They were on the access road. Trees blocked the highway from view.

"Are they gone?"

"Not yet." Violence still sounded in his voice. "There." Pointing to a dirt road that wound into the trees, he killed the headlights and slowed. Pulling into a thicket, he parked.

Then they waited, the sound of their mingled breathing harsh and loud in the quiet interior.

A moment later a vehicle sped past, too quickly in the darkness for Brenna to make out its type.

"Hummer," Carson said, as if he'd read her mind. "Dark colored—black, brown or blue. Whoever they are, they've got money."

Swallowing, she nodded. Still her heart pounded in her chest. She willed it to slow.

"We need to go," she said.

"In a minute." Leaning against his door, Carson spread his arm comfortably along the back of the seat. "Why don't you start talking? Are these the same people who shot at us?"

"I don't know."

"Enough lies." His tone lined with steel, he sat up and dropped his arm.

When she only stared silently at him, he swore again, his mouth twisting. With a savage flick of his wrist, he started the ignition. Once out of their hiding place, he pulled back onto the highway, continuing north.

Brenna watched the speedometer climb to eighty again, unable to resist a quick glance behind them at the now-deserted highway.

"No headlights," Carson confirmed. "Tell me the truth. Are you working with them?"

"Working with—" She shook her head. "Of course not. I don't believe in random violence."

He regarded her strangely. "Your brother does."

"My brother's in trouble," she muttered. "I don't know how or why, but he is."

His short bark of laughter contained no humor. "In trouble? Of course he is. Besides having the DEA, ATF and FBI after him, he has to worry about rival gangs. It's only a matter of time until one of us finds him. I wouldn't want to be in your brother's shoes right now."

There was something in his voice. Pain. Bitterness. Rage.

"It's more than that with you," she said, keeping her eyes on his shadowed profile.

At that his head snapped up, his gaze icy again. "What do you mean?"

"You're too angry. With you, it's personal."

She thought he might deny it, even as the fury that momentarily darkened his eyes betrayed him. But after a moment of chilly silence, he gave her a cold smile and nodded.

"My wife and daughter are dead because of Hades' Claws." He might have been discussing the weather, so remote was his voice. "They thought they'd killed me, too."

His unspoken anguish sliced through her, sharper than any knife. "Were you shot?"

"In the back. I nearly died. Now I want the ones who killed my family."

She swallowed. "Surely you don't think Alex was part of that."

"Yeah, actually, I do."

She couldn't believe it. There were a hundred reasons why Alex couldn't be the killer he sought, but she couldn't give him any of them.

"Now." With one hand on the steering wheel, he grasped her chin with the other. "I want the truth. Are those goons who shot at us and chased us Hades' Claws?"

Furious, Brenna tried to pull away, but he wouldn't

let her. "How would I know? If Alex is, as you say, involved with this gang, he wouldn't let them endanger me."

His expression turned dark. "They want me dead. They should have killed me when they had the chance. Now they'll have to wait until I'm done."

"Wait until—" She stared at him. "Are you saying you want to die?"

"Not until I find the people who destroyed my life."

He hadn't said no. What kind of man…? But she knew. He hurt. Like a wounded animal, Carson would seek death rather than continue to endure horrific pain.

Shaken, she looked away. There was no way she could fathom such grief.

"If you're in on this, now's your chance to come clean. I can get you government protection if you testify."

"I'm not in on anything. Alex would never…" She didn't bother to finish.

"I'll shut up about it for now," Carson finally said. "But if you're not with them, you're in danger. Hades' Claws mean business."

This time she smiled. "I can take care of myself."

"Sure you can." His mocking tone belied his words. "If you really are Alex's sister, you'd be real good at looking out for number one."

Every time he spoke her brother's name, she could taste the hostility.

"I *am* his sister," she said. "And if you knew him at all, you would understand why I can't believe my brother killed your family." The words stuck to her tongue. She tried again. "I don't understand how you can think he did."

He spoke a vile word under his breath. In the dim light, his features appeared savage, so like one of her people at the moment of change that she stared.

"Understand this, then. I was there. I was shot, but I saw Alex. He had a gun."

Chapter 2

Stunned, Brenna swallowed. "Alex couldn't," she stammered, her words trailing off at the cynical certainty she read on his face.

"The killing was a test to determine Alex's loyalty. They said he passed with flying colors."

A sound escaped her, something between a plea and a moan. She had read about this case. "The newspapers said 'an unnamed biker.'"

"Innocent until proven guilty. How could you not know? You're his sister." He made the simple sentence sound like a curse. "Or so you claim."

He thought her brother was a murderer. Worse, he believed she knew and was lying through her teeth. Her throat felt tight, closed in. She couldn't seem to get enough air. She forced herself to breathe deeply. To swallow then lift her head and look directly at Carson

Turner, unflinching. Alex couldn't have done what this man claimed.

"There has to be some other explanation," she said. "You were shot. In pain. Maybe you saw wrong. Alex isn't a murderer."

Though in effect she'd just called him a liar, to his credit he didn't threaten or sneer. He didn't open the door and shove her out with a wave and a quick *hasta la vista,* baby. No, Carson did none of those things. He merely continued to regard her much like a wolf watches a rabbit caught in a snare, waiting for her to prove her statement.

But she couldn't, not in words he would believe. She hadn't been there; she hadn't seen her brother with a smoking gun. Carson had. Or thought he had.

"What kind of trouble are you in?" Carson asked, breaking into her chaotic thoughts.

Still silent, she shook her head, raising her hands, palms up, in a gesture meant to convey ignorance.

His mouth twisted. "If you want me to help you, you're gonna have to tell me."

Startled, she met his gaze. "Help me? Why would you do that?"

"Because whoever you are, I'm stuck with you right now." His sour tone left no doubt as to his feelings about the situation. "If you really are Alex's sister, having you with me might help me get his attention. If you're not…" he shrugged "…you still seem to care deeply for him. Either way, your being with me can't hurt."

His eyes narrowed. "If you know something about the shooting or those guys in the Hummer, you'd better tell me now. Traveling with me is dangerous. You're putting your own life in danger."

"No," she told him. "I don't know anything." In more ways than one, she thought. Whatever Alex had gotten himself involved in, *dangerous* didn't seem to begin to describe the situation.

"Okay. I consider you warned." He sounded oddly agreeable—pleasant, even—making her wonder if he used this tone on a daily basis to trick suspects under interrogation into admitting guilt.

"You really think I'm a criminal." She spoke her thoughts out loud.

"The men in the Hummer weren't with law enforcement." He spoke as though he had no doubt. "Neither was the shooter."

She shook her head. "Hades' Claws?"

He snorted. "You tell me."

"Hey, I don't even know them." She could tell from Carson's skeptical expression that he didn't believe her. "Seriously, I never heard of Hades' Claws until you mentioned them."

"How long have you been looking for your brother?"

She narrowed her eyes. "A few months. I haven't heard from him for six. Why?"

"Surely you read the papers."

"Some." She gave a halfhearted shrug. "But I don't remember seeing anything about them."

He laughed then, lightening the grim atmosphere in the Tahoe. "Are you from around here?"

"No. Upstate. I came down here looking for my brother. Why?"

"Because they make the paper here all the time. Maybe your local paper isn't interested."

"So they aren't that bad?" Keeping her expression haughty, she resisted the urge to chew on her fingernail.

This was a habit she'd broken in her teens, right after she'd passed the Pack tests that made her a full-fledged huntress. Odd that a habit she despised would try to resurface now.

"Oh, they're bad, all right. Unless you don't count murder, smuggling—" he ticked the words off on his fingers "—illegal weapons, drugs and robbery as wrong."

"And they want to kill you," she said softly.

"Oh yeah. And even if you can't get a grip on the idea that your brother is one of them, while you're with me you're a target, too."

"I'm not worried." She ran her fingers through the back of her long hair, combing it out from force of habit. "As I've said, I can take care of myself."

"So you claim." He lifted one shoulder in a quick shrug. "Either way, I have no intention of letting you out of my sight. So don't even think about taking off."

"The thought never crossed my mind," she drawled.

Instead of replying, he accelerated. At her questioning look, he flipped his fingers at the dark road ahead of them. "We need to get off the interstate."

"Do you think they'll catch us?"

One corner of his mouth twisted. "Eventually. For a while they'll keep going down that access road, thinking we're just ahead of them. But once they realize we pulled off somewhere..." As he spoke, he glanced in the rearview mirror.

His profile seemed hard and angry. No doubt he still believed she'd lied about her connection to the biker gang.

Biker gang. Alex a murderer. Hard to even think

of using the words together in a sentence. Never mind DEA and FBI. Another shiver went down her spine.

"I'm not a member of Hades' Claws." Her words came out in a furious, staccato burst.

"A rival gang?"

"Of course not. No."

"You don't sound too certain. What about this 'pack' you mentioned?"

Alarm clogged her throat. He'd caught her accidental slip. "It's a nickname, an inside joke among my relatives," she said. "It's what we call ourselves. No gang, just family. You know how family can be."

"Yeah. I had a family once." The grim savagery in his voice made her catch her breath.

"How long ago?" she asked softly. "How long ago did it happen?"

He shook his head, a muscle working in his jaw. With a white-knuckle grip, he held on to the steering wheel. "It's been eighteen months."

Eighteen months. Last year, early spring. Alex had called her, told her he'd taken a new job, one that would let him move from the city back to the Catskills. Still only a few hours away, he'd said, knowing she missed him. After they'd graduated from college, he'd left her once before to go alone on an extended winter tour of the northern cities. Seattle, Vancouver, Boise, Helena, Bismark. Then east to check out Phillie and Boston and New York. His absence had made her sad, then furious, wishing she'd gone with him.

When he'd finally returned to the small town of Leaning Forest, he'd told wonderful stories. Not of blood or murder or mayhem, but of ordinary, city-human things. Rush hour and crowded subways, poodles with painted toenails and corner hot-pretzel vendors.

They'd laughed together over his tales. In her quiet life as the town librarian, she'd secretly envied him the adventure, the experience, never dreaming that one day she would venture forth from her comfortable existence in search of him. Never expecting him to go missing, be accused of murder. How peaceful her old life seemed now.

"Eighteen months," she repeated. "And you've looked for revenge ever since?"

"I've been looking for your brother," he said. "As soon as I got out of the hospital, I started searching. Alex went underground. Obviously, he doesn't want me to find him."

She let that one go, focusing on the word *hospital*. He'd said he'd nearly been killed. "Did it take you a long time to recover?"

He gave a curt nod.

Less than two years. In her own life, a lot had happened in that time. She'd lost a fiancé, misplaced her brother. Meanwhile, this man's entire family had been ripped away, brutally murdered in circumstances that made her brother look guilty.

"I'm sorry." She knew her words were inadequate, but she meant them nonetheless.

In response, Carson accelerated again.

Brenna got the message and closed her mouth. The digital clock on the dashboard showed 1:30 a.m. Late for humans, but prime hunting time for those of her kind. Glancing at the shadowy woods as they flashed past, she wondered if any of her people roamed there. Snow had begun to fall, the dainty white flakes becoming thick, heavy ones the farther north they traveled. Soon Carson slowed the vehicle to a crawl, his headlights reaching only a few feet ahead of them on the snow-covered road.

A sign proclaimed they were on the outskirts of Albany, the state capital.

"Where are we going?" she asked.

"I got a lead that some of the gang is holed up in Hawk's Falls, near the Vermont border."

Mostly wilderness. Her kind of place. She allowed herself a small smile. As a huntress, her tracking skills were unparalleled. If Alex hid anywhere in a forest, she would find him.

"How long before we get there?"

He shook his head in the clumsy manner of a wolf cub shaking off snow. "We won't get there tonight," he said, his deep voice sounding gravelly. "It's late, and the storm's getting worse. I need some sleep."

She sat up. "I'm not tired. I'll drive."

He drummed on the steering wheel. "I don't think so."

"I want to find him as much as you do," she reminded him. "You sleep, I'll get us there. It's not too far."

"We're pulling off at the next town. We'll take a motel room for the night."

"But—"

"We have to stop sometime."

"I'll stop when I find my brother."

He shook his head again. "We'll start fresh in the morning."

"If we're not snowed in."

"I've got chains." He shrugged. "And there's always a plow."

She tried not to grind her teeth. "Look, I really think—"

"Enough." His tone was sharp enough to cut a coyote off in mid-howl. "This is not a democracy. We're stopping and getting some rest. End of subject."

Brenna glared. "Fine. You get a room. I'll stay in your vehicle."

"Right." He snorted. "It's ten below and snowing, and you want to stay here?"

Put that way, her words did sound…unusual.

"I don't want to waste money on a motel room. I can rest here. This is comfortable enough for me."

"Money?" He gave her a long look. "Don't worry about it. I'll pay. We're sharing a room, anyway."

At her sputter of protest, he flashed her a bleak, tight-lipped smile. "Look, I'm not going to attack you. I don't want sex with the sister of my family's killer. I'll make sure we have two beds."

Safe. If only he knew. She suppressed the desire to growl. "I'm not worried."

"Of course not." His tone mocked her. "But like I said, until we find Alex, I'm not letting you out of my sight."

"I don't want to be that close to you."

"Tough."

She took a closer look at the intense man beside her.

"Fine," she conceded. "I want to keep an eye on you as badly as you do me."

"Then it's settled." In silence he drove on, windshield wipers slapping ineffectively against the blinding snow. He handled the vehicle with the ease of long familiarity. In the blizzard, the streetlights shone like dim halos, the occasional car or semi looming up huge, then lumbering away, like brief scenes from a surreal, homemade movie.

An exit sign indicated available lodging. They left the freeway, turning right and fishtailing on the snowy road.

"Slow down," she said.

Instead of commenting, he pointed. "There." Clustered together were several older motels. A red neon sign at the first one indicated a vacancy.

Carson pulled into the snow-covered lot, parking around back, out of sight of the brightly lit office. With the snow coming down fast and furious, the place looked cozy, inviting, though Brenna knew in harsh sunlight the weather-beaten exterior would seem tired and worn.

With an innate caution that came as naturally as breathing, she took stock of her surroundings. The frame building appeared badly maintained, its fading green paint peeling. A few pine trees, bent and sickly, grew near the office. The weight of the snow on their branches made them seem about to topple.

Despite the storm, or perhaps because of it, the parking lot contained five or six other vehicles, all older, all rapidly disappearing under white shrouds of snow. From the iron bars on the office windows, she judged this would not be a safe place for a woman to wander at night, at least a human woman unable to change.

Carson killed the ignition and pocketed the key before turning to face her, his expression flat.

"Let's go." He squeezed her shoulder, effectively cutting off her last attempt at refusal. "Give it up. You're staying with me."

"I'm your captive?" Both amused and angry, she couldn't help but wonder at his reaction if she were to change right here, right now. If she were her powerful wolf self, he wouldn't be able to contain her. No man on earth could hold her then. Even as a human, she was a formidable opponent. Years of martial arts classes had made sure of that.

For now she could only let him think he had won. The force of his glare told her he didn't appreciate her amusement or her anger.

"Fine," she said. "Let's go."

"Brenna, I'm warning you." Illuminated by the flashing neon hotel light, his gaze was as cold as the night and twice as harsh. "Don't try to escape. Your brother destroyed my family and ruined my life. I *will* make him pay. Neither you nor anyone else will be able to stop me."

Releasing her, he pushed open his door and strode around to her side. Before he reached the door handle, she pushed it open herself and slid to the ground in front of him. Squaring her shoulders in the bulky parka, she lifted her chin and stared him in the face, snow swirling around both of them in a heavy cloud.

"My brother is not the man you're looking for."

"Unwavering devotion," he drawled. "That's good in a sister." Pausing, he looked her over once. "That is, if you really are Alex's sister."

Her breath came out in a hiss. Narrow-eyed, she glared at him with such ferocity that he took a step back. Then she spun on her heel and marched over to the hotel office, yanking open the dirty glass door. She went inside without waiting to see if he would follow.

A few minutes later, metal key firmly in hand, Carson allowed her to precede him toward their room.

On the ground floor, 119 sat at the very back of the building, as far away from the growl and snarl of the normal freeway traffic as the hotel offered. Though the blizzard muffled sound, she was still glad, as the noise, utterly foreign, made her uncomfortable and restless.

Come to think of it, the utter absence of sound, normally welcome, had her feeling skittish as well. Or maybe she owed her heightened awareness to her companion. With his grim-jawed features, he appeared oblivious to her discomfort as he unlocked the door.

Once inside, he flicked the light switch. A single dim lamp illuminated the well-used room.

Brenna went in. She sniffed, wrinkling her nose at the foul smell. Though he'd asked for nonsmoking, the stale scent of cigarettes hung in the musty air. Coughing, she looked at the window. Carson shook his head.

"Too cold." A battered heat/air unit, faded yellow, sat under the window. With the twist of a knob, he turned on the heat. She could only hope the warmth didn't intensify the nauseating smell.

"I've been in worse," he said. Never having stayed in a motel, Brenna didn't reply. She waited to see what he would do next.

Two double beds took up nearly all the space in the room. Once he'd pulled the door closed behind him and turned the dead bolt, he had to turn sideways to get past her. Their chests brushed. He jerked away as though she'd given him an electrical shock. She couldn't help it—a quick chuckle escaped her at his discomfort.

Ignoring her, he moved quickly, turning on every lamp. The cheap clock radio on the nightstand blinked red—2:05 a.m. Then Carson went to the bed nearest the door and yanked back the sour-smelling bedspread.

"Nice and comfy, don't you think?" His tone mocked both her and their surroundings. The heat overpowered her. The sickening odor made her head spin. Because she didn't trust herself to speak without giving her true nature away, she went into the tiny bathroom and closed the door with a sharp click.

Chipped turquoise tile decorated the walls and floor. The porcelain sink, though old, appeared clean. She turned the faucet. The tap water felt icy and refreshing. Splashing her face, she drank deeply from her cupped hands. Then she finger-combed her hair, eyeing herself in the distorted mirror. Exhaustion and worry had made faint circles under her brown eyes and carved new hollows in her narrow face. She craved a long hot shower, but she didn't want to leave Carson alone for too long. If he made a phone call, she wanted to hear every word.

By the time she came out of the bathroom, he had pushed one of the beds snugly up against the front door, effectively blocking them in.

"Yours?"

He nodded.

"Give me a break. What if there's a fire?"

"Then we'll move it."

Unable to resist pointing it out, she said, "There's always the window."

"You'd have to go over me to get to it."

Over him. The air felt suddenly charged. Brenna shrugged away the unfamiliar feeling of awareness with a quick toss of her head.

"We can keep this up all night," he said. "Or we can get some rest. It's late." Massaging the back of his neck, he indicated the other bed. "That's yours. Go to sleep. We'll start again early in the morning."

"If the plows show up."

He gave her a tired smile. "They will. They always do."

He watched while she gingerly tested her mattress. She pinched a corner of the faded bedspread between her index finger and thumb, yanking it back so it fell on the floor at the foot of the bed. The nappy blanket, though, she turned back neatly. Then, still fully dressed, she lay down on her side on top of the sheets, trying to ignore the faint musty scent that tickled her nose. Still facing him, she kept her eyes open. Watching.

"Tap on the wall," he said.

Blinking, she sat up. "What?"

"I need to go in there." He indicated the bathroom. "I want you to tap on the wall until I come out."

Amused, she let her mouth curve in the beginnings of a smile. "You really think I'll run."

"Won't you?"

Exhaling loudly, Brenna lifted one shoulder. "Turn down the heat." Moving with deliberate slowness, she peeled off her heavy leather vest and tossed it on the bed. Then she lifted her hand to the wall and rapped three times, the plaster rough against her knuckles, repeating until she'd found a simple, primitive rhythm. Oddly, this soothed her.

After flipping the dial to Off, he nodded curtly. Leaving the door slightly ajar, he spent less than a minute in the tiny bathroom before he emerged. Without glancing at her, he went around the room, extinguishing the lights one at a time. That made Brenna want to laugh again. She saw as well in the darkness as she did in the light.

She let her arm fall, watching him as he readied for bed.

Like her, he didn't undress. She heard the rasping

sound of his jeans as he slid between the sheets, fully clothed.

In the silence, she listened for his breathing to slow. Instead his restless movements indicated he was as far away from sleep as she.

"Let me tell you about my brother," she said finally, keeping her voice low and nonconfrontational.

He grunted. "Go to sleep."

"Maybe I can tell you something you don't know."

"I doubt it."

"Alex and I are twins."

He sat up at her words, his bulky shape ominous in the dim light. "Listen, quit the lies. You're not even his sister. Alex had no family. Believe me, I would know if he did."

She sighed, reaching over and clicking on the light. "Maybe you don't know him as well as you think."

"You don't even look like him." Disgust colored his words, and his hard tone would have shaken even a career criminal. "He's blond and you're dark."

"We're fraternal twins."

"Sure." He folded his arms across his chest. "You live in fantasy land, lady."

She sighed again. "This is getting old. I'm telling the truth. Alex is my twin. I have no reason to lie."

"Don't you now?"

Ignoring his skepticism, she continued doggedly. "Alex and I are different in a lot of ways. Of the two of us, he is calmer and more rational."

"Alex is an unemotional man," he agreed, the savagery in his voice surprising her. "And I still don't believe you're his sister."

She leaned forward to peer at him through the dim

light. "Did you ever see his birthmark? The one on his arm?"

Surprise briefly lit his face. "Yeah, I did," he said grudgingly. "I thought it was a tattoo at first."

Turning her back to him, she lifted her shirt, pushing down the waistband of her jeans so he could see. "The shape of a wolf," she said, giving him a clear view of her own birthmark above her left hip. "Maybe you'll believe me now."

He swore at the unmistakable evidence. "He never mentioned family. Any family. At all."

Ignoring that, she let her shirt fall back into place, turning once more to face him. "You never told me. Where do you know Alex from?"

"DEA." He spat the single word. "We were undercover together. Alex was my partner."

Chapter 3

"Partner?" For a moment she didn't understand. Then, once she realized what he meant, she wanted to call *him* the liar. "You're telling me that my brother was working for the FBI?"

"DEA."

"Whatever." She swallowed. "He would have told me."

With a wry twist of his mouth, Carson shook his head. "He couldn't. Right after we graduated from Quantico, we were sent out together. We were both undercover."

Her heart skipped a beat. "Isn't that dangerous?"

"Very." From the hitch in his voice, she knew he was thinking of his murdered family.

"No wonder he didn't mention me," she said. "He didn't want to put me in danger."

With a pointed glance at the clock, which now showed 2:45 a.m., Carson made a rude sound. "Who knows? Who cares? Turn off the light and go to sleep."

Stung, she glanced away. No matter what precautions her brother had taken, she'd managed to put herself at risk by traveling with Carson. Judging from the shooter and the men in the Hummer, danger had found her.

Reluctantly she clicked off the light and closed her eyes.

Morning came quietly, with bright sunlight peeking through the heavy curtains. The second she opened her eyes, Brenna lay motionless, instantly alert, and listened for activity outdoors.

"The snow's stopped." Carson spoke from near the door. How had he known she was awake?

Slowly she raised her head. Even with his five-o'clock shadow and sleep-mussed hair, the man looked devastatingly attractive. Dangerous. She licked her lips. "I haven't heard the snowplows."

"They haven't made it through yet." He ran a hand through his disheveled hair. "I think we got maybe a foot."

Forcing herself to look away, she swung her legs over the side of the bed. "Powder?"

"I can't tell. Probably, under the crust. We'll find out. There's a coffee shop across from the motel office."

She stretched, yawning. Though her jeans were snug, they were comfortable and she'd slept well in them.

"I'd like to take a shower." She rubbed the palms of her hands on the faded front of her jeans. "That way I'd feel more human." Now there was a laugh.

Carson opened his mouth to reply, but whatever he'd

been about to say was drowned out by a burst of static as the clock radio alarm on her nightstand went off.

The previous occupant must have set it. Shocked, she saw it read 10:00 a.m. They'd slept late.

"Breaking news." The radio announcer's stern voice broke into the dying strains of the music.

"Drugs were involved in a multiple murder in the small town of Welkory near the Vermont border."

They looked at each other. Swallowing, Brenna grimaced and reached to turn up the volume.

Details followed. In the midst of a bank robbery less than an hour earlier, two groups of people had opened fire on each other, killing several innocent bystanders. One of the getaway cars had been captured, trunk loaded with cocaine. Supposition was that the robbery had been an attempt to gain money to pay for the drugs.

"Damn," Carson said as the news announcer switched to another story. "That's north of Hawk's Falls. We need to check it out."

"The Claws?"

"Hades' Claws," he corrected absently. "And yes, I'm willing to bet they had something to do with it, especially since Welkory is so close to their hideout. Add the cocaine, and it's pretty much a given."

Again she met his gaze, letting him see her fierce determination. "You think Alex was involved, don't you?"

He shrugged, turning away. "No doubt."

Brenna took a long look at the man who'd claimed her as his captive. In the small room the pain radiated from him so strongly it made her own heart ache with sympathy she could ill afford. She needed to focus only on finding her brother and ensuring his safety.

"Let's go," Carson said.

"Wait." She held up a hand. "We need to get something straight. Your family is gone. You want revenge. I've got that. But I want to know the truth. You said you knew Alex well, that he was your partner. Well, why would he go bad? Is it possible there was some other explanation why he was at your house when it happened? Some other reason he had a gun?"

The absolute silence in which he glared at her was the embodiment of rage. Though the muscle that ticked in his clenched jaw should have been adequate warning, she couldn't stop herself from continuing.

"What do you think he did? Really? Murder, rape, torture?" The mere notion of someone thinking her twin could hurt anyone for no reason, anyone at all, made her furious. "He's incapable of those things. You should know that, too—if you truly know him as well as you say."

Despite her taunts, Carson said nothing. His features seemed cast in stone. Implacable. Angry. Hurt. She noticed he, too, wore the same faded jeans and dark flannel shirt as the night before. And boots. The man wore cowboy boots made of some kind of exotic leather.

"Somehow I have to prove to you that my brother is not the devil incarnate."

"You only have to prove it to yourself." Bitterness coated his words with acid. "Grab your coat. We're hitting the road. Since the robbery was less than an hour ago, the investigation will be in full swing." He consulted his watch. "The interstate should be plowed. If we leave now, we'll get there in time to talk to them."

For the space of a heartbeat, she merely looked at

him. “Logic,” she drawled. “The one thing I can’t argue with.”

A few minutes later they were back on the road. He’d been right about the snowplows. Piles of snow lined the one open lane on each side. Carson constantly pressed the seek button on the radio, looking for more news about the robbery.

The farther north they went, the less deeply the snow appeared to blanket the ground. The highway opened up, too, all lanes, though the traffic seemed considerably lighter than the day before.

Welkory, Exit One Mile.

As they approached the turnoff, he reached behind him and yanked a wrinkled black jacket from behind the seat.

“Here,” he said, shoving it into her lap. “Put this on over yours.”

Noting the yellow *DEA* on the back, she guessed the coat would provide cover as well as warmth. Shrugging out of her own parka, she slipped on the lighter jacket. “What about you?”

“I’ve got a cap.” His tone discouraged conversation.

The two-lane road that led to Welkory was curved and lined with towering, leafless trees. Coated with a light dusting of snow, they appeared both majestic and threatening. Brenna sensed the presence of animals in the woods, though she and Carson sped by so fast that she had no time to communicate with any of them. Before long they rounded the final curve and found themselves smack-dab in the middle of Welkory.

Downtown seemed oddly deserted, as though at the first hint of danger all the shops had rolled up their carpets and locked their doors.

Carson slowed the car, though every one of the four stoplights turned green at his approach. First Street, flanked by well-maintained, charming historical buildings. Then Second and Third, until finally they reached the intersection of Main Street and Fourth. Yellow police tape squared off the corner of Welkory First Bank and Trust, and a yellow fire truck, lights flashing, was parked next to the drive.

Brenna counted no fewer than seven police cruisers, two of them local, the rest state police.

Carson rolled down his window to flash his ID at the officer blocking the entrance. "DEA," he barked, and was rewarded with an immediate wave past the barricade. They barely glanced at Brenna. Wearing Carson's jacket made her look like another DEA agent.

He parked between two police cars, right next to the building. After turning off the ignition, he pocketed the keys and grabbed a battered black cap and crammed it on his head. The *DEA* letters in yellow made the cap a mate to her jacket.

"Ready?" he asked, his voice raspy. All traces of emotion had vanished from his face. He looked every part the professional government officer, stern and unforgiving in his quest for justice.

She licked lips suddenly gone dry before she replied quietly, "Yes."

"Then let's go," he said. "More than anyone else, you need to see this."

She heard the unspoken second part of his sentence: so you'll understand what kind of man your brother has become.

Eager to prove him wrong, Brenna pushed open her door. Ice-coated gravel crunched underfoot as she walked beside Carson to the squat brick building. Crisp air carried a chill that had nothing to do with the temperature and everything to do with the grim mood radiating from the uniformed officers who congregated inside the bank.

Brenna froze, sensation overwhelming her. The interior of this place smelled strongly of fear, of blood and death, like a hunt gone brutally wrong. She wanted to cover her nose, so nauseated did the scent make her. The odor of evil hung in the air so strongly she thought she might be sick. More than anything, she wanted to break away, lunge for the door and run. But she was a huntress, strong, not weak. Though her sense of smell was ten times more powerful than a human's, she would force herself to stay.

She breathed, though each lungful of air felt cloying, full of decay and hate. She swallowed, tasted bile and concentrated on not being weak. Nothing, not the hunting rituals of the Pack, nor any of the limited television shows she watched, had ever prepared her for the carnage here.

Mindless savagery. Hate. Pure evil.

It felt surreal and simultaneously more real than any experience she had ever felt. She despised every minute, wishing she were somewhere, anywhere, else.

Three sheet-covered bodies lay in front of the long, paneled counter. One man, probably the coroner, knelt beside the nearest one, making notes. Quiet sobbing came from a group of people clustered in the back.

"Tellers and other customers, most likely," Carson told her, *sotto voce.* "The ones who survived to tell their stories to the police."

Heart in her throat, Brenna managed a nod, trying

to hide her trembling. Though hunters by nature, her people did not believe in mindless violence or senseless slaughter.

Two uniformed locals intercepted them.

"DEA," Carson said again, touching the brim of his cap. They looked at Brenna, eyed her jacket and relaxed their stances. One, a younger man, met her gaze and blanched. Some humans always reacted so to one of the Pack.

"Where's the FBI?" the shorter of the two officers asked, his tone disapproving. At Carson's shrug, he grimaced and moved aside to allow them access to the witnesses.

Striding across the room as if they belonged, they moved into the edge of the group surrounding the survivors.

Then she smelled it, mingled with the acrid, coppery scent of blood. His scent—faint, but definitely Alex. She felt an instant of panic. Was he hurt? She nearly turned to Carson, then, remembering he was not like her, glanced casually around the room instead.

There. A faded jean jacket lay crumpled on the floor next to the wall, splattered with blood. It carried her brother's scent. She would have to inspect it, smell it better and touch the cloth before she could determine if the blood belonged to him.

Carson's hand on her shoulder kept her in place.

An older, heavyset woman, bright spots of color high on her pale cheeks, talked quietly. "The leader was a tall man, built like a wrestler or something. Muscular, and he liked to show those muscles off, I think. Despite the weather, he didn't wear a shirt or coat, only a black leather vest. And jeans."

The officer taking notes nodded. "Any other distinguishing characteristics, ma'am?"

"His hair was long—longer than mine. Oh—and he had a tattoo."

Carson looked at Brenna. She knew he was thinking of Alex's birthmark, shaped like a wolf.

"Tattoo?" she asked, keeping her voice professionally level. "What did it look like?"

Eyes wide, the woman waved one plump beringed hand. "Oh, it was very intricate, some sort of curly snake thing, evil-looking, that wrapped all the way up his arm."

Not Alex's birthmark. With an effort, Brenna kept her relief from showing on her face.

"Hades' Claws." One of the troopers muttered to another. "It's their mark."

Carson gave Brenna a narrow-eyed look, and she saw that he already knew about this tattoo. Again she wanted to open her mouth, to tell him Alex would never defile himself like that, but too many others surrounded them, so she held her silence.

"Eye color? Hair color?"

Ah, now was the important part. Brenna held her breath.

The woman didn't hesitate. "Dark eyes. Brown, I think. And that hair, why it was so inky black it didn't reflect the light. It had to be dyed."

Another officer had begun to question two more tellers, who responded with similar answers to the first. Carson watched and listened, intent on their answers.

Brenna had heard enough. Glancing around the brightly lit interior of the bank, she wondered at the creepy feel of it, as though the room had taken on a texture both clean and sharp, yet tainted and foul. She ran her hand along the faux wood surface of a desk, the smoothness an odd contrast to the rough menace that still hung in the air.

Moving as unobtrusively as possible, she went to the jacket and lifted it, resisting the urge to bury her nose in the cloth and breathe in the familiar scent. Carson made no move to stop her, though she could feel his watchful gaze boring into her back. Instead she held the coat a few feet away, inhaled deeply and breathed.

Another's smell tainted the material, mingling with and overriding her brother's. This other man, a human who had left the sharp smell of anger and fear embedded in the fabric, had worn it recently. Though it might once have belonged to Alex, someone else had worn it here. With a quiet sigh, she let it fall back to the floor and turned to rejoin Carson.

Something else… Teasing her sensitive nose, the scent came strong, alive instead of dead. Not human nor of the Pack. She stopped before reaching Carson, carefully looking around. A high-pitched whimper from under a nearby desk caught her attention. Crouching down to peer underneath, she let her breath out in a quiet hiss. A tiny black puppy of mixed heritage, eyes huge and frightened, stared up at her from the floor, shaking.

Here, then, was something she understood, one in many ways closer to her kind than the myriad assortment of humans inside this place. Still kneeling, Brenna held out her hand, letting the small creature absorb her scent before she reached out to stroke the softness of his midnight-colored fur, noticing the contrast of his white paws.

Touching the animal, Brenna felt a sensation of noise and terror. She shivered with the aftershocks of what the small creature had experienced and even now still felt. This young dog had been with his human companion when he died. Glancing at the sheeted bodies, she received a brief image of love, burst apart by a single gunshot to the head. The noise, the blood, the hatred, had terrified this young animal. Grieving and fearful, he was alone now.

Without a second thought, Brenna scooped him up in her arms. "I will be your protector now, small one," she promised, whispering the ancient words that had always bound her people to their animal companions.

"Has anyone viewed the tapes?" Carson asked the nearest officer.

"Not yet." The cop indicated another man, a plainclothes detective from the looks of him. "We were waiting for him."

"He's here, let's go," Carson barked.

The other two men conferred, then moved toward a darkened back office. Carson signaled Brenna to follow. Head held high, she did, the pup cradled in her arms, trying to burrow under her jacket.

"Where'd that dog come from?" one of the local officers asked, eyeing her suspiciously.

She lifted her chin to reply. "He was under the desk. I think he might have belonged to one of the victims."

The officer gave her a skeptical frown. "Do they allow pets in here?"

"Who cares?" the detective snapped. "Let's go."

With the lights dimmed, they had already set up the equipment to play the security tape.

"Ready?" At the collective nod, he hit Play. Grainy

images began to move on the monitor as the horrifyingly brutal robbery was reenacted in black-and-white.

From the general area outside the office, Brenna could hear a woman sobbing.

"There." One officer pointed to the tallest man in the video, the obvious leader, the one with the bare chest and intricate tattoo twining up his muscular arm.

"Can't see his face," another man grunted, leaning so close to the monitor his nose touched it.

A grumbled complaint from the others moved him back.

Brenna held her breath, letting it out with a loud sound as she got a better look at the criminals' leader. He was built like her brother, yes. But there the resemblance ended. Though she couldn't make out the killer's features, she could tell from the way the man moved that he was not her twin.

Relief flooded her. Carson's unwavering certainty that her brother had gone bad had given her doubts. But the man in the video was not Alex. A quick glance at Carson told her he knew that, as well.

"Hey." Catching the interaction, the detective moved closer. "Why didn't you come with the other DEA guys who called this morning? They're on their way in."

Carson went still. "We wanted to be first," he said. "We wanted to check around on our own."

Though the other man nodded, Brenna got the distinct impression he knew Carson was lying.

"As a matter of fact, I think we're gonna head into Hawk's Falls and look around there. We'll check back with you guys tomorrow to see if anything new turns up."

As they left the room, Brenna heard one man

comment, "DEA or FBI, they're all the same. Always want to sweep in and steal the glory, even from their own."

"What was that all about?" she asked, as soon as they were outside. "Why *aren't* you working with the other DEA guys?"

He didn't answer, just yanked her truck door open with a brusque motion. Without protest, she climbed into the cab, the puppy still tucked in the curve of her arm.

"Just a minute." Carson indicated the young dog with a wave of his hand. "Leave the animal here."

"No. That's not negotiable. He comes with me or I don't go at all."

Carson frowned. "That puppy doesn't belong to you."

"He does now." She pulled the door closed behind her with a thunk. Adjusting her seat belt, she made sure the dog was comfortable before turning to look at Carson, who was still standing outside the truck. Finally, as she continued petting the pup's soft fur, Carson shook his head and strode around the vehicle. He climbed into the driver's seat and slammed his own door. Without another word, he started the ignition and put the vehicle in Reverse.

"Tell me one thing," he said, one arm draped over the back of the seat. "Are you bringing that dog because he's your brother's?"

Brenna laughed. "You really think Alex would bring a puppy with him to rob a bank and kill a bunch of people? And then leave his pet behind?"

Carson lifted one shoulder in a shrug. "Why not?"

In his tone she heard what he did not say: If The

Wolf didn't value human life, what would the life of one small animal matter?

"Not my brother's," she told him finally. "I think the owner was probably one of the people killed in the robbery. Now it's your turn to answer a question. Why aren't you working with the other DEA agents? You lied. You didn't even know they were coming."

Carson drove as if a demon were chasing him, rapidly increasing their speed until they were hurtling down the highway. They took the left lane by storm and passed every other vehicle they encountered.

"What are you hiding?" Brenna heard the taunt in her voice and lifted her chin. "Tell me, Mr. Level-With-Me. Why aren't you working with the other government people?"

"I work better alone," Carson snapped. "I'll find him and bring him in before they even get their heads out of their asses."

"You never stop, do you?"

His expression grim, he shook his head. "No. And I never will. Not until he's in custody."

"Did it ever occur to you that he might still be undercover?"

"Yeah." His mouth twisted. "It did. Briefly. But I saw him. I'll never forget that. He shot my family, then threw away the gun. And he never contacted me. Ever. Not even the day of the funeral, the day I buried Julie and Becky. He was my partner, damn it. My friend."

The bitterness of betrayal rang in his voice. Unable to take the stark desolation in his eyes, she looked away.

"That wasn't Alex in the video," he said finally. He eased up on the gas pedal and moved into the middle lane.

Staring at him, she nodded. "I know."

"That doesn't mean he wasn't involved."

"He wasn't."

The puppy whimpered, shifting in her arms. Some of her tension must have communicated itself to the animal. Taking a deep breath, Brenna forced herself to relax.

"You'll see," she told him. "Once we find him, I'm sure he'll have a reasonable explanation for everything."

Ignoring her, Carson exited the freeway and pulled into a service station.

While he refueled, Brenna concentrated on her new companion. He had to have a name. For now she would call him Phelan, little wolf.

As she spoke the name out loud, three times in the custom of her people, the puppy raised his head. He lifted a small foot, accepting the naming with quiet dignity. As she took his paw in her hand, Brenna saw a splotch of rust marring the white fur. Blood, dried and flaking. Surely Carson had tissues or something in the glove box. A sidelong glance showed her that he had his back to her.

She opened the glove box. Inside there were no tissues, only a few sheets of paper, crumpled and wadded into a ball. One of those would have to do. Smoothing one out, she glanced at the words printed on it and froze.

"Leave of Absence—Medical." Swiftly she scanned the rest of the document. In disbelief she read it again, before crumpling and tossing the paper back. Carson Turner had lied. Whatever he did, he was no longer acting under the auspices of the DEA. Since early summer, he'd been on forced medical leave. Six months ago. That meant that in his hunt for her brother, he was acting alone and unsanctioned, his reasons personal rather than official.

A private vendetta. Now, more than ever, she knew she had to find Alex first.

Chapter 4

Outside, the sharp ice of the wind cut straight to the bone. Shivering, Carson regretted giving Brenna his work jacket. Quickly he fitted the icy gas nozzle into his tank, setting the metal pin so the gas would run automatically. Then, turning his back to the wind, he punched a number into his cell phone. Warm as it was inside the Tahoe, he needed to talk to his informant privately yet still keep an eye on his reluctant passenger.

Three rings, a click, then a muffled answer. As usual, the man he knew only as Jack didn't want to talk. Carson kept his voice low, rational, cajoling. He did the usual song and dance with the normal promise of payment, and finally got the information he needed. A potential sighting of Hades' Claws. As he'd thought they might, they were heading north, toward their compound in Hawk's Falls.

Jack believed Alex traveled with them.

Snapping the cell phone closed, he got back in the truck, shivering, and turned up the heat. A quick look at Brenna told him something had happened in the brief time he had taken to make the call. Her entire demeanor, posture and expression had changed. From the rigid line of her back to the way the sharp edge of her glare touched on him before skittering away, he read a simmering anger.

He swept the gas station at a glance. Two or three other vehicles were parked at the pumps, their drivers bundled against the cold while pumping gas. Nothing seemed out of the ordinary, and no one had approached the Tahoe while he was on the phone.

Then why was his new companion spoiling for a fight?

"What's up?" He avoided her gaze as he turned the key and started the engine. The less eye contact, the less chance for an argument.

"You used your cell phone. Who'd you call?" Her tone sounded surprisingly pleasant, even with contained anger.

He suppressed a smile. Damn, she was good. Answering a question with another question. One of the oldest avoidance tactics in the book.

"Informant." Signaling, he pulled onto the road. With one hand looped over the top of the steering wheel, he fiddled with the radio, finding a station that played soothing classical music to calm her. Small tricks like that had become ingrained, something he did without conscious thought.

Her face still averted, Brenna made a sound low in

her throat. It could have been either pleasure or disgust; he didn't know her well enough to determine which.

Nor did he care. Again he reached for the radio. One flick of the dial increased the volume to a level loud enough to discourage conversation, and he settled back in anticipation of a nice, quiet ride. Alex's sister seemed inclined to cooperate, watching the snow-covered landscape go past with no attempt to speak further.

But when the melody on the radio switched to Liszt's "Hungarian Fantasy," she swung around in her seat to face him. The swiftness of her movement, in keeping with the ominous crash of the music, startled him.

Even more alarming was her degree of anger. One quick glance told him the shoulder restraint was all that kept her from launching herself at him. Even her exotic eyes glowed caramel with fury. She took a deep breath, baring her white teeth, before exhaling loudly.

She looked almost like a wild animal.

"What the h—" Imagination. Had to be. He took a deep breath himself, blinked and took another look.

The furious glare remained. Quickly he turned the radio off.

"Now what?" he asked. "You got a problem?"

"Why did you lie to me?" Simmering rage trembled in her voice. "You said you had an official reason for looking for my brother, but you're not even working for the DEA."

Damn. He shook his head. "You snooped in my glove box."

"I was looking for a tissue. Instead I found a crumpled piece of paper that says you're on medical leave."

He clenched his jaw. "None of this is your business."

"I think it is." She tilted her chin, contempt blazing

from her gaze. "Tell me, Carson Turner, have you become the thing you profess to hate?"

"What?"

"A criminal."

"Lady, I'm no criminal."

Again she blew out her breath. "You're acting without the sanction of the Justice Department. You're on medical leave. Impersonating a federal agent is a crime."

"You just did the same thing at the bank."

"That was different. You led me to believe you were there on official business, and I was with you. You've been doing it for…what? The last six months?"

Carson felt his face heat. "I have good reason—"

"Sure you do." Scorn sharpened her tone. "Even Ted Bundy thought he had good reason."

"Give me a break." He ran his hand through his hair, his earlier expectation of a peaceful drive evaporating. "You can't compare me to him."

"Why not? He's a murderer. You could be. Do you intend to kill my brother?"

A low growl rose in his throat. It sounded enough like an animal to cause the puppy to raise his head from Brenna's lap.

Oddly enough, Brenna smiled as though she found comfort in the sound.

"I'll bring The Wolf to justice. By whatever means necessary."

Brenna forced her jaw to relax. She would simply have to wait and see what other lies he might have told.

Carson turned his head, looking directly at her for the first time in what seemed like hours. Holding his gaze, she resisted the strange, shivery sensation she got whenever their eyes connected. She didn't know if it was because of the threat this human represented or some other, inexplicable reason. Whatever the cause, she didn't like the feeling. She focused on the threat.

"I will not let you harm Alex."

His lips twisted into a mocking smile. "Hmm."

Brenna let that pass. Carson had no idea what he was dealing with. Most men took one look into her eyes and knew better than to toy with her. "Why aren't you afraid of me?"

He laughed. "Should I be?"

She tried a different tack. "Are you afraid of anything?"

Instantly he sobered. "I told you. I live for one thing only. Finding the people who destroyed my life and making them pay. Nothing and no one can keep me from that goal."

Back to that. Fine. "You want answers, right?"

"I want the truth."

"Then we're on the same side."

He quirked a brow in question, alternating his attention between her and the road. "How do you figure?"

"We both want facts."

"Yeah." A shadow of savagery remained in his tone. "That's why we're heading toward the Vermont border."

All right, she would bite. "Why? What'd you find out?"

"My informant told me that Hades' Claws is having a big meeting. Hundreds are assembling in a week's time in a place they have north of Hawk's Falls."

"How do you know you can trust him?"

"Trust who?"

"The informant."

"I've worked with him before. His tips have always panned out. As long as I pay, he tells me the truth."

"I thought you didn't pay for information," she said.

"Seldom." He smiled. "Sometimes I bluff."

"And if you don't pay?"

"Then he'd sooner let me die."

For some reason that touched her. "You live a sad life, Carson Turner."

His expression froze, the falsely pleasant mask slipping slightly to reveal hard ruthlessness underneath.

"Sad?" He shook his head. "Angry, maybe. Mad. Oh yeah, definitely furious. But not sad, not anymore. Not ever again."

She saw that her words had hit some deeply hidden mark. "I meant," she said, "it's sad that you have to pay people to help you."

He shrugged, a quick jerk of his shoulders. "Not in my line of work."

"And this?" With her hand she indicated the road ahead. "Is all this work, too? Pretending to be an active DEA agent, lying to other law enforcement guys, making me a captive?"

Holding her breath, she waited to hear his answer. Though he'd lied to her initially, since she'd caught and confronted him, perhaps now he would tell her the truth.

"This is my life," he said, after a long silence. "Finding Alex, finding *them,* keeps me alive."

"Vengeance?"

He nodded.

Bleakness settled in her chest, icier than any northern blizzard. "You do mean to kill him."

"Maybe. I don't know. If he was the one—"

"'If'?" She pounced on the word. "You have doubts then?"

He continued as if he hadn't heard her. "If he was the one who betrayed me—us—and had Julie and Becky killed, he deserves to die."

She seized on the word. "'If.' You said 'if' again."

"I saw him, Brenna."

"No." She remembered his exact words as clearly as if she'd written them down. "You said you saw him with a gun. But you never saw him shoot, did you?"

"Semantics," he snarled. "It's not like he tried to help me, now, is it?"

"And you have the right to be his judge and his jury?"

"The right?" Raw savagery burned in his expression, from the hard set of his chin to his burning gaze. "I lost any rights long ago. I should have been the one to die, not my family. They were blameless, damn it. It was because of me, because of my job. They died without warning, without protection. They'd done nothing—" His voice broke, and he swallowed. White-knuckled, his hands gripped the steering wheel while he struggled to regain control of his emotions.

Such pain. Raw anguish. As quickly as it had begun, her protective anger faded. What must it have been like to lose everyone he loved? Brenna could only imagine.

"What about your parents?"

He continued to stare straight ahead. "What about them?"

"I imagine they care what happens to you."

"Imagine all you want. They're divorced. My mother lives in Seattle. She calls me once in a while, or I call her."

"Your father?"

He made a rude sound. "Remarried. New family. He doesn't need any of this."

"Any brothers or sisters?"

"Look, what is this?" His gaze raked her before he turned his attention back to the road. "Why are you asking so many questions? Why does any of this matter to you?"

His reaction stung. "I'm trying to figure you out, that's all."

"Well, stop. All the relatives in the world can't make up for the loss of my wife and daughter."

"I didn't think they could," she said softly. "But having them to depend on sure helps."

"Like you depend on Alex?"

She ignored the mockery in his tone. "Yes, exactly. Like I depend on Alex."

"I wouldn't depend on him too much. Looks like he ducked out on you, too."

She heard the unspoken: like he ducked out on me.

Though she tried to tear herself away, she found her gaze drawn to him. Despite the painful emotions still plain in the hard cast of his features, he handled the Tahoe with deft precision, moving in and out of lanes with the confidence of a skilled driver. His law enforcement training, no doubt.

Watching him channel his agony into driving, Brenna knew Carson meant what he said. The more she learned about him, the more she realized he wanted the truth and meant to find it, no matter what. This man took no half measures. He would be absolutely certain he had the right person before he started any course of action. Given that, she couldn't blame him for wanting to find her brother.

A thought struck her so hard that for a moment she couldn't catch her breath. What if Carson was right? What if her brother *had* been the one who'd murdered Carson's family? Just thinking such a thing felt disloyal and impossible, yet…

The evidence seemed damning. Carson himself had seen Alex with the gun. He was still involved with the biker gang. If he wasn't undercover, why was he with them? There had to be some sort of rational explanation.

"I don't understand why Alex hasn't contacted you," she mused. "Unless he's in danger."

"Because he's guilty." After a quick glance at her face, his tone softened. "Believe me, that's something I've wondered, too. Hell, Julie loved him like a brother. Becky called him Uncle. And he was my best friend."

Was. Once again, past tense. Did Carson see no possibility that he might be wrong? That someone else might have killed his family?

"When I was lying on the floor bleeding, I raised my head and looked at him. He knows I saw him. That's why he's trying to have me killed."

Brenna started. Though he spoke without inflection, she heard no doubt in Carson's voice. He truly believed that Alex… She couldn't complete the thought.

Again Phelan whimpered, shifting in her arms. Instantly she stilled her heart rate. She didn't want to alarm the puppy. In a moment he snuggled into her warmth, drifting back into a fitful doze.

"You should have let him out when we got gas," Carson commented. Since he was right, Brenna merely nodded.

With the radio off, the ebb and flow of traffic combined with the Tahoe's engine in a soft roar. Twice

Brenna's eyes drifted closed. Both times she forced herself to sit up and stretch her neck and shoulders.

"How much longer will it take to get there?" she asked, not from any real need for conversation, but merely to break the silence and stay awake.

"An hour, maybe less." From his terse response, she doubted he wanted to talk any more than she did. Tough. She had to prepare herself for the situation they were headed into.

"Tell me about Hawk's Falls. What kind of situation are we going to find?"

Another sidelong glance. "Dangerous. If Jack—my informant—is right, a lot of money and drugs are going to change hands in a couple of days. They're smart. The big rally is a cover. With hundreds of bikers in town, no one will be able to tell when the deal goes down."

"So the bikers will be on edge?"

"Only the ones involved. The rest of them will be too busy partying to pay attention to anything else."

She sighed. "What kind of place is this?"

"Hawk's Falls? Typical small town. I've been through it once or twice. Nothing exciting."

"Then why do they allow this biker gathering?"

"Hey." Amusement sparkled in his eyes. "Most bikers are decent people. Their money's as good as anyone else's."

"What are we going to do once we get there? Do you have a plan?"

"We?" Carson shook his head, still watching the highway.

Amused, Brenna hid her smile. "Yes, we. Unless you plan to tie me up and leave me in here."

"Don't tempt me," he growled, though the slight lift

at the corner of his mouth told her he was joking. So the man *did* have a sense of humor.

"Seriously, what are we going to do?"

"We have to be careful. Once we get to Hawk's Falls, we're going to play it by ear."

"You don't have a plan."

"I have a plan." A quick grin came and went on his face. "I just don't know what it is yet."

"We'll look for my brother."

"No." No trace of a smile relieved the hard cast of his features now. "We most definitely will *not* be looking for Alex."

Brenna's breath caught in her throat. If he was still kidding, he had an odd sense of humor. "Why not?"

He shrugged. "Basically, you're my bait. I want him to come to us, but I don't want to alarm the entire gang. So we pretend we don't care. Keep things low-key."

"Bait?" Her voice rose. "As in setting a trap?"

"I want to talk to your brother. I told you it would be dangerous."

She waved away his words. "I don't care about me. I want to make sure we don't put Alex in danger."

"Danger? He'll probably be surrounded by his cohorts. I doubt I could get close to him. I mean to force your brother to talk to me. Having you with me in the line of fire is the best way I can think of to make sure that happens. So, yes, you're my bait. We're going to go into downtown Hawk's Falls and pretend to enjoy each other's company."

That galled, too. "What's the point? If Alex wants to find us, he will. His tracking skills are excellent. I'd like to find him first."

"No." Impatience sounded in the gravelly timbre

of his voice. “With so much going on, he’ll be busy. Distracted. I need to get his attention. Having you with me should do it. I want him alone, not surrounded by his gang.”

“Alone.” Brenna repeated the one word that bothered her. “I won’t let you hurt him.”

“So you’ve said.”

“Then—”

“Try and understand. I need to talk to him. I want him to look me in the eyes and tell me, in his own words, what happened that day. Why he was there, at my house, holding the gun. Why he shot.”

“And then you’ll kill him.”

“I’d like to think I’m better than that. I’d like to think I’d see him arrested, make sure he stood trial.”

“But you’re not sure.”

He met her gaze. “I don’t know. If he was the one who killed my family…”

“If he’s as evil as you seem to think, he’d shoot you first.”

He lifted one shoulder. “Then I’d know, wouldn’t I? But before I died, I’d make sure to take him with me.”

His violent words echoed in the interior of the Tahoe. Or maybe, she reflected, they bounced off the walls of her bruised heart. Carson didn’t really care whether he lived or died, as long as he found out the truth and exacted vengeance. Hell of a way for a man to live.

Why his pain touched her so deeply, she couldn’t say. Yet one thing stood out in all he’d said. Despite his seemingly firm conviction, Carson still didn’t really know the truth. Even she was beginning to wonder what exactly had happened that day.

But Alex was her twin. She knew him nearly as well

as she knew herself. He would have an explanation for everything. And, unless the danger was too great, once he knew of her presence, Alex *would* find her. Even if he had to change to do so.

Phelan lifted his head, watching the exchange between them with interest. Now, apparently having decided he wanted to check Carson out more thoroughly, he wiggled from her lap and sank to his stomach. Sniffing furiously, he stretched his stubby little body until his neck was fully extended. Still unable to reach Carson over the console, he began a slow belly crawl up and over.

"Hey." Gently Carson pushed him away. "If you're gonna let that dog travel with us, keep it away from me."

Brenna gathered Phelan back in her lap, making quiet soothing sounds while she stroked his soft fur. She hadn't imagined the flash of panic on Carson's face when Phelan licked his hand. Carson had built such a wall around himself that he couldn't even let a puppy get close. Again she felt her chest tighten; again she forced the feeling away. She couldn't afford to let pity—or any other emotion—cloud her judgment where Carson was concerned.

She'd always been a sucker for the underdog. The forgotten ones, the quiet children who remained in the background while the others shone, the formerly beloved pets that waited, ignored, in some suburban backyard while the television inside the house blared.

Her first concern had to be for her brother, but she couldn't walk away until she knew Carson had his answers and maybe, finally, peace.

How stupid was that? Thoroughly annoyed with

herself, Brenna crossed her arms and glared at her oblivious companion.

She let her gaze wander as her glare faded into a perusal. He was a fine-looking man. His shoulders pleasantly filled out his sweatshirt, and his muscular arms spoke of more than a passing interest in physical fitness. Dark, shaggy hair and craggy, masculine features combined with his lean, athletic build, making him the kind of man most women drooled over.

His scent pleased her, too. Before she thought better of it, Brenna inhaled. Masculine, crisp and slightly musky, he carried the enticing smell of one who would make an excellent mate—if he were a shape-shifter, that is, she added hurriedly to herself, not liking the direction her thoughts had been heading. Mate indeed! After what had happened in her one attempt to marry a human, Brenna definitely wasn't up to that kind of agony again. Ever.

"Are you done?" he drawled.

Her gaze flew to his face. "What?"

"I asked if you were finished looking me over like I was your next meal?"

Deliberately she smiled, showing her teeth. Some humans—no, most humans—recoiled instinctively when they saw her in predatory mode.

Carson simply stared back, unsmiling.

"Don't get any ideas," he said.

For a moment she couldn't understand his meaning. When she did, she felt her face color. Still, because she rarely backed down, she challenged him.

"What kind of ideas? Enlighten me."

Was it a trick of the light, or did his own tan complexion turn red? His sensual lips thinned, and his eyes turned flinty as he glared at her.

"You know exactly what I mean."

"No." She batted her eyelashes for good measure, ignoring the unaccustomed butterflies in her chest. "I don't. Really. What kind of ideas do you not want me to have?"

For a moment she thought he might cry uncle. But evidently Carson Turner, renegade DEA agent, was every bit as stubborn as she.

"Sex." He spoke crisply. "You looked me over like a woman with sex on her mind."

Sex. Him. Her. A tangle of bodies. Hot, passionate— No. He was wrong. She laughed, unable to keep from choking midway through.

Still, her best response had to be humor. A pitiful attempt at laughing off his right-on-target remark.

"Hey, it's been a long time." She tried for a teasing tone and found it.

The darkness in his eyes deepened. "Look, I admit you're an attractive woman. And it's been a long time for me, too." His husky voice did strange things to her insides. "But I loved my wife. I couldn't even think of anyone else that way—"

The cell phone rang, interrupting him. Unlike the sometimes annoying specialty rings some phones had, he'd chosen a plain, unvarnished tone. Somehow she wasn't surprised.

"Unidentified caller." He glanced at the silver faceplate where the caller ID showed. "Only a few people have this number. We'll finish this conversation later." He stabbed the on button. "Hello?"

Was that a threat or a promise? Brenna settled back

in her seat, trying to sort out her confused reactions to him.

She could smell her own desire. Mingled with that, despite his words to the contrary, she could smell the heady scent of his.

Complications like this she did not need.

Though she tried, she couldn't make out the voice on the phone. Listening, Carson narrowed his eyes.

"Alex?" The single word was full of shock—and fury. "Alex, is that you?"

Chapter 5

Alex?

"Give me the phone." Grabbing for it and missing, Brenna clenched her jaw as Carson snapped the flip top closed.

"Damn," he swore.

"Was it him?"

"Yes." The grim set of Carson's mouth exposed his agitation. "I could barely hear him. He was whispering."

Whispering? "He must be in danger and trying not to be overheard."

"Damn." Carson cursed again. "I don't believe this."

"Tell me what he said."

With a savage flick of the turn signal, he moved the Tahoe into the middle lane. "He gave me an order, plain and simple. 'Get Brenna out of here.'"

Alex. Concerned about her welfare. How did he even

know she was here? Maybe by using the same internal sense that told her he was in danger.

"Did he say anything else?" Leaning forward, she watched while Carson focused intently on his driving, trying unsuccessfully to change lanes again, this time into an unbroken line of traffic. Finally he negotiated an opening in the right lane and moved over. Their speed was now barely sixty.

"We have to exit in a half mile," he said. "After this we'll take mostly back roads."

She waved his words away. "Carson! Did Alex say anything else?"

The look he shot her was dark. "Not much," he drawled. "I'll repeat it. 'If Brenna gets hurt, there will be hell to pay. Get her out of here. Now.'"

"He's worried about me. And not just because I'm traveling with you. Whatever he's involved in is dangerous," she said. "Was that it?"

His expression turned cold, watchful and alert. "Did you expect a personal message? Something in code?"

Suspicion tainted his voice and gaze, forcibly reminding her that they were still on opposite sides of the fence.

"No." She sighed, wishing Alex had thought to give her some sort of signal. "I would have thought you two had a code, since you did undercover work together."

Carson shook his head. "All field agents use abbreviated speech for emergencies. He didn't use it."

"Did he sound okay?"

Carson made a sound of disgust. "Hard to tell from a whisper."

Phelan whimpered and lifted his small head to peer up at her. Absently she stroked his soft fur. What kind of trouble was her brother in? Bad enough that he didn't want her anywhere near him, even though they both could change for protection.

"I don't get this." Speaking her thoughts aloud, she looked at Carson. "How long have you had that cell phone?"

"A couple of years. Why?"

"Because Alex still remembers your number. I don't understand why he hasn't contacted you before now."

"Here we are." Ignoring her, Carson jabbed his thumb toward the exit sign. Behind a beat-up, dirty, white panel truck, they slowed to nearly forty miles per hour.

"Come on." He drummed his fingers on the steering wheel. "We haven't got all day."

Brenna bit back a flash of anger. "Carson? Any thoughts? Why do you think Alex never called you?"

"Importance." He ground the word out between his teeth. "Until now he obviously didn't feel anything was important enough to merit a call."

The unsaid words hovered in the air. *Even when my wife and daughter were murdered and my world ripped apart.* Even then his partner and former best friend hadn't called.

She fought rising panic. "Something is terribly wrong."

Carson snorted. "You think?"

Without thinking, she placed her hand on his forearm and felt his muscles tense at her touch.

"I know my brother. If he called you his friend, he wouldn't rest until he helped you."

With a deft motion he shook off her hand and drove. Now the road curved sharply, and the panel truck in front of them slowed further. Carson muttered under his breath.

They passed a weathered wooden sign. "Welcome to Hawk's Falls. Population 1,240."

"Twelve hundred and forty?"

"Yeah."

"It *is* a small town. That's weird."

"I know. You would think that would make them more obvious. But most of this area is rural wilderness. People mind their own business here."

After the curve, the road widened to four lanes, with a concrete median. The panel truck remained on the left. Carson swung around to pass on the right.

"Damn idiot is speeding up."

It was true. As they drew abreast of the dirty, unmarked truck, the driver matched his speed to theirs. Alongside them, the truck rattled and bumped as it kept pace.

"What's up with that?" She envisioned men leaping from the van with machine guns spitting, just like in the movies. "I don't like this."

"Neither do I." Now Carson gripped the steering wheel with both hands, tension evident in the stiff set of his shoulders. "They were behind us for miles on the interstate, then got in the right lane and wouldn't let us cut in front of them when it was time to exit. At first I thought they were following us—"

"Is it a government truck?"

"Maybe." Carson gunned the Tahoe, then eased off. A speed limit sign flashed past. "These days, anything goes."

"We're up to fifty-five, and the speed limit is forty

here," she said. She could practically taste his agitation. Or maybe that was merely her own.

"Yeah, there's one more sharp curve ahead, then it will be thirty, because we'll be downtown."

The white truck slowed to take the curve. As it did, it drifted across the solid line into their lane.

"Look out!"

Carson stomped on the brake, causing the Tahoe to fishtail. They missed clipping the truck's bumper by inches, coming to a sliding stop just behind it.

It proceeded on a few hundred feet, weaving across both lanes of the deserted road.

"Something—" Before he finished speaking, the truck swerved and came to a screeching halt, blocking both lanes completely.

"They're waiting for us." Jaw set, Carson put the Tahoe in Reverse. "We'd better get out of here."

"How? You can't see."

"I think I can."

"It's a blind curve. We'll be killed."

Two men dressed entirely in black jumped from the cab of the truck. Both carried shotguns.

Carson put the Tahoe in Drive. "You want to take your chances with them?"

Brenna sat up straight. "We can take them."

He stared hard at her. "Are you crazy? They have guns!"

She exhaled, forcing away the adrenaline pumping in her blood, hoping her eyes didn't show how badly she wanted to fight. "You're right, but I don't care. Let's go."

With a short bark of savage laughter, he gunned the engine. The Tahoe surged forward, directly at the gunmen. One of the men jumped to the side, out of their path. The other remained where he stood, cradling the gun—good, that meant he wouldn't shoot it. He lifted his arm to throw something.

"Get down!" Carson yelled.

Instantly, Brenna obeyed, dropping her head and touching her nose to her knees.

They bumped across the median and sped past on the wrong side of the road. As they did, the rear window shattered, showering her with glass.

"What the—"

"We're past them. We lucked out. No one was coming from the other direction." Carson sounded irrationally calm. Too composed. Still, she sensed his rage.

"Are they following us?"

He checked the rearview mirror. "No, they don't appear to be. Maybe they just wanted to scare the hell out of us."

"Did they shoot? Is that what broke the window?" Sitting up again, Brenna shook her head, sending tiny bits of glass flying. Gingerly she brushed herself off.

"No gunshots. That one guy threw something through the glass. You need to see what it is."

Brenna looked over her shoulder. A large brick covered in shards of glass rested on the back seat.

"A brick." She brushed more glass from the upholstery before leaning over the seat to retrieve it. "You'd think they could have been a little more creative. Look," she mocked. "There's even a note attached."

She lifted the brick and undid the rubber band holding a white piece of paper in place.

"A note?" Carson glanced at her, then back to the road. "Read it to me."

Carefully she unfolded the crumpled paper. Made

from letters cut from a magazine and pasted on the page were two simple sentences, which she read aloud. "'The Lamplight Motel, Hawk's Falls. Meet me there.'" At the bottom of the page, a name—The Wolf. Her brother's nickname.

"That doesn't make sense," she mused. "First he calls, warning us away, then uses goons to break your window to send a message asking us to meet him? No way."

"He's nuts."

Brenna sent him a savage look. "This note isn't from Alex. We're being set up. I think it's a trap."

"You do, do you?" Carson whistled, the sound causing Phelan to try to stand in her lap. "Still trying to protect him?"

"I don't get it. Protect him how?"

"You want me to think this rendezvous is a trap so I won't go to the Lamplight Motel. Then you can slip off and meet your brother without me."

This time Brenna laughed, a bit wildly, since adrenaline still coursed like a jolt of caffeine through her blood. "Get real. Why would Alex resort to such drastic action to send a simple message? For that matter, why would anyone?"

"Exactly." Carson narrowed his eyes. "But then, why would anyone kill my wife and daughter?"

Carson snapped his fingers. "Bingo. I know why. He's insane."

Brenna bit her lip. None of this made sense. Alex wasn't a criminal, nor was he crazy. She knew him better than anyone, Carson included. If only he would *talk* to her, she knew she would get to the bottom of things.

Like why he'd never contacted Carson.

Someone else was involved, thus the old-fashioned, heavy-handed brick through the window. But who? Most likely the same people who wanted to kill Carson.

Glancing up, she saw the dense undergrowth in the trees had thinned out. They went around another bend in the road. Myriad brick buildings, many of them restored, decorated the outskirts of the town.

"Here we are," he said. "Hawk's Falls. Now we need to find the Lamplight Motel and check in."

Brenna stared. "Look, Carson. While I can take care of myself, I don't know if I can protect you. I *know* this is a trap. If Alex truly wanted to meet me somewhere, he'd make sure I knew without a doubt the message was from him. And he wouldn't sign the note 'The Wolf.'"

"Does insanity run in your family?"

For a moment she only gaped at him. "What?"

"Look at you. What are you, five feet tall?"

"Five-one."

"And I'll bet you're a hundred pounds soaking wet."

"So?"

"You really think you can protect yourself from these people?" His tone left no doubt what he thought of that.

"I'm tougher than I look. But like I said, I don't know that I can protect you."

"Is that a threat?"

"No." She sighed. "Just the truth. The letter isn't from Alex. You say people are trying to kill you. I think they're setting a trap. I can't protect you from guns."

"You can't protect me from guns." His cool tone indicated his disbelief. "You're as bad as he is. What kind of life do you people lead?"

"I'm trained in martial arts."

He glanced at her sideways. "Martial arts, right. What exactly do you do for a living?"

"I'm a librarian." She grinned. "I live upstate, in a small town called Leaning Tree."

"For a librarian you have strange hobbies," he said.

"Jujitsu classes were Alex's idea. He wanted me to be able to protect myself. Always."

She glanced at him. Anger simmered underneath his skin, radiating from him. Furious, he looked deadly, like one of the lead hunters in the Pack. Again she felt an unwelcome tug of sexual attraction.

"You're lying." He made a sound of frustration. "You know more than you're saying."

Instead of responding, she studied the town. Hawk's Falls was a charming place, with neat, well-tended buildings and a quaint air. Small-town America at its best.

"I can't see why a biker gang wants to meet here," she said.

"Changing the subject?"

"I've told you everything I know," she said.

"I'll let it go. For now."

"Good." She lifted her chin, daring him to accuse her again of lying. "Now tell me why this biker gang would want to congregate here."

"Their leader, a guy named Nemo, has a farm north of town. Over a hundred acres, isolated and fenced."

The name took her by surprise. "Nemo? Like in *Twenty Thousand Leagues Under the Sea?*"

"Yeah." One corner of his mouth lifted. "Kind of sappy for such a dangerous man. He's deadly, though, make no mistake about it. I met him when Alex and I were undercover." A pained expression crossed his face, and whatever else he'd been about to say died.

"There." He pointed. "The Lamplight Motel."

A weathered sign hung from a seven-foot-tall, black cast-iron lantern. At the end of the cracked blacktop drive, the motel itself had been painted a cheery yellow.

Brenna sighed. "Here we go again. Two rooms?"

"One."

He still didn't trust her. "Fine."

After they were settled in their room, which this time smelled blessedly free of stale cigarette smoke, Brenna began to pace. It had been a while since she'd changed, and she was beginning to feel the need. Since she couldn't, she needed to do something else to dispel her nervous energy. A two-mile jog sounded wonderful, but she doubted Carson would go for it. Still, the outdoors beckoned.

"I need to go for a walk." Crossing her arms, she gave him a look that left no room for argument. "You can come with me or not. I don't care. But I'm going. I need exercise."

On the floor near her feet, Phelan cocked his head. He whimpered and pawed at her leg, tongue lolling.

"He needs a walk, too." Without waiting for Carson's response, Brenna picked up the puppy and headed for the door.

"Wait. I'm coming with you."

Hand on the knob, she paused. "Well, come on, then."

"Don't you want this?" Her coat dangled from his hand. "It's twenty-seven degrees. The wind chill is probably in the teens."

A coat. Brenna had nearly forgotten. She seldom

wore jackets unless the temperature dipped far below freezing, as her internal body heat was much higher than a normal human's. That enabled her to stay warm even in subzero temperatures.

"Here." He tossed it to her. "I brought it in. I thought you might need it."

"Thanks." After placing Phelan on the bed, she slipped it on, leaving the zipper undone. Then she scooped up the puppy and stepped out, lifting her face to the cold slap of the chill breeze.

The air contained the scent of snow. The wind blew crisp and exhilarating, beckoning to her to enjoy winter, her favorite season. She increased her pace, heading for the fringe of trees to the west.

"God, I hate winter." Beside her, Carson turned up his collar. "That wind cuts like a knife."

Ignoring him, Brenna continued to scent the air. No danger here—yet. Only the chill sharpness of winter and the silent call of the woods. Exhilarating. The longing to change, to run as a wolf, shook her. All that she was, her very nature, seemed contained in this slight expanse of forest. Here she belonged. Still, she must remain human for now. She suppressed the urge to change, pushing it deep inside herself.

Phelan squirmed in her arms, feeling the pull of nature just as she did. Stooping, she let him loose, watching with envy as he romped and rolled in the snow. If she were free to change she would join him, frolicking without a care.

"Keep one eye open," Carson said, his voice low. "If they've been tracking us, we'll be an easy shot out here, unprotected."

Brenna started. "What did you say?"

"We'll be an easy—"

"No. Before that."

"Keep one eye open?"

She jerked her head in a nod. "When I was a kid, my mother used to put it a different way. 'Sleep with one eye open,' she always said."

With a puzzled look, he studied her. "Why would a mother say such a thing to a young child? Seems like it would scare the daylights out of you."

"It was meant to." Brenna laughed softly. "Who knew what kind of threats we might face?"

Carson stopped, frowning. Hunched against the cold, he had his hands in his pockets. "Where did you grow up?"

Guarded now, Brenna forced a smile. "Alex and I grew up on a farm upstate, near the Canadian border. Very remote and isolated. There were lots of wild animals and dangers you city folk never have to deal with."

Not entirely a lie. But the real danger always came from humans. Though members of the Pack integrated well, if humans were to discover the Pack's ability to shape-shift, they would panic and attempt to destroy them. Such a thing had happened before, long in the past. Because of that history, they always had to be guarded and abide by the unbreakable laws.

"Your brother never mentioned a farm." Though steady, Carson's tone sounded suspicious.

"Apparently Alex kept a lot of things to himself." Though she meant to be flippant, her remark served to remind both of them that perhaps she hadn't truly known her brother at all.

"I know."

To the left, a twig snapped. Phelan barked, then set off after the sound. Brenna jumped, even though she still detected no danger. "Phelan!" she called, glancing at Carson, knowing if he weren't with her, she would investigate herself.

"It might be a rabbit or a raccoon," Carson said, his wide-legged stance reminding her again of an alpha male in the Pack.

"It might. But on the off chance that it's something bigger, I want to keep the puppy near." She called again.

"Good luck. If it's a deer, you'll never get him to come."

"A deer," she repeated. *Prey.* Though she longed to hunt, Brenna called Phelan a third time. This time the young dog instantly obeyed, running full tilt until he crashed into her leg. He sat expectantly in front of her, tongue lolling, a blissful expression on his face.

"What the hell?" Narrow-eyed, Carson looked from her to the dog and back to the woods. "How did you make him do that?"

"Do what?"

"Come instantly when you called him? You haven't had time to work with him."

"He's smart."

"Maybe. But still…"

She smiled. "It sounds like you know a lot about dogs."

"Some." He looked away. "I… We used to have one." He swallowed. Fascinated, Brenna watched the movement of his throat.

"Used to?"

"Yeah. His body was the first thing the responding officers found when they arrived on the scene. Cody died protecting my family." Hunching his shoulders, he turned away.

Her first instinct was to comfort him. But would he accept consolation from the sister of the man he believed responsible for so much pain?

"I'm sorry," she said instead, keeping her hands to herself.

His back to her, he made no response.

"I'm good with dogs." She began to speak, saying anything to distract him from his anguish. She rumpled her pup's fur. "Phelan understands me, and I understand him. Don't you, boy?"

Phelan grinned up at her. He knew what she was.

Turning, Carson looked at his watch. "How much longer do you need to walk?" His hawk-like features were once again expressionless. Rubbing his hands together, he blew on them. "It's colder than a well digger's butt out here."

Looking from him to the gray sky that still promised snow, then to the unexplored shadows of the woods, Brenna sighed. The powerful craving to shake off her human form, to change and run free, unbridled and unbound, still simmered in her blood. She actually trembled, so strongly did the desire consume her.

"See." Carson took her arm. "You're shivering."

For a moment she couldn't speak, afraid she would snarl or make some other nonhuman sound. She took a deep, shuddering breath, then another, watching the white plumes of frost hover in the air each time she exhaled.

When the longing decreased enough so that she felt human again, Brenna pulled her arm free.

"I could use—" Her voice broke. Clearing her throat, she tried again. "I could use something to eat."

Phelan barked. His intent gaze was focused on the woods.

Quickly, she picked up her puppy. He squirmed in protest and barked again, trying to lunge out of her arms.

Now the back of Brenna's neck tingled a clear warning. "Someone's there. Human, not animal."

Instantly Carson straightened. One hand slipped inside his jacket, and Brenna saw the glint of black metal holstered there.

"Let's go back to the motel." He kept his voice low. "I'm going to move close to you, for cover. Walk slowly, like you haven't noticed anything out of the ordinary."

Quieting the still-protesting Phelan with a sharp word, Brenna did as Carson asked. He moved in behind her, his broad shoulders effectively cutting out the wind.

Silently they retraced their tracks across the snowy field, then the parking lot. When they reached the door to their room, some of the tension left her shoulders. Phelan remained agitated, squirming in her arms.

Once inside, she let him go. He raced to the window, trying to see over the bulk of the heating unit and making little yapping sounds low in his throat.

"He saw something." Pulling off his jacket, Carson kept his holster on, gun in plain view.

"Whoever it was, he meant to harm us."

Suspicion caused Carson's expression to harden. "You know this because...?"

How to explain the sixth sense that kicked in whenever she was in danger? The warning had been clear, but not urgent. Brenna shrugged. "At least he didn't shoot at us."

"Did you expect him to?"

She squared her shoulders. "Could have."

"But didn't," Carson mused. Some of the hostility left his face. "Still, he didn't show himself, either. The note said he would contact us at the hotel. Here we are. Where's The Wolf?"

Sighing, Brenna removed her own parka. Already she felt too hot, with the heater blowing a steady stream of warm air. "I told you, that note's a fake. Alex didn't write it."

"Whoever did wants to meet. Maybe it's an informant." Carson shrugged.

"Or a killer. We need to take precautions," she said. "There's no sense in being sitting ducks."

His gaze sharpened. "Like we were a minute ago in the woods. Tell me, Brenna, was that deliberate? You wanted to go for a walk. Did you set me up?"

Biting back a sharp retort, she marched across the room and grabbed the plastic ice bucket. "You really are the most annoying man. I warned you out there. If I wanted to set you up, you'd be dead by now. I would have killed you myself."

"Are you going to throw that at me?" He indicated the ice bucket, one corner of his mouth lifting in the beginning of a smile.

She stared at him. At the bucket. Then she laughed. "No. We need ice. A couple of diet colas would be nice, too."

As he reached to take the bucket from her, the room phone rang. Brenna jumped, then looked at Carson. They both started for it at the same time.

Carson reached the phone first. Elbowing her out of the way, he plucked it from the receiver. He listened intently, then slammed the phone back in its cradle.

"Alex?"

He nodded. "Interesting. Now instead of just wanting you gone, I've been ordered to get myself the hell out of town, as well—and I have until midnight tonight to do it."

Brenna studied Carson's face. Judging from the muscle that jerked in his jaw, the call had infuriated him. "Or?"

"That's the thing." The bleak fury in his dark eyes froze her. "He knows there's nothing else he could do to me. So he's trying to bribe me instead. If I do as he asks, he says he'll turn himself over to me on Friday."

Chapter 6

He didn't know which pissed him off more—the fact that his former partner thought he was an idiot, or the utter lack of reaction with which Brenna took the news. Obviously, she still didn't believe her brother had become a vicious criminal. Talk about blinders.

"Why Friday?"

"It's the day after the big drug deal is supposed to happen."

"Tell me exactly what he said," she demanded.

Carson took a deep breath. Struggling to keep his voice flat and unemotional, he jammed his hands in his pockets and looked at the ceiling. "He repeated what he said earlier on my cell. 'Get Brenna out of here. I don't want her hurt. And I want you gone, too. Get out by midnight, before you get yourself killed. Don't mess this up for me.'"

"By midnight, huh?"

"Yeah. By midnight tonight." Carson ran a hand through his hair. "Though, as threats go, it was pretty ineffectual. He didn't back it up with anything except his stupid promise. More than anyone, I know his word is no good."

"What else?" Determination colored her tone. "I need his exact words. Please."

Carson turned to study her. "'Tell Brenna I'm all right. But she has to leave right away. No ifs, ands or buts.'"

She sank down on the bed, relief, worry and joy all at once showing on her face. "Alex."

So much love in her voice when she said his name, Carson thought, infuriated. But he himself was alone in the world because of her brother, and that infuriated him even more. "What was that, some sort of code?"

"In a way. Our mother used that expression, too; just like keeping one eye open. Alex and I made fun of it our entire lives. He said it for me, so I would know without a doubt it was him."

"Yeah, well, your very considerate brother's been trying to kill me." He knew he sounded savage, and he felt absurdly guilty as he watched her smile vanish. "Does he really think I'll turn tail and run when I'm so close? Turn himself in on Friday—right."

"He's worried about your safety as well as mine." Brenna stood and crossed her arms. Worry darkened her eyes. "He has a reason for everything. I know he has."

"I'm not leaving," Carson said, dark promise making his voice nearly a growl. He could have softened it, but he wanted to make sure she understood he meant what he said.

"Neither am I." Now she wrapped her arms around herself, in a hug. "Until I talk to Alex and find out the truth, I'm not going anywhere."

"I know." Feeling compelled by some strange impulse he didn't understand, in three steps Carson crossed the room to stand in front of her. Cupping her chin in his hand, he forced her to look up at him.

"As long as you're with me, he has to come to us. You're my insurance."

She stared at him, shock making her eyes widen. "You mean to use me against my brother?"

"I—" At first he thought she was trembling from fear. Then her gaze pinpointed on him, narrowing. Too late, he realized she was shaking not from fear but from anger.

He released her chin and stepped back.

"I shouldn't have said that," he admitted. "I just meant—"

She moved toward him. "You plan to use me to make Alex suffer."

"No." He meant it.

"It will never happen. I won't let you use me." The flat certainty in her tone both intrigued and infuriated him.

"What kind of monster do you think I am?" He turned away before she answered, telling himself he really didn't care, but still not willing to see the stark condemnation on her face.

"No more innocent lives will be lost because of me. I've got enough stains on my soul." He hadn't meant to reveal so much. Since he had, he might as well finish.

"I'm not like your brother."

"Listen to me." Moving silently, she came up behind

him and placed her hand on his shoulder. He held himself still only by sheer effort of will. “You’re a desperate man. I understand you want revenge. I’d want vengeance, too. But you’ve got to look for the truth in all this or else none of it will matter. You need justice, not a blind settling of scores.”

His throat closed. Each word she spoke increased his confusion. How simple it had all seemed before he’d met her, when he’d been a hundred percent certain Alex had been the one who betrayed him and killed his family.

“I still think he did it,” he muttered. He couldn’t summon enough strength to brush her hand from his shoulder. Until now, until Brenna, he hadn’t realized how much he craved human contact.

She squeezed. “But you’re not positive.”

His gut twisted. “No.” The single word burst from him. “Because of you, now I’m not positive.”

He heard her swift intake of breath and slowly turned to look at her. She let her hand fall. He wondered if he would see amusement or—God forbid—pity on her expressive face. But he saw only warmth and compassion, two things that had been absent from his life for so long.

Their gazes met. Locked and held.

“Brenna.” He spoke her name as a warning.

She chose not to take it. With her chest nearly touching his, she gazed up at him, the obstinate tilt of her chin somehow endearing.

Maybe because she smelled of a long-forgotten spring, or because her soft mouth parted and her pupils darkened, or maybe because he just plain wanted to, Carson bent his head and kissed her.

After her first startled hiss of breath, she reached

up and drew him closer. Her lips moved under his, unbelievably, delectably sweet. His body responded with a violence that stunned him. Desire slammed into him, heating his blood, thickening his body. Guilt—what the hell did he think he was doing?—surfaced, clawing at him. Out of reflex, he tried to picture his dead wife's face in his mind. That always brought him some measure of comfort.

But for the first time, he couldn't see her. He saw only Brenna, with her warm smile and freckled nose. Panic replaced craving. He pulled himself away, breaking the kiss and stepping from the intoxicating circle of her arms.

She, unlike the hell of his memories, let him go without a word.

Ignoring his body's insistent ache, he chose to focus on the smile that trembled at the corners of her mouth. How could she regard this kiss as somehow amusing, while to him it felt like the epitome of disloyalty?

"Another trick?" His voice dripped ice. He felt a pang as confusion clouded her eyes, but he pushed it away.

Meeting his gaze without guile, she combed through her hair with her fingers, mussing it in a way he knew was unconsciously sexy. "I won't bother to answer that," she said. "You're furious. With me or with yourself?"

He set his jaw and crossed his arms, feeling an absurd need for self-defense. "Sleeping with me won't help your brother."

"Sleeping with—" Lifting her hand as if to slap him, she apparently thought better of it and shook her head instead. The light went out of her lovely face. "You're crazy."

"Am I?" He should stop, he knew, but his guilt and

the erratic beat of his heart goaded him on. "Then why did you kiss me?"

"I kissed you *back*." Scorn rang in her tone. "You initiated it."

Suddenly weary of the entire thing, he turned away.

"I'm a fool," he said. Crossing to the small window, he lifted a corner of the curtain and peered outside. The parking lot was empty, and the late-afternoon sky once more threatened snow. The pewter of the sky matched his mood.

"Let's forget this ever happened," he told her, unable to keep the anger from his voice. Looking back over his shoulder at her, he saw that she was crouched on the floor, petting her small puppy's belly. The dog looked comical, all four paws in the air waving madly, tongue lolling to the side of his mouth. His eyes were closed, and he appeared to be grinning in sheer bliss.

Carson felt a pang. Both for what he'd lost and for what he would never have. For an instant he could imagine her hands touching him, stroking, sensual…

No. No more mindless lust. He forced himself to remember. Doing so would bring back the pain, then the welcome numbness that had turned his world to gray. Damn Brenna for even thinking she could make him feel.

Movement outside captured his attention. A man, dressed in a nondescript black overcoat, crossed to the room alongside theirs. Though he kept his head down, his pace unhurried, the way he moved was as familiar to Carson as the generic dark blue or black car he bet the man drove. If one was here, there were always others. Carson would bet his last dollar that federal agents were their neighbors, though whether FBI or DEA, he didn't know.

Either way, since his supervisor had already warned him off this investigation, it didn't look good for him. If they saw him, they would consider him a rogue and place him under arrest.

Once more the stakes had been raised. Not only did he have to keep himself and Brenna alive, but he also had to remain invisible to the Feds.

Another thought occurred to him. If federal agents were converging here, his informant had been right. Something big was going to happen in Hawk's Falls in a couple of days. Perfect. Maybe Hades' Claws—and Alex—would be too preoccupied to make any more attempts on his life.

Though he wouldn't bet on it.

"What is it?" She reached him, moving in that soundless way of hers that would be an asset in his line of work. Right now he found it a liability.

He turned abruptly, blocking the window. "Just the people in the room next door."

"Oh," she said.

"Were you expecting Alex?" With an effort of will, he kept himself from glancing back outside. "I thought you didn't expect him to show up here."

The disgusted look she gave him nearly made him laugh. "I don't. If Alex could come to me, he would."

"Such faith," he mocked. "I used to trust him like that, too. But now I know better."

She smiled. "Tell me about what it was like when he was your partner."

For a moment he was so dumbfounded that he couldn't speak. His chest suddenly felt tight with too many memories: Alex playing with Becky, bringing her a huge, floppy rag doll—her first. Alex at his dinner table, joking with Julie over pot roast, helping with the dishes. Drinking Bud Light and munching on pizza while the two of them watched football. Alex always cheered for the Vikings while he rooted for the Giants. Now the memories felt like quicksand, dragging him down.

"No," Carson said. "I'd rather *you* tell *me* about him." At her startled look, he elaborated. "About his life before I knew him."

As she watched him, her smile broadened. "Only if you return the favor later. I want to know about when he was your partner. He never told me about any of that. His degree was in marketing."

"I used to tease him about that." The words slipped from him before he thought better of it. "At least I knew about his marketing degree."

"There's so much he never told me." She sounded so hurt that he felt an impulse to comfort her. Knowing how easily one touch could lead to folly, he suppressed it. Instead, he twisted his mouth in what he hoped would pass for a smile.

"I know."

She sat down on the edge of her bed, still watching him with a thoughtful expression. "What exactly did you want to know?"

How could he answer, when he didn't really know the answer himself? Why even try to understand the man who'd been like a brother to him, then betrayed him so horribly? Yet how many sleepless nights had he paced, trying to do exactly that? To understand the why of it?

He glanced at her, at Alex's sister, the woman who

still believed in fairy tales. She couldn't begin to understand the depths of the horror he'd witnessed. Blood and death and evil were as foreign to her as love was now to him. She didn't belong here.

But love and worry for a brother who surely didn't deserve it made her place her own life in danger.

Unabashedly he studied her. She met his gaze, the same intent look on her mobile features. He saw it now, the resemblance to his former partner, every so often when she turned her head a certain way or smiled at her puppy's playful antics. They had the same dark brown eyes. Their profiles were similar. But there the resemblance ended. Alex stood over six feet tall, while Brenna barely cleared five feet. Her hair was the color of sable, while Alex was blond. Brenna's bones were delicate, nearly fragile in appearance, while Alex had the lean, sturdy build of a fighting man.

"I want to know all of it." He cleared his throat. "Like I said, Alex never mentioned any family."

"He didn't have any family left, besides me. Our mother died when we were still teenagers." Her gaze never wavered from his face. "We were seventeen. After Mom passed away, all we had was each other."

"What about your father?"

She lifted one shoulder in a gesture he thought was meant to be a shrug that somehow fell short. "Who knows? We never knew him."

"So—"

Holding up her hand, she smiled. "My turn. Tell me when you first met Alex."

"Training." He thought back to that crisp autumn day. He'd been full of exuberance and naive hope. His dream job was finally within reach. "Like the FBI boys, we trained in Quantico, Virginia. Alex was in my class."

"I didn't even know," she marveled. "All he told me was that he had a new job. One he was excited about."

"Yeah." Carson tried not to remember how Alex had been the star of their class. His keen intelligence and enthusiasm had been contagious. The mysterious fascination women had for him was a plus for the guys who'd hung with him. "Women flocked to him."

Brenna laughed. "Even when he was a teenager, he had that problem. Though he did come to like it eventually."

"You must have had a similar reaction from guys." Carson hadn't meant to blurt those words, but he saw from the odd shadow that crossed her face that he'd touched on something sensitive.

"There weren't many guys," she said, drawing out the word as if she found it distasteful, "in the small town where I live. I was engaged once, but it didn't work out. I never went out into the world like Alex."

Out into the world. Odd choice of phrasing. He studied her face, looking for clues. Though he could have sworn he'd seen a brief flash of pain in her dark eyes, now her expression might have been carved in stone. He opened his mouth to ask his next question.

"Nope. My turn," she said. "I'm counting that as a question. Since Alex was your partner, exactly what kind of work did you do together?"

"Not office work," he shot back. "And I really didn't see my earlier remark as a question. It's still my turn. I want to know about this fiancé."

"Wait." The shadow had returned to her eyes, telling him that he hadn't imagined it. "I would rather not talk about him. He's…" She paused for so long that he began to imagine all sorts of crazy things to finish the sentence.

"He's what?" Carson cocked his head. "A biker? A cop? A—"

"He's dead," she said, her expression as bleak as he imagined his was when he talked about his lost family. A thousand other questions came to mind, first and foremost the need to know how he'd died, but Carson decided that could wait for another time. Asking her would have felt too much like tearing the wings off an innocent butterfly.

"And that's not about Alex. That's personal."

"You're right." He dragged his hand through his hair. "I don't know why I asked. It's none of my business. I'm sorry. Go ahead and interrogate me." He gave her a quick smile, meant to ease the sting of his word choice.

She nodded, relief lightening her gaze. "Okay, then, elaborate, please. You said you and Alex were in the field. You mentioned undercover work. Like police officers or what? Did you assume other identities, different names? What exactly did you do?"

"We were in the Drug Enforcement Agency." He emphasized the first word. "Our job was to find the people who transported and smuggled drugs. The big guys. We let the local police go after the small fish. And, yes, of course we had false names and identification."

She looked at him, chewing her bottom lip. Something still bothered her, and Carson thought he might know the reason.

"Did Alex do drugs?" she blurted. "Is that maybe why—"

He'd guessed correctly. "Not that I know of." He

took another look at her face. Again he saw the quick flash of pain in her eyes. "Maybe why…what? Why he killed my family? Wait a minute. You believe me now?"

"I don't know what to believe."

He felt the oddest urge to comfort her. Though he couldn't pinpoint the exact moment when his own innocence had been destroyed, he knew he'd been a better man before. Now, not only was his innocence gone, but the very reason he had for drawing breath depended on gaining vengeance from the same man who'd had a part in ripping out his heart.

Carson began to pace, the hotel room suddenly seeming too small, too warm, too much like a trap.

"Believe this," he said, the words coming out raspy, instead of strong, as he'd intended. "Your brother is not the same person you knew. Sometimes when we work undercover—" he remembered the instructor's lessons in Quantico "—we run the danger of losing our original identity to the new one. Especially if that identity is more exciting, more dangerous. I think that's what might have happened to Alex."

"If that were true, Alex would have forgotten I existed. Obviously, he hasn't."

He gave a noncommittal nod, risking another quick look out the window. The courtyard now appeared deserted. The parking lot held only his Tahoe and the government-issue sedan.

"Carson?" Brenna's voice no longer sounded uncertain.

Turning, he saw she'd regained a bit of color in her face.

"How did you know Alex?"

Jamming his hands in his pockets, he forced himself to stand still. "We met at the academy. Why?"

"You knew him well?"

"I thought I did." He frowned. "But obviously I didn't."

"There has to be something," she persisted. "If you didn't see him shoot you or your family, you must have some other reason to make you suspect a man you once trusted."

"I have plenty of reasons."

"Pick one." Her tone dry, Brenna crossed her arms.

"I didn't see anyone else at my house that day."

"Were you shot first?"

Swallowing, he forced the word out. "Yes."

"Did you remain conscious?"

Now this was an interrogation. Though he didn't want to relive that day, he felt as if he owed Brenna the facts. After all, he was asking her to believe horrible things about her beloved brother.

"No. They—he—shot me in the back. I blacked out. When I came to, the rest was already over."

Her eyes looked huge. Once again her face had gone pale.

God help him, he couldn't move. Couldn't breathe, couldn't think. "Enough," he said. "No more."

She inhaled, her chest heaving. "I'm sorry. Let me ask this, then. Do you have any other reason to suspect my brother? Did his behavior change? Did he do anything that seemed weird?"

"Yes." Relief flooded him. Back on solid ground, he could talk about anything but what had happened on that awful day. "Alex first started to change when his wife left him."

"Wife?" She looked blank. Stunned surprise? Her shock seemed genuine.

"How many sisters don't even know their brother has gotten married?" he drawled.

"He couldn't have. He would've told me."

Carson simply shook his head.

"Are you sure we're talking about the same person?" Her dazed look faded, replaced by one of determination. "I have a snapshot of him in my wallet. Let me get it—"

"Brenna," he said, "you saw the picture on that datasheet. Face facts. Alex got married, and you didn't know about it."

"He didn't tell me," she whispered. "How could he not— Where? When?" Brenna took a step toward him, puzzlement clouding her eyes. "Who was she? What was she like?"

He thought back to the three times he'd met Lyssa. "She was a looker," he said. "Tall and slender, with long, blond hair. Her name was Lyssa. It must have been a whirlwind courtship, because he never really mentioned dating her. One day he just showed up and announced he'd gotten married. We were best friends, and he never even brought her over to my house."

Brenna swayed. He watched as she visibly took hold of her composure. "Did he—" she licked her lips "—love her?"

"I guess." Carson shrugged, watching her closely. "How long did you say it was since you last saw Alex?"

If his question surprised her, she didn't show it. "Less than a year. Six months. Not long enough for all this—" she gestured vaguely "—to happen."

"I've been looking for him for eighteen months. He was married two years ago," he said gently. "For whatever reason, he didn't tell you."

She closed her eyes, her stunned hurt evident in the way she tightly compressed her lips.

"I don't understand," she whispered. "What on earth has happened to my brother?"

He should have felt victorious or, at the very least, a small bit of grim satisfaction. But as he watched her, one more person The Wolf had managed to hurt with his actions, he felt only aching weariness.

"Don't try to rationalize. He lied to you. Betrayed me. Alex has changed."

"I'll say." Straightening, she gave him a dark look full of blame as she stalked to the bathroom. "And I mean to find out why."

With that parting remark, she closed the door firmly. The knob rattled enough to let him know she'd locked it. He didn't care. The bathroom had no window. If she wanted to blame him, he would let her. Brenna seemed like an intelligent woman. She would realize soon enough that he'd had nothing to do with her brother's choices.

His cell phone rang. Jack. He wanted a face-to-face and named a restaurant in town.

After one more look out the blinds—still nothing—Carson let the curtain fall back. With a tired sigh, he dropped into the room's one chair, a burnt-orange monstrosity. He pulled off his alligator boots, setting them neatly side by side under the table.

Just when he'd thought he knew everything, the situation had grown even weirder. Brenna's shock had been genuine. She truly didn't know her brother had gotten married. What reason could Alex have had for keeping his marriage a secret? Carson had doubted the marriage from the moment he'd heard about it. He found it even stranger now, since Alex hadn't even told his own sister.

When Lyssa had run off barely a month after the wedding, his partner had seemed devastated. But Alex had managed to pull himself together. Undercover, a distracted man made deadly mistakes.

In an operation the scope of the one that they'd been part of, neither of them had wanted to jeopardize things. The DEA had been after Hades' Claws for years. They'd been too close to blow it.

A remembered wave of pain swamped Carson. He ran a hand across his mouth. Once he'd thought his job defined his existence. He'd found out otherwise after his cover had been blown and his family brutally murdered. His job had meant nothing to him then. Nor did it mean anything to him now. Nothing but a vehicle for self-recrimination and blame.

The bathroom door opened. Brenna had run a damp comb through her hair and washed her face. She looked achingly young, though fierce determination shone from her eyes.

"Do you know how to get in touch with this woman?" She made a face. "Alex's wife?"

He let her have a moment to cross the room, waiting until she sat perched on the end of one bed.

"No one does, and that's saying a lot," he said. "Despite hundreds of government resources at my disposal, I couldn't find her. Though I can't say for certain, I think she might be dead."

Chapter 7

Brenna didn't believe him, not at first. Twisting her hands in her lap, she stared at Carson. Hard. With all the anger and defiance building inside her. She gave him the kind of predatory stare that made most humans back away.

But he seemed oblivious. Either that, or he simply didn't care.

"Dead," she repeated, when she could find her voice. "How convenient. Are you… Are you *sure?*"

He shrugged. She wasn't fooled by his nonchalance. Pain carved lines in his face. "Alex thought she might be. He worried."

"Was there a—" again she struggled to find the words "—a funeral?"

"No. We never found a body."

Her stomach roiled. "This is ridiculous."

"Yep." Unsmiling, he watched her. "She disappeared off the face of the earth."

Again hurt blossomed in her, bringing unwanted tears to her eyes and a need to strike out at something—anything. With an effort she stayed seated, for though she wanted to attack Carson, none of this was his fault. She took several deep breaths and was able to push her feelings aside.

"Seems I'm the bearer of bad news," he said.

"I was just thinking that," she said, startled at the way his words mirrored her thoughts. "I can't help but think—"

"That Alex's bad luck began when he met me?" His voice sounded harsh; his expression was even more so. She recognized the anger in his tone, mixed with guilt and hurt.

She jumped to her feet, jumbled emotion propelling her as she padded across the room to stand in front of him. Impassive, he regarded her, expectation plain in his face. His emotions fed her own. She couldn't tear her gaze away. They breathed in unison. Intensity flared from him to her and back again.

Brenna unclenched her fists, her heart pounding. Her anger leached out of her, becoming something else. Something that vibrated between them, silent but equally powerful.

"There's no sense in this," she said quietly, her body thrumming with desire. Though she wanted to, she seemed unable to look away. Despite his closed expression, she sensed a certain vulnerability in him.

Before, he had kissed her. Now *she* wanted to kiss *him.* She took a step closer. Then another. Reaching out, she buried her hand in his thick, sable hair.

A shudder ran through him. She felt its echo in her own thundering heartbeat. Inhaling, she took in his scent. Spicy, musky, male.

One more small movement and they met, chest to chest. She wanted more, wanted to strip off her clothes and his, then wrap herself fully around him, belly to belly. She felt him quicken against her in a rush of hardness, felt her own body respond with warmth and moisture. Flicking her tongue against the corded muscles of his neck, she tasted the salty desire on his skin, breathed it in the air.

He groaned. "Brenna, no—"

Standing on tiptoe, she covered his mouth with her own. "Shh." Urgency and need, confusion and sorrow all combined in her kiss. Her body heat increased, as it always did when she became aroused. Making wordless sounds of desire, she drank of him deeply, drawing out of him the bottled emotions he'd kept to himself for so long.

Again he groaned. Nestled snugly in the juncture of his thighs, she felt his body surge against her, even as he used his arms to push her away.

"No." Shoulders heaving, he turned his back to her, visibly struggling to regain control. "Damn it, I want to forget, too, Brenna. Believe me, I do. But not this way, not by using you."

Stung, she said the first thing that came to her mind. "It's not a betrayal, you know."

He swung around so quickly that she sucked in her breath.

"Every breath I take is a betrayal," he ground out. "*I* should be dead, not them. And though there is a certain kind of irony in me screwing their murderer's sister, I can't do that to their memory."

All that had burned inside her went still at his words. "It's been eighteen months," she said quietly. Her throat ached. The pulse pounding in her temple, the conflicting emotions that flooded her made her head hurt. How could she want to attack and comfort someone all at the same time? How could mere words cause so much pain?

Face grim, he held up an unsteady hand. "Enough. You've had a lot of surprises today. I understand what you're feeling. You want a channel for your anger. That's understandable."

His clinical observations amused her. "And what of your own body? You wanted me, Carson. Lie to yourself all you want, but you can't hide your arousal."

"You're a beautiful woman," he said quietly. "And it's been a long time since I—"

"Made love?"

"Had sex. Think about it, Brenna. You'll realize this isn't what you want."

Though his clearheaded logic irked her, she considered his words. He'd made it clear that this would have been sex, sheer lust. Her breasts still tingled. She crossed her arms to cover her pebbled nipples and inhaled. Why had she thought that when the two of them came together, it would have been making love? Carson was right. Damn it. Though he aroused her, she didn't want a fleeting sexual fling. Much like the wolves they became when they changed, her kind mated for life.

"We need to eat," she said, changing the subject. "I'm starving."

Slowly he nodded, still watching her. "Right. We do."

Glancing at the window, he frowned and consulted his watch. "Let's wait until after dark."

That made no sense. "I thought you wanted to be seen with me."

"No need." He shrugged. "Alex knows you're with me."

"You have an answer for everything, don't you?"

He dropped into the chair and he pulled on his boots. "In my line of work, you have to."

She looked at his feet. "What's with the cowboy boots?"

Running one hand lovingly over the ridged leather, he sighed. "They were a Christmas gift from my wife. I sold the house, the furniture, everything. They're all I have left of her."

Again she felt his sadness. "You must have loved her very much."

Though Carson didn't answer, he didn't have to. Brenna found herself wondering what it would be like to be loved like that.

She changed the subject. "What about the midnight deadline?"

"What about it?"

"Do you think Alex will do anything?"

His quick flash of a smile reminded her inexplicably of her brother. "I hope so."

"Sorry to disappoint you, but I don't think he will. Not with me here."

Jaw clenched, he raked his hand through his hair, reminding her of how surprisingly thick and silky it had felt when she'd touched it. Her mouth went dry. Swallowing hard, she lifted her chin.

"Do you think we need to change motels?"

He frowned. "No. Whoever threw the brick said to meet him here. As long as we watch our backs, we should be safe."

She noticed he no longer seemed to believe Alex had written the message on the brick. "So you don't think it's a trap?"

"If it is, I'm ready." Though he sounded perfectly reasonable, she detected a hint of savage anger behind his voice.

He stood, pulling on his DEA jacket from force of habit; then, apparently having second thoughts, he yanked it off and tossed it on the bed.

"No sense in being more of a target than I have to be," he said.

She smiled. "I agree."

His expression remained deadly serious. "Brenna, I'm not joking about the danger. These people mean business. If this is a trap, we've got to be exceptionally careful. If we're lucky, we might be able to grab one of their guys and use him for leverage."

"That's your strategy?"

"I haven't come up with much of a plan yet, other than meeting with Alex."

Brenna reached for her coat. "It's just about dark," she said. "Let's go eat. We'll bring something back for Phelan."

At the sound of his name, the puppy came running. He jumped first on Carson, then, when Carson ignored him, ran to Brenna. Lavishing kisses on Phelan's small head, Brenna shook her head at Carson.

"He likes you, you know."

"Whatever." His surly tone revealed his thoughts on that subject. "What do you want to eat?"

"I don't care," she said. "As long as it's red meat."

He raised a brow. "Red meat?"

She nodded, still scratching Phelan's neck.

Just as he picked up his jacket, they heard the sound of tires squealing, then the sickening crunch of metal hitting metal.

"Wait here," Carson ordered.

Hand already on the knob, Brenna yanked open the door first. "Like hell I will."

They rushed outside shoulder to shoulder, just in time to see the brake lights of a battered El Camino exit the parking lot and speed away.

Carson kicked at a rock with the toe of his boot. "My Tahoe."

Together, they walked toward the vehicle. The entire passenger side was crumpled. That, in addition to the shattered back windshield, made the vehicle look ready for a junkyard.

"You'd better call a tow truck," Brenna said, speaking her thoughts out loud.

Running his hand over the black metal, Carson shook his head. "It's drivable." His tone left no room for argument. "Not pretty, but I bet it'll still run."

The door to the room next to theirs opened, and a man with a shock of curly red hair peered out. After a quick look, he ducked back inside and closed the door behind him with a firm thunk.

"Carson?" One minute he'd been standing beside her, the next he'd disappeared on the other side of the Tahoe.

"He's gone," she said. "Didn't even seem curious."

Carson came around the front of the vehicle. "He's a federal agent. He doesn't want to get involved."

Hands on her hips, Brenna glared at him. She didn't

need to ask how he knew. "A federal agent? So that's why you didn't want to be seen. Why didn't you tell me?"

He lifted a brow. "No reason."

His churlish growl didn't faze her. "Are they here because of the biker meeting your informant mentioned?"

"Probably. I don't know. I'm out of the loop. I'm on medical leave." He crossed to the undamaged driver's side. He held the door open for her. "Come on."

She went around and climbed up in front of him. He didn't offer to assist her, for which she was oddly grateful. She wasn't quite sure how she would feel about having his hands on her body so soon after that scorching kiss. Clambering over the console felt ungraceful, but she made short work of it, settling in her seat with an *oomph.*

He got in and started the engine, put the transmission in Reverse and backed from their parking spot. Other than a few rattles, clunks and clangs, the Tahoe appeared to be in sound mechanical condition.

Carson, on the other hand, appeared about as talkative as a rock.

"Do you think this was an accident?"

Carson didn't even look at her. "Get real."

"Another warning?"

"Maybe."

As they drove down Main Street in search of an open restaurant, Brenna decided to ask the question that had been nagging at her ever since she'd found that crumpled paper in his glove box. "Why are you on medical leave, anyway?"

His hands clenched on the wheel.

"Hey." She kept her voice soft. "You owe me at least that much."

A brief shadow came and went on his face. "Why? Afraid you might be traveling with a crazy person?"

She watched him, waiting.

"Fine. You want to know? They said I was losing it." Though his tone was fierce, Brenna detected bewildered hurt underneath. He made a sound of disgust. "They felt I was too intense, too focused on this investigation. That I was in danger of turning into some kind of vigilante." He shot her a grim smile. "And you know what? They were right."

From the jumble of her conflicting emotions, Brenna searched for a response. Finding none, she contented herself with watching out the window.

On the outskirts of town, a neon sign indicated that Jean's Coffee Shop was open. They turned into the parking lot.

"Vigilante," she repeated, rolling the word around in her mouth, trying to get a sense of it. "Because you want to find the man who killed your family?"

If he noticed she didn't say Alex, he gave no sign.

"Yep." Again the grim smile. "Imagine that."

"You know, I think the killer wants you here."

Carson gave her a startled look. "Why do you say that?"

"If you were a killer, wouldn't you want to finish the job?" She waited for him to make the connection.

Which he did. "But Alex wants me gone."

She wished she could ring a bell. Instead she settled for a small smile. "Bingo."

"Ergo Alex can't be the killer?" His face had gone grim again, his eyes dark and hard.

"Right." She nodded, refusing to let his obvious disbelief deflate her.

"Or maybe he regrets what he did."

Trust Carson to come up with his own kind of logic.

"You're wrong. I have a strong feeling about this. I get those sometimes."

With a savage flick of his wrist, he killed the engine. "Woman's intuition?" His tone made the words sound like a curse.

Determined to keep her smile from slipping, she nodded. "Sort of. More like animal instinct."

"Oh, yeah? Then use your sixth sense and stay alert while we grab dinner. My informant's meeting us here, and you never know who might be watching us."

Stay alert. He was right, though she doubted whoever threatened them would make a move in a public place. Still, she scanned the exterior of the small restaurant. Several cars and pickup trucks were parked outside, some snow-covered except for the windshields. The front sidewalk had been recently shoveled. Through the big front window, she could see that several others had chosen to eat their evening meal in the homey coffee shop.

"It looks okay," she told Carson.

He gave her an odd look. "If the locals eat here, the food is bound to be good."

"I meant safe."

He made a rude sound. "I don't think anywhere in this town is safe for us."

Together they walked to the door. The oddest wish struck her—she wanted to slip her hand in his. A quick glance at Carson's hard profile told her how foolish such an action would be.

A bell over the door jingled as they went inside.

"Sit anywhere." A cheerful woman with short brown hair waved her pad at them. "I'll be with you in a minute."

Aside from a few curious glances, none of the other diners paid them any mind. Brenna studied them out of the corner of her eye. Most looked like retirees or farmers. None of them remotely resembled members of a biker gang. Nor did any appear to be government agents, though she really had no idea what a federal agent should look like.

She glanced at Carson. Openly casing the room, he hid his thoughts behind an implacable facade, no emotion showing on his masculine face. He hadn't worn a jacket, only his gray, nondescript sweatshirt, which she had to admit he filled out very well. With his broad shoulders and muscular arms, he looked dangerous, yet he moved with an easy grace that spoke of authority, determination and confidence. She wondered how he'd made it undercover, because a man like Carson would attract attention wherever he went.

They'd just settled into a booth when the waitress bustled over.

"Do you want coffee?" She set down two filled water glasses, then turned over their two cups and poured from a pot she carried with her. After sliding their steaming cups in front of them, she plunked down a couple of laminated menus and then a small pitcher of cream.

"Look these over and yell when you're ready."

Brenna glanced at the menu for steak but found only a chopped-meat version.

"The burger will be better," Carson said.

Startled, Brenna smiled. "How do you know?"

He jerked his head. "Look around."

Most of the other diners had hamburgers.

"Specialty of the house. But I'm partial to liver and onions myself."

One of her favorites. "Since there's no T-bone—" Brenna leaned forward "—I guess that'll have to do." She glanced over her shoulder. The waitress had vanished.

Looking at Carson leaning back in the booth, Brenna asked the question that had been bothering her. "Why do you suppose Alex hasn't come to talk to me himself?"

Disbelief shone in his eyes. "Come on. First off, I'm with you. He knows I want him. Then there're the Feds. Mix in bikers and drugs. It's too dangerous for him to show his face."

She sat back. "Alex knows I can take care of myself."

"You seem to have lived a pretty sheltered life." His expression doubtful, Carson took a long drink of water.

"Don't equate sheltered with weak," she warned. "I might be a librarian, but I work out four times a week. And as I said, I have a brown belt in jujitsu."

"Brown?" His lips twitched. "Why not black?"

"I'm working toward that. Give me another year," she said. Then, because she knew unless he saw her in action he would never believe her anyway, she changed the subject. "Explain what you said about not being able to find Lyssa. How can that be possible?"

"I don't know. I used every resource I had, even the FBI database. She'd vanished. Worse, I couldn't find any trace of her. I didn't have fingerprints to run. She must have used a fake name or something. It was like she'd never existed."

Dead? Or had someone erased her records?

Disturbed, Brenna mulled over the possibility. She would ask Alex about it when she saw him. That and numerous other things.

"She was mixed up in it somehow," Carson continued. "Though I haven't been able to figure out exactly how."

"Was she a member of Hades' Claws?"

"Are you folks ready to order?" Smiling expectantly, the waitress appeared at their table. They both ordered the liver and onions. The waitress wrinkled her nose but wrote the order dutifully on her pad.

Taking another drink of water, Brenna waited until she was out of earshot before continuing. "Do you think this Lyssa set my brother up?"

"How?"

Disappointed, Brenna crossed her arms. "I don't know. You're the DEA guy. You tell me."

Carson shook his head, making a quick cutting motion with his hand. A young man dressed in a heavy down parka and knit cap slid in beside him. His long, dirty-blond hair hung loose around his shoulders.

"Hey." He cut his gaze toward Brenna. "You must be the girlfriend. Carson told me you'd be with him tonight."

She stiffened. Carson held up his finger, warning her silently to keep quiet.

"I got a message for you, man." Turning back toward Carson, the man watched with an expectant look on his bony face. "Along with some info. Freakin' great stuff."

Carson fished in his pocket, removing a crinkled bill and passing it over. "This better be good, Jack," he warned. "We've already gotten a couple of conflicting messages today."

So this was the informant. Carefully keeping her expression bland, Brenna pretended to be intensely interested in the chipped Formica tabletop.

"Busy day, huh?" Jack smiled, showing crooked teeth as he stuffed the money in his pocket. He let his gaze travel slowly over Brenna, making her skin crawl. "Hope everyone is all right. You don't wanna mess with some of these people. 'Specially the dude sending those messages."

Did he know who that was? Brenna lifted her gaze from the table. Tempted to stare him down, to intimidate him into telling her if he'd seen Alex, she leaned forward.

"Cut the crap." Impatience sounded in Carson's tone. "If you have something for me, let me have it."

With another lecherous look at Brenna, Jack leaned over and whispered in Carson's ear. Despite her excellent hearing, Brenna could not make out the words.

The waitress, carrying a heavy tray, headed for their table. Jack pushed himself up.

"Wait." Carson grabbed his arm. "Here." He pushed another crumpled bill into the other man's hand. "Buy yourself something to eat."

Jack smiled. "Thanks, man." Head down, he strode toward the door without a backward glance.

"Well?" Brenna asked, unable to contain her curiosity another second. "What did he—"

"Here you go." Setting their meals down in front of them with a thud, their waitress also refilled their water glasses. She took an inordinately long time to do it, so much so that Brenna opened her mouth, ready to ask her to leave.

"Thank you." Carson beat her to it. With a stiff nod, the woman bustled off.

"She's not happy," Carson said. "I wonder if our visitor had something to do with that."

"Who cares? So what did Jack have to say? Was his info any good?"

With a slow smile, Carson nodded. "Oh, it was good, all right. Though I suspected Alex might be here, Jack confirmed it. He told me how to find your brother."

"What?" Food forgotten, she bounded to her feet. Her stress brought on the need to change. Fighting that, she practically snarled her next words. "Come on, what are you waiting for? Let's go."

With his mouth full, he jerked his thumb in the direction of her seat. Chewing, then swallowing, he shook his head. "Calm down and don't get crazy. Eat first. You need your strength."

"What?"

"We're not going out there tonight. It's not safe. We've got to plan."

She dropped back into her chair. "I don't understand. He could be gone. He could—"

"Brenna."

She closed her mouth, trying not to inhale the tantalizing aromas of liver and fried onions.

"Eat. He's not going anywhere."

Instead of complying, she glared at him. "How do you do that?"

"How do I do what?"

"Make me feel like a little kid who's just been chastised?"

Lifting a big piece of liver to his mouth, he grinned,

then ate. Chewing with gusto, he swallowed before popping some fried onions in his mouth.

"We've got to do this right. Rushing in on them in an unplanned, impulsive action could get us killed. Now eat."

Her stomach growled. He was right. Both about the need to plan and the food. She was hungry, and she needed her strength. She'd finished two-thirds of her meal before she tried again.

"So tell me—" she leaned back and blotted her mouth with the paper napkin "—why do you feel there's no hurry? How do you know Alex won't leave?"

"Though it was helpful to get confirmation, Jack didn't tell me much that I didn't already know. He gave me directions to their hideout, Nemo's place in the woods. The Hell Hole, they call it." One corner of his mouth lifted in a mocking smile. "Thursday, the date of the big meeting—that I already knew."

"If you know how to get there, let's go."

"No." His flat stare told her that he wouldn't back down. "Too dangerous. No one's going anywhere, at least not tonight. After we eat, there's another place I want to check out—a bar where they all hang."

"Do you think Alex will be there?"

He shrugged. "Who knows? It won't hurt to check it out, and any public place will be a hell of a lot safer than the hideout. If Alex isn't there, I want someone to tell him *I* am. And you." He tacked on the last as an afterthought.

Brenna sighed. "You know, planning *is* all well and good." Fighting back the need-to-change-fueled energy, she clenched the edge of the table and leaned forward. "But we can make a plan in a few minutes. Why don't we go out to the Hell Hole now, instead of this bar? I don't understand why we can't simply show up and force a meeting."

"You *are* crazy," he said, no humor in his deep voice. "That place is probably protected better than Fort Knox. They'd shoot you before they'd let you get within fifty feet of them."

"You don't know—"

"I don't want to be such an easy target." He spread his hands on the table. "With such an important drug buy about to happen, tension is pretty high. Anything could set off violence. Their old enemy showing up on their doorstep would rank pretty high on their list of triggers."

She sighed. He was right, but she had one advantage that he didn't know about. She could change.

"Then let me go alone. They don't know me. They have no reason to mistrust me."

"You don't know what kind of people you're dealing with."

"No." She swallowed. "Nor do I much care. All I want is to talk to my brother."

"Even if doing so could endanger his life?"

Chapter 8

That stopped her cold. "What do you mean?"

"If Alex is still undercover and you reveal you're his sister, what happens then, with his cover blown? Do you want to give them ammunition to use against him?"

She hadn't thought of that. "Do you think he is? Still undercover?"

"Of course." But the bitter twist of Carson's mouth told her he didn't really believe it. "Anything's possible."

She sighed. "I want to help Alex, not hurt him."

"Then we stick with my original plan. We need to bring him to us, not the other way around. That allows him to choose the time and the place when things are safest for him."

She nodded reluctantly. What he said made sense, damn it. If she were a mere human woman. While he had a point—no sense in endangering her brother—

Carson had no idea what she could do. If she could get close enough to the Hell Hole, she could signal her brother. He could change and meet her in the forest. As wolves, they would blend into the shadows. No one would see; no one would know.

Decision made, she took another bite of the tasty liver. She would pretend to agree with Carson's plan, wait until he slept, then sneak out under the cover of darkness. Alone.

Glancing up to find Carson watching her, she forced a smile. "Did your informant—Jack—tell you anything else?"

"No." He polished off a few more of the greasy onions. "Same old stuff."

"Then why'd you pay him? If his information wasn't useful, couldn't you get your money back?"

He laughed. "There are no 'satisfaction guaranteed' deals in this kind of thing. And he's my link with Hades' Claws, because he knows a couple of them. I want to keep him talking."

Confused, she shrugged. "I don't see what else he could possibly tell you."

"You'd be surprised. Sometimes the most interesting information comes out when you think there's nothing left to learn. Excuse me." Signaling the waitress, he smiled pleasantly. "I'd like a to-go box, please. And the check."

At Brenna's questioning look, he pointed to her plate. "For Phelan," he said. "I saved some, too."

So he had. Between his leftovers and hers, the puppy should have enough to eat. Still, it was surprising—and touching—that Carson had cared enough to remember. He'd seemed so determined to keep even the affectionate dog at a distance. She still planned to pick up a bag of bona fide puppy food later, but decided to keep that fact to herself for now.

After he paid the check, they headed into the now-dark night. The parking lot wasn't well lit, and Carson winced when they rounded the corner and he saw his battered, black Tahoe.

"What a beater," he said, shaking his head. "That SUV is only three years old. It was in such great shape before all this."

Staring at his vehicle, Brenna couldn't manage a laugh. With every minute, every hour, her sense of urgency increased. She needed to talk to Alex. Not tomorrow, not in a few days, but *now.*

But how would she ever find the compound if Carson didn't show her the location? She decided to make one more attempt to convince him of the need to act immediately.

"No one will know if we drive out to the compound. I just want to see where it is. It's dark, and we don't have to stop."

He didn't even look at her. "Tomorrow," he said.

Fine. She'd tried. Now she had to figure out a way to make him tell her what he knew. Once she had the location of the hideout, she would wait until Carson was asleep and go out there herself. This would give her a much-needed opportunity to change, as well—a wolf could lope through the forest much faster than a human.

Phelan smelled the leftover liver the second they walked in the door. Wagging his tail, he began to drool. Brenna emptied the pungent bag on the bathroom floor, letting the eager puppy gobble his fill.

"Hey." Carson put his hand on her shoulder. "Don't

worry so much. We'll drive out to the Hell Hole tomorrow, in broad daylight. Hiding nothing. Though we won't—" he shot her a warning look "—go in. I want Alex to feel sufficiently threatened so he'll arrange a private meeting, but not enough to make some crazy person start taking potshots at us."

"Broad daylight?" She echoed his words. "Since they're trying to kill you, do you think that's wise?"

Letting his hand fall, he shrugged. "We need to check the place out thoroughly. We can't if it's dark. We'll just have to be careful."

Brenna nodded. "I hope you're right," she murmured. "How far away is this place?"

"About five miles north."

Five miles. A long way for a human to walk. Not so far for a long-limbed wolf. Still, she needed more specific directions. She couldn't go wandering around town after she'd changed.

"How far are we from the Vermont border?"

This time her question earned a hard look. "Why do you want to know? Planning on seeing if you can make it to Canada?"

Though the Canadian wilderness was home to many of the Pack, fleeing had never entered her mind. "Not without Alex."

They stared at each other for a moment, neither speaking. She felt like a lone wolf unexpectedly meeting a larger wolf in the forest. Finally Carson looked away, a muscle working in his cheek.

"How long will it take you to get ready?"

Perplexed, she looked at him.

"To go check out the bar." He glanced at his watch,

silver gleaming against his tanned skin. "It's nine-thirty."

The biker bar. She'd forgotten about that. With a sigh, she smoothed her hands over the front of her faded jeans. "I'm ready now. I don't have any other clothes. Besides, jeans and boots seem to fit in well in bars."

"Where's your vest?"

"Vest?"

"The black leather one you wore in the bar where you met me." With a wicked smile that came and went too quickly, he crossed to the door. "It looks good on you. If you can find it, put it on."

Was that a teasing note in his voice? Had pigs learned to fly?

"Was that a compliment?"

He shrugged.

After locating the vest where she'd tossed it on a chair, she slipped it over her arms. "I need to let Phelan out first."

"I'll do it." The quickness of his gruff response brought an involuntary smile to her face.

"He'd like that," she said.

"I'm only taking him so you'll stay in here." With a grimace, he looked at Phelan. "Come here."

The puppy didn't move. Cocking his head, he looked up at Brenna, then at Carson.

"He's confused. You sound too angry."

"I'm not." Carson snapped his fingers and whistled. "Let's go." He reached for the door. "Outside."

Starting forward, again Phelan hesitated, studying Carson with his head cocked.

"Go," Brenna ordered softly. "Be a good dog."

Tail held high, the puppy trotted over to Carson, sitting at his feet and gazing up at him.

"How old do you think he is?" Carson regarded both Brenna and Phelan with a frown.

She shrugged. "I don't know. Pretty young, I'd guess. Close to a year maybe."

He shook his head. "You stay inside." Opening the door, he stepped out, Phelan trotting at his heels.

For about ten seconds she resisted the urge to peek out the window at them. Then she gave in and looked. When she did, she watched Phelan romping in the shadowy field next to the parking lot. He found a stick and ran to Carson. Carson hesitated. Phelan jumped, stick still between his teeth, and pawed at Carson's jeans. Finally Carson crouched low, ruffled the puppy's fur and then tossed the piece of wood. The two played this game for a few moments before they started back toward the room.

Hurriedly, she let the curtain fall. With a peculiar ache in her chest, she went into the bathroom to study herself in the small mirror.

"Not good, Bren," she muttered. With her hair curling around her shoulders in an untamed riot, she looked like a wild woman. Biker mama, hoochie-coochie. Not at all like the prim-and-proper librarian the people of her hometown knew. Even her own brother might not recognize her, with her tight jeans and leather vest. With a touch of bright-colored lipstick she could easily pass for a biker groupie, hunting in a biker bar for a man to take home for the night.

She looked, she thought with a sigh, exactly as she needed to look. But part of her wondered if the vixen she saw in the mirror was the way Carson saw her.

Though she didn't like Carson's plan, she was glad he'd decided to go to the bar. Action was always better than inaction, as far as she was concerned. She didn't have much patience for waiting. Unless she was on a hunt, which meant perpetual motion, no matter how stealthy and slow, she felt restless and unfocused. Which also might help explain her unwarranted fascination with Carson himself.

The front door opened, and Phelan bounded inside.

"Ready?" Carson glanced at her. A slow smile spread over his rugged face. "I'll be damned."

"What?"

"You look…different." He cocked his head. "Not sure how you did it. Maybe it's the hair."

She lifted her chin. "Or the vest. Do you think I look biker-mama enough?"

His smile faded. The appreciative glow in his dark eyes vanished. His bleak, determined expression returned.

"Yep." He sounded gruff, cold. The original Carson was back.

Slowly she studied him, hating the ache behind her throat, the tightness in her chest. She'd always had a compulsion to heal wounded creatures. She had to remember he wasn't an animal—not like her. He hadn't asked her to heal him, wouldn't even welcome her interference in the tight-fisted grip he had on his own suffering.

"Let's go." As he reached for the doorknob, they both heard the door from the next room squeak open.

Carson froze, then held up his hand. Silent, they listened.

Speaking in low voices, several men walked outside.

Brenna could only make out a few words, including *Hades' Claws.* With her overdeveloped sense of smell, she detected that they all wore too much aftershave, a spicy scent often worn by teenage boys.

"Damn," Carson swore in a whisper. "What the hell are they doing?"

She wrinkled her nose in a grimace. "Do you think they're getting ready to raid the Hell Hole?"

He swore again. Tension radiated from him. "I hope not. That'd be stupid. They must be FBI—they sure as hell can't be DEA."

"Why not?"

"Because the drug deal isn't until Thursday. Unless it's been changed, which I doubt. I would have heard about it if it had. They'd have to wait until then if they wanted to collect the evidence and all the players."

The men outside continued to argue, their voices low. She heard footsteps—a single man walking away, not the entire group. A car door slammed; an engine cranked. Still the small group stayed outside the door, continuing their discussion more quietly, even as the car sputtered off. Finally they went back inside, slamming the door behind them so hard the walls shook.

"Gotta be FBI," Carson repeated. His teeth gleamed white in the darkness. "At least if *they* see me, they won't recognize me."

He stayed put, his wide-legged stance still blocking the way out.

Brenna didn't move, either. "What just happened?"

Lifting one shoulder in a shrug, he snorted. "Who knows? Maybe one guy went out for pizza."

Or maybe that one guy had gone to case the Hell

Hole under the cover of night. Like she still planned to do.

Carson's cell phone rang. Exchanging a glance with Brenna, he answered. The conversation was brief and monosyllabic, at least on Carson's end.

"Yes. No, sir. I won't. In the city. Yes, sir. That's great. Yes."

As he snapped the phone closed, he grimaced. "My boss. Says someone called him, thought they saw me. He wanted to make sure I was nowhere near here."

"Where'd you tell him you were?"

"New York City."

"Do you think he believed you?"

"I don't know." He rubbed the back of his neck. "He's given instructions to the guys on the team—if they see me, they're to arrest me, no questions asked."

"That's not good." She sat down on the edge of the bed and yawned. "Does your neck hurt?"

"Tension."

Exhaustion washed through her. The near-violent urge to change that had assaulted her in the coffee shop had passed for now, leaving fatigue in its place. She needed to rest before attempting to sneak out later. Turning her head, she glanced at the bedside clock, numerals glowing red. Ten o'clock.

"Maybe going to the bar right now isn't a good idea. I'm tired, and you look worn-out, too. Let's get some sleep." She spoke before he could, muffling another yawn with her hand.

"I'm not hiding. There's just one more group of people we have to watch out for, that's all. Let's go." His gaze bore into hers. His sharp tone indicated he thought she'd lost her mind.

She suppressed a smile. “Leaving right now is a bad idea, with those guys so close. We can check out the bar tomorrow, after we go to the Hell Hole.”

He stayed where he was, though he made sure the door was closed, sliding the dead bolt into place. “I don’t like this,” he muttered.

“But you said they’re FBI and won’t recognize you, so why are you so worried? Or do you think there’s some kind of bulletin out on you, too?”

“Bulletin?”

“You know—” she kept her voice casual “—like the fake one you showed me on Alex.”

As she’d expected, he answered instantly. “It wasn’t fake.” Frustration showed in his clipped tone. “What is it going to take to convince you?”

Hands on her hips, she faced him. “How easy would it be to forge one of those things?”

He crossed his arms. “Give me a break.”

“I want to know.”

“Why would anyone want to forge an FBI datasheet?”

This time she waited for the implication to sink in.

When it did, Carson only shook his head. “The datasheet was real. Don’t lie to yourself,” he said gently. “It’ll only hurt more in the end if you do.”

Her heart sank. “I’m going to bed.”

“Suit yourself.” Though he sounded as though he still intended to hit the bar, he made no move to leave. He watched her while she prepared her bed, pulling down the discolored bedspread and brushing off the sheets. She padded over to the bathroom, chin held high, and closed the door.

After she emerged, Carson sat on the edge of the

bed opposite hers, head down, hand pressed against his temples. He'd pulled off his boots and placed them neatly underneath the table by the window.

"Look, I—"

"This is not a game," he said, interrupting her. "You need to understand that. You could be killed."

"So could you."

"Yeah, I could." He lifted his head to look at her and the bleakness in his dark eyes nearly made her cry out. "But the difference is, I don't care."

"*I* care." The words slipped out, words she'd had no intention of saying—ever. Mortified, she swallowed hard.

"Don't." His one-word response said it all. She should have thanked him for reminding her of the chasm between them. He didn't want or need her pity *or* her friendship. She ought to be grateful that she couldn't give him love.

Love? Was she so foolish as to let herself care for such a wounded man? And a human, at that. Horrified, Brenna thought of her former fiancé, Jeff, and his reaction when he learned she could change. Finding out about her had cost Jeff his life.

She climbed into bed, hating the heat she felt in her cheeks. She'd nearly hung herself out to dry, telling him she actually cared.

Meanwhile Carson's one-word warning hung in the stuffy air between them.

She closed her eyes. She couldn't think straight, not with the ever-present desire to change simmering faster in her blood again. If she got a brief nap, she would awaken in a few hours refreshed and ready to go. To think, to decide. To change.

Carson clicked out the light, plunging the room into welcome darkness. The faint but pungent scent of their dinner hung in the air.

"I can't protect you, you know," he said finally, his acrid certainty final.

"Protect me?" She sat up. "How many times do I have to tell you? I can take care of myself."

He made a sound, the strangled sound of a wild animal in pain. She nearly went to him. Only by holding on to his warning was she able to keep herself immobile.

"Get some sleep." She rolled onto her side in an attempt to do the same. The room felt unbearably hot, and finally she struggled out of her jeans and sweatshirt, covering herself with only the sheet.

An hour later, still awake, she gave up. Since counting sheep only made her hungry, she tried not to listen to Carson's restless tossing and turning, and focused on relaxation techniques instead.

They didn't work, either. Restless and impatient, she couldn't stand it any longer. Sending Phelan a quieting thought, she rose soundlessly. Dressing in the dark was easy. She stepped into her jeans, shimmying them over her hips. Her sweatshirt came next, then her socks and shoes, and she was done. She left her parka behind. She would be warm enough once she changed. With one last look at the puppy curled up on the end of her bed, she made her way toward the door.

"Going somewhere?" Carson's scent suddenly filled her nostrils as he loomed up in front of her, blocking her with his body. His sleep-roughened voice seemed deeper, more suggestive. Startled, Brenna jumped, fighting back the instinctive urge to change.

"Outside," she said, managing not to growl. "I need some fresh air."

"Right." He didn't move. She blinked, taunted by an insane urge to run her hands down the length of him.

Desire, or the haunting scent of need, filled the space between them.

"I'm going outside." Attempting to push past him, she felt a spark as her hand connected with his bare stomach. She jerked her hand away as if the feel of him burned her. Sometime in the night he, too, must have removed his jeans. An ache started deep within her, pulsing with her accelerated heartbeat.

"Move," she snarled, furious at her body's reaction to him. Instead, his arms came around her and crushed her against him. Her sweatshirt rode up, giving her bare skin a touch of his.

Naked except for his boxers, he was muscular and hard in more ways than one. A thrill went through her, even as she debated using her martial arts training to free herself. But, unable to resist, she gave an experimental wiggle against him, as though she were only a helpless human female, trying to free herself. Immediately his body responded. She bit back a moan as he surged against her belly.

Adrenaline, frustration, desire. The urge to change always made her other animal instincts more pronounced. And she wanted him—badly. She could still scent her own desire. Though his sense of smell couldn't be as developed as hers, Carson could surely detect her urgent need. If not from the scent of her, then from the way her nipples pebbled against him. In the darkness, she could see only his silhouette, though his heartbeat thundered under her cheek.

He broke out in a sweat, the light sheen only adding to his appeal. Unable to resist, she licked his neck lightly, the salty taste heady. He moaned, a strangled curse as he ground himself against her.

Now she wished she hadn't gotten dressed.

He captured her wrists with both hands. She saw images of him tethering her to the bed, ravishing her eager body with his mouth, before he covered her with his body and made savage love to her.

Instead he released her and pushed her gently toward her bed.

"Back to sleep."

She laughed, the sound almost a purr. "Is that an order?"

"Brenna…"

With slow, deliberate motions, she kicked off her shoes, peeled off her jeans. He swore again, still motionless in front of the door. Without hesitation she removed her bra and panties, thrilling to the feel of herself naked, desirable, powerful and aroused.

She moved silently, knowing he couldn't fully see her in the darkness. He still wanted her, she knew in an instant, as she rubbed her cheek against his chest.

"No," he said, but his body disagreed. Delighted, Brenna let herself touch him, chest and arms as well as there, and was rewarded by his groan.

She kissed his corded shoulders, then his neck, pressing her bare breasts into his chest.

One minute he was with her, the next he pushed her away and moved toward the bathroom.

"Fine," he said, disgust and anger in his voice. "You win. If you want to leave, I won't stop you. Just don't try to seduce me again." And he slammed the bathroom door, leaving her shocked and aching.

Five-thirty in the morning. Only masochists rose at this hour. Carson punched his pillow and listened again for the sound of Brenna's breathing. He'd had a torturously rough night. Fitful dozing only, hanging on to the sharp edge of awareness so he would know if she tried to climb into his bed. Asleep, he could not resist her, though even the thought of her silky limbs intertwined with his made him uncomfortably aware of his own hard and aching body. His own need and desire.

Guilt filled him. He shouldn't want her, but he did. Pushing away his erotic thoughts, he gave up his futile attempt to go back to sleep and sat up.

If he focused on what he'd come to do instead of what he wanted to do to Alex's sister, maybe his raging hormones would subside.

Today. Today they would drive out to the encampment, the last thing those murderous thugs would expect. And, since Alex seemed so intent on warning him away, Carson wanted to show him beyond a shadow of a doubt that he wouldn't let Brenna go anywhere. Not until he got answers. He found it hard to believe that a man as cold-blooded as Alex had become would worry about her at all. And if he did, surely Alex knew Carson. He wouldn't let her get hurt. Not on his watch. Two lives lost had been more than enough. He would die before he let that happen again.

Alex had offered a trade—himself for his sister. Right. Like Alex would really turn himself in on Friday, the day after all the drugs and cash were supposed to trade hands. No, Carson would bet his last dollar Alex would be on some plane to an undisclosed Caribbean country.

The rising sun leaked around the edges of the heavy, dust-covered curtains. Padding to the window on bare feet, Carson drew back the drapes, letting the fresh light of the new morning in through the dirt-streaked glass.

Today would be a good day. He repeated the words like a mantra. Though he hadn't had a truly good day since he'd lost his family, each hour that brought him closer to achieving his goal he deemed a success.

In the bed next to him, Brenna stirred, stretching her supple, slender body like a cat. She'd kicked off her covers in the night, and the sweatshirt she wore rode up one shapely hip. He stared, unable to resist, drinking in her unconscious sensuality like whiskey and feeling it burn in much the same way.

Whiskey had been his salvation once, when every day had seemed like the darkest night. No more. He needed every sense sharp and ready to bring down his enemy. The need for such oblivion still haunted him, especially when his stomach ached and he wanted to forget.

He focused his attention away from the bed next to him.

Brenna. Damn her. When he'd woken in the night and found himself holding her, fully aroused, he'd wanted her with a savage mindlessness that stunned him. Later, after he'd rejected her, she seemed hurt. No doubt an act; yet he couldn't let go of the knowledge that she wanted him as badly as he desired her. Still.

Later again, watching her try to sleep, at times she'd seemed as if she were burning from the inside out. She'd seemed like a wild animal, predatory, fierce. Looking at her, Carson had thought for one startled second that he still lingered in some weird dream. Then she'd rolled over, stretched and become Brenna again, and he'd felt even more foolish.

Time to get back to reality.

"Hey." Reaching down, he shook her shoulder, ignoring the leap his heart gave in reaction to her soft skin. "Wake up."

She came awake instantly, moving away from him and rising with a compact movement that made him remember her claim to martial arts training. The more he came to know this woman, the more he questioned his sanity.

He shouldn't even care, didn't care, not really, but sometimes, just watching her made him remember how sweet his life had once been.

"Take the first shower." His voice sounded gruff, brisk, a drill sergeant who'd actually taken that imaginary shot of whiskey. "Make it quick. We've got a lot to do today."

After her first surprised look at his sharp tone, she narrowed her eyes. He was almost disappointed when she didn't argue, merely ducking her head in a quick nod before grabbing her duffel bag and disappearing into the bathroom.

The shower started. For a moment he entertained the enticing image of her naked, water sluicing over her creamy skin, the soapy washcloth touching her breasts. Then, muttering a curse, he forced his thoughts to the target at hand—the internet maps he'd obtained of Nemo's isolated estate, the Hell Hole.

The shower shut off after five minutes. The bathroom door opened a moment after that.

"Your turn." She matched his earlier tone, toweling her hair with one hand. She'd donned a beige T-shirt and a pair of olive khakis, again making him think of the military.

With a nod, he grabbed a clean pair of jeans and a shirt from his own duffel, and turned sideways to go past her into the bathroom. Though he had no doubt she'd planned to sneak off in the night, he closed the door behind him. If she wanted to go it alone, on foot, more power to her. However, no matter how badly she wanted to find Alex, he didn't believe she would do anything that stupid. And he needed space to clear his head.

But even here, he couldn't escape her. He took a deep breath and smelled…flowers. A floral, feminine scent filled the small room. He shook his head. Chest tight, he turned on the water, setting the knob to hot, and stepped inside the shower.

A few minutes later, clean and dressed, he pushed open the door and stepped into the bedroom. Empty.

Refusing to believe she'd really gone, he caught himself about to peer under the bed. A glance at the front door showed the chain had been taken off, the dead bolt unlocked.

His heart began to pound. He wanted to curse his own stupidity. He battled the urge to run outside after her, to see if she'd left tracks.

Damn! She'd left. And he'd given her the opportunity. Now she would warn her brother, and Alex would disappear, exactly as he'd disappeared eighteen months ago.

Or, worse, Hades' Claws would see her, know she

was with Carson and kill or capture her. Once again he would have failed to keep an innocent safe.

He'd blown it. His careful planning—gone. All for nothing. All because, for the first time in years, he'd allowed himself to think with his body—and maybe a little bit of his heart.

Chapter 9

He would find her. Plain and simple. Holstering his gun, he grabbed his jacket just as the front door creaked open. Wearing the black DEA cap at a jaunty angle, Brenna brandished a couple of white bags in one hand, grinning.

"I brought breakfast." Her wide smile faded when she got a good look at his face. She kicked the door closed, juggling two takeout cups of coffee in her other hand.

"What is it? What's wrong?" After setting down her burden on the dresser, she crossed her arms and studied him. "Are you all right? What happened?"

"You went outside. Unprotected." His words came out in a snarl.

"I was hungry." She shrugged. "So sue me."

"Hungry?" An explosion built inside, but he tried

to contain his anger, worry and, yes, relief as he strode across the room. When he reached her, he gave in, grabbing her small shoulders and yanking her into him. Holding her tight. "What the hell were you thinking?"

She froze, completely still in his hold. Unable to help himself, he breathed in her scent, the flower-like aroma of spring. No doubt she felt the still-too-fast thumping of his heart in his chest, the lightning-swift catch of his breath as his anger shifted into desire. Unwanted desire, sudden but razor sharp just the same.

She lifted her head to look up at him, long lashes shadowing her coffee-colored eyes. Though he wanted to step away, to drop his arms and let her go, she gave a soft cry and wound herself around him. The invitation of her parted lips was more than he, no saint for sure, could even begin to resist.

As he bent his head, she lifted her mouth, and he was lost.

Lifting her arms, she twined them around his neck. Belly to belly, they kissed. She tasted of spearmint toothpaste and woman. He wanted her. Like an eager youth in a roadster, his body urged him to take her. Now. Hard and fast and deep. Impossible, without them stripping off their clothes. Would she let him inside her? The way she curled into him, sinuous and willing, told him she might.

Brenna. Heat and musk, no longer spring but the lush heat of summer. Brenna.

Think. He needed to think. Through the red haze of desire, he forced himself to use common sense. He couldn't do this—*they* couldn't do this. Cursing under his breath, he pushed her away. He would have laughed cynically at himself if he didn't hurt so damn bad.

And she—what must she think? Lately all he'd done was paw at her like some horny adolescent, then push her away. He, of all people, should know better.

Unable to look at her, his every sense on overloaded overdrive, he spun away, staggering like a drunk. One step wasn't enough, so he took two. Then three, until he stood as far away as the motel room would allow. Wiping a hand across his mouth, he took a ragged breath, exhaled, then took another.

Behind him, she made a sound. Not a whimper, not exactly, but a sound of regret, nonetheless. Even so, he refused to turn around, afraid if he did he would drown again in the frank sensuality of her gaze.

"This isn't acceptable," he said harshly, furious with himself and with her for the lure she represented. He should have been beyond such temptations.

Paper rustled. He smelled eggs and ham and croissant. That must have been what she'd brought for them to eat. His stomach, which, like the rest of his body, had taken on a mind of its own, growled.

"Breakfast," she said. If her voice sounded overly bright, he pretended not to notice. "And coffee. Hot."

While she fussed with the grease-spotted bag, he stalked to the dresser and snatched up one cup. As he pried off the lid, the steam told him it was still scalding. Good. She'd brought it black. Even better.

Moving back to the window, he peered out. He took a quick gulp, letting the coffee scald his throat.

"We need to talk," she said, sounding determined and angry and scared all at once.

"No." He took another swallow. "We don't." If, like most women, she pressed the issue, he would simply apologize and tell her it wouldn't happen again. Hell, he would make damn sure it didn't happen again. No matter what.

Even now, guilt still lay coiled in his gut. Not guilt because he'd taken unfair advantage—no, that wasn't it. Brenna, with her eager mouth and roving hands, had been more than willing. This self-directed loathing was because he shouldn't have wanted her. Shouldn't have, couldn't have but still did. Right this very moment his blood still burned with desire for her. If he was stupid enough to close his eyes, he knew he would still see her, knew he would still dream at night of the yearning on her mobile face, dream of pushing himself deep inside her. Knew he would still want her with every breath he took.

"Damn it all to hell." He had to get a grip—no, not that kind of grip. A grip on the crashing crescendo inside his chest.

"Do you want to eat?" Her voice sounded normal now, clear and unaffected. Which both angered and pleased him.

"Yeah." He forced himself to meet her eyes. Seeing nothing but pleasant concern made his gut clench.

Holding out one of the white bags, she flashed a small smile. "It's okay, Carson. Come eat."

Her cool-and-collected look almost fooled him. Almost. But her nipples still poked against the front of her faded T-shirt, and the irises of her eyes were dilated.

And he was hard again, just from one look.

"This has to stop."

"Yes," she agreed. He hadn't realized he'd actually spoken the thought out loud.

"Your food's getting cold." She tossed him the white bag.

Suddenly ravenous, he pulled out the croissant and

took a huge bite. While he chewed, Brenna wadded up her bag and napkin and tossed them at the trash can. They bounced off the rim and went in.

"Two points," she muttered. Then she glanced at the nightstand clock. "Are you about ready? I want to get this show on the road."

He nearly choked on his food. Then he laughed, feeling the tension ease. "Let's go," he said.

Following her outside, he tried not to notice her sexy behind or the gentle sway of her hips. Together, they climbed into his vehicle. After clicking the seat belt in place, she folded her hands in her lap, as prim as if they were heading to church.

Once out of the parking lot, the Tahoe's rattles and creaks attested to its recent beating. Carson found a radio station that played oldies and turned the volume up louder than usual. The last thing he needed was Brenna continuing in her earlier we-need-to-talk vein.

The drive north down Main Street took less than five minutes. At the end of the town square, they took a left. On the outskirts of town, the forest took over, scraggly branches of leafless trees giving the road a stark, primitive appearance. The houses, few and far between, were set back at the ends of long, tree-lined driveways that snaked away from the road. In the summer the trees would shield these brick monstrosities from view. But right now dappled sunlight mingled with the bare branches, exposing the massive homes in a sort of primitive beauty. Even so, the limited sunlight was unsuccessful in melting the snow and ice alongside the road.

"Beautiful," Brenna said.

He glanced at her and saw she was studying the

landscape, an intense look of yearning on her face. He recognized that craving—identified with it, as well. He, too, often longed for what he'd lost—a home. But for him it was like crying over spilt milk. But Brenna had a home somewhere upstate, where she worked as a librarian. That is, if her story was true.

As they followed the curve of the road, the houses became fewer, the trees thicker, the scrubby underbrush wild.

He consulted his handwritten directions and slowed to a crawl.

"It should be right about…there." An uneven stone wall wound between the trees. Flanked by two towering cement monoliths, the wall ended at a huge, black iron gate, which guarded the long driveway that disappeared into the trees. The rock wall looped and dipped, high and low, some areas crumbling, others tall with the look of haphazard repair, as though installed by a crew of inebriated men.

It appeared to be five feet tall at the lowest point, well over eight at the highest. With its varying height and width, the wall had only one constant that Carson could see—the flat stone top was inlaid with broken glass, bright colors sparkling in the winter sun. All the shards pointed outward, sharp and deadly.

"Hell of a deterrent," he said. "I've seen a few walls like that before, but only in Mexico and Brazil."

Though she nodded at his words, Brenna continued to study the wall. Too tall for her to leap in her wolf form, impossible to climb as a human, the barricade seemed insurmountable. No doubt that had been the builder's intention, she thought with a wry smile. She would have to figure out a way around it.

"How do they open the gate?"

"By remote." Carson pointed to a small speaker box set into the stone. "You have to be admitted. And they have cameras, see?"

Not one but two cameras were aimed at the gate.

"They probably have motion sensors, too, don't they?" Her heart sank. "The place is well guarded."

"Yeah." His gaze searched her face, as if he knew what she was considering. "Of course it is. They have too much to lose to be careless."

She studied the wall again. Somewhere there had to be a spot low enough for her to jump. As a wolf, if she took a running start, she might be able to leap over. Of course, the consequences were she to fail could be deadly—or merely a scraped wolf belly. Either way, she had to try.

Just thinking about changing brought the urge so strongly that her mouth went dry. For a moment Brenna battled herself, hoping Carson wouldn't notice. It had been far too long since she'd assumed her wolf form.

"Okay, so that's it." After making a U-turn in the road, he accelerated back toward town. "We can't drive in there unannounced. And with the cameras aimed at the gate, they'd spot us. We're just checking the place out. I don't want them to know I was here."

"We," she corrected automatically. "We were here." She craned her neck for one last look, marking the stately oaks that guarded the gated drive. Though a good distance from the motel, the Hell Hole was not too far for her to run in a single night. To lope there and back would certainly be exhausting, but such a distance was well within her capabilities once she'd changed. Breaching the wall would be her main problem.

He broke into her chain of thought. "What are you thinking?"

Suddenly aware of his scrutiny, she turned in her seat and said the first thing that came to mind. "This bar you want to check out, do you think it will be safe?"

He shrugged, watching her from the corner of his eye. "No place is safe for us. Especially if they know we've been out here, casing their hideout. If you're worried, you can wait in here."

"Right." She drew the word out in a sarcastic drawl. "Since they're shooting at you, why don't *you* wait in here and let me check out the bar?"

To her surprise he laughed. Not the cynical, no-humor sound he'd been prone to since she'd met him, but a deep peal of belly laughter that made her smile in return.

"You didn't dress in your biker-babe outfit," he reminded her. Amazed at the way humor lit up his craggy face, she was so busy staring that she nearly didn't respond.

"Didn't feel like it," she said. Noting again the sharp tug of sexual awareness, she tore her gaze away from him.

"With you wearing that DEA jacket—" she touched the brim of her cap "—and me in this DEA hat, we don't need to look like bikers anymore, do we?"

He laughed again. "No. Now we look like targets." Still chuckling, he reached over and took the hat from her head. "I think we'll leave the DEA gear in the Tahoe."

Bringing one hand up to comb through her flattened hair, she smiled back. "Okay. Now let me in on the joke?"

He shook his head, the grin fading, though traces of

humor still sparkled in his eyes. "I just had this mental image of you in a packed biker bar, doing a *Crouching Tiger, Hidden Dragon* routine and taking them all out."

Since that was perfectly within her capabilities, Brenna still didn't see what was so funny, but she let it go. The shadows had lifted from Carson's eyes. However briefly such a thing might last, she wouldn't question it.

Suddenly conscious of biting her lip so hard it throbbed, she tilted her chin up and pretended intense fascination with the sun visor.

"Do you think that bar serves food?"

He glanced at his watch, a black-banded Timex. "Are you hungry already? We just ate breakfast."

She nodded. With the urge to change came fierce hunger, a strong need for red meat to sustain the body. Glad he hadn't noticed her inner struggle, she settled back in her seat.

Then Carson cast her the sort of sideways look males of all species can give, and she knew she hadn't entirely fooled him. He knew something was up. He just didn't know what it was.

"I'm starving." As if on cue, her stomach rumbled.

"It's a biker bar," he said. "A lot like the one upstate, where you found me. Greasy hamburgers are probably the best they have."

"A greasy hamburger sounds wonderful." She meant every word. Her mouth watered thinking about it.

"And about the bar being safe, if any Hades' Claws are hanging out there, I doubt they'll expect us to walk right in among them. They're used to terrifying their prey. So going in there will probably be a lot safer than if we sat on the bench in front of our motel."

Unnerved by his use of the word *prey,* she nodded.

A few minutes later he made a right turn into an unmarked lot. "Here we are."

Barely four miles from the gated compound, towering pine trees surrounded the uneven parking lot. A faded, hand-painted sign hung on the weathered gray building, proclaiming they'd arrived at a bar called—appropriately enough—Dante's.

If she were simply driving by, she wouldn't even take a second look, so unassuming was the structure. Most notable about the place was the way the winter sun reflected off row upon row of gleaming chrome handlebars and exhaust pipes. Only two cars and a pickup shared the parking lot with the sea of motorcycles.

"There must be fifty." Brenna couldn't take them all in. "When you said biker bar, you weren't kidding."

Flashing her another quick smile, he parked as far from the rows of bikes as the lot would allow.

"In case we have to make a quick getaway." This time his brittle smile took on a sharp edge.

Stepping from the Tahoe, Brenna inhaled deeply, searching for the scent of trouble. This time the chilly afternoon air carried only a vague promise of snow, nothing more. Cocking her head, she listened, but heard only the faint sound of music and raucous voices from inside the bar. Maybe Carson was right. Maybe Hades' Claws wouldn't bother them here, so close to their den. She bared her teeth. The violence of the urge to change had her spoiling for a fight.

"Are you okay?" Carson's deep voice broke into her thoughts. He'd been watching her. Again. Had she been too careless, revealed too much of her true nature?

Chastising herself under her breath, she gave a curt nod. When he opened the heavy wooden door, she squared her shoulders and swept past him into the dim, smoky interior.

Wincing at the acrid odor of cigarette smoke, she glanced around. The rolling swagger with which she walked had taken weeks to perfect.

At her entrance, several men looked up with interest. Two of them immediately headed her way, their eyes gleaming. Neither noticed the other, so she braced herself for the inevitable clash when they both reached her at the same time.

Immediately Carson slung his arm across her shoulders and pulled her close. The possessive message was plain. *Back off.*

Both men stopped, sized Carson up and turned back to their companions.

Brenna turned to glare at Carson. "What the—"

"Shh." His breath warmly tickled her ear, sending a shiver down her spine. "I want them to know you're with me."

"I won't learn as much," she growled back. Still, she forced a smile. Odd how his touch seemed to be able to take her mind off the need to change. Usually nothing and no one could do that. The urge would lessen only once she'd given in.

"Hey, you look like you want to fight me. Relax," he said, keeping her close.

As if. Across the crowded room, she spied two empty chairs and a rickety round table. "There's a place."

"Great," he said. "We'll order a drink."

"I want something to eat," she reminded him. He left his arm around her as they slowly crossed the room.

She found it much more difficult to do her stroll this way and, after two steps, gave it up. As they wound their way through the crowd, though some continued to watch them, most people paid them no mind.

Checking for danger, she continued to breathe deeply. Mingled with the yeasty scent of beer and ever-present cigarette smoke, the air smelled of male sweat. A quick glance around told her she was one of maybe five women to fifty or more men.

"Such odds," she murmured. "Ten men to every woman."

He leaned his head close, still carrying on the charade, she supposed. "Some women would like it." He licked her ear.

Damn the man. Even here, he could still make her knees go weak.

"Stop," she hissed. "Let go."

They'd reached their table and finally Carson released her. With a sigh, she dropped gratefully onto the hard wooden seat.

A waiter, his gray braid longer than Brenna's, leaned close. On his forearm he had a shotgun tattoo, and his hand bore the insignia of a large, hairy spider. This time her shudder was from distaste. She despised spiders.

"What d'ya want?"

"I'll have a hamburger." Steeling herself, she let her gaze wander over him, as though she found him attractive. He lifted an arm, and she discovered he'd neglected to put on deodorant that morning.

"And water," she added, unable to keep from wrinkling her nose at the odor.

"Budweiser." Beside her, Carson smelled it, too. She could tell from his choked tone.

The waiter managed to leer at Brenna and smile at the same time. "Gotcha. Be right back." He lurched off toward the bartender.

"Why'd you check him out?" Carson asked gruffly. "If you say he's your type, I'm outta here."

Was he making another joke? "Are you all right?"

He frowned. "Why?"

With a shrug, she lightly touched his hand. "Nothing. You seem different, that's all."

His frown deepened, making her sorry she'd mentioned his mood. Now he would probably revert to the surly, bitter Carson she knew.

"Thank you," he finally said, looking off into the roomful of people.

"For what?"

He leaned back, crossing one booted foot over his leg. She was struck by how well he fit in here, despite his lack of tattoos or earrings.

"For reminding me who I am. And who you are."

His words stung. "You're welcome," she retorted.

He continued to ignore her. She watched as he scanned the crowd.

Some demon drove her. "So…you forgot who I am?"

At first she didn't think he would answer. He didn't turn his head, even when the waiter reappeared with his beer and her water. The few cubes of ice were already melting in the large plastic glass. Once the waiter had threaded his way to the next table, Carson took a long, deep drink of his beer. When he met her gaze, she saw that the self-reproach was back in his.

"I never forget," he said. "Anything."

His words sounded like a threat.

A moment later the waiter brought her hamburger.

The tantalizing scent of meat drove all other thoughts from her mind. Seconds after he'd deposited the full plate in front of her, she grabbed the burger and began to devour it. Though she preferred meat slightly rare, and this had been cooked until it was nearly rubbery, she ate half in three bites, washing it down with gulps of lukewarm water.

Well on her way to finishing, she became conscious of Carson—and several other men—watching her eat. She ignored their avid interest—and Carson's speculative stare. She didn't much care if human women ate as quickly. The protein filling her blood with a rush of power felt good. The energy coursing through her—red meat, without the hunt—empowered her with optimism.

The hamburger went too quickly, so she started on the fries. Carson had barely finished half his beer by the time she'd cleaned her entire plate.

A reluctant smile pulled at one corner of his mouth. "Hungry?"

"I was." Smiling back, she licked her lips. His gaze, following her tongue, intrigued her. With fresh energy flowing through her veins, she felt the sensual connection between them much more strongly, supplanting even the ever-present urge to change.

His pupils darkened, and she knew he felt it, too.

He leaned forward. She scooted her chair closer.

"Brenna—"

Behind them, glass shattered. She jumped. The entire room erupted. Men scrambled to their feet, a few heading for the door, more heading for the knot of bodies in the back corner of the room.

"Fight!" someone shouted.

Pushing back his chair so hard it clattered to the floor, Carson stood, blocking her view.

"Don't move," he ordered. "Things could get dangerous. I'll be right back." Pushing through the crush of bodies, he disappeared into the crowd.

For the space of two seconds she sat, staring after him. Shouts—egging the two combatants on—and the splintering sound of a chair breaking. Danger brought exhilaration, mingled with the trailing remnants of lust, all fueled by the fresh vigor in her blood.

No way she could simply sit and wait while everyone else got in on the action. She jumped to her feet, getting ready to duck and dodge in Carson's general direction, and found her way blocked by a tall, male form.

"'Scuse me." She attempted to skirt around him without making eye contact.

"Brenna," a deep and achingly familiar voice said, "what the hell are you doing?"

She froze. Looked up. And met brown eyes so much like her own. "Alex?"

Chapter 10

"Alex." Her heart thumped so hard she feared it might burst from her chest. "I can't… I've been—"

"Shh." He enfolded her in a tight hug. "You always worried too much."

Normally those were fightin' words. And he knew it.

She held on to his forearms with a death grip. "Where have you been? What have you done? You disappeared. You scared the hell out of me, you know. You'd better start talking."

A crash—the back corner again. Two more men ran to join the fray. Alex glanced back. Then, apparently satisfied that they weren't being observed, he shook his head in warning at Brenna. He wore his blond hair long, the cut shaggy. The shadow of a beard darkened his chin and cheeks. He looked like Brad Pitt gone bad.

"I don't have much time. Shh," he said, when she opened her mouth to speak. Tension radiated off him.

"I just need to know—"

"Questions can wait." He grimaced, his expression dark. "It's bad here right now. Deadly. I want you safe. Gone. Go home."

"But—"

"No." His eyes blazed. "Leave, Brenna. Now."

"Well, well, well." From behind them, a bitter voice. Carson. "I thought you might show."

Releasing Brenna, Alex turned to face the other man. Brenna noted Carson's set jaw, clamped mouth and intent gaze. Her brother's expressionless face she could not read.

Her insides clenched. Though it seemed as if she'd been waiting for this moment forever, the roiling emotions inside her made her feel ill.

Carson. Alex. She looked from her beloved brother to the man she'd come to care for.

"Not here," Alex said, his harsh words a clipped order. "Not in front of my sister."

Carson laughed. His hand hovered near his shoulder holster. Near his gun.

Both men glared at each other.

"You're coming with me," Carson growled. "I'm placing you under arrest."

"Don't pull your gun in here."

"If I have to—"

"No." Expression unchanged, Alex glanced once more around the crowded room. "I'm not going anywhere. Not yet. Not today. Friday we'll talk. I want you to get out of here. Take Brenna home."

"Brenna!" Carson exploded. "This isn't about your sister, damn you. This is about my wife, my little girl. I've been looking for you for eighteen months. I saw you there—the day Julie and Becky died. I saw you, Alex, you…my partner. You killed them, and then you tossed the gun away. Right after you shot me in the back."

Chest tight, holding her breath, Brenna prayed for her brother to deny Carson's horrible accusations.

Instead, he shook his head, his narrow-eyed gaze revealing nothing.

"This is not the time to talk about what you think happened that day. Take Brenna home, Carson," Alex said. "They meant to kill you then. They failed. You might not be so lucky this time. They want you dead. And they'll take my sister with you."

"Lucky?" The single word shook with rage. "I want answers." Carson stood his ground, one hand now resting on the handle of his gun.

After glancing around once more to make sure the rest of the room remained occupied by the fight, Alex shook his head. His next words came in staccato bursts. "Not now. It's big…huge. I'm on it, man. The killer—I'm gonna bring him down. Don't mess it up. And don't involve my sister." He took a step closer. "Get her out of here before she gets hurt."

"You're serious?" Carson's lips twisted in an imitation of a smile. "You expect me to believe you're worried about your sister when you can't even tell the truth about what happened?" He looked at Brenna. "How does it feel, knowing your brother is a coldhearted murderer?"

She recoiled, still reeling from her brother's lack of defense. Carson's words stung.

"I'd like to beat some sense into both of you," she muttered. They both looked at her, Carson still expressionless, Alex registering a brief moment of surprise.

"Brenna—" Warning sounded clear in Alex's sharp tone. "You have no place in this."

"But I do." She touched her brother's shoulder lightly. "I'd like to see this settled. Let's go somewhere else and talk, someplace private."

"No time." He looked once more at the crowd still gathered in the back corner.

"You're coming with me." Carson's hand still rested on the pistol. "Under arrest. For murder."

A shout came from the back of the room. One of the combatants lifted a chair and bashed another on the head. The man crumpled to the ground. Shouting, several others moved in to restrain the first man. The fight was winding down.

Alex looked around them yet again, his actions furtive and earnest at the same time. He stared at Carson with such deadly intent that Brenna's entire body stilled.

"Shoot me, then," he growled, baring his teeth. "Shoot me and be done with it. But, buddy, if you do, you won't ever know the truth, will you?"

Carson drew his gun.

With a savage snarl, Alex stood his ground. "I didn't kill Julie and Becky. It wasn't me, damn you. But go ahead, shoot me now. Get it over with. Do you want the blood of the wrong man on your hands? Do you?" He poked Carson in the chest, hard.

His free hand clenched into a white-knuckled fist, Carson stood frozen, his expression shattered, and let him. Slowly, without taking his gaze from the other man's face, he holstered his pistol.

"I sure as hell don't," Alex said. His hard voice

cracked, and Brenna knew that no matter what had really happened that awful day, Alex blamed himself for Carson's loss.

As the fight broke up, the first wave of men scattered, returning to their seats or making for the exit. A man moved in front of Brenna, and for a moment she couldn't see Alex or Carson. Two or three more burly bikers shoved each other—and her. She pushed back, ignoring a challenging glare from one man, squeezing around another. When she could see Carson again, he stood alone. Alex had gone.

"Damn." Pushing a man out of his way, Carson turned and began elbowing his way to the door. Grabbing hold of his shirt, she followed in his wake, continually scanning the crowd in vain for a glimpse of her golden-haired brother.

Along with twenty or thirty others, they spilled out the door, trapped in the stream of exiting bikers.

Outside, dusk had fallen. Men congregated in the parking lot, laughing about the fight, standing around their gleaming motorcycles. There were bikers of every size, portly men in leather and short men in jeans. Long-haired and short, tall or thin, the crowd looked menacing. Brenna saw no sign of Alex.

"He's gone." Carson swore. "With this many people, we won't even find footprints in the snow."

"Look!" someone yelled, pointing toward the field across the road. At the edge of the snow-covered grass, where the tangle of forest began again, a large, silver wolf watched them, silhouetted in the approaching darkness.

"That's one big dog," another man commented. Someone whistled, and the animal lifted his massive head.

But Brenna knew the shadowy figure was not a dog. The wolf was her brother. Alex had changed. As they all watched, he turned and slipped into the underbrush.

Ignoring the latest commotion, Carson still scanned the crowd. Two men sidled up behind him. Distinctive snake tattoos decorated their forearms. Hades' Claws. She saw the glint of metal. One of them held a weapon in his hand.

Correctly recognizing the threat, Carson spun. Too slow. The metal edge of a knife glittered and slashed. He grunted in pain.

Brenna lunged forward. Arms came around from behind her, pinning her in place. Pretending to struggle, she twisted instead and dropped her shoulder, freeing herself. Out of his grip, she spun and aimed a hard kick at his shin. Violence—the scent of blood… Change. She felt an inner shifting. So it always began.

No. Not here. Not now.

Carson.

Another man blocked her. One swift chop and he went down. She pushed past him. Outnumbered, Carson tried to draw his gun. Another cut—like slow motion—knife raised, Carson's arm, wrist, a slash of crimson. Blood. The urge to change roared inside her. She froze, occupied momentarily by her own savage inner battle.

Carson grimaced, held on to the gun a moment longer, but the second man knocked it from him. It fell, clattering to the ground. The first attacker reached, and Carson kicked it away.

Blood. Carson's blood. She could smell the coppery scent of it. She took a step forward.

Change.

Again she fought the compulsion. The laws of the

Pack were strict. She could not change now. Not here. There were far too many witnesses.

Still fighting, Carson swung. Missed. Grunted. An awful look on his face, he staggered. Straightened.

Internal battle won, she used her martial arts training. A twist, an elbow. She sprang forward. Picking himself up off the ground, one attacker took off, running. The other man followed suit.

No. She couldn't let them get away.

Change. The urge slammed into her.

She felt the change begin in her. With a snarl, she shook it off. With the energy rush giving her strength, she began to run. Half wild animal, with each pounding step she regained control of herself.

Someone shouted. Others came toward them. The two attackers rounded the corner of the building. The crowd surrounded Carson, blocking him from her view. Brenna stopped, breathing hard. Carson. She had to make sure he was okay. No one else must be allowed to hurt him.

Abandoning the chase, she went back, thrusting herself between him and the others.

"Give him room," she ordered. "Back off. Let him have space."

Carson still stood, his eyes bleary and hot and furious. The only signs of his pain were the deep furrows at the edge of his mouth. That, and the blood from the slash on his wrist.

She pushed back his jacket. The side of his shirt was sticky and crimson. Glaring at her, he held his hand pressed to his side.

"Someone call an ambulance," Brenna ordered. When

no one moved, she raised her voice. "An ambulance. Now."

"No hospital." Carson's jaw worked. He touched her arm. "It's not as bad as it looks."

She flashed him a look of disbelief. "You must be delirious."

"No." He shook his head. "It's not serious. A surface wound. Just get me out of here." He grimaced. "Please."

That simple word, more than anything else, made up her mind. He must be badly hurt. For now, she did as he asked, leading him across the parking lot, waving off the curiosity seekers who came to try and help or simply gawk.

A few scarlet drops had fallen on his boots, staining the leather. She wondered if he noticed. A quick glance at his set profile told her Carson was hurting far worse than he'd admitted.

"I'll drive." She struggled to get the rear passenger door open, succeeded, then helped him climb up. Leaning heavily on her shoulder, he breathed hard. She closed the door, went around to the driver's side, and once behind the wheel, held out her hand for the keys.

"Don't..." He swallowed and grimaced. "Don't go back to the motel. Not yet. I'm too vulnerable." He drew the key chain from his pocket and clumsily tossed it to her.

She caught it easily. "The motel? Are you crazy? We're going to the hospital."

After turning the key in the ignition, she backed out of the lot, zigzagging past the clustered knots of bikers. No one tried to stop her as she peeled out onto the road.

"No." He sat up. Winced. Lowered his voice. "No hospital."

Men. Pack or human, they were all the same. "Cut the macho crap. You're hurt."

"Not really." He lifted his hand, showing fingers covered with blood. Reaching into the glove box, he grabbed a few paper napkins, pressing them against his ruined T-shirt.

"I've had it. Really had it. Don't lie to me." Resisting the urge to bare her teeth, she allowed herself a furious growl.

"Don't worry about me. It's not your problem."

She glared at him. "I can't stand stupidity. This *is* my problem. *You* are my problem. You need medical help."

All at once the anger left him. The merciless planes of his face smoothed out. His mouth twisted in what Brenna guessed he must think looked like a smile. It resembled a smile as much as her low growl resembled a human sound. Not at all.

"No hospital," he said again. "I'm okay."

"Carson..." she warned.

"I'm not lying. It hurts like hell, but it's just a cut. Not much more than a scratch. I think it's almost stopped bleeding. No hospital. I don't trust anyone here."

"Fine." She sighed. "No hospital."

"Thank you."

"They stabbed you." Dividing her attention between the road and Carson, Brenna shuddered. The aftershocks of denying the need to change would last awhile. "Alex was right. They mean to kill you."

"Yeah. Probably on his orders."

"Get real. He warned us. He doesn't want you to get killed."

"Right," he drawled. "Let's see. I've been hunting the man for eighteen months, and he slips right by me.

Then, while I'm preoccupied looking for him—bam. Knife to the ribs. Out of nowhere. I sure as hell didn't expect that. Carelessness nearly cost me my life." He sounded so disgusted that she nearly smiled. Nearly. But she was too wound up to smile much about anything.

"Alex is—"

"One of the bad guys," he interjected. "That's obvious."

"Obvious?" She clenched the wheel to keep from snarling. "It doesn't seem obvious to me. If he's one of them, then why would he risk himself to warn us?"

"You."

She looked sideways at him. "What?"

"He showed himself because of you. He's worried about you, about you being in danger. He didn't warn *us,* he warned *you.* Alex doesn't give a rat's ass about me."

"You're wrong. Did you see his face when he mentioned your family? Did you?" This time she did bare her teeth, just a little. "He's hurting, too, Carson. Having witnessed that, can you honestly say he doesn't care?"

His face contorted. "Stop the car."

"Like hell I will," she snarled back, matching his tone exactly. "Not until I think it's safe."

He leaned forward, maybe meaning to reach over the seat and grab for the wheel. But his sudden movement made him grimace. He gave a strangled cry, jerking up short.

"That was stupid, damn it. I ripped my side wide open." He fell back in the seat. "Now it's bleeding again."

Brenna's stomach clenched. She wanted to pull the Tahoe over right then, so she could assess the extent of his injury. Instead, she lifted her chin and forced herself to drive on, staring straight ahead at the road, trying to calm the churning inside her.

"He killed my family." Carson's voice was thick.

The pain she heard in his tone made her wince. Still, she had to defend her brother. "You don't know what happened. You didn't see. How do you know who shot them?"

"Maybe I don't, but he let them die." His expression was bleak. "I don't remember much of what happened that night, especially after I was shot. My cover had been blown and I didn't even know it. But Alex stayed with the gang, still undercover. How was my cover blown when his wasn't?"

She didn't answer.

"He had to know what they meant to do."

"I'm sure he didn't or he would have stopped it."

She eyed Carson, letting conviction round out her voice. "I know Alex. He would never have done such a thing or allowed it to happen if he knew. I'm surprised you can think so, if you were as close as you say."

"I told you. I saw him holding the gun. The pistol that killed my wife and little girl. He was there. He shot them. It was a test, a test for him to prove his loyalty. If he failed, they wouldn't have let him stay in the Claws."

She shook her head. "I don't believe it."

"Believe this—he disappeared." Self-recrimination showed in the deep lines on the sides of his mouth. "I was in the hospital a long time. Nearly died. When I found out Julie and Becky were gone, I went a little crazy. By the time I—" He shook his head, raw emotion glittering in his dark eyes.

Chest tight, Brenna looked away. "I'm so sorry," she murmured. "I can't imagine—"

"My wife never knew," he said softly. "She didn't suffer. At least, that's what they told me. They shot her from behind, one shot, straight through the back into her heart. She died instantly. Didn't even have time to scream."

Brenna's throat ached. "Your daughter?" she heard herself whisper.

"I can't talk about my daughter." His voice cracked. "She was only five."

He took several deep breaths. When he spoke again, his tone was flat and unemotional.

"Alex made no effort to contact me. Today was the first time I've seen him in a year and a half."

There were no words she could speak to ease his pain. Blinking back the tears that stung her eyes, tears he would hate, she simply gripped the steering wheel and drove.

"There." He pointed to an unmarked road that led directly west, into the setting sun.

She slowed the Tahoe and turned. After a few hundred feet, the pavement became dirt. They plowed on ahead. The road was full of potholes and ruts. They bounced, and more than once bottomed out. Carson groaned, and Brenna saw he'd gone white.

On one side of the road, a grassy shoulder led to an old, untended cemetery. Coasting to a stop in front of the haphazard stone fence, she shifted into Park and killed the engine. With a sigh, she opened the driver's door and went around to the back. Leaning in toward him, she nearly laughed out loud at the puzzled look he gave her.

"Let me see it." She pointed toward his side.

His expression shuttered, he slowly shook his head. “I’m fine.”

Carefully keeping her face impassive, she gave him the sort of look mothers all over the world could relate to. “Let me see the damn wound.”

His slight recoil made her want to smile. She didn’t.

“I’m fine,” he repeated.

Ignoring him, she slowly pried away the hand he kept pressed against the bunched-up and bloody shirt.

“It’s a clean slice.” Only by pretending he was like the injured animals she’d treated in the past could she objectively examine the cut. Carson had told the truth. It was a narrow slice, not deep enough to have caused serious damage.

“Yeah.” His voice sounded distant. “Hurts like hell.”

“We need to get some disinfectant.” Matter-of-factly she ripped away a clean part of his T-shirt, then folded and pressed it into his gash. “No telling where that knife had been.”

This elicited a grim smile. “I don’t see a drugstore anywhere around here. So unless you happen to carry around a bottle of hydrogen peroxide in your purse, I’d say we’re out of luck.”

“No first-aid kit?”

He shook his head. “Didn’t care.”

Brenna thought of the Pack and the way wolves licked their injuries to clean them. She sighed, envisioning Carson’s horrified reaction were she to suggest such a thing.

“I’ll be fine,” he told her, again giving her the eerie feeling he had read her mind. “It’s just about stopped bleeding again.”

She glanced around to get her bearings. The spot she

had chosen was not only isolated but deserted. Not even a single house could be seen through the thick tangle of leafless tree limbs.

A perfect place for a wolf to run. She pushed the thought away.

"Did you pick this place for a reason?" He indicated the tumbled gravestones, some of which were so ancient the engraving had been wiped clean by time. "Is this a hint?"

This time, she let herself smile. "No hint. If I'd wanted you dead, I would have killed you a long time ago."

He whistled, giving her a long, slow perusal. "You sound like you mean it."

"I do," she said. "What now? You said no hospital, and you don't want to go back to the motel." The deepening purple of the sky told her night would soon be upon them. Without a single streetlight, their parking spot by the cemetery would be dark indeed. She looked again at the jumble of tombstones, unease prickling under her skin.

"Maybe this isn't a good place to stop," she said.

"We'll sleep in the Tahoe."

The back of her neck tingled. Not a good sign. No telling what other sorts of beings might roam such a deserted cemetery in the deep part of night. Though she had never met a vampire, she knew they were out there. She had no desire to meet one now, with Carson fairly reeking of blood.

And, more important for her, being this close to nature would intensify the desire to change. She was struggling enough with that as it was.

Of course, she could tell him none of those reasons.

"You know," she said, keeping her voice casual, "I really think we should go back to the motel. We've already made it plain we're not leaving."

Immediately he shook his head. "Too easy. Let them think I'm scared. Or seriously hurt. Whatever. We need to throw them off a little. That'll buy me time to come up with a plan."

"I thought you had a plan."

"Things have changed. I need a better one."

Because he'd seen Alex. Clearly that hadn't gone the way he'd expected.

"I think you need stitches."

He lifted his hand from his side. "I'm fine."

She gave up. She supposed another scar on his body wouldn't matter. Why should it, when he already had so many scars on the inside?

"Your call," she said.

"My call? Fine. We sleep here."

She studied him. The stark beauty of his profile, silhouetted in the waning sun of winter, made her ache. Even now, seated so close to her, he had an air of isolation that seemed almost physical.

She couldn't stand it. Wolves ran in packs. A solitary animal was unheard of. How could she make Carson understand he was no longer alone? She was with him now. Suddenly, fiercely, she wanted to break through his barrier and touch him, really *touch* him. More deeply than merely her fingers on his skin.

Glancing at him, she saw he was watching her.

"Brenna…" The warning in the way he spoke her name told her he somehow knew. No longer caring, she climbed in and scooted close, heart thudding in her chest, never taking her gaze from his face.

With a sound—a cry of resistance?—he reached out and met her halfway. Though no doubt meant to stop her, his touch felt oddly gentle. His hands tight on her shoulders, he held her off, but for only an instant; then he slowly slid his hands down her arms to bring her closer.

"Brenna," he said again, breathing hard. At first she thought the movement had caused him pain. Then a quick glance at his fully aroused body assured her that what he felt was an entirely different type of pain.

He spoke her name again, and she understood this was his way of giving her a second chance. She could pull away now if she wanted. Pull away? She would sooner die. Instead, she leaned into him and moved her lips over his, openmouthed, an invitation.

With a groan he captured her mouth with his, hard, demanding and…searching? Yearning. Or was that only in her head, a projection of her own emotions onto him? She didn't care.

Both trembling, they kissed, tongues intertwined, bodies straining. Passion arced between them, as strong and as violent as the winter lightning that sometimes rent the sky. She let her bewilderment, anger, confusion fuse into this one point of contact, mouth to mouth, Carson to Brenna, mate to mate.

Mate to mate? No! This was nothing so serious, no bonding, no binding, not mating at all.

Fighting panic, she raised her head. He grabbed her hair and pulled her back, claiming her with a deep, searing kiss. He drank of her, taking her essence into him and exchanging his own. Such a thing, new and fascinating, thrilled her, making her already-overloaded senses reel.

Mate? No, this couldn't be what it felt like, couldn't be what it seemed. Animal instinct, nothing more.

To her mingled relief and disappointment, Carson finally lifted his mouth from hers. The cadence of his harsh breathing matched her own.

"We'd better stop." He ground out the words, his eyes smoky with a heat equal to hers.

She didn't answer, not so readily capable of speech as he, afraid that if she opened her mouth she would end up begging him to make love to her. Instead she jerked her head in a tiny nod, wondering why she felt such an aching sense of loss.

Chapter 11

Carson decided that he needed to get Brenna to go. Anything to keep his already overheated body from reacting to her incredible sensual lure.

Damn. Now was one hell of a time for his libido to go into overdrive.

Closer to finding his family's killer than he'd ever been, so near to the end he could taste the sharp, metallic tang of victory, Brenna was a distraction he could ill afford. If he were a different man or a less cynical one, he would have laughed out loud at the bitter irony.

Instead he found himself wanting to weep.

Damaged in so many more ways than the small stab wound in his side, he had no right to take what Brenna so passionately offered. Not now, not ever. Used up, hollow, he had nothing to give in exchange. The quick fix of a one-night stand would create more problems than it would solve. Despite her self-sufficient attitude and attempts to appear tough, Brenna was a forever kind of girl. An emotionless, no-strings-attached, sexual encounter would hurt her. His wife had been the same way.

Brenna shifted, running her hand through her long, dark hair. Watching, he realized he knew the exact texture of each smooth strand. He thought how erotic a silken curtain her hair would make, cascading over them when they made love.

When? How about *if* they made love?

No. They would not make love. Ever. He shook his head, tearing his gaze away from her. Damn! He still wanted her. Badly. He groaned out loud.

"Are you all right?" Her concerned expression told him she'd mistaken his frustration for a sound of pain.

"Yeah, I'm fine." Steeling himself, he gave a pointed glance at the front seat. "If we're going to sleep tonight, one of us needs to move up front. It's crowded back here."

"Crowded?" Her cool tone matched his. She studied his face, probably trying to figure out what made him tick. He couldn't blame her. One minute he was all over her, the next he couldn't get far enough away.

Tough. Squaring his shoulders, he looked at the growing darkness outside the window. He couldn't afford to get distracted—not by her, not by anything. He knew what mattered. Finding the killer, whether Alex or some other man. Finding him and bringing him to justice. Nothing else.

His priorities firmly back in place, Carson refused to watch as she started to scramble forward between the two front seats. He was admiring her perfect rear end—in the abstract, of course—when she appeared to have second thoughts.

After a pause, she moved into the driver's seat, fastened her seat belt with a click, then started the engine and pulled onto the road, tires spinning, all without even once looking at him.

"What the—"

"We're going back to the motel." Her no-nonsense tone told him she meant it. "Phelan will need to go out, and he'll need to be fed."

He'd forgotten about the puppy. "We'll get him and take him with us."

This time she did look at him, a quick, hard stare that told him not to give her any flak. "We're staying there. I don't like this graveyard."

Suddenly tired, he didn't feel like arguing. He had to try, anyway. "I told you, the motel isn't safe."

"Is anywhere? I mean, come on. This gang seems to know where we're gonna be before we do."

He sat bolt upright, causing another painful pull to his side. "I can't believe I didn't think of that."

"Of what?" Her exasperated tone told him that she still wasn't buying whatever he had to say.

"A tracking device." He didn't bother searching the inside of the Tahoe. It had to be in a wheel well or underneath. When they stopped again, he would find the damn thing and yank it off. "They're tracking us."

"Sure they are." Now she sounded as though she thought he was delusional. "And maybe little green men are hiding under the seats."

Though he really shouldn't care what she thought, for some reason her snide comment rankled him.

"Even your brother said they weren't taking any

chances I'd get near them," he reminded her. "This way they can be sure."

Silence while she digested his words. Finally she gave a slow nod. "Alex is usually right," she said.

He hated that it took a mention of Alex to make her pay attention.

Back at the motel, they both emerged from the Tahoe in silence. His side aching like hell, ten times worse than he let on, Carson bent over to inspect the undercarriage of the vehicle.

"What does a tracking device look like?" she asked.

Straightening, he dragged his hand across his dry mouth. His rib cage was on fire. Perspiring heavily for no good reason, he straightened. The entire world swayed and tilted on its axis.

"It could look like anything." He heard himself speaking as if from a distance. "Most likely—"

He saw a burst of black; then the ground rushed up to meet him.

Change of scenery. Inside the motel room. Ugly green shag carpet. Unmade bed and lumpy pillow. How much time had passed? Confused, he tried to lift his head, and the room spun.

"I'll bet that hurt." Brenna's voice, soothing and low, sounded close to his ear.

Swallowing, he opened his eyes and found her. "What happened?"

Her expression seemed grim. "You passed out. I had to drag you inside."

She was lying. Had to be. No way could she, all of five feet tall and a hundred pounds soaking wet, manage to move his bulk.

"Who helped you?"

Ignoring the pain in his side, he watched the emotions flit across her face. Worry, confusion, frustration, then, finally, comprehension.

"You don't think I could have moved you by myself." Not a question. She wasn't stupid. She knew it would be a Herculean task, even for a much larger female. He said nothing, waiting.

"I'm very strong." Color stained her cheeks. He wondered why she would lie to him, especially after what had just happened. Then a thought hit him, a possibility so infuriating that he pushed himself up on his elbows to glare at her.

"Alex?"

Instantly her entire posture changed to one of watchful alertness. "What about Alex?"

"No." He had to grind his teeth to keep from shouting. "Did your brother help you get me inside?"

"Of course not." She waved his suggestion away, shaking her head and sending her dark hair flying. "No one helped me."

Another thought, equally plausible, equally bad. "The guys in the room next door? The federal agents? Damn." Surprised he wasn't in handcuffs, he let himself fall back onto the pillow, rubbing his eyes to clear the cobwebs. The blackness receded, then surged again, causing him to keep himself immobile, fighting to keep from drifting in and out of consciousness.

When he opened his eyes, Brenna had moved away. He could hear her rustling through a plastic bag on the other side of the room. With an effort he managed to lift his head and next, his aching shoulders. With his elbows for support, he struggled to sit up again.

"Here." She propped two pillows behind his back. "Maybe this will help."

He didn't thank her. Since even his own traitorous body wanted to betray him, he fought the grayness and concentrated on the fiery ache in his side.

"Aspirin?" He croaked the word with a grimace. He still meant to find out how she had gotten him inside, though right now all his efforts were focused on not passing out.

"Here." She brought him three pills and dropped them into his palm, then handed him a can of diet cola. "I still think we need to go to the hospital."

"Where's your dog?" Deliberately changing the subject, Carson choked down the aspirin, washing them down his dry throat with the lukewarm cola.

Recognizing the word *dog,* the small animal placed his front paws on the side of the bed, cocking his head in enquiry.

"Have you fed him?" Carson let the puppy sniff his hand, then lick. "Has he been out?"

She flashed a smile. "Yes, he's eaten. How's your side?"

"Better. What about the dog?"

"He needs to go outside. I'll take care of him in a moment. Carson, we ought to have a doctor look at you."

"No." Squinting, he tried for a hard stare. "Pack up your stuff. We're leaving."

"You're delusional." She expelled her breath with a noisy puff. "If we're going anywhere, we're going to the hospital."

"I'll take the dog out."

"You can barely stand."

"I'm fine." He swung his legs over the side of the bed,

ignoring the crazy tilt the room took at the movement. "And we're not going to a hospital. Since you don't want to sleep in the Tahoe, we're changing motels. This one's not safe."

She stared at him, her expression unreadable. "Give me a realistic rationale, and I might agree. Otherwise, no."

"I've given you plenty of reasons."

"I don't think there's another motel in this town."

"We'll find one."

A reluctant smile tugged at her full lips. "Whatever you say. Did you find a tracking device?"

"No." He watched her closely. "Did you?"

"I didn't look." She gave a shrug, oddly graceful. "But I wouldn't know what to look for."

"Hmm. Tell me who helped you move me inside."

She froze. As he had intended, throwing the question at her from nowhere ambushed her. Maybe now he would get a straight answer.

"I need to know where I stand," he pushed. "If Alex is helping you, or if you've alerted the Feds that I'm here, I deserve to know."

"Alex didn't help me. And I didn't ask the men next door." Standing rigid, head held high, she met his gaze with a frank look of her own. "I'm telling you the truth. I dragged you in here by myself."

Next she would expect him to believe she could fly. Right.

"You heard my own agency warn me away from this investigation. They could be trying to stop us," he reminded her.

"I told you, I didn't even talk to those guys."

He tried another tack. "How long was I out?"

"Long enough," she said. "I didn't time you."

"Fine." He would accept that for now, since she gave him no other choice. "Get your stuff."

Pushing himself to his feet, he stood, swaying slightly. He gripped one side of the bed for support. Hoping she wouldn't notice, he squared his shoulders. "We'll take the dog out together."

"Phelan," she said, and shook her head. "He has a name. You might try using it."

Ignoring her, he opened the motel room door and went outside. Brenna and her pet followed.

Though Brenna had been right about the lack of lodging, they'd finally found a small place on the other edge of town and gotten a room. After a quick meal of more greasy takeout, they'd showered—separately. Then, exhausted and hurting, he'd taken a couple more aspirin and dropped into a deep, dreamless sleep, for once not tossing and turning all night.

The deep sleep seemed to have helped. The next morning Carson woke feeling almost normal. The night before they'd picked up some bandages and antiseptic at a local pharmacy and doctored his side. Now the bleeding had stopped and the pain had subsided to a steady ache. He stretched, then grimaced at the sharp jab in his side. As long as he didn't make any sudden moves, he would be all right. He'd been lucky.

He'd also searched the Tahoe both inside and out, finding nothing. Maybe he'd been wrong about the tracking device; more likely he hadn't found it yet. Still, he was glad he'd insisted they change motels.

In the bed next to him, Brenna still slept. For a moment he studied the even motion of her chest, her glossy hair fanned out on the white pillow. Somehow, some way, she'd managed to get under his skin. Last night he'd dreamed of her. Startling thought, but he remembered the dream vividly. After all, he'd awoken from it hard and aching. Wanting her.

And, he realized as let himself drink in her sleeping form, he still ached with desire. He wanted to crawl under the sheets and roam his hands over her soft, pale skin, explore her slender shape. As he contemplated doing exactly that, guilt gnawed at him, reminding him once again how easily Brenna was able to distract him.

He shook his head, deliberately moving in a way that brought him fresh pain from his cut. Pain, in this case, might serve a good purpose, that of keeping him focused and on track.

She shifted, and the cadence of her breathing changed. Any moment she would open those big brown eyes and blink sleepily up at him, hair tousled.

At the thought, his body stirred again. Maybe a cold shower would be a good idea.

He sat up, once more welcoming the stab of pain, and slowly swung his legs over the side of the bed.

Phelan poked his head out from under Brenna's covers.

Tongue lolling out of his mouth, he appeared to be grinning. About to reach out and ruffle the dog's fur, Carson reconsidered. Such softness was more than he could stand right now. And touching the pup would bring his hand too close to the temptation of Brenna's body. So he stood, hating his unsteady wobble, and made his way into the bathroom for a much-needed cold shower.

The soft click of the bathroom door, followed by the

flush of the commode and the shower starting, brought Brenna fully awake.

Carson. She smiled, remembering the soul-searing intensity of the kiss they'd shared. Then frowned as she realized the direction her thoughts were taking.

With a heavy sigh she pushed back the blanket and discovered Phelan. Tugging at the sheet, the puppy wiggled mischievously. He wanted to play tug-of-war with the bedding.

Brenna laughed. Such wonderful innocence, so much like the young cublets in the Pack, made her long for her own childhood. Made her long to be—

A tremor shook her. Even being around the puppy increased the desire to change. The triggers were becoming more frequent, the need more consuming. She shook herself in frustration, gritting her teeth. This was the longest she'd remained totally human. Yet she had no choice. Somehow, until she'd settled things with her brother, she would have to suppress the urge. If she could.

The shower cut off, and a few minutes later Carson emerged. This time he wore only his jeans—not just a towel, hounds help her, as she didn't know how she would be able to keep from jumping his too-sexy-for-his-own-good bones then. Still, bare-chested, he looked good. Without looking at her, he crossed the room to his duffel bag. She couldn't keep from staring as he tugged his T-shirt over his head. Her mouth went dry even as she called herself names—dumb Brenna, really dumb. He used his fingers to comb out his still-damp hair.

Something about the quiet domesticity of the scene lifted her heart and brought an unfamiliar happiness.

He caught her watching and raised a brow. "What?"

"Nothing," she said, unable to keep from grinning. "I was just thinking something good is going to happen today."

He paused and studied her. "Any particular reason?" His casual tone told her the question was anything but.

"No." She gave a slow shake of her head. "But enough bad stuff has happened to us that I think the universe has got to cut us some slack."

"It doesn't work like that." One corner of his mouth twisted. Turning away, he grabbed the remote. Brenna indulged herself, admiring the view from the rear.

He clicked on the television. A diet cola commercial with a loud, inane jingle came on. Channel up. The local news anchor excitedly described a fire. Camera footage panned in on a roaring blaze. The building collapsed as they watched, despite the fire department's attempt to save it.

"That's the motel we were staying in until last night." Brenna stared, her heart beginning to pound. "I don't believe it."

Carson swore. "They torched it. They must have thought we were still there." He thumbed up the volume.

"At least two known dead," the news woman intoned. "Several more injured."

"Maybe I was wrong about the tracking device," Carson said slowly. "Obviously they didn't know we'd moved."

"The federal agents." Unable to peel her gaze away from the television, Brenna's eyes ached. "Do you think they made it out?"

"If they didn't, Hades' Claws will have hell to pay. The Justice Department doesn't take kindly to the murder of their own."

Witnesses claimed they'd seen nothing. Heard nothing.

Most had been awakened by their smoke alarms going off.

"We need to put a stop to this." Brenna stood, tearing her gaze away from the screen to meet Carson's eyes.

"Oh, yeah?" He lifted a brow. "How do you propose to do that? Have you got a cadre of men with AK-47s that I don't know about?"

"No." Glancing back at the news, she bared her teeth, knowing Carson couldn't see. "But there has to be some way."

"When you think of one, let me know."

Another commercial came on. Carson stabbed the off button. The sudden silence seemed poignant—and threatening.

Brenna exhaled. Inhaled. Repeated the process. She had to strive for calm, especially now. The momentary instant of violent rage that had bubbled up inside her had triggered her body to begin the onset of change. Each time, the craving intensified. Each time, subjugation proved more difficult.

Too bad. She had more important things to think about right now.

"So what's your plan?" she asked.

Carson took his time answering, rotating his neck while massaging the back of it. "I don't have one," he said. The stark words sounded bleak.

"It's got to get better," she repeated. "It certainly couldn't get any worse."

His grim expression told her that he thought it could. "Don't tempt fate."

As if on cue, Carson's cell phone rang. Keeping his

back to her, he answered. The conversation was brief. She could only make out a few of his monosyllabic replies.

He snapped the phone closed. His sudden tension indicated the information he'd received hadn't been good. With a major effort of will, she waited.

"You were right about one thing." He flashed her a humorless smile. "Something good *is* going to happen today—for you. You're going home."

For one heart-stopping second she thought he meant something had happened to Alex. But no, his savage expression contained no satisfaction, just anger.

"Only if you go with me." She smiled, knowing he would do no such thing. "And since we've covered this before, I'm not going anywhere."

"You've got to leave," he said. "It's too dangerous for you. If you won't listen to me, listen to your brother. He warned you. He was right. Pack your stuff. I'll take you to catch a bus."

Her heart stuttered. "Was that Alex on the phone just now?"

"No." Jaw clenched, he bit out the single word. "That was Jack."

"Your informant?"

"Yeah." His hooded gaze was bleak. "Only, this time he said he had a message for me from the Claws."

"They know he talks to you?"

"Apparently so."

Moving forward, she touched his arm. "He's in trouble, then."

To her surprise, though he went very still, he didn't shake off her hand.

"More than trouble. This isn't like some TV show. He

has something to tell me. He thinks they're on to him. I'm meeting him at the bus station in an hour. He's got to get out of town, too, or he's a dead man."

Chapter 12

Her hand on his arm felt like a brand. When she touched him, Carson froze. They had sixty minutes before they had to meet Jack. Suddenly, fiercely, he wanted to make love to her, take her swiftly, furiously, mindlessly.

Her small hand on his arm wasn't nearly enough. He could cover her hand with his, slide his palm up her arm to her shoulder, then cup her chin. One step would do it. One step, one move, and he could have her in his arms, where he could kiss her senseless. One touch, one kiss, would be enough to make both of them temporarily forget about this mess.

The light floral scent she wore made him think of Easter in the dead of winter. Renewal. The phone call, Jack's panicked voice, had brought everything into focus, made his emotions, desires and needs more intense. Enough was enough. He was tired of death. Once, just once, he longed to celebrate life.

The ache in his side felt inconsequential now. The cramped room, the trouble with Jack, all of it faded as he contemplated giving in to his newly awakened, raging libido and taking her, hard and fast and furious.

"What did Jack find out?" Brenna's worried voice broke through his thoughts.

Jack. He'd always tried to take care of him, slipping the kid a little extra so he could eat. How could he think of sex when Jack was in trouble? Furious at himself, he moved away. Though they had an hour, he needed to use the time to figure out a way to help Jack, to make sure he got out of town safely. Since Jack had been helping him, the younger man's trouble was now his responsibility, his fault.

"Hello, Carson?" Brenna repeated. "What about Jack's message?"

His priorities finally in order, he swallowed and hoped she wouldn't notice his raging arousal. He edged toward the bathroom.

"I think he's worried about you. He warned me to get you out of here. You're next, he said. His voice was shaking. First time I've ever heard him rattled."

"He's young." Her voice had gone soft, similar to the gentle way she spoke to Phelan. When she noticed Carson looking at her, she started toward him. Out of reflex, he stepped back, ignoring the pang he felt at hurting her. Then she lifted her chin, eyes flashing, and he told himself he'd only imagined it.

"We've known all along they're after me." He held up a hand to prevent her from moving. "And Jack, too, because of me. Now they want you, too. They'll kill you, do you understand? *That girl,* Jack specifically said."

"Why?" Her clipped tone showed anger, which surprised him. He would have expected fear. "Did they give a reason?"

She constantly surprised him. Most women would have reacted with fear. But then, nothing about Alex's sister was ordinary.

"It's like I've been telling you all along. You're with me. You might be my girlfriend, for all they know. You might know too much. Who knows how the hell they think? Most of them are borderline psychopaths."

"Psychopaths?" She sounded disbelieving.

"Yeah. Most killers are. So pack your stuff. I'll dress and then take you to the bus station. Jack thinks I should put you on the bus with him." He headed for the bathroom again.

"It could be a trap to distract you. They want you more than me."

He didn't turn around. "Could be. But that doesn't change anything. You're leaving."

She didn't reply. Maybe she finally understood. Hah—that would be a good one. He closed the bathroom door, sagging against it. Though Brenna hadn't seemed to notice, the front of his jeans still bulged conspicuously. Muttering to himself, he ran a hand through his longish hair.

"Ready?" he called, opening the door. "The bus station is downtown, near Main Street. If you need bus fare, I have it."

"Quit it." Crouched over, stroking Phelan, she didn't raise her head to look at him. He noticed she'd twisted her hair into a knot on the back of her head.

"I'm not going anywhere."

He should have known. "But—"

"Carson. I'm staying. Live with it."

Her casual choice of words cut deep. "I can't live with it, Brenna. There's no way I can live with another death on my hands."

She lifted her head and rose, graceful in tight jeans. Barefoot, she padded over to him. Before he understood what she meant to do, she wrapped her arms around him—careful of his side wound—and laid her head against his shoulder.

He tensed—couldn't help it—and tried to summon up the strength, the desire, to push her away. He couldn't find it. So he stood, frozen, knowing she could feel the proof of his desire for her. He waited for her to speak. When she didn't, merely held on, he breathed in her scent. Brenna. She'd somehow stormed her way inside his heart.

He should have felt angry. He should have felt miserable. Instead, he felt a dawning sense of wonder. She made him feel as though he had a future to anticipate, as if he still had hope. Such possibilities shouldn't exist—not in the gray aftermath of his bleak world. Since he knew them to be utterly, completely false, the very thought hurt a thousand times worse.

Still, he couldn't summon up the necessary will to make her release him. Maybe he'd become a masochist of sorts, for in the midst of such pain he found a bright blossom of pleasure.

Brenna.

How long they stood that way, he didn't know. Forever. Not long enough. Then, with a soft sigh, she finally released him. Silently moved away. Now, his weakness revealed, he couldn't bring himself to look at her, to meet her eyes. He'd stupidly made himself vulnerable, and there was no way he could deal with the pity he was sure to see. And pity she must feel. Compassion could be the only reason for her tenderness, though he'd certainly done nothing to deserve it.

Not quite steady, he tried to regain control of himself. The scent of flowers—roses? tulips?—lingered, out of place in the dingy hotel room. In the course of his job he'd stayed in a hundred similar places, each of them impersonal, a stopping place, a bed to sleep in. How he'd longed for home then, the brightness of his family's laughter and the comfort of knowing he was loved. He'd known how lucky he was each time he returned to the aroma of fresh-baked bread and his daughter's soft kisses, though he'd never truly appreciated the scope of his blessings. Not until they were savagely ripped from him.

Afterward, while he'd lain in his hospital bed willing himself to die, he'd had one question. The same question that surely plagued every other person who walked away from a fiery car crash, the lone survivor. Why? Why them and not him? Why had he lived while they died? Why?

Unable to find an answer, he'd finally gained some measure of understanding. He must have lost them because he'd never deserved them to begin with.

"Let's go save Jack," Brenna said, bright-voiced, as if nothing untoward had occurred.

He glanced at his watch. "We have forty-five minutes. I'll take the dog out before we go."

"Phelan." Her quiet tone rebuked him. "His name is Phelan."

"Fine. Whatever." He grabbed his jacket. In the small room, with her scent still fresh in his lungs, he felt uneasy. Maybe, if he went outside and breathed in deeply, the sharp air of the winter afternoon might clear his head.

If he let the scattered patches of unmelted snow dampen the bottom of his boots, he might be able to remember what was most important. Justice. Vengeance. Not gentle brown eyes and soft skin. Not a beguiling smile and come-hither body.

He spun, meaning to scoop up the puppy and go. But Phelan had heard Brenna say his name and was right there, under Carson's foot. He stumbled, the puppy yelped, and Brenna rushed over. They both bent at the same time to comfort the young dog, heads nearly colliding.

The front window shattered. Something hit the carpet, rolling into the bathroom. A second, a heartbeat. Carson recognized the oddly shaped gray cylinder—a pipe bomb.

"Down!" He jumped on Brenna, pushing her to the floor and covering her body and Phelan's with his own.

The world exploded.

After that, time existed only in flashes.

Searing heat. Fire. Move. He scooped up the shocked puppy, grabbed Brenna's arm. Smoke. Couldn't see. Burning.

Flames reached for them, attempting to lick at their jeans, hair, skin. Hurt.

Stop, drop and roll. No time. Need air.

More smoke. Heavy and blistering. More heat. Fire. Frantic, he sought a way out. An exit. There. An opening where the wall had been. Furious, hungry, the fire roared in front of them, behind them, surrounding them. Death.

Brenna clutched his hand. He caught a glimpse of her face. Her eyes were red and wide with terror.

"Jump," he shouted, throat raw. "Our only chance. Now!"

Together they leaped.

Then they were through. Free. Outside.

Run. He felt each footstep as they pounded the ground. Lungs burning, he sucked in air, cool and fresh. He rubbed his eyes. They were full of soot.

Brenna stayed with him. In the shimmering mirage caused by the heat, her movements seemed animal-like, powerful. Alien.

He didn't care. *Live,* he silently urged her, urged himself. *Live.* His heart pumped, pounded. Proof of life.

The sharp bite of icy air seared his lungs. Still running. Away from the motel. He'd parked the Tahoe around back, out of sight.

In the distance, sirens screamed.

Run.

At the edge of the trees, he collapsed. Brenna dropped to the wet ground beside him, coughing. Phelan whimpered, struggling to be free. Carson let him go, and the puppy staggered a few feet before dropping to the ground.

"Is he—"

Brenna crawled forward. She ran her hands over Phelan's immobile body. "He's all right, except his fur." Her voice sounded like sandpaper. She combed her fingers through the dog's short coat. "Singed."

"Check yourself," Carson ordered, discovering he,

too, was unable to speak above a hoarse whisper. "For cuts. Burns."

He coughed, causing a sharp jab of pain in his side. The knife wound. Minor. Ignoring it, he pushed himself to his knees and crawled over to Brenna, hacking and wheezing like an old man.

Damp and clammy, the ground was still snowy in spots, though mostly from old moldering leaves and mud. The numbing moisture felt good on the palms of his hands, dampening his jeans at the knees.

He couldn't seem to stop coughing.

"Are you okay?" She squinted at him.

When he could speak again he managed a nod. "Getting the smoke out of my lungs."

Though the night air felt crisp, he removed his jacket and spread it on the ground for her. "Here. Sit."

Once she was settled, he dropped down next to her. Phelan had staggered away, sniffing. He seemed intent on exploring the trees.

Brenna straightened and opened her mouth. Now she coughed, the spasms doubling her over. Feeling awkward, he reached out, patting her back. She jerked away, glaring at him, still hacking. Finally she wiped her mouth with the back of her hand.

"They found us," she said.

He nodded.

"Maybe we should go to the police."

"You know we can't."

"Phelan," she called. "Phelan."

The sirens grew louder. Across the field, a fire engine raced into the parking lot, lights flashing white and red.

His stomach clenched, remembering another time, another ambulance. That time help had come too late to save his family.

Brenna touched his arm, bringing him back to the present. "What do you want to do?"

"The Tahoe," he said. "It's all we have. We've got to get to it now."

She nodded and pushed herself to her feet, staggering slightly. Joints protesting, Carson did the same.

More sirens—police cars following the ambulance and fire truck. It wouldn't be long until the Feds from their last motel showed up, if they were still alive. If not, there would be others. Since a bomb had been used, ATF would be called in, as well. That meant DEA, FBI, ATF, as well as local and state police, would be swarming the place. Exactly what he—and, he would have thought, Hades' Claws—wanted to avoid.

A crowd began to gather in front of the burning motel. More cars raced up—most likely curious civilians—and pulled into the parking lot. Others stopped on the shoulder of the road, onlookers emerging to gawk at the inferno. Now, before the rest of the circus started, would be their only chance.

"Wait here," he said. She nodded, and he sprinted for the Tahoe. Gasping for air, he felt the beating his lungs had just taken. But he made it to the edge of the parking lot, slowing his pace, pretending to be another curiosity seeker watching the fire. Hoping the firefighters were too intent on the blaze to notice him, he unlocked the door and started the engine. In the confusion, no one paid him any attention. Slowly he drove to the edge of the pavement and stopped.

Brenna emerged from the darkness, Phelan in her arms. She climbed in, yanking her door closed with a resounding thunk. She smelled of smoke and soot.

Both silent, they pulled onto the highway, heading north. Lights flashing, sirens wailing, two police cars sped past them on the way to the disaster. No doubt this and the fire the night before were the most excitement Hawk's Falls had seen in years.

Leaving the fire behind, Carson finally exhaled. Driving with blind luck, he located another of those deserted dirt roads that appeared to lead to nowhere and turned on it.

Because his hands and arms felt like rubber, he only went a couple of miles before he pulled over on the shoulder and killed the engine.

He looked at Brenna. Wide-eyed, she stared back.

"It's cold," she said, her voice husky.

Was she in shock? Most likely, though the dampness of the chilly night did tend to seep into the bones. He gathered her in his arms, holding her tightly in his lap. Only to keep them both warm. Nothing more. Unable to help himself, he dropped a kiss on the top of her head.

She stiffened. "What was that for?"

Strong emotion rushed him, constricting his chest and clogging his throat. Unprepared, he shook his head and simply tightened his arms around her.

"You could have died." He stared blindly at the top of her head. Brenna, beautiful, bold Brenna, had nearly become an innocent casualty in his quest for justice. He'd failed to protect her, despite his vow to make sure no more lives were lost because of him. The thought of her perishing nauseated him. Made him want to fight something. Someone.

"*We* could have died," she corrected. "But we made it. You, me and Phelan. We're all right."

Avoiding her direct gaze, he reached over the console and gave the puppy a rough pat. Blinking up at him, Phelan licked his hand, then curled into a ball and went to sleep.

Carson felt Brenna shiver in his arms. Delayed shock. He'd been right the first time.

"God, I'm sorry," he said. "I never intended—"

"It wasn't your fault." She sounded so sternly reproving that he couldn't help but smile.

"We were lucky."

He thought of another time, when he hadn't been so lucky. The shot in the back had taken him down. Down and out. He'd nearly died then, but instead had recovered to live with the reality that he'd lost his entire world. Most days since, he'd wished he had died. Only vengeance kept him alive. Only the search for justice kept him going.

After that, he didn't know. Until now, he'd always planned to end it all, to join Becky and Julie in the afterlife.

Now…he wanted to live. Again his own thoughts stunned him. He shied away from the notion, not sure he trusted himself. The very idea seemed foreign. He just didn't know how such a thing could be possible—awakened desires, longing, feelings he'd believed long dead.

Once entirely certain of his own path, now he simply didn't know. All he knew was the soft beauty of the woman he held in his arms. Letting the past go, he buried his face in her hair and breathed in her smoke-tinged scent. Through the soot and ashes, he could still detect the unwavering aroma of flowers clinging to her skin.

"Those Hades' Claws people are nuts," she said.

"Yeah, and dangerous. I tried to warn you." He glanced at his watch. His heart skipped a beat. "We'll never make it to the bus station on time now. I hope Jack gets out okay."

"Jack! How long—"

"By the time we get there, his bus will have already left."

"What about the message he's supposed to give you?"

Carson pulled out his cell phone and punched in a number. After the ninth ring, he hung up. "No answer."

"Maybe we should go."

Checking his watch once more, Carson sighed. "No point."

His throat still burned. He swallowed, anyway. "He can call me later. I'm sure he's all right—guys like him know how to survive. He'll call."

Turning in his arms, she raised her chin. In the dim light of the wintry sun, her skin looked like cream, her eyes huge and dark, her mouth full. Never had she seemed more hauntingly, achingly beautiful. And fragile.

He wanted her safe. Yet she wouldn't let him protect her. "I'll take you to the bus station if you'll get on the next bus out of here."

"No." Her eyes flashed.

Frustration made his stomach clench. "Look at

what's happened. They won't stop until they kill us. You have to go. I can't let you die because of me."

"Hey. We're alive." Leaning into him, she brushed her lips across his. "Alive. Go with it. We're all right."

His heart thudded in his chest. Stunned, he accepted her kiss. She was right. Even now life thickened his blood, stirred his body to readiness. He held himself still, frozen. Alive.

Afraid to breathe, afraid to move. With her mouth she explored his. With sensual slashes of her tongue she tasted. She stroked him, caressed him, teased him. Brought him to an achingly hard readiness, close to losing control.

Adrenaline. It fueled both of them, he knew. In his line of work, such a reaction to a close brush with death was normal. They lived, they breathed. The first rush of shock had left her. With energy still pumping through her veins, Brenna wanted to reaffirm life. With him.

Because he knew better, he fought, but desire and wonder and joy exploded inside him, bubbling up from a long-forgotten place. His pulse pounded. He wanted… He needed… Yet somehow he kept himself utterly and completely still. Under control. Waiting. She touched him, and he surged against her, letting her feel the strength of his desire for her. Her call now, her move.

At his lack of any overt response, she gave a frustrated cry and, completing the turn she had only half started, straddled him. Settling her soft warmth over him with a quiet sigh, she touched him, her small hands everywhere at once, soft and hard, gentle and urgent. Each stroke, each caress, brought him closer and closer to the edge of his iron control.

"Brenna..." He couldn't understand how she, so vibrantly beautiful, could want a broken man like him. That thought, and only that thought, kept him from ripping her clothes off and taking her.

"Carson."

He heard the naked longing in her voice and shuddered. She moved over him, and his body stirred. Her heat seared him through their clothing, wet and warm and willing. His own need escalated—it had been so damn long since he'd felt this way—desire mingling with uncertainty. He closed his eyes, lost in sensation. Inhaling sharply, the scent of smoke from the fire reminded him of things he could not forget.

How he longed to forget. Just once.

He slanted his mouth over hers, hard, demanding. With a glad cry she met him, her passion equal to his, her movements frenzied and urgent.

"Alive," she gasped once more. This time, his heart, his soul, his body, echoed the word.

Alive. Never had he felt more so.

"Brenna." His voice thickened as he gave her a final warning. "Last chance," he said. He knew that if they kept this up, he would take her here, mindless and savage in the front seat of his truck. She deserved better. A soft bed, candlelight, wine.

Turning his head, he attempted to push her away. She resisted, the steering wheel at her back.

"No," she said, and kissed him again.

Finally he surrendered. Lost, he followed where she led. The bleak abyss that had shadowed his days for so long receded, as did the cold, hard leather seat beneath him. He touched her through her clothes, his hands warmed by the heat she radiated. She arched into him, crying out, and with one stroke he felt her come apart under his fingers.

Too much between them—jeans and zippers and sweatshirts. Unnecessary clothing. He wanted silky skin, flesh slick with desire.

As though she'd read his mind, she yanked at his shirt, pulling it over his head and tossing it in the backseat. Caressing his bare skin, she tugged at the edge of his jeans. Guiding her, he helped her find the zipper, helped her pull it down over his swollen body. When she freed him and curled her fingers around his heat, he gasped. So long denied, he surged into her hand, uncontrollable.

"Wait." He grabbed her fingers to keep from embarrassing himself right then and there like an eager adolescent. "I don't have a condom."

She smiled, a slow and sensual thing that held a tinge of sadness. "You haven't, er, been with anyone since—"

"No."

Her kiss took away the sting of that simple word. When she raised her head and met his gaze, she looked solemn. "Then I think we're safe. It's been over a year for me—"

"I'm not a careless man."

Touched, she stroked him again. He moaned and pulled her back for another deep, drugging kiss.

"Enough talking," she growled against his mouth. She arched her back in a long, sensual stretch, head back. One look at her and he lost his battle for control. With her eyes half-closed, she settled over him. Heat. He gave a hoarse cry, struggling for control. She made a sound, then sheathed him deep inside her warmth.

Home. The absurd thought slammed into him with the subtlety of a brick. Brenna. Hot. Wet. Wonderful. *Home.*

How could he ever let her go?

Then he forgot to think, couldn't think, as she began to move.

Chapter 13

How could he sleep? Brenna eyed Carson's form in the uncomfortable passenger seat next to her and shook her head. Inside the vehicle, the night's chill air made the leather seats hard and unforgiving. She shifted, trying to find a comfortable position. Carson apparently had no such problem. Head back, he slept sitting up, a slight smile softening the harsh planes of his face.

Gazing at him, she felt again that softening inside. Longing to glide her fingers over his skin, she clenched her fists to keep from touching him. Instead she watched the even rise and fall of his chest, inhaling the faint musky after-scent of their lovemaking.

Though she had seen many men, both shifters and human, never had she found one as beautiful as Carson. Beautiful. She pondered the word, knowing it was an odd choice to describe a man so hard and wounded. Yet she fancied she saw a new contentment on his face, as though the slaking of his body's hunger for hers had eased a few of his burdens.

Beautiful. Her chest tight, her heartbeat a steady thump in her ears, she envied him his moment of peace.

Sleep was the last thing she wanted. Though sated, she felt energized, charged. Restless, she wanted to run and jump and laugh out loud. Oddly enough, she also wanted to weep. So much had changed between them. They could never go back to the way they had been.

Their lovemaking had been explosive, wild and abandoned. She'd felt like a virgin again. Jeff had been her first and only, yet the one time they'd had sex couldn't hold a candle to this. No one had told her such pleasure was possible. She blushed, feeling a remembered tingling as she contemplated the things she and Carson had done. They hadn't even bothered to remove all their clothing, their passion had been so frenzied.

Yet they'd made love. Carson had possessed her, put an indelible stamp on her soul. It wasn't only the way he'd brought her to her first release. No, they'd forged a bond, a thread that would tie them together now and always.

Always.

The very thought frightened her, even as she exulted in the certainty of it. Things had changed and, hounds help her, she should have known better. Their coming together was everything she'd ever imagined lovemaking could be and more. So much more. Like finally finding the place where she belonged.

A shattering, painful thought, especially since she knew Carson would not want her the same way.

She had to find some distance. She could not allow this to happen again.

Her heart sank. Letting him go would be difficult. How could it not be, when even his masculine scent brought her pleasure? Watching him now, she immediately hungered for more. She desired to touch him, taste the salt of his skin. She wanted to love him again with her body, since he would not accept her soul.

Fool. Though she wanted what had happened between them to be mere lust, nothing stronger, she knew she had given more than her body to Carson. She now felt naked, exposed. Vulnerable.

One final look assured her he still slept deeply. That was good, for if he looked at her, she was afraid he would be able to read the powerful emotion thrumming through her body.

Love. Unable to lie to herself any longer, Brenna admitted the truth. She loved him. With all her heart, all her soul.

Love. Covering her face with her hands, she shifted in the seat and again called herself a fool. There were a thousand reasons why she shouldn't love Carson. He was human and she—she was not. He was broken and bitter and probably incapable of ever loving another woman. Especially one such as she, who could change into a wolf at will. What future could they possibly have together? None.

Yet in her heart of hearts she'd named him her mate. There would be no other for her. Once he had gone, she would remain alone to the end of her days. Alone and childless.

Another thought struck her. Had they made a child

together? They'd used no protection. Pregnancy was entirely possible.

Even now, she could be carrying Carson's child. She spread her fingers protectively across her stomach, pondering.

A child. How would Carson react to such a thing? For that matter, what would *she* do?

A child of theirs would be half shifter, half human. She'd heard of such children, though she knew none personally. While the shifter gene was dominant, children born half shifter were not as powerful as full shifters while in their wolf shape. Still, because they had the ability to change, they were accepted unequivocally into the Pack, welcomed and loved like any other cub.

Carson's child. The thought brought a rush of another sort of pleasure. A child of her own. Though her work as a librarian brought her daily human contact, she'd been lonelier than she'd cared to admit.

Her head hurt. Kneading her temples, she gazed out at the black night and felt a primal call. She still needed to change. To slip soundlessly through the woods, unencumbered by human thoughts and emotions.

In the backseat, Phelan stirred, whimpering. He needed a quick trip outside to relieve his bladder. A perfect excuse for her to briefly disappear into the woods to become a wolf.

Quietly, hoping not to disturb Carson, she reached into the backseat and got Phelan. Though at first he wiggled in excitement, a quiet word calmed him. Together they stepped into the night forest.

The woodsy scents of earth and bark and winter gave her immediate comfort. Phelan bounded ahead, plowing through an occasional snowdrift, tail wagging. Moving more slowly, Brenna followed. She wanted to make certain she was out of sight of the Tahoe before she allowed herself to change.

The moon provided a silvery light, eerie through the leafless trees. Here. Stopping in a small clearing, she turned and lifted her arms to the stars that glittered in the icy sky. Quickly she shed her clothing, making a neat stack next to a large oak.

Power hummed in the crisp air. Finally. A thrill ricocheted through her as she gave way to the craving. Her bones sang as they began to elongate, her heart pumping as she felt the necessary shifting begin to course through her blood. Eventually it would consume her. In a few minutes she would run through the deserted forest, glorying in her full power as a she-wolf. Full-fledged huntress. One of the Pack.

Leaves cracked. Phelan barked, alerting her. Too late, she spun around to face the threat, her energy locked up in the beginnings of the change. Not Carson, but some other man. She saw his shadowy face reflect horror a second before he grabbed her. She tried to fight but, in the middle of changing, with not enough time to complete the process, she was vulnerable, exposed. She had no energy to resist. Nor to complete the change.

Arms clamped around her. He held her, fumbling for something—a weapon. Weakened, she attempted a kick, but it fell far short. Cursing, he tightened his grip. When he covered her face with a sweet-smelling cloth, she tried to bite him. He shoved some of the material in her mouth, gagging her. A sharp taste, metallic and bitter. The rag—some sort of drug. Must. Not. Breathe.

But, inevitably, she had to have air. One gasp to fill her lungs and she felt herself spiraling into oblivion.

Carson jerked awake. Somewhere outside, a dog barked, shrill and furious. Phelan? A quick glance around the Tahoe showed him Brenna had gone, her pet with her.

As he reached for the door handle, he saw headlights coming toward him on the dirt road. Instinctively, he ducked, but not before he saw the front of the van barreling toward him. Ford. Brown. His law-enforcement-trained mind automatically recorded the make and color. The vehicle sped past, bouncing over the rutted road until it vanished from sight.

From deep within the dark forest, Phelan began to howl.

Brenna. Yanking open the door, Carson jumped to the ground and ran.

Here. A tangle of footprints in the snow. Brenna and Phelan and…someone else. A large man. One who wore at least a size thirteen boot.

Phelan barked again, and Carson veered left. Ignoring the nagging pain that blossomed in his side, he headed toward the sound.

Reaching a small clearing where the trampled snow showed signs of a struggle, he cursed. Swiftly he followed the tracks. Abruptly Brenna's footprints ended. Only the stranger's trail led away, followed by Phelan's paw marks.

Brenna. She'd been grabbed. Like Jack had warned, Hades' Claws had come after her. Again moving faster than he'd anticipated, they'd caught him unprepared.

Despite Jack's warning, he'd been so sure their next move would be against him.

He hadn't been vigilant. One incident of great sex with Brenna and he'd dropped off to sleep like a man who had a right to. He'd relaxed his guard. Stupid. Now Brenna had been taken. They would kill her if he didn't get to her in time.

Still barking, Phelan rushed into the clearing, straight to Carson. Clearly agitated, the young dog jumped again and again, then ran toward the trees and waited.

Phelan wanted to show him something. Following, Carson went into the trees, surprised to find the road twisted near on the other side. Tire tracks showed where Brenna's abductor had parked.

Carson grabbed his cell phone, hitting Redial. Even though Jack should be on the bus, he might know something. Three rings. Four. Still no answer.

On the sixth ring, Jack answered.

"Jack, they've got Brenna."

"Help me." Jack's voice, a full octave higher than normal, sounded terrified. "I missed the bus, and they sent someone here, he's going to—"

Over the phone line, Carson heard the unmistakable sound of a gunshot. Heard Jack's muffled scream, the awful sound of his body as he fell.

"Turner." Another voice—Jack's assailant? "You're too late to help the snitch. He's dead. We've got your girlfriend. She's next."

Then a final click as the man snapped the phone closed.

Forty minutes later, Carson pulled up to the bus station. Three squad cars, lights flashing, blocked the entrance. Yellow police tape fenced in a square near the entrance. Like at the motel fire, a crowd of curious onlookers had gathered.

Carson parked the Tahoe as close as he could. Leaving it running, he crossed to the edge of the crowd, keeping watch for anyone who looked remotely like a biker.

"What's going on?"

A man turned to look at him, his graying, short beard and lined face perplexed. "Man was murdered," he said. "Young guy, too. From the city. Heard he'd just bought a bus ticket to Brooklyn."

Jack. Carson took a deep breath. What about Brenna?

"This man, was he alone?"

"Far as I know." The man peered at Carson. "Why?"

"I knew him. Was he shot?"

"Yes." The man shuffled his feet. His sparkling white sneakers and neatly pressed jeans proclaimed him a tourist.

Carson's cell chirped. "Excuse me." Making his way toward the nearest brick wall, he kept his back against it while he answered.

"Talk to me."

"She's not at the bus station." It was the same voice—Jack's killer.

Carson scanned the crowd. "Is she alive?" He could hardly get the word past the knot in his throat.

"For the time being."

"Are you here?" Carson clenched his fists.

"Nah. Not me." No hesitation in the guttural voice. "If I was, you'd be dead. Like your girlfriend will be soon. Did you know she was naked?" The caller chuckled. "Though the boss made us put her clothes back on."

Swallowing back his rage, Carson kept his voice level. “Where is she? Tell me how to find her.”

“Why bother? She’s as good as dead.”

With a snarl Carson shifted his grip on the phone. “Cut the bull. Let the girl go. I’ll offer myself instead. You name the time, the place.”

The biker sneered. “A sacrifice?”

“If that’s what you want to call it.”

“What if we want you both dead?”

“Then I go down shooting. I’ll take some of you down with me.”

“I’ll get back to you.” Again that click as the other man disconnected.

Heart hammering, Carson punched the wall. If the man delivered his message, Carson might finally get what he wanted—a face-to-face confrontation with Alex or whoever had killed his family. If he could only work out a way to save Brenna at the same time.

They would never cut a deal; Hades’ Claws didn’t play by rules. Never had.

Then neither would he. Let them think he was waiting for them to set up a meeting. Meanwhile, he would ditch whoever was watching him and head out to the Hell Hole, figure out a way to get in and rescue Brenna. If he got really lucky, while he was there he would find the SOB who’d ordered her taken and get some answers.

Alex. Brenna’s brother. What part did he play in all this? Did he know his own people had taken her? If he did, she ought to be safe. Surely her own brother wouldn’t let her come to any harm, or would he?

Carson knew what he would do in Alex’s place. If they’d given him a choice eighteen months ago, he sure as hell would have traded his life for that of his wife and child.

After, when all that he'd lived for had been savagely ripped away from him, he'd longed for death. Prayed for death. Hell, until recently, he still would have welcomed oblivion, once he'd gotten his hands around the murderer's throat. But not anymore.

So many deaths. Because of Carson, Jack had been killed. Now his enemies had Brenna.

No more.

The killing would stop.

Giving the still-gawking crowd one final look, Carson walked away quietly and got in his Tahoe. The battered vehicle creaked and sputtered as he drove slowly away.

He slammed on the brakes as a horrible thought occurred to him. What if Brenna was already dead? What if he was too late to stop them from killing her?

His head began to ache. Since he'd lost his family, he'd lived for the day when he could finally look the bastard who'd killed them in the face. The renegade side of him wanted to pull the trigger himself. The lawman in him voted for arrest and justice.

Even he wasn't a hundred percent certain what he would do when the time came. He just wanted to know.

But not at the risk of yet another life.

He wiped his hand across his mouth, unsurprised to find it was shaking. After being focused on one goal for so long, his grip on reality had been disturbed. He no longer recognized facts or lies, reality or fantasy.

But one thing he did know—Brenna Lupe was special. She'd crept into his heart and stayed there. He wouldn't be too late to save her. Fate couldn't be so cruel. Brenna was the one person he wholeheartedly believed in since he'd lost his entire family. She was good and innocent and blameless. He would stake his life on it. Now he might have to.

Determined, he pressed the gas pedal to the floor and headed north, toward the Hell Hole.

Brenna woke in a dark room. She came awake fighting. Sucking in great gulps of air, she attempted to ward off an absent enemy. Her fists came up short, unable to move. Any attempt at movement brought sharp pain.

A look at her wrists showed her why. She'd been handcuffed, one hand to each side of a headboard.

Shaking her head, she blinked furiously, trying to clear her sight. The room appeared to be shrouded in fog. She swallowed, grimacing at the metallic taste. The objects in the darkened room receded, came closer, then danced away. Blurry. No sharp edges. Her heartbeat felt sluggish, her limbs heavy.

Finally she understood why. She'd been drugged. One of the worst possible things that could happen to a shape-shifter. If she lost control of her body's ability to change, she could mix the molecules. The end result could be death or worse, a horrific maddened creature out of mankind's worst nightmares.

Deliberately she calmed herself, using relaxation techniques to focus. She'd always prided herself on her control; she would call on that ability now to aid her.

The dark room didn't bother her; like others of her kind, smell was her dominant sense, enabling her to see in a way her eyes did not. She sniffed, groaning aloud.

Whatever drug she'd been given had dulled even that important faculty.

Still, though unable to probe deeply, she was able to detect the first layer of scents. The room smelled musty, as though it had been unused and closed up for a long time. The clogging scents of dust and decay made her sneeze.

Next she attempted to listen, blocking out the sound of her own heartbeat and labored breathing, trying to hear voices, a radio, some conversation—anything to give her a clue as to where she might be.

She heard only silence. Felt only confusion.

She could not change to save herself. All she could hope was that Alex would learn of her capture. Once her brother knew Hades' Claws had taken her, she would be safe.

She hoped.

With a groan, she swallowed. She hated that now even she doubted her own brother's intentions, thanks to the way he'd behaved around Carson.

Carson. A fresh wave of emotion swamped her. Would he look for her? She didn't want to put him in danger because of her own foolishness. Bottom line: she would rather her life be at risk than his.

She loved the man.

Her eyes filled with tears. The drug? Or her own burgeoning sensitivity? She sighed. What a time to fall deeply, hopelessly in love with a human.

At least, she thought, she could find some humor in this horrific mess. Things couldn't get any worse. Or could they? She remembered a similar thought she'd shared with Carson the day before. The room had blown up then.

Yes, things could certainly get worse. She had to find a way out. Closing her eyes, she ignored the pitch and roll of the floor, knowing it was the drug wreaking havoc with her senses. She must regain control. She needed to come up with a plan. She had to figure a way out.

Carson didn't stop to plan, or even to think. This time he couldn't lose, couldn't afford to fail. To rescue Brenna, he would have to act solely on gut instinct and impulse. He had to get her out—now. No time to waste. He'd delayed in getting to Jack, and now Jack was dead. He wouldn't make the same mistake again—not with Brenna's life at stake.

Once he reached the Hell Hole, he drove past and parked off the road, near a copse of leafless trees, even though the dark night hid the car well enough.

Leaving a protesting Phelan in the truck, he slipped on his black work jacket, thankful the bright yellow DEA logo was emblazoned only on the back, and began to walk toward the gate, taking care to stay near the trees in case he needed to take cover.

No cars disturbed the late-night peace. The faint moonlight turned snowdrifts silver, bathing the trees in a ghostly luminescence. Yet danger lurked here, in the depth of the dark forest, in the compound where evil slept.

There had to be a way in. Encircled by the odd fence, the perimeter of the Hell Hole was clearly marked. He studied the stonework, looking for a break. There, where the wall made a slight turn—one place looked less intimidating than the rest. At roughly four feet tall, some of the rock had crumbled, leaving a gap. This low point would be his best bet in scaling the glass-shard-protected fence.

Ice in the breeze made him shiver. The end of his long journey waited inside these walls.

Focus. Center. One thing at a time.

First—get inside, find Brenna and get her out.

Once she was safe, then he would hunt down his former partner and settle things once and for all.

He placed his hand on the stone, feeling the cold seep into him. Focus.

How to breach their security and remain undetected?

When a survey of the surrounding trees failed to reveal any other security cameras besides the ones aimed directly at the gate, he let out breath he hadn't even realized he'd been holding. Despite what he'd told Brenna on their trip out here earlier, he doubted the woods were filled with motion sensors. It would make a lot more sense to outfit the fence itself with an alarm rather than try to monitor the entire forest. Half-assed security, but still more than enough for an ordinary home.

This place was far from normal. He was pinning his hopes on the fact that Hades' Claws wouldn't believe anyone would be foolish enough to invade their headquarters. He hoped to use that arrogance against them now.

Limited planning session finished, he backed up. He took the low point of the fence at a dead run. Vaulting over, he made it with only one shard of jagged glass stabbing his palm. The cut bled, but he ignored it and stood still, heartbeat a loud thumping in his ears.

No alarms sounded; no spotlights began to sweep the woods. All remained quiet and still. He'd been right, then—they only monitored the gate. Apparently he hadn't triggered the sensors. So far, so good.

Slipping from tree to tree, just in case they posted guards, he finally saw the house through the tangled branches. Still a good fifty yards off, the low-slung ranch was an architectural holdover from the fifties. Unpainted and slightly weathered, the structure hid behind overgrown shrubbery. This had the singular result of making the place appear to blend with the forest, especially with all of the windows dark, as they were now. In the silver moonlight, the cedar siding appeared to glow. Overall, Carson found the effect eerie rather than truly menacing. But he, more than anyone, knew better than to trust simple appearances. Nothing was ever what it seemed. If he were to trip an alarm, he had no doubt that bikers would swarm over the yard, armed to the teeth.

He crept closer. There had to be a way inside without alerting any of the occupants. His next step would be figuring out where they were keeping Brenna.

Moving silently, he made his way around to the side of the house. Checking his watch, he stumbled. Caught himself. Nearly midnight. He took a deep breath, blew it out in a frosted plume. His nerves jangled. With an effort, he steadied them. Years of undercover work had taught him to trust his gut reactions—and his gut said something was off-kilter. There was something...wrong about the situation.

He took inventory. Midnight. Dark woods. Even darker house. Too quiet. No dogs. He found it hard to believe a bunch of bikers went to bed so early. Unless they were expecting him, he couldn't imagine them sitting around in the darkened house.

Unless they were gone.

He froze, unable to consider that possibility. If they were gone, they'd taken Brenna elsewhere. He would have a hell of a time trying to find her.

As he stared at the house, a light blinked on, spilling bright yellow light into the backyard. No blinds or curtains shaded the window. Ducking behind a thick oak, Carson watched a large man enter the room, bending over as he fiddled with something out of Carson's line of sight. Carson moved forward.

A leaf crackled. He spun. Too late.

Chapter 14

A loud crash came from the hall. Startled into wakefulness, Brenna attempted to sit up, yelping in pain as the handcuffs yanked her back to the bed. Footsteps pounded. She heard a thump, a curse, another crash, sounds of a scuffle.

Two men, maybe three, fighting. Were there guards outside her door? Straining to hear, she went very still. She heard a low voice give a guttural order but could not make out the words. The walls shook from another huge thump. She heard grunts and the horrible resonance of fists connecting. Finally there was an ominous-sounding thud, followed by silence. Then she heard only the steady drum of her own heartbeat in her ears.

Her door squeaked open. The light clicked on again. Blinking against the sudden blinding brightness, she squinted at the man standing in the doorway. Shorty, the sour-smelling man who earlier had brought her food, grinned at her before disappearing briefly. When he returned, he backed into the room, dragging an unconscious body under the arms. Though his head was turned, she recognized the black DEA jacket and matching cap. Her heart stuttered, began to thud erratically. Carson. They had Carson. His hands had been cuffed in front of him.

After depositing Carson in an unceremonious heap on the floor next to the bed, Shorty produced one more pair of steel handcuffs. They were twins to the ones he'd used to shackle Brenna to the bed. Since her feet were free, Shorty yanked Carson's leg up and cuffed his ankle to hers. The cold steel bit into her flesh.

"Too tight?" Leering at her, her captor shook his head, grinning.

"Yes," she said. "Too tight. And you've got him upside down."

"Tough," Shorty sneered. "He can try and fix that when he wakes up. Hell, he ought to thank me. Now you two can be together. Die with each other, too, most likely. Nemo should give me a big bonus for this one."

He aimed his steel-toed boot and kicked Carson, catching him hard in the leg. Semiconscious, Carson gave a muffled groan.

It took every ounce of willpower she had to keep herself from baring her teeth and lunging forward. Only fear of her inability to control the change kept Brenna motionless. Until she was certain the drugs had left her system, she dared not risk it.

"He's gonna wish he'd died the first time, along with his wife and kiddo." With a laugh, Shorty leaned in to chuck her under the chin. Brenna growled low in her throat, baring her teeth at him. Immediately she felt the change begin in her. Horrified, she clamped down, closing her mouth.

"Hey, girl, I like 'em feisty," Shorty said, ruffling her hair as an added insult. Still chuckling, he waved a set of keys at her. "Too bad you can't reach 'em." Dropping them with a clank on the dresser, he left the room, slamming the door closed behind him.

Brenna calmed herself. She took an analytical inventory of her system. The room no longer danced and swam through a blur. She could once more see angles and corners. Though her mouth felt as if it had been stuffed with cotton, she no longer tasted metal. Lifting her head, she tried to scent the air. This time she could detect the faint odors of perspiration and blood.

Carson. Tied as she was, she couldn't help him. He lay on his back on the floor, the leg that had been shackled to hers pulling at her like a dead weight. Hounds help her if he tried to roll over.

"Carson," she said softly. No response. She wiggled, propping her back against the headboard, trying to ease the blood flow to her hands and now her leg.

"Carson." She tried again. She had to wake him before he moved and stretched her between him and the bed like some medieval torture rack. Then it would be a simple matter of making sure the drugs were gone. She would change, the cuffs would drop off, and they would be free.

But what about Carson? If she changed, would he despise her? Vividly remembering how Jeff, the man who'd asked her to marry him, had reacted to the truth about her nature, she knew the last thing she wanted was for Carson to find out.

Jeff's reaction had killed him.

For years, Brenna hadn't been able to rid herself of the idea that he'd chosen death rather than a life with someone such as her. Ridiculous, she knew now, especially since his death had been a horrible accident, but it had happened because in his shock and horror he had run from her to his car. Reckless driving, fueled by confusion and shock, had caused him to have a head-on collision with a gasoline tanker truck. Both Jeff and the truck driver had been burned beyond recognition.

No, she really didn't want Carson to find out she was a shape-shifter. But if she didn't change, they would both be trapped and die. Unless her brother suddenly appeared with the handcuff keys and released them, she had no choice.

Carson attempted to move his leg, yanking hard at hers. She yelped.

"Brenna?" He went still. Raising his head and licking the blood off his cracked lips, he pushed himself up on his elbows. Blanching, he took in the situation with a quick glance. "Damn."

"Hey," she said softly. "How badly are you hurt?" His face had been bruised and his lip split open, but even battered, she still found him beautiful. She wanted to reach out and smooth the hair from his forehead, but she couldn't.

"Not bad." He attempted to shift his weight, wincing at the pain. "They hit me from behind. Once again, I screwed up."

"Me, too." She had no answer for him, no words to soothe the tortured self-reproach she saw in his eyes. She blamed herself enough for both of them. She had powers ordinary humans did not. Of the two of them, she should have been the most able to evade capture. Like Carson, she'd been taken by surprise.

Even the mere thought of changing made her body resonate with need. With every heartbeat, every inhalation of breath, the desire sharpened, unbearably intense.

But she had to make sure the drugs had worn off before she gave in to the urge. If some other way out presented itself, she would take it. She would only change as a last resort.

"My leg—" Struggling to rise without yanking her apart, Carson pushed himself closer to the bed. Twisting, he managed to get his knee under him, propelling himself against the side of the bed. Since his hands were cuffed, he could only use them for leverage to thrust himself up.

"Help me." He raised his head, dark gaze meeting hers. "I can't hold this position long—hurts like hell. When I come up this time, hold your leg still. I'll have to use you as a sort of anchor, but I think I can make it up there."

Swallowing, she nodded.

With a grunt, he pushed and twisted at the same time. Clearing the edge of the mattress, he landed with his chin squarely on her groin.

She froze.

"Sorry," he said, his gaze darkening. With a neat motion, he rolled to the side. That meant she had to scoot over as far right as her handcuffed wrists would allow.

"Thanks," he muttered, attempting to wiggle into the space between her and the edge with minimal contact between him. But even if he lay on his side, with his left ankle chained to her right one, it wasn't possible. With that leg underneath him, they still had to mingle ankles. He looked like a bruised human pretzel.

"This isn't going to work." His words echoed her own thoughts. She looked at him, the beginnings of desire subjugated by the ever-present urge to change, and swallowed. "You'll have to lie on my other side, partially on top of me," she said.

He narrowed his eyes. "It's the only way, huh?" he said.

"Yes."

"I'll try not to hurt you." With an awkward twist and roll, he settled his weight over her, the hard length of his body pressing against hers for an instant. He jockeyed to find a comfortable spot. Her body heat increased, making her feel as though she were burning.

"There." He sighed. Closing his eyes, he sagged against her.

"Carson? We've got to get out of here. Carson?"

He didn't answer. The dead weight of him told her that he was unconscious.

She eyed the handcuff keys on the dresser. A mere twelve feet away. So close, but out of reach. Even if she extended her leg and Carson stretched out to his full length, they couldn't reach them.

A window sat midway along the other wall. It was reachable, though only by Carson, and only if they did some contorting.

There had to be a way to escape. Had to be.

But the only way she could think of involved her changing.

Several hours later she shifted for the twentieth time. Her hands were asleep again, the painful pins-

and-needles making her grit her teeth as she forced herself to do finger and wrist exercises.

Dim light streamed in through the blinds. Dawn. Her bladder was full, though she'd only had a small sip of the lukewarm water Shorty had offered the night before.

Carson shifted his weight with her, though this time the movement caused a perceptible change in his breathing. She took a deep breath and drank in the sight of him. With his face inches away from hers on the pillow, she longed to plant featherlight kisses on the dusky beginnings of a beard on his unshaven cheeks, but she dared not. He would awaken soon. Once he did, he would be in no small amount of pain, but at least he was alive.

That had to count for something.

She couldn't watch him die. Testing her own reflexes, she felt a noticeable improvement. Even if he despised her after, she would change if she had to in order to save his life. Heck, if they didn't let her go to the restroom soon, she would change just so she could relieve her bladder.

From out in the other part of the house, she heard the early-morning noises of people stirring, the clang of a skillet, the sound of the pipes as water ran. At the faint aroma of brewing coffee, her mouth began to water.

From the hall came another sound, this time the uneven thudding of a man running. Outside her closed door, two men talked in low voices that she strained to hear but could not. The back of her neck began to tingle.

Something was up. She sensed urgency in the very air, in the faintly acrid scents of their captors' perspiration.

Danger. Excitement. Those emotions rolled off the men in the house, reaching her in waves.

"Brenna?" Raising his head, Carson sounded the way he looked. "Damn. I feel like I've been run over by a freight train."

This time she couldn't resist—she reached out and gently kissed his cracked lips. He went utterly still.

"They worked you over." She kept all traces of emotion out of her voice.

"Yeah." He laughed, though his laugh sounded more like a choked-off cough. "Hurts like hell."

She studied him. "Why'd you wear the jacket?"

With a shrug, he grimaced. "It's black, it's warm. I didn't intend to get captured."

In the hall, a man shouted. They could hear the words "Out front!" More footsteps ran past.

Carson pushed himself to a sitting position. "What's going on?"

Listening intently, she shook her head. "Something. I don't know what."

He glanced at his watch and swore. "What day is this?"

She had to think. "Thursday." Still, she strained to hear. The house seemed to be enveloped in chaos—men shouting orders and running.

"The drug deal. If we stretch, can we reach the window?"

She stared at him blankly. "Why? If they start shooting out there, the window won't be safe."

"I don't care."

Of course he didn't. Maybe the edginess in his tone decided her, or perhaps the sudden hardness she saw in his gaze. Either way, Brenna knew what mattered to Carson above all else was his thirst for justice, for revenge.

"I need to see outside and find out what's going on."

"It's on the west side of the house. Can you see the front from there?"

His face full of impatience, he grimaced. "I won't know until I try."

Hating her feeling of helplessness, she wanted to growl her frustration. Sometimes being a wolf was much easier.

"If you think it'll work, let's try." With a curt nod to indicate her agreement, she motioned for him to attempt to push away. He rolled, their legs still cuffed together, pushing himself to his knees. Shuffling, crawling, he made it to the edge of the bed, leaning on the windowsill for support.

The metallic handcuffs bit into the skin of her wrists. Pain. Out of nowhere, the urge to change ripped through her. This time she found it even more difficult to push away.

"Not yet," she said under her breath.

"What?" Carson shot her an impatient glance.

"Nothing." Gesturing at the window with her chin, she forced an impersonal smile. "You wanted to see if you could see out the window. Have at it."

As she spoke, she heard more shouts. She smelled a faint hint of smoke. Fire? She quelled a rising sense of panic. No wolf—or human, for that matter—could endure for too long the threat of being trapped in a fire. Every sense on the alert, she listened. But she heard no roaring or crackle of flames, nor felt any hint of the searing heat that such a blaze wrought. They had time. She prayed she was right.

Peering out the blinds, Carson looked so long without speaking that Brenna couldn't resist giving the leg handcuffed to his a quick jerk.

"Patience." He kept his attention focused on the window.

This time a quiet growl escaped her. He didn't appear to notice.

"The hell with patience." Though her hands were numb from the bite of the handcuffs, her arms were aching again. Her shoulders and neck felt as if she'd been stretched on a medieval rack. "Tell me what's going on."

"A black stretch limo with full biker escort just pulled up outside. Looks like Jack was right—something more than a drug deal is going to happen today."

More footsteps and voices out in the hall. The guard outside their door shouted good-natured greetings to the others.

Carson spoke again. "A bunch of the gang just went outside to greet the limo."

"Alex?" She let her worry show in her voice.

"He's there. Front and center." Carson gave her a layered look. "Has your brother been to see you since you were captured?"

"Of course not." Though she started off strong, her voice faltered. "He doesn't know I'm here."

"You're certain?"

She heard disbelief in his husky voice.

"Of course I am." Her sharp tone dared him to doubt. "If he knew, I wouldn't be cuffed to a bed. And you."

"Are those the keys?"

"Yes."

"I want to see if I can get to them."

"There's no way we can reach that far." She grimaced. "This hurts enough as it is."

His gaze raked her stretched-out body. "If you can make it a little longer, I'd like to see what else happens out front."

"I'm fine," she said. "But I smell smoke and it's getting worse. With all of them focused on that limo, this would be a good time to escape."

Now she had his full attention.

He cocked his head. "Any plans?"

The hell with it. Maybe changing now wouldn't be such a bad idea. She gave him a measuring look. He'd already turned back toward the window.

"I wonder if the DEA is here."

No sooner had he spoken than she heard a rapid staccato of sound from outside.

She tensed. "What the—"

"Gunshots," Carson said. He swore. "The guys in the suits were barely out of the limo. Looks like some trigger-happy idiot jumped the gun."

"Alex." Worried for her brother, her first thought was to escape the cuffs. Once she changed, they would slip right off a wolf's slender paws. Instinctively, she began the process.

"Brenna." Carson's sharp voice brought her back. Tamping down her impatience, she hastily rearranged herself internally.

"What?" Taking deep gulps of smoke-tinged air, she looked at him. Something in the craggy lines of his face made her pulse skip a beat.

"Alex?" she asked, her voice tight. "Please tell me Alex is okay."

"He's fine." Now he left the window and crawled over in front of her. "Stay calm."

Heart in her throat, she nodded.

"The building is on fire," he said.

"I thought so." Animal instinct—flight or fight—filled her. "Carson, I—" She needed to change. Now.

"Take it easy," he said. "Rest your arms. If we're going to figure out a way out of this, you can't panic."

Right. She couldn't afford to panic. Especially if there were still drugs floating around in her blood. "I'm fine." Lifting her chin, she swallowed. "I don't like being helpless, that's all."

"None of us do." He moved his leg, rattling the set of cuffs that linked them together. "These are too tight."

She smiled at that. "Yeah. At least you can move your hands." Then, sobering, she tugged at her arms, cuffed tightly to the sturdy wooden post of the bed.

It was time. She would give him a warning first.

"Look," she said. "I'm going to do something now to free us. Don't freak out on me, okay?"

Disbelief and hope warred in his dark gaze.

She closed her eyes and summoned her strength, ready to begin.

Change.

Outside, chaos sounded. There were more sharp cracks of gunfire, more shouts and running. The scent of smoke grew stronger. The air seemed to thicken, heavy and acrid. Again she fought to ignore the interruption, using all her strength to cleanse her blood, to start the change.

Carson touched her arm, causing her to jump. She opened her eyes and glared at him.

"What?"

"If you're going to do something, do it now. The fire's getting closer."

"I know." She glared at him. Her eyes stung; her throat was clogged. Each breath burned her lungs. Air—she couldn't seem to breathe.

Panic and instinct warred within her. Though she needed more time to check herself for drugs, she didn't have it.

"When they bombed the motel, we made it," Carson reminded her. "We'll get out somehow."

Somehow? They hadn't been chained to the bed in the motel room. Well, she would soon take care of that.

"I'm sorry," she gasped, feeling the tremors begin as her cells started to shift. She yanked again at the metal that cuffed her to the bed, a futile, final attempt to set a miracle in motion.

But the handcuffs held.

The smoke became a weapon, bludgeoning them. Fire lapped at the door, tendrils of flame seeking entrance, crackling, hissing.

Change.

Her heartbeat raced. Though the altering of her body had her swaying, still she saw the orange glow of flames, felt the heat, tasted the bitter tang of smoke. Carson's craggy face swam before her, his eyes dark with the sickening belief that this was how it would end. He thought they would die here, like trapped animals tethered in a burning barn. With every fiber, every nerve ending in her, Brenna felt savage joy that her changing would prevent that from happening.

Human. Wolf. Wholly in the grip of the change, she welcomed her animal nature, hastening the sudden shifting of molecules and cells. As her limbs elongated, narrowed, she felt the useless handcuffs slide from her bones, clattering to the floor.

Ferocious fierce strength—*wolf!*

By her actions, Carson, too, was freed, his handcuffs dangling from one ankle, useless. They could reach the keys now and free him. And because of her changing, he would finally know what she was, what she could become.

She couldn't resist, even in her lupine form, glancing once at the man she loved above all others, even though she knew if she saw horror and repulsion on his face, the pain would sear her heart as badly as a fiery death.

Their eyes—man and wolf, Brenna and Carson—met and held. In his gaze she saw disbelief. Shock. But he reached out his hand, and she felt him thread his fingers through her furry pelt. Wonder and joy exploded in her. Hope. Yearning.

Though doing so now was extremely dangerous, in an instant she changed back to Brenna, human woman. She stepped into her torn clothes, then unlocked the cuffs. Grabbing his outstretched hand in hers, she clutched him tightly. Then, through flame and smoke she led him outside the burning house to safety.

Had they given him hallucinogenic drugs? Rubbing his eyes furiously, Carson blinked through the heavy smoke as he fumbled to unlock the handcuffs from his wrists. He had to be on some sort of drug, because he could have sworn he'd just seen Brenna shimmer and somehow become a huge silver wolf. The handcuffs had slipped off, freeing them both.

She'd been a wolf. A huge, beautiful, silver wolf. Snarling. For an instant, then… He rubbed his eyes, glancing at her again. Had to be drugs. Had to be. Because after somehow slipping the cuffs, Brenna stood right next to him, her hand clutching his. Not a wolf at all. Beautiful, yes, and courageous, but human. Brenna.

"Did you…" he started to ask. But she held up her hand and shook her head, a slight smile playing across her full lips.

"Not now," she said. "We've got to find Alex."

Alex. Though she'd seemed to know what he'd been about to ask and hadn't denied it, she was right. Even though they both had different reasons, they needed to find her brother.

Still…

"I thought I saw—"

Ignoring him, Brenna started moving, tugging him along after her. He had to hurry to catch up. Side by side they crossed to the front of the burning building. Even though the gunshots had died down, he felt a moment's apprehension. The protective instinct so deeply ingrained in him told him they should take cover. But with Brenna striding boldly forward, the best he could do would be to hope to shield her. So he didn't bother to conceal himself, aware that he, with the bright yellow *DEA* emblazoned on the back of his jacket, would be an easier target than she. At the slightest hint of gunfire, he would knock her to the ground.

But, oblivious to the danger, she marched forward. Fiercely intent, she continued to search, ignoring the men milling around them, some of them in custody, cuffed and bleeding, ignoring, too, the others who were down for the final count. She cared only for one thing, had only one purpose, one goal. To find Alex.

Carson grabbed a gun from a fallen guard and went after her.

A man ran past them, head down. Two others came from the side of the burning building and tackled and cuffed him. They led the man away without paying Brenna and Carson any mind. His DEA jacket, no doubt.

Again gunfire erupted. On the other side of the house another shoot-out was going on. Still she pressed forward.

Things looked about over—after that first wild shot, the Feds had swooped in. Watching Brenna's back for threats, Carson counted no less than three different agencies among the milling men of the invading army: DEA, FBI, ATF. In an odd sort of irony, his own DEA jacket was keeping him safe from his own agency, many of whom didn't recognize him, though he knew they would drag his ass in for questions when this was all over. Should he still be standing.

But he wasn't focused on that right now. He had to protect Brenna from her own brother. Alex had been willing to sacrifice his own sister for greed. Carson had to be there for the woman he loved when she finally realized what kind of man her twin had become.

The woman he loved. Once before, Alex had taken his family from him. Carson would kill him or die before he let anything happen to Brenna.

That revelation should have shocked him, especially since he didn't know if she really had changed into something decidedly not human.

Drugs? Or reality?

It didn't matter. Whatever she might be, she was still his Brenna. *His.* For now, for this exact nanosecond in time, he would focus every breath, every heartbeat, every fiber of his being on protecting her, especially once they found his enemy. After Brenna saw what Alex had become, he was going down.

Edging around a corner, Carson finally sighted his target. *Target.* Yeah, that was how he'd come to think of this man who'd once been his partner. An inanimate object—not a person.

Alex saw him at the same instant. Narrowed his eyes at the sight of his sister, who remained at Carson's side.

Carson raised his gun.

Alex raised his, too.

Target in sights. Still, Carson's fingers merely hovered over the trigger. One squeeze, one shot to the chest, and the big man would die.

Beside him, Brenna gave a stifled cry, a gasp.

God help him, this was her brother, her blood. Carson couldn't help remembering Alex as his partner, his best friend.

This was Alex. *Alex.*

While Carson hesitated, Alex did not. He fired.

Chapter 15

Carson jerked, but the bullet went wild. From behind him, someone grunted. Another man. Whirling, Carson saw Brenna leap forward at the exact instant the other guy squeezed off a shot. She knocked away the gun, but the bullet went—where? Brenna reared back. She spun and dropped to her knees. Head down, she gave a muffled cry.

No time to think. Carson raised his gun and shot. The man fell, crimson blossoming on his shirt. Pivoting, Carson brought his weapon to bear on Alex.

"Brenna?" Keeping Alex dead center, Carson backed over to her. Hunkered down. "Are you all right?"

Her hair a dark curtain shielding her face, she raised her head and grimaced, showing white teeth. The orange glow of the flames reflected in her brown eyes. "I'm fine." She sounded winded.

He didn't believe her.

His gun arm wobbled. Steadying it, he kept his weapon on Alex while he pushed away her hands from her shoulder. Scarlet stained her sweatshirt.

"You've been shot." His gut clenched.

"Let me see."

She moved away. "Alex," she said. "He saved your life."

"No. You saved my life. We need to get you to an ambulance."

"Alex fired first," she insisted. "He didn't shoot at you. He hit that guy in the stomach. Kept you from taking a bullet in the back."

She was right, Carson realized. "Why?" He stared at his former friend, now nemesis.

Stone-faced, Alex lowered his gun. "He was gonna shoot you." His grim expression showed his awareness that Carson still had a weapon trained on him. Dead center, finger on the trigger. Then he looked past Carson to his sister, concern softening the harsh planes of his face.

"Are you all right, Bren?"

Nodding, she pushed herself to her feet. "I'll live." She kept both hands pressed against her shoulder. "You know me. I heal fast."

Carson sucked in his breath.

"He saved your life," she repeated, raising her voice to be heard over the roar and crackle of the flames. "He could have killed you, but he didn't."

"I realize that." While he'd hesitated, Alex could have taken him down with one shot. Instead he'd fired to save Carson's life, even though he knew Carson wanted to blow him away.

None of it made sense. Unless…

Part of the building went down. A side wall crumbled, giving way to the fire's fury. A man ran screaming from the inferno, his entire body on fire. Two others tackled him, knocking him to the ground and rolling.

Carson focused on Alex. "Tell me the truth. Why not shoot me when you know I plan to bring you in?"

At his words, Brenna shifted. "Bring him in?"

"I couldn't kill him." He met her eyes. "Once, maybe, I would have. Now, because he's your brother, because you love him, I'm going to arrest him and bring him in to stand trial."

Shouts came from the other side of the burning house as the roof collapsed. Flames roared into the sky, sending smoke and sparks over them in a shower.

"You're right, Carson. I didn't save your life." Alex kept his hands at his sides. "Not this time. My shot didn't take him down. Brenna saved your life. She stepped between you and his gun."

"So your shot—" Carson heard his voice go flat "—was only to protect your sister."

Alex shook his shaggy head. "And you, idiot. Put the gun down." He took a step forward, holding his own weapon loosely, hand at his side.

Carson ignored him. "Freeze. Alex Lupe, you're under arrest for the murders of Becky Turner and Julie Turner. You have the right to remain silent. You have the—"

"Stop." Alex held up his hand, his expression tortured. "I didn't kill Julie and Becky, Carson. I was too late to save them, but I tried. Damn it, they were like my family, too. I loved them. You have to know that. You saw me with a gun, maybe you even saw me shoot, but you didn't see who I shot. That day, I did save your life."

Confused and exhausted, Carson swayed on his feet, though he didn't change his position. Weapon on target. Finger near the trigger.

Beside him, Brenna made a strangled sound. She sank to her knees. Carson's heart stopped.

Brenna or Alex? If he had to make a choice, he chose Brenna.

He lowered the pistol. And went to her.

"Let me see." Tenderly he swept back the hair from her face. Capturing her hands, he moved them so he could see her wound again.

"I'm fine," she protested, pushing him away. "Alex—"

All around them, smoke and fire and noise. Men down, men being led away in handcuffs. The acrid, coppery smell of gunpowder, of ashes and fire. The flash of cameras. Reporters already? No. The crime scene guys took photos.

Occupied in fighting the blaze and rounding up stragglers, a few of the federal agents glanced their way and moved on. No one interrupted them, seeing only a fellow agent in their matching, standard-issue jacket as he talked to two others.

Alex took another step forward. "Your cover was blown. We're not sure exactly how or by whom. I heard about the hit and went after the guy. I thought I could get there in time to stop it." The lines in Alex's face reflected his own pain.

"Instead I was too late. But I got there in time to take down the shooter before he finished the job. That's what you saw. I shot the guy who'd just shot you in the back. Stopped him from putting another bullet in you."

Carson stared at him blankly, cradling Brenna in his arms. She watched his face silently, hope and love mingled with the pain he saw in her expressive eyes.

Carson shook his head, trying to think.

"Don't you remember me calling your name?" Alex came closer. "I ordered you to hang on."

"No." He searched the other man's face. "After I saw you throw away the gun, I don't remember anything until I woke in the hospital room. I never saw anyone else. Just you."

"The DEA knew there was another guy. The shooter. The guy I killed. They couldn't reveal that and risk blowing my cover. So they put the story out that I did it as some sort of initiation test."

"You didn't kill them," Carson said slowly, woodenly. "But Hades' Claws believed you did."

Immobile, Alex jerked his head in a quick nod. "I had to stay inside to find out who'd ordered the hit. I also had to excuse my dropping the guy they'd sent to do it, so I said you shot him. Since he was dead and couldn't tell, the story worked."

"I used to wish I'd died, too."

The corners of Alex's mouth twitched. "What, and miss all this?"

"I thought it was you. I've been hunting the wrong man all along. I want the name of the murdering bastard. The guy who ordered them killed."

"We got him. His game's over."

Holding himself still, Carson tensed. Chest tight, he waited to hear the true name of the man he'd been seeking for so long. Then he felt Brenna's hand on his shoulder, comforting. With only her touch, she kept him sane.

Carson kissed the top of her head. He looked at Alex. "Senator Guiley. Top dog. We've got him in custody."

"The guy in the limo."

Alex nodded. "New York State Senator and drug lord. He raked in millions. What was one agent's family to him? He ordered the hit. He wanted you dead."

With a sound of disgust, Carson looked away. "All this time," he muttered, scarcely able to take it all in. "All this friggin' time."

He buried his head in Brenna's hair, inhaling deeply. His eyes full, he breathed in her beloved scent. Despite the fire and the smoke, she still smelled like spring.

Brenna—his rock, his love. Head bowed, he struggled to regain control of his emotions.

"I'm sorry," Alex said.

Unable to speak, Carson swallowed. When he finally lifted his head, he saw the man who'd meant to kill him lying on the ground, blood drying on his shirt.

Brenna sagged in his arms.

"She's unconscious." He heard panic in his voice. He pushed back her shirt at the shoulder, gently lifting the blood-soaked material from her skin.

Alex clapped a hand on his shoulder. "It doesn't look deep. I think his shot winged her." He swallowed, visibly shaken. "But you got him in time."

"We need to get the paramedics over. I want her thoroughly checked."

"She'll be all right. She's not badly hurt."

Carson narrowed his eyes. "How do you know that?"

"She's my twin," Alex said simply. "I know."

For the first time it occurred to Carson to ask about

what he'd thought he'd seen earlier, when Brenna had slipped the handcuffs. But, he thought as he studied the other man, if Brenna could change into a wolf, Alex was capable of the same thing.

His head throbbing, Carson decided to ask. "I—"

Like his sister, Alex seemed to know instinctively what Carson had been about to say. "Not now."

Two federal agents charged around the corner, guns drawn, too late. They skidded to a halt, backing off when Alex waved them away.

"You know they'll want to debrief you."

"Later. I've got to talk to Brenna."

Alex's gaze sharpened. "What do you want with her?"

"My entire future."

"Really?" Alex's voice seemed unnecessarily curt. The steely glint in his dark eyes carried a warning.

"Damned if I'm going to ask your permission."

"He saw me change." Brenna lifted her head, her voice weak.

Alex frowned. "When?"

"To get free of the handcuffs."

Carson kept his arms around her. "You mean when you—"

"Became a wolf. Yes."

"How?"

Alex ignored the question. "Among our people, it is forbidden to change in front of a human."

"You're worried because she broke some stupid rule?" Clenching his jaw, Carson inhaled. "We were handcuffed to the bed. The building was on fire. She did it to free us. She saved both our lives."

"I won't let you hurt her. She's my sister. I love her."

"I do, too." Lowering his gaze, Carson looked at Brenna as he spoke. Her eyes filled with tears. "I love you."

She sat up, grimacing as the movement caused her pain. "Even though you know what I am?"

Carson hesitated. As an undercover agent, he'd thought he'd seen it all. Now he realized he'd barely scratched the surface.

"What are you?"

"We're shape-shifters." Brenna's low voice was edgy, yet controlled. "We're an ancient race."

"Werewolves."

"In a way." Alex shrugged. "Though we rarely howl at the moon. And we can control it, for the most part. We aren't compelled to change because of a full moon or anything like that. We try to integrate ourselves into society and live normal lives among humans. Insiders know us as the Pack."

Carson turned to Brenna. "You once referred to your family that way."

She nodded, her expression watchful.

"This all sounds like some movie of the week."

"Yeah." Alex gave a short laugh. "Or a good book."

"Yet it all makes sense. Your eyes, the way you move, your confidence."

Brenna grinned. "Like that, do you?"

Alex coughed, drawing both their frowns. "Still, we are not human."

"Are you immortal?"

"No. Though we heal much faster, our life spans are the same as yours."

Tilting his head, Carson considered the woman he

loved. "Let me get this straight. You live, you die. You eat, you sleep, you breathe. Like me. Right?"

Brenna nodded, her expression tight.

"So the only difference is that you can change into a wolf at will."

Again she gave a nod, still watching Carson with shuttered eyes.

Throat tight, Carson managed to lift one shoulder in a shrug. "So who cares?" He took a deep, shuddering breath, trying to take it all in, knowing he couldn't, not yet. So instead he focused on what he did know, what really mattered. *Love.*

"I love you." He swallowed. "And I think you love me, too. I've been given a second chance. I don't want to waste it. What we have between us is special. I took it for granted once. I won't make that mistake again."

Brenna's expression didn't change. "What about children?"

Children. For a moment Carson's heart constricted as he thought of his lost daughter, Becky. Could he have another child, take such a giant leap of blind faith? Then he remembered the love he'd seen shining in Brenna's eyes and knew he could.

"What happens with children born of a union between a human and a shape-shifter? Is such a thing possible?" he asked.

Alex answered, one corner of his mouth lifting in a wry smile. "We call them Changelings. They can change, though they are not as strong. Still, among our people, they're welcomed and loved."

Love. "That's all that matters."

"Then I give you my blessing." Alex sounded formal—and pleased.

"Wait." Brenna pushed herself away from Carson to stand. "You two are talking like I'm not here."

Alex grinned. "Sorry."

Holding her shoulder, she focused on Carson. "We've been through a lot together. I don't think you've had enough time to think this through."

"Time?" Carson ran a hand through his hair. "I've spent the past eighteen months shunning life, living in the past. I'm not avoiding life anymore. I love you. I want to spend the rest of my days with you."

She didn't move. "I was engaged once. His name was Jeff. He loved me, too, or so he said. Yet when he found out what I was, what I could do, he ran from me in horror. He lost his life that night, Carson. Because he couldn't face what I am."

"I know what you are."

"I want you to think about it." She went to her brother and placed a light kiss on his cheek. "If he has any questions, answer them."

Then, turning, she faced Carson from several feet away. "This distance between us feels like a chasm."

His heart sank. "Only if you make it one."

"Three days." Sadness clouded her eyes. "Meet me in the woods in three days. If you don't show up, I'll understand."

With an effort Carson tamped down his impatience. Not an easy task when every heartbeat, every breath, sounded out the need to convince her. "I won't change my mind."

Her smile was a pitiful attempt. "We'll see." She walked away, still holding her shoulder.

Carson started after her. Alex stood, blocking his path. "Let her go. She's right. Think about things. Then, if in three days you still want her, both of you will be certain."

Shoving his hands in his pockets, Carson swallowed. "I don't understand."

"It's not often we mate with humans. To expose her true nature to you, Brenna took a terrible risk."

"Did her fiancé really die?"

"Head-on collision. Killed instantly."

Carson grimaced. "I guess I can understand her need to be certain." He started to turn away.

"I need to ask a favor."

Something in the other man's tone stopped Carson in his tracks. A hint of desperation, tinged with worry and fear.

"Once this is all done, there will be a trial," Alex said. "I'll have to testify. I don't want anything to happen to Brenna if…"

The rest of his sentence hovered in the air, unsaid.

Pain blossomed as Carson thought of Alex, of Brenna, meeting the same fate as his family. Then, to his amazement, the pain slowly receded. He didn't hesitate. "I will protect her with my life."

"I thought you would say that." Alex nodded. "You really love her, don't you?"

"Yes." With an effort of will, Carson kept his voice even. "I'll give her the time she wants, then I'll tell her again myself."

"Three days." A fierce grin broke out across Alex's face. "Sunday evening. Meet me in the woods near the cemetery around seven. I'll take you to her then."

"That's late. Make it earlier."

"She needs time."

"You're sure she's fine?"

"Yes. Agreed?"

Though his first impulse was to argue, Carson knew what the other man asked was fair. Or would be, if he were a reasonable man. Unfortunately, he'd wasted too much time to be sensible.

"I'll be there," he said, and got up to go.

"They'll need to talk to you now." Alex jerked his thumb toward the cluster of Feds.

"Later." Ignoring what he knew he should do, Carson headed out to the road and his battered Tahoe. "I've got a pet to look after."

Still waiting in the Tahoe, Phelan barked, standing with his front paws on the door, nose pressed against the window. As soon as Carson opened the truck door, the excited puppy jumped all over him, panting and licking furiously. No matter how often Carson rebuffed him, Phelan never cared. Wiggling his entire small body to match his wagging tail, he leaped on Carson with all the fervor of any well-loved pet greeting a beloved human.

Beloved human. Gathering Phelan to him, the thought shamed Carson. Because letting anyone, even a puppy, get close had terrified him, he had devoted all his energy into pushing the pup away.

As Phelan rained wet doggy kisses all over him, he realized he had a lot to make up for. In more than one way, he would be starting over.

Immediately he took Phelan to the woods. Somehow, he meant to find Brenna.

"Three days my ass," he told the puppy. He had to see Brenna now, to touch her with his own hands and make certain she was okay.

And he wanted to convince her how much he loved her.

Phelan barked, wanting out of his arms. Gently placing the puppy on the ground, Carson had an idea.

"Phelan." He put playful urgency in his tone. The puppy cocked his head, listening.

"Where's Brenna? Find Brenna."

With a small bark, the puppy took off running.

She heard them coming long before they neared her hiding place. In her wolf form, every sense became amplified, especially the sharpness of her hearing. So she listened and waited, trying to puzzle out the whys and the hows.

Carson knew what she was. He hadn't waited, as she'd asked. What had he decided?

First came Phelan, crashing through the forest, a bounding bundle of eagerness and joy. Brenna couldn't help but smile as only a wolf could.

And behind him, Carson. Moving more slowly, cautiously, though with no less purpose.

Carson. Her smile faded. Heart began to pound. She'd asked for three days. Had he made up his mind to leave so quickly?

Wavering, she stood on shaky legs and moved soundlessly farther into the shadows, where he couldn't see her.

"Hiding, sis?" Alex's voice.

She turned, saw her brother standing in his human form and began the change herself. It took only seconds for her to go from wolf to woman and step back into her clothes: then she was able to wrap herself in Alex's comforting arms and place her head on his broad chest.

"Are you all right?"

"I've healed my shoulder wound," she said. "But my heart? I'm not certain I can heal that."

"There, there." He stroked her hair as he'd done so many times before when they were small. "Talk to him, Brenna. Everything will be all right."

She raised her face to look at her brother's implacable expression, finding, as always, comfort and strength in his rugged features, so like her own, yet so different. His gaze, full of sympathy, had the inexplicable result of making her want to cry. Even as she thought it, her eyes filled.

"I never cry," she said, lifting her chin and swiping at her eyes.

"You never did," Alex agreed. "Even when you were small."

A tear spilled onto her cheek. "I love him so much."

The barest of smiles touched Alex's firm mouth. "Then be yourself. You can't lose."

"Be myself?"

"Confident. Daring. Fearless. Don't lose your tenacity now."

"Easy for you to say," she mumbled. "One eye open, remember? Carson saw me change."

"Mama was talking about our enemies when she told us that, Bren. Keep one eye open for trouble. Trouble, not our mates."

Mates. Her breath caught at the word. Alex was her twin. He knew. "Do you think he is?"

"Could be." He lifted one shoulder. "Only you know for sure."

She registered a certain sadness in her brother's rugged features. "I heard you were married."

"Yeah." For a moment pain shone stark in his face. "I sent her away, made her disappear for her own safety. Once all this is over, I'll find her and settle things between us."

He would, too, Brenna knew. Once Alex set his mind to something, he wouldn't rest until he'd accomplished his goal. She wished him happiness.

Phelan's tinny bark echoed through the woods, closer.

Alex smiled. "It's only a matter of time before your pup finds us."

"Change," she whispered urgently.

"Brenna…"

With one last desperate look at Alex, Brenna gave herself over to the change. In her wolf form, with her human emotions subjugated, she felt more capable of doing what she had to do.

Carson saw them first, two immense silver wolves standing in the shadows. When Phelan caught their scent, he hesitated in his stride, whining as he sat back on his haunches. He looked up at Carson as if asking for protection.

"It's all right, buddy," Carson said, awkwardly reaching down and scratching the puppy behind the ears. He eyed the magnificent animals. "Just Brenna and Alex, waiting for us."

The larger of the two wolves glided forward. Phelan scrambled to hide behind Carson's leg, trembling. The wolf stopped and cocked his head, tongue lolling. Carson could have sworn he was grinning.

Then Carson slid his gaze to the second wolf.

"Brenna."

At her name she came forward, past the first wolf to halt a few feet from Carson. So close he recognized Brenna's beloved brown eyes shining in the wolf's aristocratic face.

Then she changed.

Contrary to the old horror movies, there was nothing brutal or horrific about the transformation. One moment a regal silver wolf stood before him, the next, Brenna's slender form. The air had seemed to shimmer, her image wavered for an instant, then she was there. Naked, her beauty took his breath away. Then she stepped behind a tree, reappearing in a long, flowing dress.

When she changed to face Carson as a human, so, too, did Alex. Smiling, he dressed, then reached for the surprised Phelan, scooping him up in his arms and crooning wordlessly. He winked at Carson as they walked away.

"You've come to say goodbye," Brenna said, her expression solemn, pain evident in the careful way she enunciated each word.

"No." He shook his head. "You of all people should know—" Unable to continue, he swallowed. Hard. To try for a second chance at life, at love, was not a thing to be attempted lightly. What he would do if she refused him, he couldn't contemplate.

Brenna.

When he'd regained his composure, he took one step. Only one. Watching and hoping and praying—yes, praying—she would give him some sort of sign.

"What do you want?" Her features were as blank as her tone. "If it's absolution, I give it freely."

"Absolution?" Humbled, he looked away. Then, unable to help himself, he dragged his gaze back to her face.

"For doubting my brother," she said. What she meant, he knew, was "for doubting me."

She shrugged, a careless gesture, but he wasn't fooled. He saw how much she cared in the rigid way she held her slender body, poised as though on the edge of flight.

Or of changing.

He stepped forward again, not stopping until he stood mere inches from her. She lifted her chin, false bravado evidenced by the sheen in her eyes.

"I never doubted you," he said. Then, wanting to be totally honest, he added, "Maybe in the beginning, a little. But not after that."

She opened her mouth and closed it.

He moved toward her until his breath mingled with hers. Then he kissed her. Her nose. Her forehead. Her cheeks. And finally her lips.

"I love you." He whispered the words inside her mouth, knowing she heard them from the way she went utterly, totally still. So he lifted his lips from hers and said them again. "I love you. All of you."

This time it was she who reached up and pulled his face down to hers. As she kissed him, he tasted the salt of her tears and knew himself to be the luckiest man in the world.

Still, he had to make certain she understood.

"I can't do anything as exotic as change into a wolf," he said, smiling. "But I will cherish you and love you with all of my heart."

Her eyes were bright with tears and fierce with emotion. With love.

"Wolves mate for life," she warned him.

He laughed. "I wouldn't have it any other way."

* * * * *

COMING NEXT MONTH
from Harlequin Nocturne®
AVAILABLE OCTOBER 16, 2012

#147 THE WITCH'S INITIATION

Elle James

Desperate to free her sister from a chimera monster, a fearless witch must learn to accept help from a mortal and control her special powers to overcome the beast on his own dangerous territory.

#148 KISSED BY A VAMPIRE

The Calling

Caridad Piñeiro

Two-thousand-year-old vampiress Stacia gave up on life and love long ago, but a chance encounter with a man from her present will bring unexpected love and possible death.

HARLEQUIN®
INTRIGUE®
HE WOULD DO ANYTHING TO PROTECT HER...IF ONLY SHE COULD REMEMBER.
JOANNA WAYNE
BRINGS YOU ANOTHER DRAMATIC INSTALLMENT OF
BIG D DADS
When wealthy oilman and rancher Durk Lambert sees past lover Meghan Sinclair being rushed into the emergency room he is determined to see whoever tried to kill her arrested. He's afraid Meghan won't forgive him for their breakup and his past fear of commitment enough to let him help protect her. But when Meghan wakes up she doesn't remember anything….not even Durk.
Can Meghan regain her memory in time to save herself and Durk from a killer?
Find out in
BIG SHOT
Available November 2012 wherever books are sold.
www.Harlequin.com
HI69650

Something's going on in Conard County's high school...
and Cassie Greaves has just landed in the middle of it.

Take a sneak peek at RANCHER'S DEADLY RISK *by* New York Times *bestselling author Rachel Lee, coming in November 2012 from Harlequin® Romantic Suspense.*

"There comes a point, Cassie, when you've got to realize that stuff you got away with as a child is no longer acceptable or even legal."

Linc paused, realizing he must seem to be going around in circles. Well, he probably was, between her damned scent and his own uncertainty about what was happening.

"I'll be honest with you," he said slowly. "I'm wondering what's been bubbling beneath the surface at the school that I'm not aware of. That makes me uneasy. On the one hand, I'm trying to paint it in the best light because I know these kids. Or thought I did. I don't want to think the worst of any of them. On the other hand, I guess I shouldn't make too light of it. There have been three transgressions we know about with you. Four, if we add James. I'm not going to dismiss it, but I'm not going to be Chicken Little yet, either. The mind of a teenage male is impenetrable."

She surprised him by losing her haunted look and actually laughing. "You're right, it is. And girls aren't much better at that age."

Girls weren't much better at any age, he thought a little while later as he drove her home. He'd certainly never figured them out.

"Thanks for a wonderful time," she said as he walked her to her door. "I really enjoyed it."

"So did I," he answered more truthfully than he would have liked. He had to bite his tongue to keep from suggesting they do it again.

She was still smiling as she said good-night and closed the door.

He walked back to his truck, keys jingling in his hand, and thought about it all, from the bullying to the rat to the evening just past. The thoughts were still rumbling around when he got home.

Something wasn't right. Something. He'd grown up here, gone to school here, been away only during his college years, and now had been teaching for a decade.

His nose was telling him something was wrong. Very wrong. The question was what. And who.

Find out more in RANCHER'S DEADLY RISK
by Rachel Lee, available November 2012
from Harlequin® Romantic Suspense.

HRSEXP1112

V